# DEAD TIMES REVIVE IN THEE

## A CLANCY EVANS NOVEL

M. Glenn Graves

*To Cindy, with love, from the beginning*

# ALSO BY M GLENN GRAVES

*(these e-Books are available through the Kindle Store on Amazon.com)*

*One Lost Soul More*

*Mercy Killing*

*The Peace Haven Murders*

*Revenge*

*Desperate Measures*

*When Blood Cries*

*Outcast in Gray*

*Out Jumps Jack Death*

*The Dish Ran Away With the Spoon*

# To the Reader

This story is a work of fiction; although, unfortunately, it is true to life. This particular story was written after I discovered the character of the adult Clancy Evans. Once I had been introduced to Clancy the adult young woman, I had the idea of going back in time to see if I could find the reason that she became the kind of investigator, detective, person I knew her to be after a few stories were developed. This is that story which shaped her life. These are the events which occurred when Clancy was eleven years old, prior to her twelfth birthday. These are the events which altered the direction of her life. I hope you enjoy this glance backward in time, even if you have never read any of the other Clancy Evans stories. Hopefully, you either will see the adult Clancy in the young girl Clancy in this story (if you have already met her), or you will be enticed to read some of the other adventures of this dauntless detective who both charms and exasperates many of the people she meets in her work. At any rate, I hope you enjoy this crucial story which shows how she became the feisty and fierce investigator. Some of the Clancy Evans Murder Mysteries are available as e-books through Wolfpack Publishing online at the Kindle Store (amazon.com).

M. Glenn Graves
Mars Hill, North Carolina
2017

# Acknowledgements

John Donne's often quoted line that "no man is an island" is especially apropos to my writing life. There is no way this book could have happened without the significant editing, proofing, and seemingly endless manuscript readings accomplished by my spouse and partner, Cindy. She has had the unenviable task of reading through each subsequent revision of the stories I write. Her tenacity, love, and encouragement can be found throughout the pages of this story especially, but all of the other Clancy Evans Mysteries as well. My appreciation for her tireless efforts has no end to it.

Since this book is my first attempt to "put something in print," I am indebted to Maggie Powell who has labored on my behalf in reading, suggesting, formatting, and endeavoring to aid me in exposing this work to a larger readership. There is no way this book would have been created without her professional touch, to say nothing of her encouragement.

The cover is an original work of art by Connie Kramer. It is an oil on canvas entitled "Butterfly on a Thistle." I am thankful to Connie for allowing me to use her painting on the cover. The original art does not include the smaller butterflies around the cover. These were added with Connie's permission.

Finally, I must acknowledge the support of my small readership from the e-book community, many of whom have encouraged me to create a printed book which they could "hold in their hands." I am grateful for their loyalty and support over the last several years.

*STAY near me—do not take thy flight!*
*A little longer stay in sight!*
*Much converse do I find in thee,*
*Historian of my infancy!*
*Float near me; do not yet depart!*
*Dead times revive in thee:*
*Thou bring'st, gay creature as thou art!*
*A solemn image to my heart,*
*My father's family!**

* The first stanza from the poem *To A Butterfly* by William Wordsworth.
This poem was first published in 1807 in *Poems in Two Volumes*.

# CHAPTER ONE

The summer was more than just hot that year. All the yards looked like brown toast. The leaves on the trees were withered by early July. An occasional breeze would rattle them, sounding much like a sack full of decayed locust shells. The dogs refused to leave the shade trees or from under the front porches, and the cats stayed inside of everything that they could get inside. Folks generally did not move around much either, except for the kids. We kids could handle the heat better than the older folks. Besides, we had important things to do. We kids had business. We had fishin.'

One yard was the exception to the toasted grass. Mr. Joe's grass wasn't like that. My brother and I walked by his place almost every day on the way to our important business of fishing. We walked by his lush, green grass on the way to our favorite spot on the river. A person couldn't help but notice his lovely, healthy, vibrant lawn of jade. While the rest of the small town sported brown toast for yards, Mr. Joe had nothing but the color of emeralds growing around his place.

Mr. Joe's grass was thriving and beautiful. When we asked him why his grass looked so good and everybody else's looked like parched earth, he would give us a big smile and say, *I prays*. I used to wonder why others didn't pray as well. Sounded easy enough to me. If that was all it took to make the grass look good and green, and since we were living in what some folks called *The Bible Belt*, well, it made a body wonder about such stuff.

"Mr. Joe," I said to him because I wasn't permitted to call him Black Joe like some in our community would say, "Reverend Flowers prays and his grass looks like … dirt."

"Maybe he's a prayin' fur the wrong thing," he said.

"I reckon he prays for rain-water like everybody else," I said.

"'Reckon so," said Mr. Joe, "but that ain't what I prays fur."

"Well, my goodness," I said, since I was completely surprised at his revelation. I was a member of a family that got up every Sunday morning and drove a few blocks to the largest church in town. It was a slow and sometimes painful indoctrination, but I was part of the church family even though I was not officially a member. I knew some things.

"So, what do you pray for?" my little brother Scottie asked before I could pose the same question. Scottie was two years younger than I.

"Scottie, don't ask that," I said, chastising him as if I had no intention of asking such a thing. "Prayer is private. Don't you remember what Daddy told us?"

"'Dats okay, Miss Clancy. Yur daddy is right, but some folks don't mind sharin' their prayer-talk. Least-wise I don't mind tellin' you and Mr. Scott here. Yur daddy done taught you prudy well about prayer," Mr. Joe said.

"Yessir, Mr. Joe. He says what a person prays is between that person and God. He says it's sacred and none of anybody's business," I said.

Mr. Joe laughed and nodded his head as he shifted his walking stick from his left hand to his right. He had no noticeable limp in his walk, and I often wondered why he used the cane. Maybe he had it to get rid of bothersome kids from our small Virginia town since I never saw any other kids around him. Just me and Scott.

"'Dats what it is, Miss Clancy. 'Hits sacred." Mr. Joe leaned heavily on his walking stick and looked towards the small hill rising behind his house and barn. He just stood there gazing off towards that small rising in our otherwise rolling terrain. He seemed to be lost in thought, or praying, or something. I became uncomfortable standing there in the hot sun waiting on Mr. Joe to come back from wherever it was he went to in his mind. I could see that Scottie was restless.

"What do you pray for, Mr. Joe?" I finally said, more out of impatience than anything else.

My voice had interrupted Mr. Joe from his thoughts. He hadn't heard my question at all.

"What'd ya say, child?"

"I asked you what you prayed for. You said you didn't mind tellin' me and Scottie."

He smiled pleasantly and patted me on the top of my bright red hair. I smiled up at him. He was a tall man, even bending slightly with his cane.

"Miss Clancy, you shore do get to da point right fast," he chuckled a little more.

"Daddy says there's no point in beating the bush to death to get to the facts," I said.

"I reckin' so, Miss Clancy. Jest remember to be easy on some folks. They has a hard time tellin' the truth right off, ya know. They'll git to it in time, they jest need some coaxin' and warmin' and soft-talk before they's ready to say what it is they has to say, or what they needs to say. That's what my mammie used to tell me."

"I reckon that's the truth, Mr. Joe. Do you know old man Silas Mayhew?"

"I herd tell of 'im."

"Well, it takes that man a good day of saying nothing in particular in order to get rid of an idea. Daddy told me it took him nearly two weeks to get the truth out of old Silas a while back. Silas had witnessed a robbery. Daddy said Silas saw the whole thing happen, but he just couldn't remember the details without going through Arkansas with his stories. Daddy could have solved that crime a lot faster if Silas had remembered quicker," I said.

"Yessim, that's the way 'tis for sum. Ya got to be patient and give 'em lots of room to say their mind."

"You gonna jabber all day Clancy! The fish are waitin'!" Scottie said.

"Quiet! Mr. Joe and I are talkin' here," I whispered too loud, irritated at my brother.

"Mr. Scott's right, Miss Clancy. Fish won't be bitin' all day. Why don't you stop by here on your way back home? We'll talk sum more then. How dat be?"

"Okay. We'll see you late this afternoon. Can we bring you some fish?" I said.

Mr. Joe grinned a little as he rubbed his chin, seriously contemplating my offer of fish coming later on.

"If you has plenty, Miss Clancy. I can't take yur catch if you don't have 'nuff fur your family."

"Oh, don't worry 'bout that, Mr. Joe. We'll have plenty. Scottie and I have a secret hole with plenty of fish. Cats are always in that hole. I never fail to catch less than three or four. Scottie often does better than that. How many would you like?"

Mr. Joe smiled broadly, fully engaging his entire face in an expression of complete enjoyment with our conversation, or with my offer of unlimited catfish.

"Two's nuff," he said. "I can't eats likes I used to. Two's more than kind."

"Two it is," I said. "Be back late this afternoon."

My confidence was brimming. I had no doubt that Scottie and I would bring back an ample number of fish for Mr. Joe and our own family.

"Y'all be careful at the river, Miss Clancy. Some places' real deep, ya know."

"Yessir, we know. We'll be careful."

"Good day to both of you."

Scottie and I walked maybe ten paces before I turned to look back at the elderly black man who was always so kind to us. Mr. Joe waved slightly, turned, and entered through the small gate into his verdant front yard. I returned his wave.

My brother and I walked on down the hot, dusty road toward the Staunton River. No doubt both of us were filled with great anticipation.

When we were out of ear-shot of Mr. Joe, Scottie posed a question.

"Why do you call him Mr. Joe when everybody else around here calls him Black Joe?"

"Daddy says we shouldn't call him Black Joe. Says it's disrespectful. Says that everybody deserves some measure of esteem."

"Esteem? You sound like Daddy when you talk like that," Scottie said. "But Black …uh, Mr. Joe is black and most everybody I know calls him Black Joe. They never put that mister stuff in front of it either."

"That's their problem. I think it best that we live by Daddy's rules. Besides, he'll bust our butts if he ever hears us say Black Joe."

"That's a fact!" Scottie said.

I could hear the police siren off in the distance. It woke me from my fishing nap. My red and white float was resting just under the water but not moving. Scottie was down a few feet from my shade-tree spot, wide awake and fishing hard.

"How many do you have on your stringer?" I said.

"Seven," he said. "You?"

"Counting the one on my line I'm fixin' to take off, … I think it's six."

"You can't count the one on your line. You ain't caught him yet." Scottie reasoned.

"Wanna bet?" I said. I reeled slowly and surely so as not to disturb the catfish too much. I figured the fish had been sleeping just like me and it would serve no good purpose to start reeling in frantically at this hour of the afternoon. I eased my whole fishing rig out of the water with that big cat just following along without so much as a whimper. I would have sworn that the fish was still asleep by the time I got him to the bank.

"Say, what time is it anyway?" I said. Scottie was the keeper of the watch. Daddy had given him his old pocket watch and Scottie wouldn't even go to the bathroom without it. He loved to tell me the time, and did so even when I didn't care to know the time.

"A little after four," he said.

"You ready to go home?"

"In a little. I'd like to catch one or two more since you already promised two of our catch to Black … Mis-ter Joe. Why can't he fish for himself?" Scottie said.

"I think he does fish for himself. I don't know. But what difference does that make? Can't we be nice to people? Daddy says that —"

"Clancy, don't you ever get tired of saying of what Daddy says?" his question interrupted my Daddy-wisdom.

"Not yet, not until someone comes along with more horse sense. Do you know anybody smarter than our daddy?" I said.

"Mama should get honorable mention, I 'spose. But, outside of them … naw, I guess not. But you know that some folks probably get tired of hearin' you say what Daddy says."

"Well, some folks are ignorant. I figure they need to know as much as we know, Scott," I said. I seldom called him Scott, unless I wanted to get his attention and make him feel more grown up. It was my formal acknowledgement of his status as my baby brother. I also used it when I was upset with his behavior.

"Did you hear those sirens?" Scottie said.

"Yeah, they woke me up a few moments ago."

"That's Daddy's car. Wonder what he's into?" Scottie said.

"Don't know, but I think we ought to go and check it out," I said.

Just then his float took a deep dive and whatever was on the other end jerked his line so hard it nearly pulled him off the bank into the river. He caught himself from his potential fall and began his mortal combat with what had to be the largest catfish ever in the history of the Staunton River. At least that was the story he told our parents later after he had failed to land the Big One.

# Chapter Two

Scottie and I gathered up all of our fishing gear and headed towards home. We stopped at Mr. Joe's to deliver his two large catfish. It was close to five o'clock by the time we arrived at his place. We stayed with him a few minutes and watched him milk Bessie Mae. Scottie and I both tried our hand at milking. It wasn't as easy as it looked when Mr. Joe did it. Our success was best termed moderate.

We stopped at our house to deposit our catch of the day in some water while we hurried into town to see what was happening. I didn't want to cart our caught jewels all over Clancyville. I placed all eleven catfish in a bucket of water and placed the bucket inside the old shed behind our house. I moved quietly around so as not to make enough noise to alert my mother to our presence. She would not have given us permission to walk into town and check on our daddy. I managed my stealth quite ably, which permitted Scottie and me to get away without our mother's knowledge.

By the time we arrived in downtown Clancyville it was a little after six and we saw nothing unusual going on. Small towns in Virginia have a way of settling into boredom and enjoying it. Scottie and I figured it must have been one of those hundred and one false alarms that our father told us happen to him almost every day. Such is the imaginative crime wave of our little village.

Our daddy's official county car was parked in front of the jail. I felt the hood to see if it was hot or cold. It felt lukewarm, which indicated to me that he had gone somewhere, but it had been some time since he had left his office and then returned. Fishing on the river causes time to move faster than I would prefer.

Our daddy's office was next door to City Hall. That building was a massive, two-story construction with four large columns across the front. Impressive. The Sheriff's Office next door was of a lesser nature—small, with only two rooms. The first room one entered was the office proper. It contained two doors, two chairs, one window and one desk. The second door allowed entry into the jail portion of the small building. The jail had three cells which were seldom occupied.

"False alarm," I said to Scottie. He touched the hood just to be sure I was telling him the truth.

We decided not to bother our father.

It was a short walk back to our house from City Hall. It was basically a short walk between any two points in our town. Clancyville was the county seat even though it was small. Small is an overstatement of the size of our little settlement. I once heard my daddy say that we had close to two thousand living around the greater Clancyville area, if you allow the dogs, cats, and fish to be in that count.

"Mama, where's Daddy?" I asked when I entered the kitchen. Scottie stayed outside to admire the fish we had caught. He was probably out there talking to them as well. My brother had some strange habits.

"He's working. Where do you think he'd be?" she snapped. She was busy fixing supper and didn't like us asking a lot of questions while she was busy, sweating over the hot stove. When she was bustling about in the kitchen, questions from her children were considered useless items and wholly bothersome.

"We heard Daddy's siren while we were fishing, so we came into town to investigate," Scottie said as he entered the kitchen and using a word larger than his vocabulary normally handled. He'd been with me long enough for some of my word-education to rub off.

I noticed that my little brother was carrying the bucket of fish.

"Yeah, I'd like to see you two *investigate*," she said, emphasizing that word far beyond what I thought to be acceptable. "You keep your noses out of whatever it is your daddy is into, you hear?" she said.

At the end of her mandate, she allowed her voice to level off rather than accelerate. I figured she was already sweating enough and didn't want to get all worked up while she stirred the green beans on the stove, turned the heat down on the mashed potatoes, and checked on whatever meat she had baking in the oven.

"Mama, you want these fish for supper?" Scottie asked as he held up the bucket for her approval. Another one of those useless, bothersome questions coupled with a visual aid. I figured that this was not going to be pretty. My poor little brother was trying so hard.

"Get those stinkin' catfish out of my kitchen this minute," she was starting to lose it. "You know better than to bring those smelly things in here while I'm fixin' supper."

We let the screen door slam behind us as we hurriedly escaped her wrath. Slamming the back door screen was a major item on our mother's list of things not to do. However, Scottie and I quickly decided that we would rather hear her scolding us about the screen door from a safe distance outside, than to feel the touch of that long wooden spoon she used to stir her pots on the stove. That utensil in her hand was more of a weapon than a kitchen utensil.

"Clean those fish outside and then put them in the freezer," she called after us. "How many do you have?"

"Eleven," I said loudly as I walked towards the woodshed where Daddy first showed me how to clean fish. That would have been nearly five years ago. I never understood why he called it the woodshed since he didn't keep any wood in it. In one end it was full of rusty garden tools which he and Mama said that they would one day use whenever all the relatives died and stopped providing vegetables for us each summer. The other end contained his motorcycle which he used some in his work as Sheriff. The end of the woodshed which housed his precious motorcycle was locked all the time. Even I didn't know where the key was. I had searched in vain, but so far had come up empty in my quest to unlock his treasure for viewing.

"You usually catch more than that," Mama said later in a calmer voice after she had time to settle down while Scottie and I cleaned fish.

She was standing, looking out the screen door, watching us finish up skinning the cats.

"Clancy gave two away," Scottie said as he glanced up at Mama.

"Who'd you give 'em to?" she asked.

"Mr. Joe," I answered.

"That old colored man who lives near the river?"

"Yes, ma'am," I said.

"Why'd you give him your fish?"

"He likes catfish," Scottie answered. I poked him in the side, hoping my emphatic nudge was out of my mother's vision, and he giggled softly as he covered his mouth. Our mother didn't like us smarting off with any flippant answers, so we had to be really careful when we tried to be funny in answering her. It was a fine line which we crossed more often than not. Sometimes the answers to her questions were more than a little obvious. I had noticed this pattern earlier in my life, maybe last year, that in regards to the questions adults often ask children, the answers are painfully apparent.

This time Mother made no comeback to Scottie's cute response. We were lucky. I looked towards the back porch to see if she was still standing there. She was not. She must have returned to the kitchen stove to check on the beans, or the potatoes or on the cornbread in the oven. I deduced that whatever meat she had prepared was completed by this point.

Her absence from watching us clean those final few fish probably saved Scottie from her wrath. Next time we might not be so lucky.

"You're gonna get a whippin' for smartin' off like that," I scolded him softly along with a smile.

"Well, it's the truth. Old Joe does like catfish," he snickered again at his own cleverness.

"Yeah, but you know she meant something different. And, it's Mr. Joe. Drop that word *old*." I could tell that my brother's education was going to take years to complete.

I retrieved a plastic bag from a box on the shelf directly above our old rusty chest freezer that sat unevenly on the ground next to the shed. I handed it to Scottie and told him to put the now-cleaned catfish in the bag, tie it off, and then place them in the freezer.

My job was to make sure that the area behind our house was thoroughly spotless after our post-catch fish-cleaning tradition was finished. I was hosing down the remains when Daddy pulled up in his official car. His vehicle, provided by the county, was one of those oversized Fords, 1966 vintage, and painted a less-than-colorful black and white. It had an antenna that stretched from the front to the back of the car. I hated it, and so I referred to it as the *black-and-white*. No other name fit it like that, at least for me. It became a symbol for my daddy's authority in the town and county. And the truth of the matter, with my daddy inside, it didn't matter to me what he drove, or what color it was. It could have been a Rolls Royce for all I cared. Or even a Nash Rambler painted some gosh awful green. As long as Bill Evans was driving that machine, I was proud of him.

On the side of the car it read *Sheriff's Department, Pitt County, Virginia.* That was the thing, that was the most important thing … to me.

"Big catch?" he asked taking his cap off and wiping his brow.

"Medium size, I reckon. Thirteen. We should have done better," I said.

"Sounds like enough to eat for us," he said.

"Not tonight, though. We got home too late. Mama has some other meat prepared for supper. We'll enjoy them another day," I said.

"We gave two away," Scottie added.

"Sharing is good. Who was the lucky person?" he asked.

"Mr. Joe," I said.

"Good."

That's all he said. That was usual. Daddy didn't talk much until after supper. He seldom questioned our judgment about giving things away like fish and stuff. He was always giving stuff away himself. Mama called it a character flaw. I called it goodness.

Daddy leaned back in his chair and laced his fingers together behind his head while he stared at the ceiling fan above the kitchen table. That was his usual way of showing his satisfaction with the evening meal.

"Great supper, dear," he said to Mama.

She smiled and nodded, but without comment.

"What was all the commotion in town today?" I asked.

We were allowed to ask questions at a meal as long as our questions didn't lead to some inappropriate subject for the dinner table. Mama was the judge for all questions and all answers as to their appropriateness. I gambled that my question was safe enough now that everything but dessert had been finished, just in case there were some deliciously sordid details my daddy might want to share. Like Mama would ever allow Daddy to share any sordid details between regular food and dessert. She wouldn't permit it before, during or after the meal. We talked a lot behind her back.

"Two kids are missing," he said.

"Who?" Scottie asked.

"Buster and Micah Scruggs," he said.

"Buster and Micah?" Scottie said. "They're always running off and getting lost. How long they been missin'?"

"Well, Mr. Donald Scruggs came in today and told me that his sons didn't come home last night. He was up all night looking for them. No luck. He and his brothers stayed at it until after lunch today and then came to see me."

"Seems like a long time to wait," Mama said.

"I agree," Daddy answered.

"What'd you do?" Scottie asked my daddy.

"I took Deputy Hines and a couple of men in town, and we began searching the area where Mr. Scruggs thought was the last place they had been seen. I had Mary Lee call all the members of the Town Council for an emergency meeting this afternoon. I organized them into small groups to begin canvassing the whole area in and around Clancyville. I've got to go back out after supper. We might be small, but there's a lot of land to canvass in a search like this."

"What'd Donald say to that?" I asked.

"You mean what did Mr. Scruggs say to that?" Daddy corrected my informality.

"Yessir, that's what I mean."

"I can't tell you what he said," Daddy said.

"Whataya mean you can't tell us?" Scottie asked.

"Your mother wouldn't be happy with me if I used words like that in the house."

"You shouldn't be using words like that outside of the house either," Mama said, just to be clear.

Scottie looked bewildered. His mind was racing towards something.

"So, he didn't like your idea about organizing and meeting," I said.

"You got that right. He wanted a vigilante committee, as in whoever would go home, get their gun and then follow him and his brothers to find his boys."

"Well, you understand how they feel, don't you?" Mama said.

"In a way I do. But there's a right way and …," Daddy paused.

"The Scruggs' way," I said.

"Clancy!" Mama's tone was stern.

"She's right, dear. You know how they are. But I do understand their anxiety. But we have no reason to suspect anything has happened to his sons yet. Boys sometimes go off in the summertime and return home later. It's been like that for as long as I've been around."

"You'll be gone all evening, I suppose?" Mama asked.

"Sorry, dear. We have to find those boys, sooner rather than later."

Daddy looked at his wristwatch and jumped to his feet. His was out of his chair and through the backdoor before we had much time to realize that he was leaving.

"Can we come, Daddy?" I yelled after him.

"No, you may not. You both help me clear the table and clean up the dishes. You'll hear about it when your father returns," Mama's tone was definite.

We watched our father drive away in that ugly black-and-white. I was so proud of him. He was the Sheriff of our small county. There was no better lawman in all the world as far as I was concerned. I'd take my daddy over any of those cops on television, but I did like David Jansen in that Harry O show. The major difference being that my daddy was the real thing.

# CHAPTER THREE

It must have been very late when Daddy came home that night after the special town meeting. I stayed awake as long as I could but finally fell asleep around midnight. That was the last time-check I recall before waking the next morning.

I heard him talking in muffled tones with my mother sometime in the early morning hours. I couldn't make out what they were saying. Scottie was talking in his sleep by that time. His room was next to mine and I could hear him much too clearly through the walls. It was much too difficult to separate my father's muffled tones from Scottie's clarity.

I went back to sleep. It was a deep sleep. When I awoke later in the morning, Daddy was already gone to work. After breakfast I pleaded our case with my mother.

"Can we go fishing, Mama?"

"That's all you two seem to do these days. Don't you have anything better to do than fish?"

"What's better than fishing?" I asked. I was not being wholly truthful with that question.

"Try reading, studying, going to the library. Or maybe you could go over and play with Molly. How about that new girl down the street? What's her name?"

"Sally Trumples," I said.

"Sally Trumples? That's an unusual name around here," she said.

I wanted to ask which of those two names was strange to her, but I was afraid she would smack me for being smart. I let that opportunity pass.

"You know that Scottie and I like to fish. It's summertime. I study enough during school. I do okay, don't you think?"

"You could do better. Besides, you're a bad influence on Scott. He's not as —" she stopped abruptly. Whatever she was thinking was not to be said, at least not aloud for my ears to hear.

By the time Scottie had entered the kitchen, Mama had finished making and wrapping up two tomato sandwiches. I watched her put each sandwich in a paper sack along with a handful of homemade chocolate chip cookies. Scottie meandered around the kitchen area like a sailor with a next-day hangover who had spent too many hours in the bar the previous night. He flopped down in his chair and put his head in his hands with his elbows resting on the kitchen table. He looked completely out of it.

I nudged him in a forceful way hoping to get his attention before Mama saw his elbows perched on the table. It was the wrong place to perch one's elbows. Never mind that we were not eating a meal at the time. It was still wrong for the elbows to be stationed on the table in the presence of my mother.

I failed.

"Young man, I don't care how tired and sleepy you are. When you sit at that table you had better use good manners. That means keep those elbows off the table and in your lap like a human being should!" She was moving towards him with the fly swatter faster than I could get his eyes to meet mine. Likely enough, he was still dazed from sleep.

I jumped up at the last moment and stood between the onslaught of the swatter and the intended victim. It was a daring move and my heart was pounding faster than usual.

"Mama, can I have some more milk before we leave to go fishin'?" I shoved the empty glass toward her face like Oliver Twist pleading for more food. She stared at me for a moment, no doubt wondering what I was up to. Without thinking, almost like a reflex, she took the glass, turned toward the refrigerator, and started fussing about fishing and eating and elbows and whatever it was that she could think of at the moment.

I grabbed Scottie in his drunken stupor, swiped the two sacks of sandwiches from the kitchen counter, and hurried out the back door while she was retrieving milk from the refrigerator. Since our escape was in haste, I let the screen door slam. Twice in a twenty-four hour period I had violated one of her ten commandments, and I did it intentionally. Usually my sins were simple carelessness. Not today. First, I figured that it would notify her that we were out and gone before she had actually poured the milk. That way I wouldn't get a spanking for wasting food. Otherwise, she would have kept that milk outside of the refrigerator all day and would have made me drink warm milk when I returned that afternoon. At least I had some faint recollection of having to drink warm milk once upon a time in an earlier part of my life. Second, I was hoping that by the time Scottie and I returned from our fishing with two stringers full of fish, she just might forget that we left under the cloud of guilt and haste without being properly excused from the table or disciplined for the errors of our ways. It was long shot, but I had to do it to protect Scottie from the fly swatter. That sucker could sting you something fierce.

To her credit, Mama seldom yelled after us when we made one of our daring escapes. We didn't do it often, but from time to time we would test the fates and venture into that dangerous world of hiding out in the shadows of the world away from her wrath. She was too proper to yell outside. But inside, well, that was another matter.

We were well on our way toward the Staunton River by 9:30. It was another hot, dry day, even at that early hour. The grass looked darker than the day before. If possible, it actually looked deader. No rain was in the forecast. I wondered about the fish. It might even be too hot for them.

About halfway to our favorite fishing hole, Scottie finally spoke after he had gulped down two cookies. He was holding his third one contemplating something deep.

"You can't put your elbows in your lap."

"What?"

"It's impossible to put your elbows in your lap. Your elbows have to hang by your side, or be propped up on the table. I prefer the table."

"I will not rescue you again from the pain of the flyswatter. If you are dumb enough to put your elbows back on the table when Mama is around, then you deserve the mutilation you surely will receive."

"Mutilation? What does that mean?" he asked.

"First cousin to death."

"Too many rules in our house," he concluded. He ate his third cookie.

Mr. Joe was in his yard as usual when we passed by. He was working with some type of hand-pump apparatus spreading a black liquid around some bushes near his house. The rest of his yard had signs of that same black liquid on it.

"Morning, Mr. Joe," I said.

"Gud mornin' Miss Clancy and Mr. Scott. How be the two of you today?"

"We be fine, Mr. Joe," Scottie said.

I nudged Scottie and gave him a frown. It wasn't kind to mock the way people talk, especially friends. Mr. Joe laughed at him and seemed to take no offense.

"Fishin', huh? Well, I 'spect dat dey be bitin' all over today. You should catch a plenty. I might join you later."

"I was thinking it might be too hot," I said.

"Yes 'im, it be hot. But you know, 'dose cats love hot. Tell ya wat, go to dat spot of yours and they be waitin' on ya. Dat's a promise. Old Joe don't make idle promises. Jest go there and fish like always. Plenty of cats to catch today, fur sure."

"Say, Mr. Joe. You never did tell us what it is you pray for that makes your grass so green. We forgot to ask you yesterday evening when we brought you the fish."

"You said you didn't pray for rain, Mr. Joe," Scottie said, as if to remind him.

"Well, dat's true, fur the most part, young man. But now and then, I prob'ly slips up and axes for a mite of moisture, maybe even sum rain, ya know, like a good soaker."

"Aw, Mr. Joe, everybody prays for rain, especially this time of year," Scottie said. "Does God just answer your prayers and send a little cloud out here to water your grass?"

Mr. Joe laughed. He put down the hand-pump spray thing, grabbed his walking stick that was leaning against the front porch, and walked slowly towards us. Still no limp. He was one of those people who move along in life in a purposeful manner. I don't ever remember seeing Mr. Joe in a hurry. He never seemed to need to be in a hurry, I suppose. His manner of moving was more of gliding along effortlessly.

"Come here, yung'ins. Don't be feard."

He stopped at the gate and leaned his walking stick against one of the pickets. He held out both of his hands, palms up, toward our faces.

"Smell dem," he said.

"Smell your hands?" Scottie was skeptical.

"Yessir, smell dem."

We both moved very cautiously toward the extended palms in front of our faces. They were pink, or almost pink. They certainly weren't black or even brown. My nose got within a few inches and I took a deep breath.

"What ya smell, Miss Clancy?"

"Manure," I said. "Your hands smell like manure."

Immediately a broad smile appeared, and then he laughed.

"You pray for manure?" Scottie asked.

"Sorta. I pray dat da Gud Lawd will be kind to me, forgive me, let it rain when he takes a liken to it, and help Bessie Mae stay healthy," Mr. Joe said.

"What's your cow got to do with green grass?" Scottie said.

"She's the reason my grass be green."

"I don't understand," Scottie said.

"He uses the manure from Bessie Mae to fertilize his lawn," I explained.

"How'd you know that?" Scottie asked.

"I recall reading something about it in the fourth grade science book. It's supposed to be good for gardens and stuff," I sounded like I knew more than I did.

"Dat's right, Miss Clancy. Good fer grass. Really good fer grass and bushes and stuff that grows. Puts all kinds of good stuff in the ground for the things dat need 'em."

"Is that what you're doing with that spray thing over there?" I pointed toward the apparatus he had been using when we had arrived.

"Yessim. Dat's exactly what I be doin'."

"You already put it on the yard?" I asked.

"Oh, yes. I did that twice before. Furst, last fall I put it on to winter over. Then jest before spring come a budin' out, I puts a little bit more. Then I prays for rain."

"It come straight out of the cow and you put it on the ground?" Scottie wondered.

Mr. Joe laughed.

"No sir. Not quite that po'ent. Dat might kill everything. No sir, I ha' been workin' wif this stuff for a few years. Adds some manure to it now and again. Bessie Mae adds to it on her own from time to time. I adds water. I adds a few other things for flavor. Then I mixes it up in the back in one of my big old drums. Ya know, stir it up a lot, then thin it out and put it in the sprayer and puts it on the yard. Been workin' very well for a few years now. Don't ya agree?"

"Sure do, Mr. Joe," I said. "You have the only green grass in the whole town."

"But your hands stink," Scottie said. I poked him in the ribs with my right elbow.

"Oh, for a little while. Mostly gone the next day or two. Jest wash regular, and it goes away in time," Mr. Joe said. "Dat odor never lasts more than a few days. I gets used to it."

"Want us to bring ya some fish from the hole?" Scottie asked. I was proud of him for offering before I offered.

"Same as yesterday, if ya can spare 'em. Don't trouble yurselves. I be fine without any. But two'd be nice, in case I don't get o'r that way later. I got some chores needs doin', some more spreadin' to do, more green to keep. It'd be nice to have sum delicious cats to feast on this evenin'."

"Two it is, Mr. Joe. We'll see you later," Scottie led the way and I followed. I couldn't get that manure smell out of my nose. I liked his green grass, but I'd be a monkey's uncle before I'd want to get that manure on my hands even if it does come out in a few days of good washing.

We caught fish hand-over-fist that day. Mr. Joe's prediction was more than a little accurate. We caught so many fish that we were dragging a bit by the time we returned to Mr. Joe's place late that afternoon. His small, white-framed house was located in a grove of trees less than a mile from the river. In addition to the small house, Mr. Joe owned an old barn and several acres around the two buildings. Bessie Mae used the barn in the winter time, but Mr. Joe once told us that it was empty except for some hay for the cow. Mr. Joe's farm contained grazing lands, but mostly it was forest. He had inherited the place from his grandfather who had been a slave in our county. It would have gone to Mr. Joe's father except for the fact that his father was lynched when Mr. Joe was about twelve. He was accused of stealing by one of the local farmers, and they hung him one Saturday evening. The farmer had lots of anti-Negro friends who got together and had nothing better to do than lynch a *nigger*. That was their word, not mine. My daddy would have whipped me good if I ever said that word anywhere, anytime.

Mr. Joe's father had been hung in that barn, according to my daddy's story.

In all the times we had been walking by Mr. Joe's place to fish, we had never investigated his barn. I had been curious about it, naturally. However, Scottie was the one who wanted to go check it out, but I had fishing on my mind when we walked by in the mornings, and by afternoon we were generally too tired or too much in a hurry to get home for supper. Besides, I had been in other barns and this one was pretty much the same on the outside as the others I had seen. I figured that the inside would be similar to other barns as well. Scottie was more curious than I was. This summer he had really been pestering me to see inside of Mr. Joe's barn.

Mr. Joe was resting on his front porch when we arrived with our heavy stringers of fish.

"Looks like y'all ketched 'em all," he smiled at us. His voice sounded tired.

"Naw, we left some for you, Mr. Joe," Scottie said.

"Too tired to fish. Ain't that sump'in? If a man's too tired to fish, he be workin' too hard. Dat's all I got to say 'bout dat. Too hard," he sighed and wiped the sweat from across his forehead.

"What's in the barn, Mr. Joe?" I asked. I wasn't sure exactly how to broach the subject of our curiosity about his old structure. I had noticed moments earlier that one side of it was leaning as if it might collapse. Once upon a time in the barn's life it had been painted red. My guess was that it had been decades since a paint brush with any color of paint had touched the building.

Since I was unsure of how to maneuver the barn question subtly, I used the direct approach.

"Jest hay for Bessie Mae," he said. "I reckon there be a tool or two, nothin' 'portant."

"Can we go look at it?" Scottie asked. I started to poke him for such a direct question, then realized that I had been the one who initiated this frontal attack on Mr. Joe.

"Sure. It's jest a barn. With hay. Bessie Mae's over ther somewhere, nearby. She never gits too far away from home. She likes to bed down inside the barn whenever a storm is up, or the wind turns cold. That's why the door be crack'd open wide enough to allow her inside of her own accord. Go on up and have a look-see. Jest don't close the door shut."

"Here're your fish, Mr. Joe," I said handing him four big cats.

"Whoa, Miss Clancy. I don't needs this much. Two be fine, like I told ya."

"We had a really good catch today. Fish were bitin' something fierce. We must have caught two dozen. Please take 'em, Mr. Joe. Mama will make us clean 'em all and fuss cause we caught too many. Besides, with what we caught yesterday and these, we have more than enough for supper tonight."

He nodded, smiled appreciatively at us, and accepted the fish.

"You two can go on up to the barn and explore if you like. Jest keep ya eyes out for rats and snakes. They likes it, too. I don't go up ther' too much in the summer months, jest now and again to check on the hay supply for Bessie Mae."

I stood there holding the other stringer of fish wondering what to do with them. It was getting heavy.

"Here, Miss Clancy. Give dem to me. I'll hang 'em up till you and Mr. Scott be ready to head home."

Mr. Joe took both stringers and headed slowly towards the back of his house. Scottie and I walked toward the barn.

"Why do you want to explore his old barn so much?" I asked.

"I don't know. It seemed like a good idea at the time. I just like barns. Ain't you curious?"

"A little," I said, not committing myself to anything akin to what he might be feeling.

"And besides, I ain't in no hurry to get home and clean fish," he confessed.

"Well, I'm in no hurry to run into the likes of snakes and rats. We need to find a big stick to take inside with us. Just in case."

"Oh, don't sweat the snakes and rats. They're probably just as afraid of us as we are of them, at least that's what Daddy says," Scottie informed me. That was only part of the story. Not only did my strange little brother talk to dead fish, he also was spotted once or twice talking to a cornered snake. On another occasion, Mama found him in dialogue with a family of rats. They seemed to be listening to what he had to say, or so she said.

While I trusted my daddy's wisdom in nearly every instance, I still looked around for a good-sized stick to aid my cause. Despite his wisdom, Daddy was known to be wrong from time to time, or so Mama suggested now and then.

# CHAPTER FOUR

The old, long-ago-red barn was small, but it was a perfect fit for Mr. Joe's farm. Mr. Joe's house was a quaint four-room wooden structure painted white, and his land covered only "sum ten acres or so" he said, maybe less. I never did ask him why he didn't know exactly how much land he had. Bessie Mae had enough grass to eat and Mr. Joe must have had a few acres set aside for hay to be cut. He didn't own a tractor, so I guess someone else cut it for him.

Mr. Joe's barn was a good seventy-five yards, if not more, from Mr. Joe's house. It was also just about the same distance from the path we used to get to the river. If it had been directly on our path, or just a few yards away, we would probably have explored it before now without permission. Too convenient for us to ignore.

Scottie and I trudged slowly toward the barn. He was a few paces ahead of me. I suspected that he was more anxious to have a look inside than I was. I concluded that it was simply a worn-out building that would likely stand for another ten to twenty years unless a storm came through sooner rather than later and attacked that one leaning side. I also figured that Mr. Joe was not the kind of man who would spend any money on repairing it. Most likely he didn't have the money to spend on repairing it.

I decided early on that Mr. Joe was poor but clean. He nearly always wore a white shirt and faded bib overalls. His boots were old and brown with lots of scuff marks, but that was to be expected of a person who lived and worked on a farm. I noticed the scuff marks because Mama would always make me polish my shoes whenever I got the smallest scuff on them. I noticed other people's shoes a lot because of my mama's insistence upon my shoes looking so good. If Mr. Joe wasn't going to polish his brown boots, he surely wasn't going to rebuild that barn.

"Let's find Bessie Mae," Scottie said as he ran the last few yards towards the barn.

I was still looking around for a long, sturdy stick. Those snakes and rats never left my focus.

Scottie ran around the left side of the barn and disappeared from my sight. A few seconds later he emerged on the right side, still running.

"I can't find Bessie Mae," he yelled at me without looking.

"Maybe she's inside," I called back.

"I'll hide and you try to find me," Scottie said and then disappeared through the narrowly opened barn door. "Count to a hundred and then come after me," he added.

I started to yell out something about snakes, but decided it sounded too much like my mama. Scottie wouldn't pay much attention to me anyway since he seemed to have no fear of any type of animal. I began counting to myself while still searching for that essential stick. I moved over to the fence line hoping that maybe some old tree had given up a suitable limb for my purposes. I walked along casually enjoying the late afternoon sunshine and the freedom of Mr. Joe's wide-open spaces. The whole setting gave me a warm feeling inside. It wasn't much of a farm as farms go, but it felt like home to me. It had that comfortable, welcoming feeling about it. Maybe that was Mr. Joe's added flavor to the place. He made us feel welcome. When a body feels welcomed, that's a lot like home.

He and Bessie Mae worked together to keep the grass at a good height and the weeds in check. The fences were all standing, too. That barn was in a desperate need of some paint and repair, but from a distance it seemed sturdy enough despite the serious leaning on that one side. As far as I could tell, the tilt was its only flaw. I was allowing for several boards to be missing after I had learned of its early beginnings with Mr. Joe's grandfather and father. The barn had been around for several decades by now.

Finally, I found the perfect stick. One of the many oaks near the fence had given up a good-sized limb probably during one of our rare, pre-summer storms back in late May or early June. I used my foot as leverage to break it so it would be just the size for me to wield in case I needed to do battle against any vicious vipers or slinking rats. I hit it against the top rail of the fence to test its strength The sound of wood on wood ricocheted off the side of the barn, then seemed to bounce back against the trees near me, and then finally scattered out into the acres of Mr. Joe's forest. It gradually faded into oblivion, one of those lonely, hollow sounds.

I struck the stick against the fence once more before I turned toward the barn. I knew that Scottie would be well hidden by now even though I had ceased counting.

"Clan-cy!" Scottie screamed out my name in one, long desperate cry. His voice sounded different from his usual cries for help. He and I played together almost every day and I knew the sound of his desperation. We had played together since he was about five or six, I don't remember which it was. Mama told me that it was my job to look after my brother. I was a cheap baby-sitter. I didn't really mind, at least not the last two years. He was old enough to be some company, and, as far as boys go, he had a good mind when he used it. My singular issue with him regarding his brain was that he so seldom used it.

I clutched the stick tightly and began running toward the barn. I figured that he must have cornered a large snake or vice versa. I was not excited about the potential battle for me, but I had to protect my baby brother from all varmints. My mother would have my hide if I did any less than save Scottie.

"Scottie, stay where you are. Don't move. Stay calm," I called out instructions before I even got to the barn door. I tried to sound like I knew what I was talking about. I had seen a few snakes in my life but I had never had to do battle against one. That was Daddy's job. Daddy would tell us never to kill a snake until you had identified it. Like people, some snakes are good and some are dangerous.

"Never kill a black snake," he once said.

"Why not?" I had asked.

"They kill the poisonous snakes. They also take care of the rodents around. They're good to have around the house."

"Do I let them inside?" I was teasing him.

"No. Your mother might get a little excited if we did that. Just let them be ... outside. That's safe enough."

I was hoping that this monster Scottie was facing inside the barn was one of those black varieties, and he had simply forgotten Daddy's teaching.

I was running full speed when I entered the barn. I slowed to a cautious walk immediately upon entering. The lighting was dim and the territory unfamiliar. I scanned the first floor as quickly as I could. I couldn't locate Scottie. There was a foul odor lurking about, but I halfway expected that in barns. Still, this particular odor was severe.

The ladder to the loft was to the right of me and I headed towards it. I was three steps up when I heard a moaning sound behind me. I turned and spotted the top of Scottie's head back in a corner of the barn. A beam of sunlight had just caught a portion of his short, blonde curls. He seemed to be frozen in that corner.

I couldn't imagine why he had screamed out only once, nor why he hadn't elected to run out the door to safety. Scottie was usually vocal and animated in matters of danger.

I moved directly toward my brother without making much noise. I didn't want to frighten the snake so that it might strike him. My only approach was to his side. The bad odor intensified.

Scottie was on his hands and knees still moaning. There was vomit everywhere. He had thrown up all around himself. Some of it was on him as well.

"What happened?" I whispered in his ear after I knelt down close to him on a clean spot. While I was talking, I was searching for the snake.

He moved for the first time since I had arrived. He sat back on his haunches and stared straight ahead into a dim corner of the barn. He lifted his left arm and pointed into the shaded area. I expected a King Cobra to be lurking there and waiting for some unsuspecting kids to show up and be eaten alive. There was no King Cobra, of course. I knew that. In fact, there was no snake of any variety in the corner.

Buster Scruggs and Micah Scruggs were in the shaded corner.

I dropped my weapon and put my hand over my mouth and nose. The release of my fears and imminent danger for Scottie were now passed and the reality of that smell came on me with a vengeance. The odor was coming from the corner where Scottie had pointed. Buster was hanging from one of the barn's rafters. A large rope was around his neck and his body was swaying slightly, moving gently as in a slight twisting motion. The rope was making a kind of stretching noise as Buster's body weight created the movement. His hands were tied behind his back. He was naked and quite dead.

Micah, the little brother to Buster, was slumped over in the corner and looked like a rag doll that had been tossed there and forgotten. He was naked and dead, too.

I moved slowly towards the two boys trying to take in the whole scene as best I could. The smell of decay became worse the closer I moved to their bodies. Scottie was still moaning a bit but he was no longer throwing up. I squatted down close to Micah and waited for my eyes to adjust to the dark shadows of the corner. I could see some bruises on his small body. Micah must have been about seven or eight years old. I didn't know exactly. I knew him to be younger than Scott. I saw a little blood around his mouth and nose, but not very much. There were no open wounds, just lots of bruises. I noticed some dark spots around his neck. He had been in a scuffle of some sort and had lost.

Buster's body had more bruises than Micah's. It occurred to me that maybe he had put up more of a fight in whatever conflict might have occurred. Buster was my age and slightly larger than most eleven-year-old boys. As I stared at his dangling corpse gently swaying from the large beam, listening to the ominous, twisting rope-sound of an eerie creaking, his body rotated so that I could now see his badly bruised buttocks. He had been whipped with something heavy. There was a large dark splotch on the left side of his abdomen. His whole body was slightly swollen, like Micah's.

It was an awful sight—both of them. The now nauseating smell was way beyond bad. I finally was able to stop staring at the two lifeless forms in that small chamber of the barn. I had to leave and I had to take my brother with me.

I moved next to Scottie, placed my arms around his midsection, and then lifted him to his feet. He had a hard time standing and gaining his equilibrium. I held onto him and maneuvered the two of us out of the barn.

The fresh air was a powerful relief. The smell of death was now faint, but still present. The air outside was a gift.

"Take a deep breath," I said.

He tried, but ended up coughing instead. I thought he was going to throw up again, so I gently set him down close to the barn and leaned his head against the side of the old structure, and then moved away. I watched him for a few moments. He looked exhausted and ill.

"Try to take a breath. It'll help," I wasn't real sure about my advice. It made sense to me, but I wasn't sure that it would do him any good at the moment.

He finally took a breath and let his body slowly slide down from my positioning of him until he was nearly prone on the ground. The exception was that his head was pushing against the barn now. That posture looked uncomfortable. I felt sorry for him. He was probably too young to have seen what was inside that barn. I was too young, too. I guess I was luckier than Scottie. I had a stronger stomach for stuff like that, although I didn't know it until my encounter with those dead boys. I might have made a good doctor or nurse, except that I was more concerned as to the cause of the marks on their bodies, and why both of them were naked. In my young, ever-developing intuitive mind, I ruled out suicide rather quickly. I also ruled in torture, anger, and a vicious killer.

"Y'all okay?" Mr. Joe yelled out from the porch of his house.

I had forgotten about Mr. Joe. I left Scottie sitting on the ground with his head leaning against the side of the barn. I ran as fast as I could to Mr. Joe without saying a word en route. Some things you can't yell out even if you are in the country and no one is around for miles.

"You have to come to the barn, Mr. Joe. We found something awful."

"Show 'nuff," he said, and then mumbled some indistinguishable sound beyond my cognitive processes. I had noticed previously that many adults do this often.

He moved slowly but purposefully as he followed me to the barn. I wanted to run, but I knew that he couldn't keep up.

"Can you walk a little faster, Mr. Joe?"

"No ma'am, I can't. I hurt my leg pretty bad some years back and it don't do me no good nowadays. I couldn't run, child, if my life depend'd on it. Tell me what ya found."

"You know Buster and Micah Scruggs, those missing boys, Mr. Joe?"

"No, ma'am. Don't believe I do. But I did hear 'bout two youngins being looked for," he said.

"They lived over towards Renan, out that way. They were reported missing yesterday," I said.

"What dey doin' in my barn, Miss Clancy?"

"Nothing."

We walked on in silence until we reached Scottie leaning against the barn, just to the left of the entrance.

"What da matter wif you, child. You looks like ya seen a ghost or sumthin."

Scottie had now shifted a little so that his head was turned toward the ground as if he were looking at something below him, close to his face. It was the first time that I had noticed my brother's color was a pale yellow.

"Is he sick, Miss Clancy?"

"Yeah, you can say that. He's pretty sick. I think he's okay out here. Come on, Mr. Joe. I need to show you what's inside."

I led him into the barn and guided him back to the corner where the two boys were still resting in the aftermath of horrific violence done to them. Nothing had changed from the minutes before except the smell seemed worse now that I knew what was causing it.

"Oh, my God. What on earth has happened here?" Mr. Joe said in a voice that I had never heard come from him. His tone was rich and distinct, like a professor at a university. The sound from his mouth was so unusual that I turned and stared directly at him just to be sure it was Mr. Joe talking to me. Despite the chaos of the scene in front of us, I was fixed on Mr. Joe and his new voice. Where had that voice been hiding before now?

"Clancy, you go to my house and call your daddy. Now. Don't wait. You know where the phone is. Quickly. Call him, girl," Mr. Joe said in his wonderfully new and distinctly different voice.

I wanted to ask questions but the occasion would not permit such. I ran quickly to the house and called the Sheriff's Office. Susan Chaney patched me to Daddy's patrol car.

"Daddy, you must come out to Mr. Joe's house immediately," I said panting for breath before I could continue.

"Slow down, Clancy. Get your breath and tell me what's happened," he spoke calmly to me. He seemed to always be calm, no matter what was happening around him.

"This is bad, Daddy. We found those missing boys, Buster and Micah. You know, the Scruggs. You'll need an ambulance here. No, not an ambulance," I was still in a hurry, and couldn't think. I tried to slow down and force myself into calmness.

"Are they alive, Clancy?" he asked in his composed manner.

"No," I said, as I shook my head, and then started crying softly.

# Chapter Five

I heard Daddy's black-and-white approaching long before I saw it. The siren was blasting away down the oak-lined lane that led to Mr. Joe's house. Those huge oaks extended their presence all the way to the river. It was called Mossie's Point and it was the only road we ever used to get to Staunton. It was the most convenient. I never could find anyone who knew where the name Mossie's Point originated. I wondered if Mr. Joe's grandfather had known or had something to do with naming it since his house was the singular one along that road. The other trivial detail about Mossie's point was that there was no moss attached to any of the trees, or anything else along that route.

Clancyville had many names that few people could remember why they were called what we called them. Some traditions are simply so old that folks don't bother to pay attention to why a thing is called a thing, or a place is named whatever it is named. I figure that a name given to something should be important, important enough to know why a thing is called that. I guess that meant I liked a little history now and then. It also meant, I suppose, that I preferred rational and reasonable attachments to things. That, and the fact I was insatiably curious.

My daddy arrived at 5:36 that afternoon. I was watching Mr. Joe's mantel clock when he came through the door with Ralph Hines, his deputy, following close behind. Mr. Joe's clock was one of those hand-carved wooden types with a beautiful chiming unit that sounded every fifteen minutes. We heard it once before Daddy arrived.

No one had been talking while we waited. I had lots of questions, but Scottie was still a milky ashen color, so I thought better of asking questions while we waited for my father to arrive. I could do that later. The three of us just sat on Mr. Joe's old sofa. I was on one side of Mr. Joe leaning against his shoulder and Scottie, on the other side, had his head in Mr. Joe's lap. Mr. Joe was stroking Scottie's hair in what appeared to be a soothing kind of movement. At least it was working on Scottie. My brother's eyes were closed, but I could tell that he wasn't asleep. He just lay there without moving anything except now and then he would open his eyes. He hadn't spoken since he called out my name in that cry of desperation. That seemed like days ago.

I was thinking about Buster and Micah. Scottie was probably trying to forget about Buster and Micah. I have no idea what Mr. Joe was thinking.

Daddy nodded at Mr. Joe as he came through the front door. Deputy Hines stopped at the door and went into some kind of parade-rest posture. Deputy Ralph Hines was an idiot. All the kids in town made fun of him. If he had been funny, like a person with a sense of humor, he could have been the next Barney Fife. Deputy Hines wasn't funny. Hines took himself much too seriously and made life miserable for the rest of us. He looked uneasy standing there in the doorway, like he wanted nothing to do with this place. My guess was that he assumed he was guarding the door. I had no idea why he might be guarding the door into Mr. Joe's house.

Daddy tolerated Hines because no one else wanted the job; that, and the fact that he had gone through the training and passed. Hard to find good help when the county paid such a paltry sum for the deputy sheriff position. Hines was decent enough when Daddy was around. But my daddy wasn't around all the time. That was the bad part of having Ralph Hines in law enforcement in our county. I was just glad that Daddy was around that day we found Buster and Micah.

"What happened, Mr. Joe?" Daddy asked.

"Your chillin' axed to go up to the barn. I was cleanin' the fish for 'em. Wanted to surprise dem, ya know. Clancy and Mr. Scottie here said dey don't cotton to fish cleanin' and I thought I'd do it fer 'em. Jest a way to thank her for givin' me all dose fishes."

"Scottie ran on ahead of me, Daddy," I interrupted his interrogation.

"Let Mr. Joe finish, honey," he said calmly.

"Dat's okay, Sheriff Evans. She knows more 'bout dat."

Daddy turned his head to me as if to say *okay, go ahead and tell me.* It was a look I had grown accustomed to through the years.

"Scottie ran into the barn to hide. I was counting outside and looking for a big stick. Mr. Joe had warned us to keep a lookout for snakes and rats in the barn, so I was preparing for that."

Scottie hadn't moved yet. His eyes were focused on something across the room from the couch. His head was still resting comfortably in Mr. Joe's lap. Mr. Joe continued stroking Scottie's blond hair, offering what comfort he could to my brother. Scottie never liked people to touch him, except for Mama and Daddy. Either he was deep into shock or he was enjoying Mr. Joe's therapy.

"Next thing I knew was that Scottie yelled out my name and by the time I arrived inside the barn he was moaning. He threw up all over the place near where we found... Buster and Micah, Daddy. They're up there in the barn. They're dead. Buster is hanging from the rafters and Micah is lying in the hay. It's bad, Daddy. Really bad. The smell was awful and those poor boys...," I stopped talking. I couldn't finish what I was saying.

"Is that what you saw, Mr. Joe?"

"Yessir, Sheriff. Dat's what I saw." He nodded in agreement as he spoke.

My father stopped his interrogation and walked toward the door.

"Wait here. I'll be back."

Deputy Hines stepped out of the way and then followed my daddy out the door.

I ran out the door and onto the front porch and yelled, "Should I call the funeral home, Daddy?"

"I've done that, Clancy. They'll be here directly," he called back to me without breaking his stride.

Daddy was running full throttle towards the barn with Hines huffing and puffing behind him. Deputy Ralph Hines had a problem and couldn't jog around a bathroom. His problem was that he was skinny and had no muscle tone. It made me wonder how Hines could have passed that physical required as part of the police course he had taken. Maybe he cheated.

Since my father was tall, slender, and well built, he had no trouble running from Mr. Joe's house to the barn. I watched him glide along at a rapid pace while Hines struggled behind him. The gap between them had grown significantly as Daddy approached the barn.

I watched them all the way to the barn door. I wanted to go up there and talk with him, but with Hines around I was afraid to chance it. Like I said, Hines was an idiot and whatever I would say to Daddy would be all over town in no time. Daddy often had to be careful what he said when he conducted an official investigations. This one had all the markings of being truly official.

I heard the screen door open and close behind me. Mr. Joe joined me on the porch.

"I thinks Scottie is asleep now. He's had a long day, ya know."

We both stared in the direction of the barn for a few seconds. Nobody said anything initially.

An uneasy time passed while we stood there looking at his barn.

"Dem boys up there had a rough time of it, Miss Clancy. Whoever done this wuz mean. Real mean. And real strong, too. From da marks on der necks, I believes dey been strangled, both of 'em."

Mr. Joe's old voice had returned.

"But Buster was hanging, not Micah," I said.

"Dat true. But he could a been dead 'fo dey strung 'im up."

"Can an autopsy tell that, Mr. Joe?"

"'Spect it can, Miss Clancy."

"Mr. Joe, why do you think that those boys were in your barn?"

It was the first time it dawned on me the implications of where we had found the bodies. My question wasn't meant to imply anything about Mr. Joe or any involvement he could possibly have in this horrible mess. I knew better than that.

I turned to look at Mr. Joe just as he turned and looked at me. I think we both thought the same thing at once. I read fear on his face; likely enough, he read the same on mine.

"Maybe we'd better go up to the barn, Miss Clancy." His voice had changed once again.

Ralph Hines was trotting down toward us as we neared the gate at the edge of Mr. Joe's yard.

"Where do you think you're goin?" he said to Mr. Joe.

"We're going to see my daddy," I answered instead.

"You two got no business up there. I suggest you both git back in that there house and wait on the law to handle this."

He meandered on past us toward the patrol car. Mr. Joe and I watched the skinny Deputy Mr. Hines do his best to trot along as if he was overly exhausted from his meager exertion. If I hadn't disliked him so much, I probably would have felt some sympathy for him. But since laziness was not one of my peculiar sins, I had little sympathy for someone who moved through life at glacier speed no matter what was happening around him. In order for me to find it in my heart to tolerate him, he would have to miraculously develop a new disposition. I knew that was not going to occur in this life.

"We'd better do as he says, Miss Clancy. No need to make 'im mad at us."

"I don't care whether Ralph Hines is mad at me or not, Mr. Joe. He's an idiot."

"Now, Miss Clancy. Ever'body got der ways. Some good, some not so good. Besides, I can't 'ford to have da law angry wiff me."

I knew what he meant, or at least I thought I did. Even as a young girl of a mere eleven years, I had observed the way in which too many people treated Mr. Joe, as well as the other folks of our community who shared the same skin color with him. There was something about it that didn't seem quite right to me, and I did my best to make sure that I was kind to all people, except maybe the ones like Ralph Hines. I have my limits.

"Maybe Scottie will need you when he wakes up, Mr. Joe."

"Yeah, dats right. I gonna goes back and see Mr. Scottie. He's had a time of it."

I watched him walk back towards his house. All of sudden I had a sick feeling about this whole mess. I knew that some folks would find a way to blame Mr. Joe for the deaths of those boys. I knew it as well as I knew my own name. His land. His barn. This was not good at all. The world suddenly became a very dark place for me, and it had nothing whatsoever to do with the color of Mr. Joe's skin. Or, maybe it did.

I also knew that down deep Mr. Joe had not killed Buster and Micah. I knew that as surely as I knew that Scottie and I had nothing to do with it. Why would Mr. Joe have allowed us to go up to the barn if he had killed those boys and left them up there for us to find? That didn't make a lick of sense to me. Besides that, Mr. Joe had never been anything but kind and helpful to Scottie and me. There was no way that man could have killed those boys in such a violent way, or in any way at all, I reasoned. I was slowly being consumed by anger at the actions of a community which had not yet occurred. Still, I had this fear that what I was thinking was dead certain to happen.

I caught up with Mr. Joe. We walked back to the house together. Scottie was now asleep, stretched out fully on Mr. Joe's sofa. Joe pulled up one of his cane bottom chairs and placed it close to the couch to keep a closer eye on Scottie. I spotted a faded red cushioned chair that had been around a few decades and sank into it. It rocked gently as I settled into its softness. There was a handle on the side of the chair which I thought might open it up so I could lie back further.

"'Dat don't work no more, Miss Clancy," Mr. Joe said to me while looking over his shoulder. "Family heirloom which needs to be thrown in da dump."

He smiled and then returned his focus to Scottie. We remained silent with each other, only listening to the rhythm of Scottie breathing as we waited.

It seemed like forever before Daddy returned to the house. He appeared quite solemn when he entered.

"What time did you find them, Clancy?" Daddy asked.

"I don't know exactly, but it was before five, I think."

"Yessim," Mr. Joe added, "it was near 'bout 4:30 or so. I look'd at the clock 'fo I started cleanin' fish."

"Did you touch anything?" Daddy said to me.

"No sir."

"Did you notice anything unusual?"

"Other than the two dead bodies?" My brain was thinking much clearer now that I had had some time to rest and reflect.

"Yes, other than that."

"I noticed all of the bruises on both Buster and Micah. I noticed they were both naked. Scottie threw up right near Micah, and some underneath Buster. Lots of flies. And I couldn't help but notice the horrible smell."

Daddy nodded at me and then looked at Mr. Joe.

"Did you notice anything, Mr. Joe?"

"Only, sir, dat noose 'round dat boy's neck was …." he stopped.

"Was what, Mr. Joe?" Daddy said.

"Perfect," Mr. Joe said.

"Perfect? What do you mean?"

"Whoever done 'dis took some time, Sheriff Evans. Dey didn't jest tie a rope together wiff one of dose granny knots, ya know. Dey must've took their sweet time to string up dose kids. It wuz a perfect hangman's noose, sir. Not ever'body knows how to make a hangman's noose, Mr. Evans."

"Good point. Okay, Clancy. Let's get Scottie home. Mr. Joe, you stay close by in case I have more questions. You need to stay away from the barn. Right now it's a crime scene and we have it taped off. I'll be back out later. Do you have lights up there?"

"Jest one. One old bulb right in da middle. Not much light, ya know. But it fights the darkness."

"Yeah, better bring back some lights and drop cords. Deputy Hines will be staying until I return. They'll be lots of commotion around your place for a while, okay? Sorry about that."

Mr. Joe nodded without responding.

"Thanks, Mr. Joe," I said, as I opened the screen door for my father who was carrying Scottie in his arms. Mr. Joe followed us to the front door. He put his hand on my shoulder and patted me gently.

"Yessim."

Daddy placed Scottie in the backseat of the car, and we rode home in silence.

"What do you think, Daddy?" I finally asked as we pulled into our driveway and the car stopped.

"I think we have a real mess, Clancy. I don't like any of this."

"Do you think Mr. Joe did it?"

His eyes shifted away from whatever it was that he was staring at through the windshield, focused intently on me for a few seconds, and then quickly returned his gaze back to the scene in front of him. I looked ahead and saw nothing but our old barn.

"No, I don't. But it doesn't really matter what I think. I may have to arrest him anyway."

"Why? If you know he's innocent, why do that?"

"Two dead white kids found in his barn. Killed violently. One of them lynched. No witnesses. Just Mr. Joe's word against a few hundred years of racial bigotry. Mr. Joe's black and this is the south, Clancy. Sometimes I don't like my job."

"But if you have no proof that he did it, why would you arrest him?"

"I may have to arrest him just to keep him alive. Come on, I've got to keep moving. I don't have time to talk now. We'll talk later."

It took a while to calm my mother down. Cockroaches in the kitchen were a crisis for her. This was beyond anything imaginable. I never could figure out how my mother and father fell in love and got married. He was always calm and in control, especially in a crisis. Mother was seldom controlled or calm no matter whether there was a crisis or not. In fact, now that I think of it, my mother had a knack for making almost everything a crisis. She did not tolerate irregularities in her daily schedule.

"Should we call the doctor for Scottie?" she asked frantically.

"I don't think so. He's in shock and he'll snap out of it. He just needs some rest and some time to forget. We'll let him sleep now. I think he'll be fine."

"How long do we wait to know?" she asked.

"If he's not responding by morning, you know, talking to us, we ought to call. I have to go back, dear. I left Deputy Hines out there…."

He walked out the door without finishing his sentence.

"Are you okay?" she asked me, using a rather calm voice.

"Yes, ma'am. I'm okay. I'm just worried about Scottie and Mr. Joe."

# Chapter Six

The next morning we took Scottie to the hospital in Dan River, the closest city of any size to us. Scottie was still acting like he was in a trance, so Mama drove us over there before we had breakfast. She gave me a small glass of orange juice as we hurried out the back door. By the time he was admitted and all the paper worked signed and clarified, it was past noon and I was way past hungry.

Mama was driving her Studebaker Hawk, a car given to her sometime back in the early sixties by Aunt Nona, my Great Aunt Nona. I think it came to her about the time that Scottie entered our lives, or shortly thereafter. Mama had said, so the story goes, that she didn't need an automobile. Aunt Nona insisted, and that was the end of the discussion. Mama got used to it after a while, then it became a necessity.

I asked Mama a couple of times about eating something, but she wouldn't hear of leaving Scottie alone in the hospital room while we went to find some food. I understood that, but I also understood that I hadn't eaten since supper the night before. What with all the excitement last evening, we only had sandwiches for our evening meal. In the midst of our turmoil, we had left our catfish at Mr. Joe's. It was a safe bet that Mama was too upset to have cooked them anyway. We were lucky to have sandwiches. Whatever calories there had been from my sandwich had long since been used and my young body was running on empty.

Scottie had food brought to him, but he wasn't yet in the eating mode. Mama gave me Scottie's lunch. Settling for cold hospital food was quite a learning experience for me. I could only tolerate so much of it before I finally gave up and decided that being hungry wasn't as bad as I had first thought. By mid-afternoon I needed to get out of that building and find something to nourish me. I had a few dollars stuffed down in the watch pocket of my jeans. I told Mama that I was going to walk around a bit, and she nodded without placing so much as a single restraint for me. She had been around Scottie so long by that point that she was beginning to act a little like him.

I took the elevator to the main lobby and left the building in search of food. My nature has always been given to exploration. City or countryside didn't matter much to me. Adventure was something I craved, even if it was an adventure in search of sustenance.

There was a fast food hamburger place about two blocks down from the hospital, and I don't ever remember those window photos depicting their offerings looking so good before or since. I gulped down a hamburger, some fries and a small drink. I was thoroughly satisfied.

It was nearly four o'clock when I returned to the room to find Scottie sitting up and eating a cup of ice cream. He had that stupid grin on his face that always aggravated me because it usually meant that he was up to something suspicious.

"And where have you been young lady?" Mama said.

Her tone was not the kind that seemed to be asking for information. She was not happy that I had disappeared for more than an hour.

"I took a walk."

"Where?"

"Around."

"I had the hospital page you. Did you hear them call your name?"

"I must have stepped inside the restroom when that happened. Does that page thing work in there?" I asked. I had used the restroom when I got back from my eating ecstasy. My answer had been one of my cleverly developed half-truths, you might say; that is, half-truth over against an out-and-out lie.

"I don't know. But you were gone too long. You scared me."

"I'm sorry. I was okay. I just needed to get out. This room is kind of small."

Mother took the washrag from Scottie's brow and soaked it again in the sink under the cold water. Just then a nurse came into the room and asked to speak to Mama, outside in the hall. Mama handed me the wet washrag and left with the nurse.

"Is that ice cream good?" I asked, while moving next to his bed.

"Yeah, but not as good as I bet those fries tasted," he whispered.

"What fries?" I feigned my innocence.

"The ones you ate, silly. I smelled 'em on your breath when you came into the room."

"Don't say a word or you're dead," I threatened.

He grinned and put a big spoonful of ice cream in his mouth. Then he smacked his lips at me.

"What are you grinning about young man? You scared us to death," Mama said as she entered the room again. "It's good to have you smile again."

"Do you need anything?" I asked Scottie, hoping to avoid his having to answer her question.

"Not now, but maybe something more to eat later on. Like a … hamburger and some fries."

"They said you should start with something light. Maybe you can have some gelatin later," Mama said.

"Yuck!"

"You need to give your body time to recover," Mama said.

I was doing my best to stay out of this conversation between parent and boy-child. I knew exactly what my devious brother was scheming. I'll give him credit for shrewdness, but nothing more.

"I'll recover a lot faster if they feed me real food. Don't you think I should have something more to eat, Clancy?" he was using me. Even at the age of nine, he knew about leverage. I knew that his simple question to me was nothing more than a veiled threat. I was being coerced into playing along with him, or he would divulge my escapade to the hamburger joint in downtown Dan River.

"If he wants to eat something, Mama, maybe that means he's healing quicker than the doctor thought," I offered. My argument sounded lame.

Mama thought so, too.

"We'll go by the doctor's advice, young lady, not your opinion."

"But Mama," Scottie said, "I want a hamburger and some fries like—"

"Eat your ice cream and be quiet. The doctor may drop by and check you before suppertime. We'll see what he says then," her voice was adamant. Even Scottie knew when to stop once her voice reached a certain pitch. I was saved—for the moment—by my mother's tone and pitch, to say nothing of her sheer force of presence.

I threatened him with a slight gesture of my hand to my throat in a choking move. It was a usual sign between us, but today it was inappropriate and Scottie turned white almost immediately. He must have remembered something of what he saw, and it scared him. I stopped quickly and grabbed some water from his bedside table. I held the straw for him while he sipped. Mama had taken the wash cloth back to the sink so she missed this little episode that occurred between her two children. I was relieved. And saved.

"I'm sorry," I whispered. And I really was. I was glad he was better and I certainly didn't want to do anything to push him back to where he had been last night. Despite his peculiar, male behavior, he was my brother and I truly cared about him.

Daddy came to pick me up about six o'clock. The doctor had decided that Scottie ought to stay over one more night. That meant Mama had to stay overnight and I got to go home with Daddy.

"What's happening?" I said to my father as we drove out of the city.

"Is that a generic question or do you have something specific in mind?"

"The murder case," I said.

"Oh, that. Still thinking about it, huh?"

"I have thought of nothing else, except for a while I thought a lot about food."

He smiled.

"Any developments, is that the right word?" I said.

"A good word, … nothing much, so far. We're still looking. I've been all over the barn several times. I have found nothing useful to this point."

"No evidence at all?" I said.

"Just a rope that belongs to Mr. Joe, Mr. Joe's prints all over the place, and it would seem that they were murdered in his barn."

"Sherlock Holmes would ask about a motive at this point, I think."

"Wish we had Sherlock Holmes here. I could use the help."

"So, what would be Mr. Joe's motive for killing two boys like that?"

"I don't know yet. I'm searching. I don't have much to go on, Clancy. Not much at all." He sounded frustrated and tired. He had been on the case only a day and a night and it already seemed like a year.

"Nothing else happening?" I said.

"Oh, yes. There is plenty happening. The Scruggs' clan is up in arms and demanding the immediate arrest of Mr. Joe because *everybody knows that he did it!* At least that's what the voices say when they call me on the phone. It was hot enough this summer without all of this."

"What's next?"

He shook his head, but said nothing.

"You gonna arrest Mr. Joe, Daddy," I said.

"Looks that way, girl. I have to protect him. It's stacked against him right now. It may be the safest thing to do."

"Doesn't it make him look guilty if you arrest him?"

"He may be guilty anyway, I don't know. But, yes. I suppose you're right. Still, I have to consider the evidence."

"And the person?" I said.

"The person? You mean, Mr. Joe and the fact that he's black?"

"Exactly," I said.

"Yeah, that too. And the community. There's always that attitude of the community towards him."

"What do you think is their attitude right now?" I asked.

"I think they'd lynch Mr. Joe, given half a chance."

Daddy took me for supper at Myrtle May's Drive-In on Route 40. We had burgers, fries, and a chocolate milkshake. It was better than my lunch chiefly because I was sharing it with my daddy. I was too young to care about the difference in quality between burgers in those days. Myrtle May's hamburger was juicer than the other place's burger, if you liked juice running down your arms to your elbows. I never cared for that, but I did like the fries Myrtle served. They were larger and crunchier. But the best thing of all was the milkshake. Old Myrtle May could definitely work some magic with a milkshake.

"You'll have to come with me back to Mr. Joe's place. Is that okay with you?" Daddy asked.

I wanted to scream YES, but I decided to play it cool: "I suppose. I'm okay with going back. I was never frightened. I was only, just … well, sad to find Buster that way, you know. Buster was a pain in the butt, but most boys his age are. Still, he deserved better than that."

"I'm sure he did."

We drove toward Mossie's Point. The sun was about an hour away from setting and the whole area was glowing. We were almost at Mr. Joe's little farm when all of sudden we were surrounded by a swarm of butterflies. Neither of us had ever seen anything like it before. There must have been several hundred of them. They crossed the road in front of us moving towards Joe's house. Then they turned in unison and fluttered in the direction of the barn. We lost sight of them as they disappeared behind it.

"That was beautiful!"

"Yeah, it was. I don't recall ever seeing that many together."

"Do you call that a swarm or what?" I asked.

"I really don't know. I doubt if *swarm* would be correct. Butterflies don't really swarm, you know, like bees. Swarm doesn't sound right to use with butterflies. Maybe the word *cluster* would fit. You'll have to look that up."

Daddy was always telling me to look stuff up. I usually did, too. In fact, he was the reason that I began reading Sherlock Holmes a couple of years back. I can't recall specifically the occasion or exactly how old I was at the time. Probably around the age of ten or so. I just remember that I continually asked him questions about his work, his investigations, his routines, and all that kind of stuff. Finally, one day, he told me that I might enjoy reading about a master detective. I had heard of Sherlock Holmes but had never read any of Sir Arthur Conan Doyle's stories. Once I began, it was great fun. Daddy was right. I learned a lot from those crime stories. I began to wonder what it might be like to do that type of work for real.

"Daddy, can I go see if I can find those butterflies?"

"I expect that those butterflies are long gone by now, Clancy, but go ahead. I'll be at the barn. Don't wander off too far. It'll be dark soon enough."

When I had something to check out it didn't take much encouragement for me to be off and running. I was fascinated by what we had seen coming up to Mossie's Point. I was hoping to find those butterflies. I wanted to know where they were heading, if possible. They seemed to be moving in a specific direction. Maybe I'd get lucky. And, besides all that, I needed a distraction from what was happening in our little town of Clancyville.

# CHAPTER SEVEN

Daddy was sitting on a milking stool when I entered the barn just after sunset.

"Did you find your butterflies?" he asked.

"No, sir. They were gone by the time I turned the corner of the barn, like you told me."

"How about you, anything new?" I said.

"Not much. Too little to go on."

"Are you looking for something in particular?" I said.

"No, not really. In fact, I don't know what to look for. I guess I'm looking for anything. Clues, leads, anything. I'll know when I find it."

That made little sense to me, but I made no comment. For a small county sheriff, my father was a fairly good investigator. I could learn from him, even if I didn't understand all that he was doing or saying.

I walked over to the spot where I first saw Micah's body lying crumpled on the dirty barn floor. There were small piles of something dried all around the spot.

"What's this?" I pointed and looked over at my daddy.

"I think that's some of Scottie's contribution to the crime scene."

"Oh, yeah." I reached under the ribbon that Daddy had strung around that end of the barn to protect his crime scene from unwanted intruders. I touched the dried glob and then sniffed my finger.

"Yeah, this is the vomit from Scottie."

"Don't touch that, Clancy. I'm trying to keep the scene as pure as possible."

"It's a long way from pure," I said.

He stared at me without comment.

"Where's the rest of it?" I said.

"The rest of what?"

"The vomit."

"Ralph cleaned it up. It smelled horrible last night. The vomit mixed with the odor from the two corpses made it almost unbearable in here."

I could feel my stomach roll a little. I had a strong constitution, but a person could only take so much truth at one time. The odor which still permeated the barn's interior was like a heavy stench that made it nearly impossible to take a breath with any conviction that the air taken in would satisfy.

"It looks like he cleaned up more than just Scottie's sickness. I see several bare spots on the barn floor all around the area here where Micah was, and underneath where Buster was hanging. Should he have done that, Daddy?"

"What are you so concerned about?" he asked.

"Like you said, purity of the crime scene. And evidence. It could be anywhere. It could be anything. You said yourself there wasn't much to go on. What if that idiot Ralph Hines cleaned up something important?"

"I beg your pardon, young lady," Daddy's tone changed quickly. I had let a defamation of character slip without realizing it. You just didn't call other people names in front of Daddy.

"I'm sorry. But you know he's not the brightest star in the heavens," I said trying to recover.

"Now you sound like your mother," he smiled. Mama had learned through the years to use euphemisms whenever she slandered someone within earshot of him. I had learned some real jewels from her to hide what I actually thought about folks.

Daddy was scanning the whole barn area trying to make sense of the scene. I knew that he was trying to reconstruct the crime. He often called it the *event*. He had told me more than once that a good investigator thinks through what he or she believes happened at the scene. It doesn't mean that they know what happened. It simply means that they try to create a storyline as to what occurred.

"You're right," he said.

"About Ralph Hine's mental state?"

"No, love. About the crime scene. Perhaps Ralph did remove more than he should have."

"I rest my case," I said softly.

"Beg your pardon?"

"I'll be right back. I wanna to go outside for a breath of fresh, clean air. It's kind of stale in here, you know." I understated the severity of the lingering odor which was heavy enough to get a person down, physically. While it was true that the smell from the dead bodies was still lurking about, and the leftover vomit stench added yet another layer of heaviness about the place, what I wanted to do was search outside to find where that idiot Hines had put all that vomit-hay he had removed from the barn. I figured he wouldn't have carried it too far, considering the kind of person he was. Besides his other character flaws, he was lazy.

"May I borrow your flashlight, Sheriff Evans?" I said.

"Sure," he said, handing me his flashlight without further questioning. I knew to be extremely careful with his tools.

"I need it for close examination of what I am likely to discover," I said, as if I knew what he was thinking as well as what I intended to do. Sometimes just guessing makes a person sound more official.

The sun had set, but there was still a tiny shred of light so as to walk around safely without running into a snake or some other varmint which might be moving about as dusk settled on the barnyard.

I walked slowly around the side of the barn looking for some type of trash container where Hines might have thrown his clean-up effort. It had to be near-by because good old Ralph Hines wasn't about to over-extend himself with carefulness. As my mama often said about some folks, he was never likely to walk the second mile for anyone.

At the back of the barn, I discovered a couple of rusty drum-barrels that Mr. Joe must have used for burning. They showed signs of charred residue around the tops and sides. One of them had a lid. I removed it and the stagnant, day-old disgusting odor of my little brother's vomit immediately hit me. It felt as if someone had actually smacked me directly in the face. The powerful pungent stench was horrendous. I gagged, but managed to maintain some composure. I turned my head quickly to the side in search of some air less nauseous while I held onto my most recent meal with concerted effort.

I had discovered Ralph Hine's dumping spot.

The last thing I wanted to do was to thrust my hand down inside that day-old vomit from my brother's system, but I did want to make sure that every possible clue was looked at in this case. With Ralph Hines on his side, my daddy needed all the help he could get from me.

The flashlight aided my survey of the bottom of the barrel. Luck was with me. Ralph must have shoveled the vomit and hay and whatever else was on the barn floor into a plastic bag and then had simply dumped that into the barrel. I also checked carefully to see if there was an animal living inside or dining or whatever, either close to or inside of that bag. That included insects of all varieties. I could see nothing that was moving. I retrieved the plastic bag from the barrel, and opened it. If this was all taking place in the sunshine of the daylight hours I might have used a different system entirely to check out this evidence. But since it was dusk and growing darker by the minute, I had little time to waste, I had to hold my breath, talk to my stomach fiercely, and force myself to do what needed to be done with the crud below me, the crud that was now too close for comfort.

I lay the bag on the ground and spread the plastic opening wider. I then put my right hand into the plastic bag, inside the vomit-hay mixture, while I held the flashlight in my left hand, shining the beam on the ugliness I was feeling with my fingers.

The day-old vomit had begun to form a slight crust around itself. That thin layer of crust was not difficult to penetrate. The hard part for me was thinking about it as I was engaged in doing it. That was disgusting all by itself. Once I had penetrated the outer layer, the moist and gooey inside of the vomit felt like I was plunging my hand into a thick solution of oatmeal which required more liquid to smooth it out. There were lumps in the mixture. While it may have felt like oatmeal, it did not smell like oatmeal.

I was forced to take a breath before I had the opportunity to finish my fingering-search of the glob. I removed my hand and turned my face away from the bag as quickly as I could, hoping that I would not inhale too much of the harsh odor. I failed. I got a strong enough whiff which forced me to gag. I coughed and then returned to my work with an ever stronger tenacity as I held my breath. I kept telling myself that I had to do this. Daddy used to tell me that a good policeman leaves no stone unturned. That must also mean no vomit un-searched.

I wondered if Sherlock Holmes ever did anything like this. He probably would have made Dr. Watson do this type of stinky work. My Watson was Scottie, I reckon, but never in a million years would he have stuck his hand down in a bag full of vomit and hay, even if most of it had come from inside himself.

As I felt my way from one sticky glob to another similar object of disgust within the composition, I kept thinking of Mr. Joe and what a kind man he was. I simply could not imagine him killing anyone in the manner those boys were killed. In fact, I couldn't imagine Mr. Joe killing anyone in any manner. He just didn't strike me as that sort of man.

I suddenly felt something hard. Despite my inexperience with searching through vomit, I immediately concluded that there should not be something in it as hard as the object my fingers had discovered. I held it between my index finger and thumb as I slowly withdrew my hand. I dumped my discovery onto the ground and held the flashlight close to the object.

It was a ring. I wiped it repeatedly in some tall grass but I couldn't get it cleaned enough to see much of what was inscribed on it. I could see some writing, but I couldn't decipher it with my limited light. There was a stone in it, ruby-red, I guessed, with the ring itself made of gold. I had seen a ring similar to this worn by my Uncle Walters. I guessed it to be a class ring. I wiped it some more on the grass, and then stuck it in my pocket.

I searched the vomit-hay a few more minutes, discovered nothing significant, and then returned the garbage bag to the container and replaced the lid. I wanted to wash my hands but Mr. Joe had no spigot at the barn. I used the tall grass nearby to remove as much yuck as I could. It was disgusting work, but one does what one has to do now and then.

I smelled my hands after they were mostly clean. The smell was nasty. There wasn't much I could do about that. Removing that distasteful stink would have to wait.

As I was about to enter the door of the barn, Daddy was coming out.

"You ready to get some sleep?" he said as he passed by me in a hurry.

"Yeah, I'm a little tired."

I was also ready to get home so that I could scrub my hands and clean that ring.

"You smell like that—"

"Don't say it, Daddy. I'm sort of sick at my stomach. I shouldn't have touched that glob of Scottie's vomit and that hay in the barn. It leaves a lasting smell."

I thought I covered myself pretty well with that line of reasoning.

"Good soap and lots of hot water will have you smelling good in no time."

We walked together a few steps. I could tell that he was thinking.

"You didn't find anything around the outside of the barn?" he asked as he walked just a little ahead of me back towards his patrol car.

"A couple of barrels that Mr. Joe uses for burning," I said. I couldn't lie to my daddy. That would have been a serious error on my part. But I didn't have to tell him everything.

I probably should have told him about the ring, but I wanted to do some checking on my own. No time like the present to begin my career as an investigator. I was eleven years old and smarter than Ralph Hines. No better time.

When I finished my bath and that hideous odor was just a faint memory, I cleaned the ring as thoroughly as possible. I had let it soak in the sink while I took my bubble bath. I figured I owed myself some kind of pleasure for having put my hands inside Scottie's partly digested food. I rinsed and dried it with my bath towel. It left a faint odor on my towel, but nothing too serious. Mama would wash it anyway.

I could now read the writing on it.

It was a class ring from Freemont High School. There was some inscription on the inside that was hard to make out. It looked like some initials, maybe a B and a G or C. One was an A. The engraving on the inside of the ring was worn. The date was clear—June 2, 1956.

I had never heard of Freemont High School, at least not anywhere around Clancyville. The year 1956 placed it a few years before I was born. I had some work to do. This was the way it was with Sherlock Holmes, as I recall. One good clue always led to more work and possible leads. I hoped that any forthcoming leads would not force me to examine hay and vomit.

I reaffirmed my decision not to show the ring to Daddy for now. It might not be anything at all except somebody's lost ring. Daddy called those things *wild goose chases*. Right now he didn't have time for that. Besides, I could check this out as well as he could. I knew that I could check it out better than Ralph Hines. Besides, I knew Samuel Goldsmith personally. He was the town jeweler, and a friend. He could help me if anyone could.

# Chapter Eight

I had to wait while Mr. Goldsmith helped a young couple look at rings. The girl acted silly and the guy looked scared. She giggled each time Mr. Goldsmith showed them a different ring. The boy was wearing purple bell bottoms and some greenish short-sleeved Hawaiian shirt. His hair was dark and curly, styled like Art Garfunkel's, going in every possible direction from his head outward. He was thin and gangly. His face didn't resemble anything I could identify with quickly. He did wear ugly really well. I had never seen him in Clancyville before that moment.

The girl was wearing some very tight hot-pink pants and a large, white shirt, probably belonging to the guy. The pants appeared to be two sizes too small for her. Her shirt tails were out and tied just above her belly button. She had a purple scarf tied around her neck that almost matched his bell bottoms. I didn't recognize her either. They were probably passing through our little village on the way to somewhere.

My second thought was that they might be on their way to a costume party. After listening to her giggle and noticing the fear in the eyes of the wild-haired kid each time he saw the price of a particular ring, I finally concluded that they were going to get married. I guessed that they were maybe a few years older than I, but not many years, for sure. My opinion was that they were too young to get married, but what did I know about marriage? There is a limit to the knowledge of an eleven year old. Besides, their attire indicated that they deserved each other. If not love, then it certainly was a good wardrobe match.

Finally, they left without buying anything and I could tell that Mr. Goldsmith was relieved.

"You have many customers like that?" I said.

"More than you know, young lady. Now, how may I assist you this morning?"

Samuel Goldsmith was a kind old man. He and his wife Rachel were the only Jewish people in our small town. They had lived in Clancyville for the last fifty years, but were still considered by most folks to be outsiders. They had come south from New York City a few years after World War I had ended. He said that they were tired of big cities and wanted some peace and quiet. I wondered if there was not more to their story than what he told me. There might be other reasons for wanting to live in the south.

Mr. Goldsmith was only a few inches taller than I but outweighed me by better than fifty pounds, I guessed. He had a head full of short to medium-length gray hair that went in every direction possible, like wires searching for something to attach to. His hair reminded me of the pictures I had seen of Albert Einstein. Maybe this was the way in which the young man who had just left would look one day with gray hair instead of his present dark and curly locks. I used to wonder if Mr. Goldsmith owned a comb or ever thought about using one. He wore small glasses that rested as far down on his nose as you could place them without them falling off. All things considered, he was a charming man. I liked him.

"I found this ring and I wanted you to look at it closely and tell me all you can about it. I want to find the owner and return it."

"A good deed does not go unrewarded, Miss Clancy," he said as he took the ring and walked back to his workbench and picked up a large magnifying glass. "Let me see here," he studied the ring.

"Freemont High School," he muttered to himself. "I've never heard of that school, have you?" he asked.

"No, sir."

"1956. A few years back. Before your time, huh?"

Mr. Goldsmith had a sense of humor often expressed with his little side remarks.

"It seems so. I was interested in the inscription on the inside, Mr. Goldsmith," I said, trying to get him back to the task at hand.

"Oh, yes. Let me have a look here."

He pulled a much larger lighted magnifying glass over in front of his eyes and held the ring under it for the longest time. He kept rotating the ring and muttering to himself. The suspense was killing me.

"What is it, Mr. Goldsmith?" I finally asked.

"Well, my dear Clancy, it is obviously a class ring from that unknown high school, unknown to both of us ... and, it goes back nearly two decades. It's a girl's ring, as well."

I wanted to say something smart at this point, but I bit my tongue. I liked old man Sam. He had been my friend for as long as I had been alive.

"I'm only teasing you, Clancy. I have a hunch that you knew all of that when you came in here. However, what you may not have observed is that there's a state seal on one side of the stone and some emblem or school symbol on the other side. There are some initials here, but they are worn a bit. And there are some newer initials cut into it. They are very clear. Probably done recently. This year maybe."

"Which state?"

He paused and rotated the ring. His muttering was softer now.

"North Carolina."

"Anything else?" I said.

"Well, I think the faded initials are *B*, *A*, and ... the last one is most difficult. It could either be a *C* or a *G*."

"*B-A-C.* or *B-A-G*," I repeated to him just to be sure.

"That's what these old eyes tell me. Here, you take a look. Come around here and have a look-see yourself. Your young eyes might see something I have missed," he moved over as I came around the counter.

"That's what I think it is, too," I said cautiously. "So, who do you know with those initials?"

"Well, that's a big question. I might know several folks, or none a'tall."

"Have you ever seen this ring before?" I said.

"Can't say that I have."

"What's this?" I had rotated it under the magnifying glass until I had come across another engraving. It was a heart drawing and the initials *L* and *S*."

"That's the newer addition to the ring I was telling you about. It looks real new, maybe done in the last few months."

"So it means that *B-A-C* or *B-A-G* loves *L-S*?"

"Yes, ma'am. That's the way I read it. But with younger folks, you never know. Could mean anything or nothing."

"Thank you, Mr. Goldsmith. I guess we learned a little."

"Oh, we have learned a lot, my child. First off, the ring is 10 carats and worth a little. Not a lot, but some. It's not one of those cheap class rings. It's probably worth more to the owner than to some finder of lost rings. Secondly, it was worn by someone who had a smaller finger than the person it was made for."

"How do you know that?" I said.

"There's a sticky residue on the ring part opposite the setting. Back in the 50's and 60's it was common for teenage boys to seal their 'going steady' proposal to their fair damsel by giving them their class ring. More often than not the young lady's finger was smaller than the young man's, so the girls would take some white medical tape, cut it in narrow strips and put enough on that underside of the ring so that the ring would fit their smaller fingers, and the tape would only show when the young ladies turned their palms up. This ring had tape on it once upon a time. That would be my best guess, Clancy-girl. That kind of tape leaves a sticky residue that can only be scrubbed off with certain cleaning solutions. That hasn't been done yet to this ring."

"I thought you said it was a girl's ring?"

"I did and it is. But it just happens to be a large size girl's ring," he said.

"And she gave it to a boy with smaller fingers?"

"Whoever 'she' is gave it to somebody with smaller fingers, yes. Can't say for certain that a *she* gave it to a *he*."

I had the suspicion that Old Sam Goldsmith would have made a good detective. At the very least, he was observant and inquisitive.

"Can you tell me anything else?"

"Well, let's see. If you want to learn exactly where this high school is in North Carolina, I'd suggest that you go down to our high school and talk with Mrs. Vance Hilmar. She's the secretary and the boss down there. That old man Principal Johnson knows nothing. Don't tell him I said so. He has no humor, nor time for truth." Mr. Goldsmith chuckled a little.

"I won't say a word. And thanks for the tip on that tape thing. I thought that sticky stuff was left over from the vom—" I stopped for fear that I would tell him more than he needed to know. I trusted him, but I could only go so far with adults. Besides, my daddy knew everybody and he could easily discover that Samuel Goldsmith had helped me with my investigation of this ring.

"From the what?" he said, after my abrupt pause.

"I think I was wrong. It's not important. Thanks for your help." I turned and left hurriedly.

"Have a good day, Clancy," he called after me. "Oh, how's your brother doin'?"

I stopped at the door.

"He's coming home some time today. I think he'll be fine."

"Say, you didn't find that ring out at Mr. Joe's did you?"

I froze. I had forgotten how wily Samuel Goldsmith was. He missed nothing. That made him valuable and dangerous. My hunch about him being a pseudo-detective type was on target.

I was speechless just long enough for him to know that he had stumbled onto the truth of it.

He waved his hand across his face as if wiping away his questioning words just spoken to me.

"I won't tell a soul," he whispered across the room. "My lips are sealed. I know from nothing. Our secret, Miss Holmes. Let me know if I can be of further assistance." He smiled and waved good-bye as I opened the door. I loved the way he talked to me. It was nice to have an adult trust me; however, I chose not to divulge the truth regarding his suspicions. My guess was that he was already way ahead of me with his suspicions.

"Thank you," I said and waved back.

I let the phone ring twelve times to be sure that no one was home. It was a little past 9:30 that morning when I called and I really didn't expect anyone to be there, but it never hurts to be sure when you're trying to handle family. I loved coming into the bakery shop to smell the fresh bread even if I wasn't doing anything but using the phone.

"Here, child," Bertha said, and handed me a freshly baked roll. "You look undernourished. Is that mother of yours feeding you these days?"

I smiled faintly, playing to my audience at hand, and then nodded my head in the manner of an established, visual affirmative response to her question. I guess that was a lie since Mama hadn't fixed a meal for me in almost two days now. She had been preoccupied with Scottie and that was understandable. Besides all of that truth, I relished the rolls from the bakery in downtown Clancyville.

I took a bite of the roll and it was heavenly. The only thing better than fresh rolls from Bertha Doughton's Bakery were her fresh doughnuts. I would kill to eat her doughnuts. She offered me none of them on this day, so I was happy with the roll. Each bite made my mouth water for more. It was like eating something made of soft velvet, with a hint of sweetness. My mother could make excellent biscuits, but not rolls like Bertha. Bertha was the queen of the roll-making industry in our small town. In fact, she had a corner on the local market.

While I was momentarily lost in my food-rapture of complete enjoyment from the ovens of Bertha's magic, I spotted a wall calendar with a large, orange butterfly occupying a colorful flower.

"Do you know anything about butterflies?" I said as I pointed to her calendar just above her cash register.

Bertha had her back to me while she was busy doing something next to her cash register. She looked up at the calendar, only moving her head slightly, and then turned to face me and smiled. "They're quite lovely, don't you think?"

"They are that," I said as I chewed the last bite of her scrumptious delight. I licked my fingers slowly and loudly, as if to suggest to her that I had truly enjoyed her offering. I was also hoping that she might offer me yet another scrumptiously divine roll in light of my undernourished condition. I could've eaten a dozen of those delicacies.

My sound affects and obvious display of satisfaction failed to solicit another gift from Bertha.

"What is it you want to know about butterflies?" she asked.

"Well, Daddy and I were driving along that road going to the Staunton River, you know, out near Mossie's Point, and a whole group of butterflies appeared … seemingly out of nowhere," I said, gesturing with both of my arms to indicate a large cluster of flying insects for her.

"All the same kind?" she asked.

"I guess so. There were so many, I couldn't say for sure. But I think they were mostly the same."

"Monarchs?" she quizzed. "Like the picture, there?"

"Yes, ma'am. Monarchs. Orange and … well, I see some black as well on that one."

"Yes, and if you look closely here, Clancy," she pointed to a spot on the butterfly picture," there is a hint of yellow. Quite colorful. And they're plentiful around here chiefly because of all the milkweed that grows so freely."

"Have you ever seen a large gathering, a cluster? I'm not sure what to call them … you know, when there're so many."

"Me either, Clancy. Cluster is a good word. Quite descriptive, I'd say. But, I can't really help you with much specific information about them. I just like to look at them. And, I will tell you that when I see them around the flowers at my house, they give me a good feeling, you know, a good feeling inside."

"Yes ma'am, I know. Most of the time they do the same for me."

"Not all the time?" she asked.

"No, ma'am, not all the time." I decided not to say more at that point.

I thanked Mrs. Doughton for the use of her phone and the fresh roll. I headed towards the high school to check on the ring.

"Tell your mama that you're too skinny. She needs to fatten ya up," she called out to me as I left her bakery.

I wanted to ask for another roll, but then thought better of it. If Mama ever found out that I had asked for another one, I would have endured a long lecture. No thank you.

The secretary at the high school was not as cordial to deal with as Mr. Goldsmith or Mrs. Doughton. Besides that, she had no food to offer me. She was one of those keepers of the rules and did her best to make my life uncomfortable. I assumed that she conveyed this attitude to everyone who entered her office. Still, I would suspect that a person my age would definitely merit the treatment I received from her. Compared to her more than fifty years of life, I was practically nothing. Authority is a matter of domination for some people, and she played her role to perfection.

Everything about Mrs. Vance Hilmar was gray. Her skirt was dark gray, the sweater was light gray, her hair was a mixture of various gray tones, her glasses were some strange blend of gray and gray-blue, and her shoes were turning gray. Her blouse likely began life as white, but now it too appeared to be some version of a dismal gray, probably because of its proximity to her body. She wore no lipstick and only a hint of makeup. Her short, cropped hair made her look manly and formidable.

"Can I help you?" she asked, as if I had interrupted a congressional sub-committee meeting on some subject of national interest.

"I found a high school ring and I was wondering if you could tell me where that school is?" This gray woman was not someone I wanted to trust with vital information or my own personal secrets. I had the suspicion that she would rat me out to my father without even giving a second thought.

"Does this look like the library? Who are you?" She was definitely having a bad morning. I had made a serious mistake in coming to her.

I hated double questions. I especially hated double questions when I didn't want to answer either of them.

"What's the name of the school?" she demanded finally after I had failed to answer the first two. Nothing like having three questions waiting on me to answer.

I was hesitant.

"Belmont," I lied and I wasn't sure why.

"Let me see the ring," she ordered.

"I don't have it with me," I lied again.

"Well, I don't see how I can help you without the ring."

"But I told you the name of the school."

"That doesn't matter," she snapped. "There could be hundreds of schools with that name."

"How do I narrow it down to one?" I asked, hoping that she had given me a small door upon which to knock.

"Go get the ring and bring it back to me. I'll take care of it," she snapped.

"You look too busy to do trivial stuff like that," I said, without knowing where the courage had come from for me to speak to such an authoritarian lady.

"Don't get smart with me, little girl. Say, aren't you—"

"You've been *terribly* helpful," I said and darted out of her office before she could finish her identification.

Sometimes it was tough being the County Sheriff's only daughter. It was a small county as well as a small town, and everybody knew my daddy. I looked enough like him so that most folks could easily tell when they saw us together. We both had red hair and green eyes. My surly disposition came from my mother's side of the family.

Mrs. Vance Hilmar was helpful without intending to be. She gave me the idea of searching for Freemont High School at the County Library. I probably would have thought of that on my own, but it was nice for the old gray biddy to give me something useful since she was so bent on not helping me at all without my giving her the ring.

Instead of meandering my way to the library as I usually did when I had a mind to read, I walked purposefully and quickly to that hallowed place. It was hallowed for me. And, like everything else in Clancyville, it wasn't far away from where I was at that moment.

I loved the library. It was where I first met Sherlock Holmes. A girl remembers those wonderful encounters with a hero like him, especially one who thrilled me as that master detective had, being skilled beyond any real-life detective I had ever known or heard about. That would also have to include my own real-life hero, Bill Evans, my daddy.

When Daddy suggested that I check into the works of Sir Arthur Conan Doyle and his famous detective, Mama said I was too young. Daddy insisted in his own quiet way. The fact that my mother objected so strongly actually drove me to visit the library as soon as I could get there. I figured that there must be something sinful about Sherlock Holmes or she would have agreed with my daddy, not that they agreed about that much in life, it seemed to me.

The notable thing about our county library was that it was run by a man who had twin assistants. The man, Fred Andrews, knew everything about anything. The twin women, Elba and Melba, both sisters, both old maids, believed that they knew everything. They also lusted after the books. They treated the books like they were their own and dared us children to even open their books before checking them out. I was never clear about why opening them prior to placing my name on a card was such a vital issue for Elba and Melba. But, I had actually observed those twins chastising a friend of mine for daring to open and read prior to signing the card in back.

I tried to avoid the terrible twins whenever possible. I also made it a habit to sneak behind their backs and open as many books as I could before checking any of them out. Goes to my nature, I believe.

I was lucky. Today Fred Andrews was working the main desk. He was a jolly, portly, middle-aged man who wore a three-piece suit every day of his life, at least as far back as I could recall. It wasn't one of those matching three piece jobs. He generally wore one of five sport coats— blue, red, green, yellow or brown. His pants usually failed to match anything his jacket was doing, either in color or design. The vest was typically some wild polka-dotted, striped, or paisley designed-thing that often clashed with both the coat and the pants, to say nothing about the fight it was having with itself. I think he stumbled onto the secret of how to blend the perfect mixture of styles and fabrics each day that would cause irrevocable damage to the great color schemes of life, and to inflict both confusion and havoc upon those folk who prided themselves on maintaining the fashions of our era. His wardrobe made you want to run naked through the streets just to free yourself from his fashion statements. Matching outfits were not his forte, but he was one of the friendliest people in town. He also knew books. And, besides all that, I liked the man. I couldn't care less about his wardrobe. I had my own issues with my own fashion statements.

"Good morning, Miss Evans. And how may I help you?"

The boys all thought that Fred Andrews was a sissy and maybe more than that. Some of them called him a fag, but I never did like that term. He was different, especially from my daddy. But then, all the men in Clancyville were different from Daddy. Fred was nice, but I probably would never want to marry him. Truth be told, he wouldn't want to marry the likes of me either. My hesitancy about spending the rest of my life with him was, I think, his wardrobe. Today he was wearing brown slacks, a green shirt, a blue and yellow polka-dotted vest, and a red sport coat. I tried to look into his eyes rather than at the colors of his garments glaring at me. He looked like a neon sign behind the desk, but without the flashing.

"I need some help finding a high school in the state of North Carolina."

"Do you know the town or city?" he asked as he moved towards a small section of the library.

I shook my head without saying a thing.

I followed him, knowing that he was responding to my question by guiding me towards what was likely the answer.

Finally, he stopped, put his right hand at the base of his chin, and said something resembling "hmmm." There was a sign above our heads which read Reference Works.

He turned to face me. "Well?" he asked.

"No, sir," I said, suddenly realizing that he had probably not observed my head shaking earlier in answer to his question.

"Not really a problem. We have a reference book on high schools. It will tell you everything you want to know about the school, and," he entered the room, then walked quickly into the quietest part of the library and lowered his voice appropriately, "everything you don't want to know. It's very thorough." He pointed to a volume and turned to leave.

"The cities and towns are listed in alphabetical order. If it exists, you'll find it," he said walking away and likely heading back to the main desk. Fred always treated me like an adult. He assumed that I could find what I wanted. He obviously did not mind that I would be touching the books.

I found what I needed and it only took me about fifteen minutes. There was a Freemont High School located in Greensboro.

"Mr. Andrews, I found what I was looking for, well, at least some of it. I need some more information. It's a Greensboro, North Carolina school. How can I get a yearbook from that school?"

"That certainly did not take you very long, young lady."

"I skipped around a lot. It's sort of boring just going from A to C to D."

He studied me for a moment and then suddenly remembered my question.

"Oh, yes. The yearbook. Easy. I'll send for one. It's referred to as an inter-library loan. I'll call right now. What's the name of the school again?"

I told him and he called. I decided to walk around in the stacks while he remained on the phone in anticipation of an answer to his inquiry. I had read all of their Sherlock Holmes' books, but it wouldn't hurt to check to see if they had gotten in any new ones.

Just as I spotted one that looked new to me, I reached for it and had the uneasy feeling that I was being watched. Out of the corner of my eye I spotted one of the library twins lurking nearby, giving me the evil eye. I withdrew my hand quickly without ever touching the volume, and walked back to the main desk. I could return later when she was elsewhere. I couldn't tell which of the twins it was, but I suspected she had a sixth sense. Maybe they both had a sixth sense. Probably so.

Mr. Andrews was still on the phone when I returned to his location.

"What year, Clancy?" he whispered.

"Uh, 1956."

He gave me a strange look and relayed the request.

"Good," he said to someone on the line. He thanked them and hung up. "It might take a week or so, but they're sending it. That's a few years back before you were born, right?"

"Yes, sir. I'm doing some research about that year and needed some information." I was over my head at this point and my response to him sounded lame. What would a girl my age be doing research on a high school in Greensboro for the year 1956, and, to beat all, in the middle of the summer? He smiled and asked no further questions. Fred Andrews might dress in a peculiar fashion, but he wasn't meddlesome man. He may have acted differently than other men, but he was helpful, and not concerned with any business that was not his own. I liked that about him.

It was close to eleven and I decided that I had better head for home. Mama would send out the cavalry if I didn't show for lunch. I had a feeling that she and Scottie would be home by now.

My hunch had been correct. Mama and Scottie had been home about thirty minutes by the time I arrived. Scottie was feeling much better and so Mama was in a better humor. We ate lunch in relative silence except now and then Scottie would kick me to let me know that he was back to normal. Yes, I kicked him back.

Despite his recovery, he was confined to his room until Mama said he was officially healed. She was harder to deal with than most brain surgeons.

He wanted to know what was going on and I told him a little of what had happened. I tried to avoid talking about the dead bodies for fear that he might lapse into another dimension. I could only imagine what my mother would do to me if I caused him to re-enter his semi-comatose state. I didn't want to go there.

Fortunately he grew tired faster than his desire for being updated on the situation at hand regarding the investigation. I eased out of his room after he nodded off to sleep.

I told Mama that I was going walking. I didn't dare tell her that I was on my way to visit Mr. Joe. I figured she would never permit me to do that. Like most of the people in Clancyville, Mama believed that Mr. Joe had killed those boys. Conventional wisdom.

# CHAPTER NINE

There was no answer when I knocked on Mr. Joe's front door. I knew that Daddy had told him not to leave, so I figured he had to be close by. I called out for him. No answer.

I walked around to the back of his house, but he was nowhere in sight.

I called out again. More silence.

I looked towards the barn and felt some twinge inside me. I had been there with Daddy just last night and had had no strange feelings. But that was with my daddy. Maybe Mr. Joe was up there now. I had to go check, but a part of me didn't want to return to that place, at least not alone. It's never easy to conquer one's fears, especially when you're eleven years old, or even allowing for the fact that soon you will be a glorious twelve. Fear is fear, for whatever the age.

I stopped at the barn door. I was feeling quite hesitant. I called out for Mr. Joe and waited. Nothing. I called again. More silence. The door was ajar like always, so I stuck my head inside and called again, this time a little softer. If there were demons inside that place, I didn't want to disturb them.

The silence came back on me and I decided that Mr. Joe was not inside the barn. It was hot and still, except for the flies that are always busy in the summer. I could hear some bees off somewhere. Birds were singing in the trees that lined one side of the barn. It was one of those wonderful summer afternoons that kids sometimes remember after they're grown, part of that nostalgic stuff which occurs. We take them for granted as children. They seemed endless, and common. Then, for some reason, we become adults and they disappear mostly, returning at intervals perhaps to draw us back into childhood, or to just remind us that something beautiful and lovely is missing.

I stepped away from the shadows of the barn and into the warm sunlight. It felt good to be alive. I felt a deep sadness about the deaths of Buster and Micah. They were not friends of mine, but I hated what had happened to them. I also had some sadness for their family and what they were feeling.

As I pondered my next move, a butterfly fluttered past me and suddenly I knew what I needed to do. I gave chase. I followed it around behind the barn and then on into the high grass which formed the backside of Mr. Joe's farm. There were other butterflies by now and they were flitting about as if they had nothing better to do. It's hard to follow butterflies. They act like they are going in no particular direction at all while going in all directions at once. I was learning patience a hard way.

Slowly and erratically they led me through the tall grass and into an opening near the back fence line of Mr. Joe's farm. I stepped through the broken, wooden fence, passing through a grove of trees with the butterflies still in sight.

Suddenly, there were more butterflies than I could ever imagine or count. They were everywhere. There seemed to be several varieties. I learned later that the correct term would be species. I observed shades of blues, yellows, reds, greens, whites, and, of course, oranges, mostly oranges—nearly every color imaginable flittering around me. The orange ones clearly outnumbered the other varieties. The only one I knew was the monarch. It was the easiest to identify.

I had invaded their world, but they were behaving nicely towards me. I stood still and enjoyed the moment. It was as if I had stumbled into some magical place hidden from the world of humans. The butterflies flitted and fluttered for several minutes at my disturbing presence within their kingdom, but finally they settled back into their business at hand. They were looting the sweetness from the abundant wildflowers now surrounding me.

It looked like a breeding ground for butterflies from all over the world. I estimated the count to be in the hundreds. Mr. Joe would later tell me that they numbered in the thousands, most likely.

I was definitely in a good humor by the time I returned to the barn. Butterflies had a way of permitting me to enjoy life a little more. They were magical. I never understood my feelings about them, but they could transform almost any horrible moment by just showing up and flittering by. Colors on the move. Joyful colors looping and swooping around as if the world were their playground. Not minding a bit that I watched them on center stage. Delightful moments of enjoying soundless, extravagant, fragile colors, passing all about me.

I left that gloriously colored scene after some time had passed. I walked back the way I had come. I called again to Mr. Joe both outside and inside the barn. No answer either time.

I returned to his house and knocked once again. Silence. I was concerned that he was not around. I didn't know whether I should tell Daddy or not.

The walk home was interrupted by Daddy's approaching car. Deputy Hines was with him.

"What have you been up to, young lady?" Daddy asked.

"Chasing butterflies," I said truthfully.

Hines muttered something under his breath about all women being alike, but I couldn't hear all that he had mumbled. Daddy ignored him. The more I was around that man, the more I was able to confirm my evaluation of him. He was a rather disdainful human being and I disliked him immensely.

"Better get on home. Mama will be worried."

"Have you seen Mr. Joe?" I asked cautiously.

"He's in jail where he ought to be," Hines spit the words out.

"Jail?" I said.

"It's for his own good, Clancy," Daddy answered.

"And the town's," Hines added.

I stared at Hines without saying anything. My displeasure with the man was growing. I wished that that my father could find someone more able to help him in his work. At the very least, I wished that Daddy would hire someone with some gumption along with some culture. Hines seemed to be lacking in both.

"We'll talk at supper." He drove on toward Mr. Joe's place.

The butterfly magic was gone. I was heartsick over this turn of events. My old friend was in jail. It was not what I had wanted for him. Daddy had warned me, but I had been hoping against his reasoning. This was not a good development.

It was a long walk home.

Supper went without any major events or confrontations. Scottie was even decent. He kept his mouth shut and didn't spill his milk, two significant contributions.

"Any more evidence?" Mama said.

"Well, I called Richmond for some data on Mr. Joe. They told me to call back in a day or two. I might get some lead from that."

"What kind of lead?" I said.

"Anything. I'm desperate at this point. I need something to go on. Maybe some references, some folks who have known him and who could vouch for him. I would like some history that will help put all these suspicions and accusations to rest. Anything," he sounded frustrated.

"What's his full name?" I said.

"Joseph George Jenkins," Daddy answered.

"Did he tell you anything about himself?"

"Said he was born near Richmond, a small place called Sandston."

"That it?"

"Just about. Said he was born in 1901. Missed fighting in both world wars —too young for the first and too old for the second. Said he spent a lot of time in and around Richmond."

"Does he have any family?" Mama asked.

"He just shook his head when I asked about a family. It was like he wanted to avoid that question, or something," Daddy answered. "He did mention a sister and her teenage son living somewhere in North Carolina, but nothing more."

"Maybe he had a wife and she died," I suggested.

"Could be, Clancy, could be. We'll find out tomorrow or the next day."

"Clancy, you clear the table and then wash. I'll dry tonight," Mama said.

Chores around our place were not an option. Everybody had something to do. Daddy went outside to water the flowers before he left to meet Deputy Hines. Scottie was exempt from his chores on this night since he was still convalescing. I figured he was faking it and trying to milk all the sympathy he could for as long as he could. I said nothing because he had been through a rough ordeal, and the wrath of Mama would have descended upon my head post-haste if I had spoken a syllable against that precious boy-child.

Before it was time to turn out the lights, I visited Scottie to let him know that I was researching the ring, but had turned up nothing as yet.

"That ring might not even belong to anybody," he said.

"Oh, it belongs to somebody, but it might not have anything to do with Mr. Joe or those boys," I said hoping not to trigger any more episodes from Scottie.

He gave me a funny look and then half-way smiled.

"I'm okay, Clancy. You can talk about them if you like. I just don't want to go back there and see them like they was."

"Were," I said.

"Exactly."

"You said *was*. You should have said *were*."

"You sound like Daddy."

"I know. Just trying to help you, that's all."

"Leave my talkin' alone. I talks jus fine," he said on purpose.

"Sure thing, Scott. See you in the morning."

"What are you doing tomorrow?"

"I don't know. I guess I'll go down to the jail and visit Mr. Joe …that is, if that idiot Hines will let me see him."

"Can I go with you?"

"You'll have to ask the boss."

"Ask the boss what?" Mama said as she entered the room without warning.

"Nothing, Mama," Scottie said.

"He wants to go downtown with me tomorrow to visit Mr. Joe."

"I don't think so. And I don't want you going down there either, young miss."

"Mama, he's our friend. He doesn't have many friends around here. He's a good man—"

"You don't know that. He may have killed—" she stopped before finishing. Her eyes cut to Scottie, waiting to see if her word elicited a bad reaction. Scottie never looked at her. He was pretending to read his Superman comic book.

"I know if somebody is good or not. Scottie and I trust him. So does Daddy."

"He trusts him so much he put him in jail," she said firmly.

"That was for his own safety and you know it," I said.

"And to keep him from running off. You know how hard it would be to catch a nig—" she stopped abruptly and turned a little red. She hurried out of the room as if she was embarrassed.

I went straight downstairs to talk with Daddy. I wanted to hear it from him.

His car was still gone. Any explanation would have to wait until morning. I would talk with him at breakfast and get this straight. I would also try talking with Mama again in the morning. She could be reasonable sometimes after she had a night to sleep on something. But then again there were times when the hard-headed Clancy side of the family, the side I was named for, would suffocate any reasonableness right out of her. She was almost as headstrong as I was. I always thought it was one of my better traits, but my mother could be downright obstinate some of the time.

# CHAPTER TEN

The gods were with me the next morning. Mama relented and said I could go visit Mr. Joe. Scottie had to stay home. One more day of rest became her mantra for the morning. I wasn't about to argue with her reasoning since I had won a major victory for myself. I had the feeling that she and Daddy had talked late into the night. Daddy would have made a good defense attorney, at least before Judge Mama.

Daddy offered me a ride. I thought he was just being nice and saving me from walking. Walking was not a big deal in Clancyville, at least not one that I disliked. However, it was a big thing to ride in my daddy's police car. I don't believe all the people in our community felt that way. I felt safe in his battle-wagon no matter where we went. It was a fortress. I was the princess and he was the king. Nothing could happen when I was with him in that black-and-white. We rode off in the direction of Mr. Joe's place instead of heading towards the jail.

"What's happening?"

"Since I put Mr. Joe in jail yesterday afternoon, I have unknowingly increased my workload," Daddy said, sighing rather obviously.

"What do you mean?"

"Mr. Joe's cow has to be milked."

"Oh, yeah. Bessie Mae," I said. "I had forgotten about her."

"You know her, do you?"

"Sure. We're practically friends."

"Well, you can watch and learn, young lady. Milking a cow is not too difficult, but there is a technique to it. Some folks have it, some don't. I grew up on a farm and was made to learn the technique. My education occurred over several weeks and months."

"I've milked Bessie Mae before," I said rather proudly.

"When did you do that?" he asked, either pleasantly surprised with my newly acquired skill or my revelation of it.

"Mr. Joe showed me and Scottie how to do it the other day. It was fun, although I am sure there is a limit to the fun one can enjoy in such things. Like if I had to do it every day."

Daddy smiled and said no more. We arrived at Mr. Joe's place and found Bessie Mae behind the house looking fuller than usual. I offered to do it and Daddy backed away after handing me the stainless steel bucket Mr. Joe used for the chore. It took a few minutes, but I finally had a nice white stream flowing mostly into the bucket with every squeeze. Bessie seemed relieved. I think I heard her sigh a few times during the process.

After I had finished, Daddy unlocked Mr. Joe's back door and we transferred the milk from the bucket to a pitcher and put it in his refrigerator. After Daddy had me rinse out the bucket at the well out back, we climbed into the car and headed towards the jail.

"Would you like to handle this job for me?"

"Sure. Can Scottie help, too?"

"Twice a day. You can't forget."

"I won't forget, but that's a lot. Every day, morning and evening, right?" I asked.

"Yes, ma'am. Bessie, as you call her, will be depending on you. So will I."

"It'll be easy to remember. We can accomplish this important task in the mornings when we pass by on the way to our fishing hole, and in the evenings when we return with our catch."

"Sounds a little like a conspiracy to get your mother to allow you to fish every day," he said.

"Is there no one else we could ask to help?" I asked, trying to sound as if I had no ulterior motive in my genuine offer to do this.

"I'll do some checking. In the meantime, it's your job. You and Scottie handle this, okay?"

"Okay," I said. I decided it was the least I could do for Mr. Joe.

Daddy dropped me off in front of his office. He had some errands to run before attacking the paperwork he had to do for the day. I would have preferred for him to have entered the building with me because of Deputy Hines' presence and my bitter disapproval of that man. No such luck on this day. I had to encounter my enemy face to face with no outside assistance.

Just before we arrived at the Sheriff's Office I already had thought of a problem regarding the milking of Bessie Mae. Mr. Joe's refrigerator was going to get really full, and fast. I decided I had better check with Mr. Joe to find out what he wanted me to do with the milk overflow.

Deputy Hines was distracted as I eased into the office. I quickly moved through to the jail section without acknowledging my presence to him.

Mr. Joe gave me a broad smile when I pressed up against the bars and said hello softly.

"Mornin', Miss Clancy. How be you?"

"I be fine," I said.

I walked over and partially closed the door that separated the jail from the front office. I wanted our conversation to be private. Ralph Hines was sitting at my daddy's desk as usual when my father was out of the office. He was still occupied with something. I knew that Hines would give me a hard time if I closed the door all the way. I was testing the limits of his flawed character. He figured it was his legal duty to know everything that everybody said inside the jail. My advantage on this day was that he as yet had no idea that I was inside the jail.

"Why do you talk like that, Mr. Joe?" I said, after nearly closing the door.

"I talks like I learn'd to talk, Miss Clancy."

"But I heard you the other night. I heard you speak clearly and … differently."

"How's dat?"

"I don't know, like educated. You didn't sound—" I stopped myself. I wasn't sure of what to say next. I didn't want to offend my friend.

"Like a black man," he filled in my silence. His voice was different again.

"Yes, sir. Like most black men I know," I offered by way of some clarification.

"But I am a black man, Miss Clancy, and I'm talking to you now," he said in that deep voice I had heard the night that we found the Scruggs brothers.

"Like that. That's the voice, Mr. Joe. Why don't you talk like that all the time?"

"What's goin' on back here?" Deputy Hines pushed open the door harder than necessary and entered the jail area with his usual swagger.

No one said anything in the appropriate amount of response time. I cut my eyes sideways at Mr. Joe. He was watching Hines. I looked back at Hines and rolled my eyes heavenward.

"We're talkin', Mr. Deputy Sheriff. You think we're plannin' an escape?" I said sarcastically.

"Up to no good as usual," Hines continued. "Who told you you cud come back here anyway? You shouldn't be back here alone with that nigger."

"You shouldn't call him that."

"I'll call him anything I like, little girl. I don't care what ya think or who your daddy is, ya hear me?" His meanness was beginning to ooze. My disgust for the man was mounting, if that was even possible.

"You have no right to disrespect him."

"He's a killer and I'll treat him any way I choose," Hines said.

"You don't know he's a criminal. Nothing has been proven."

"I have all the proof I need. Everybody in town knows that he did it, Miss Smart Mouth. He's guilty as sin."

At that point I knew that I was a good match for Ralph Hines. In fact, I suspected that he was out of his league with me. However, I also knew that I would not win any of these verbal spats between us, even if I knew I had a better command of language and rational thinking.

"You could have done it just as easily as Mr. Joe," I suggested.

Hines turned white and didn't know what to say. I must have touched a nerve inside the man. His response was a look of fear. I had no idea what I had done, but I was enjoying the moment. I figured that his stupidity overcame his brain's speech center. Or, maybe something else was going on.

"She didn't mean to accuse ya, Mr. Hines," Mr. Joe offered in my defense. He must have thought that Hines' look was a prelude to rage. Maybe he had seen that look on other faces at other times. Or, maybe Mr. Joe decided that he better lighten the moment.

"If the shoe fits," I said in defense of my previous position.

Hines never allowed me to conclude my cliché.

"That's enough," Hines raised his voice and grabbed me. I was escorted out into the main office and shoved towards the front door. Daddy would never have permitted such behavior from a law officer if he had been present.

"Get outta here. Ya got no business bein' back there with that nigger. 'Hit ain't right and proper. Stay outta here, ya hear me?" His voice sounded desperate. He was searching for some authority without any success in finding it as far as I could tell.

I calmly opened the main door without responding. He deserved no answer. He was an animal. He was an idiot.

Daddy suddenly entered the office before I could exit.

"I forgot some papers I needed to show Bobby Rowland," he said as he walked past me. "You finished visiting with Mr. Joe already?" he asked.

"No, sir. Your deputy thought I had finished my visit. He said I had stayed long enough."

"Aw, let her stay as long as she likes, Hines. As long as she doesn't get into your hair and keep you from your work."

Hines grunted. He certainly didn't like this turn of events. I walked past him back into the jail room. I must say that I walked with my own swagger as I stared at Hines when I passed his desk.

Mr. Joe was surprised to see me.

"I thought the deputy had escorted you out," he said.

"Matt Dillon came along and rescued me," I answered.

Mr. Joe chuckled.

"Good thing you're the sheriff's daughter."

I nodded in agreement. Mr. Joe didn't know half of the reasons I was glad to be the daughter of Bill Evans. It's generally good to have friends in high places.

Hines didn't bother us for at least twenty minutes or so. I kept watching the door, believing that any minute now he would stomp into our area and chase me out.

"I will be milking Bessie Mae for you," I proudly announced.

"Good. She'll appreciate that. Me, too," he smiled a little.

"Your refrigerator is going to get full quickly. What do you want me to do with the extra milk?"

"Good question, Miss Clancy. I have a couple of fifty gallon drums behind the house clean enough to handle the milk you retrieve. You can pour the milk in there. If I stay in here too long, you'll have to pour the milk from the refrigerator into those drums as well. It'll sour."

"We could use the extra milk, Mr. Joe. Scottie and I drink lots of milk. Our mama insists on it. Is it okay that I asked you for it?"

"Of course it's okay, Clancy. Why would you think otherwise?"

"Well, my mama doesn't like for me to go around asking people for things, like food," I said.

"Well, I understand how she might feel. But, in this instance, it is quite acceptable for you to ask for that milk. It'll surely go to waste if somebody doesn't drink it," he said.

"You're talkin' regular again, Mr. Joe," I said when he had finished giving me his instructions regarding the milk.

"Yes 'um," he replied.

"I noticed when Hines came in and forced me to leave earlier, your voice changed back to the old way while he was in here. So, Mr. Joe, tell me what's going on."

"I don't believe the deputy cares much for me, Clancy. I had to rely on my wits years back when I moved to Pitt County. I try to talk the way people expect folks like me to talk, if you know what I mean."

"You mean like ... ah ... survival strategy?" I asked.

"Precisely. If folks knew I had more education than they did, I'm afraid it would not have set well with them, at least most of them. That old way of talking, as you refer to it, is my way of keeping my place and minding my own business. It doesn't raise suspicion. What they don't know about me, well, that's to my advantage."

"I'm sorry people are like that, Mr. Joe," I said. "It's not right."

"Plenty of things in life are not right, Clancy. And, I didn't like talking that way at first, but I've gotten used to it. I try not to think about it too much, you know, too deeply. Most of the time, it do come nat'ral."

"I think both voices you have sound natural to me. You're good at pretending."

"Maybe so," he said and smiled. It was not one of his good, strong smiles. I detected some pain in it.

"Am I being nosy?"

"Yes, ma'am, but I don't mind."

It wasn't long before my belief about Hines was proven correct. He hurried into the room and promptly ushered me out before I could mount much protest. I barely had time to say goodbye to Mr. Joe before I found myself standing on the sidewalk outside of the Sheriff's Office of Pitt County in downtown Clancyville, Virginia.

Ralph Hines was quite simply a deplorable human being, and that was a nice way of saying what I really felt about him.

"What's the matter with you?" Mama asked as I walked through the back door to our two story white house which sat serenely on Washington Street some ten blocks from downtown Clancyville. The house had been in my mother's family for seventy-two years. My famous grandfather had built the house and my mother was born in it. It wasn't the largest house in Clancyville, but was widely known because of Granddaddy. He was an icon and everything he touched became one as well.

"Nothing."

I was afraid to tell her what happened. I was afraid that she would take the side of that idiot deputy and I just didn't want to hear all of that stuff coming from her.

"Mama, do you know anything about Deputy Ralph Hines?"

"Like what?"

"Like where he's from, or, I don't know, anything at all."

"He's from here, I reckon. He's always been around here as far as I know. He was a few years behind me in school as I recall. I don't remember him before high school. His folks were raised out in the Callands area of the county."

"He married?"

"No. Not unless he's married someone on the sly in the last day or two. In fact, he's always been a loner as far as I recall. His family and ours didn't socialize, so I really can't say much more than that."

She sounded snobbish at that point and I almost hated her for saying it the way she did. Even if it was Hines, I didn't like it when Mama compared her blue blood to the lesser breeds when she talked about the people of Pitt county.

"You need to leave Deputy Hines alone. Stop bothering that man. I have the feeling that he doesn't like children, so … leave him alone."

"I generally have nothing to do with him, Mama. I simply pass him and do my best to ignore him," I confessed.

"Why are you so interested in Deputy Hines all of a sudden? I didn't think you even liked the man."

"I don't like the man. I was just curious, that's all," I said leaving her sitting at the kitchen table sipping her mid-morning coffee.

She was dressed as usual—light summer dress with a white lace collar and black flats. Her hair was impeccable. She looked like she had just stepped out of some issue of *Vogue*. Well, maybe some southern issue of *Vogue*. My mother rarely ever did any type of housework. Five days a week Sarah came in to do the cleaning, the ironing, and anything else Mama wanted done. Sarah lived on the other side of the tracks and was the wrong color, as my mama once said. I had the feeling that Mama's description of Sarah was her attempt to compliment the black lady who had been ever-present in my life from my first breath. I loved Sarah and I think that feeling was mutual.

Sarah was upstairs now making the beds or changing the beds or scrubbing the bathroom or doing the kind of work which Mama loathed. The only thing Mama did was to prepare meals. My mother loved to cook. She was good at cooking, or so her two children thought. My daddy ate whatever my mother placed in front of him without so much as a hesitation or a question. We just assumed he liked her cooking as well.

"Where are you headed now?" Mama asked.

"Thought I'd check on the invalid patient upstairs."

"Don't talk about your brother like that. He had a rough time of it, young lady."

"Yessim," I said as I ran up the stairs, taking two steps at a time.

Scottie was reading a Batman comic book when I entered his room. He looked bored and tired.

"You okay?" I asked.

"Yeah, I reckon. How's Mr. Joe?"

"He's okay. It's no fun being locked up and especially being locked up in the same building with that stupid Hines. I hate that man."

"Daddy says you shouldn't—"

"I know. I know," I interrupted him. "I don't need that now, Scottie."

"You're always tellin' me things that I don't want to hear."

"Yeah, I know. You know that Hines is … there's something different about him."

"Know what the gossip is around town?" he asked.

"About Hines?" I was suddenly interested.

"Yeah. I heard Billy Bob Doss say that Hines is as queer as a three dollar bill."

"Don't talk like that. Do you believe everything Billy Bob says?" I asked.

"Naw, but that's the stuff goin' round."

"Any proof of that rumor?"

"Proof?"

"Yeah, like have you seen something?"

"Oh, that. Billy Bob said his daddy thought that Hines had a likin' for young boys and that Billy Bob ought to stay clear of 'im. That's what Billy Bob told me, and Rufus said about the same thing."

My mind was running wild with possibilities. My brain quickly told me that Billy Bob Doss and Rufus Worley were not the most reliable of sources my brother could have referenced. Both of them had reputations for manufacturing storied details about many of the Clancyville citizens—not bad for boys who were ten years old. Let's just say that they were gifted.

"Why didn't you tell me this before now?" I said.

"You never asked me before now."

"I didn't ask you this time."

"You said you thought that something was different about Hines. I was just tellin' you what I had heard," he said.

"From those reliable sources," I added.

Scottie didn't have a comeback, so I left him to suffer alone with his comic books.

After supper that night I had a plan. I learned that Ralph Hines would be working until midnight at the jail so I had plenty of time to implement my scheme. Before I asked to be excused, Daddy scared me to death.

"I heard that you and Deputy Hines had a run-in at the jail this morning after I had left."

"Ah, sort of. What'd he tell you?"

"Said you were making a nuisance of yourself so he ran you off. Is that your version?"

"Something like that. I was simply talking with Mr. Joe and he didn't like my being there. So I left. He didn't do much running-off, except at the mouth."

Daddy smiled.

"That's sufficient young lady," Mama entered our conversation. "You will not talk about adults that way. You will learn to respect your elders."

I wanted to tell her that I respected those who deserved to be respected, but I thought better of expressing an opinion about that. Mama never was wild about too many of my insights pertaining to life and the world around me. I simply asked to be excused from the table. Scottie left with me since he felt good enough to travel, and his female warden had finally released him for light activity.

I told Scottie my plan. He was excited and frightened.

"Are you crazy?" he said.

"Probably, but I think it's worth a look-see."

"I shouldn't have told you the rumor I heard," he said.

"No, in fact you did the right thing for a change. Now I can investigate Hines. I have something to go on. Not much, mind you, but at least it is something."

Scottie and I arrived near Ralph Hines' small home on Dalton Street some ten minutes after we had left our house. We took our time. It was still light out and I knew we had to be cautious of any nosy neighbors. I decided to approach the place from Huffman Street. There was a vacant lot on Huffman which was perfect for us to hide in and wait for some darkness. The lot was densely populated with twenty year old pine trees, some tall grass, and a few wildflowers.

We sat in silence and studied the back of Hines' hovel. Actually I sat in silence while Scottie threw pine cones at some mockingbirds that were going through their repertoire in an adjacent yard. Thirty minutes later it was dark enough to make our approach.

We crossed Huffman and walked quickly through old man Rowland's side yard and worked our way to a clump of maples next door to Hines' house. This was not the direct route, but it was the best for providing us hiding places along our route. There were some bushes and an old shed sandwiched among the maples. It provided excellent cover. We sat for a few minutes to make sure we had not been seen. There was the summer evening silence. A dog barked a few streets over. It was calm and summer-quiet.

I decided to use the direct approach at first. Scottie waited behind the bushes among the maples. I walked up to the back door and knocked. It never pays to be too careful. There was no answer. I waited a minute or so, and then tried the door knob. It wouldn't budge.

I signaled for Scottie and he quickly joined me at the back door.

"I'm going inside. You go back and stay behind the bushes in the trees and watch the driveway. If you see anyone turn into that driveway, come get me!" I ordered. "No exceptions. Okay?"

He nodded without saying a word. Whenever we were out doing something daring, Scottie didn't talk much. I was the instigator on the majority of our adventures.

I studied the houses that were close enough to view the rear of Hines' place before I moved toward the back windows. I had three chances to get in. With a little luck and some carelessness on the part of that idiot who lived in the house, one of them would be open.

I waited for Scottie to get settled into his hiding place before I tried the windows. The first one was locked. Without hesitation I moved to the next window. It was locked also. My fool-proof plan wasn't going too well. I tried the final window of opportunity and it was also locked. I would have signaled Scottie of my failure, but I could only see shadows now. I assumed that he was still hiding behind the bushes. I hoped he was still hiding there.

Something told me to try the back door again. I turned the door knob as hard as I could and it gave way, the door opened. It hadn't been locked at all. It was just old and tight. I had been right about Hines. He was careless.

The kitchen was the first room I entered. There was a light on over the sink. The room was clean except for a dirty plate and a glass in the sink. I spotted some crumbs on the counter. The faucet was steadily dripping. I fought the urge to tighten the handles to make it stop.

Next came the living room. The light from the kitchen sink area helped me find a reading lamp. I pulled the chain and the room was instantly visible. It was then that I realized I had made a terrible blunder in my reconnaissance-planning. I had forgotten to bring along a flashlight. If I was going to continue in this line of work, I would need to stop making mental errors like failing to bring a flashlight to the party.

Now that the small living room was filled with light, my searching would have to be quick. I did a rapid scan of the room, moving left to right. The little place reeked of tobacco. I spotted an ashtray full of cigar butts next to an old, dirty recliner that once was some shade of a blue fabric. Hines had an oval rug the color of mud in front of the chair. Next to the chair was a dirty beige sofa that matched nothing else in the room. In front of this dingy and unmatched furniture was a portable television set. I noticed that there were no magazines or books anywhere in sight. There was a beer can sitting next to the ashtray. I took a piece of broken pencil from his cluttered coffee table and lifted the can to see if it contained liquid. It was empty. I saw Harry O use a pencil to check out something once and avoid leaving fingerprints. I thought that was a clever maneuver. I didn't want to leave any fingerprints either. You know, just in case this place became a crime scene. I did watch a few television detectives. Learn from all sources, I say.

I held onto the broken off piece of pencil in case I came across something else I needed to examine closely in my surveillance of his place.

I turned out the reading lamp after I saw a clear path to the next room. A street lamp was shining in one of the front windows providing me with plenty of light to see that this was his bedroom. It looked normal as far as bedrooms go. Some clutter but not much for a single man. He had attempted to make up his bed and there were no clothes to speak of on the floor. I spotted some shoes under the bed that didn't seem to match, and there were some pieces of paper on the floor.

I looked for some type of cloth to help me open the closet door. I found a handkerchief on his dresser top and used it. I pulled the cord hanging in front of me and the incandescent bulb burned brightly overhead. For a single man of limited intelligence and limited wardrobe, the closet was full. I used the handkerchief to move the hanging clothes to the right and to the left.

Bingo! I couldn't believe my eyes. The back of the closet wall was full of photographs of young boys, all naked. They looked to be about my age, some younger and some maybe a year or two older. Some of the pictures had been torn out of what I guessed to be some sleazy magazines. A few were in color and some were black and white. Some of the pictures were actual photographs, but I didn't know any of the boys.

There were two shelves in his closet. His photograph-wall was sandwiched between the two shelves. The top shelf was too high for me so I concentrated on the one about waist high, just underneath his hanging clothes. I gently lifted some of his garments hoping not to disturb them. I discovered a stack of sleazy magazines. I didn't want to waste my time looking at what I believed was inside them, so I left them alone. Next to them was a shoebox. I removed the lid. It was full of more photographs and more slick magazine pages of young boys. I found it all disgusting.

I put the box back, shifted the hanging garments back to their former position, closed the door, and left Hines' inner sanctum. It was almost too much for me. I had seen one or two of those so-called girlie magazines that boys like to carry around and look at, but I hadn't encountered this side of the sleaze industry.

*Why would anyone want to keep pictures of young naked boys?*

I felt goose-bumps tingle all over me as I suddenly thought about Buster and Micah.

"Find anything?" Scottie asked me as we slowly walked home.

I really didn't want to tell him. I wasn't sure that he would understand it all. I wasn't sure that I understood.

"Yeah."

"What?" he said.

"Ralph Hines likes boys."

"What?" his voice went up an octave.

"Calm down. So, Ralph likes young boys. Isn't that the rumor you told me earlier?"

"Yeah, but I didn't believe it. It was just talk. You know how kids are. What did you find?"

"Pictures, magazines ... he's really into that stuff. He collects it."

"What does he do with it?"

"I don't know. He looks at it," I said.

"That all?"

"I have no idea, but it's enough to make me suspicious of him."

"You think Deputy Hines had something to do with those boys, Clancy?"

"I don't know that either, but all that stuff in his house makes me wonder."

"How can we find out?"

"We'll ask," I said.

# Chapter Eleven

Nothing much happened for the next two days. It was still hot and most folks stayed indoors. Only a few of us kids ventured out in order to enjoy the late July summer and try to forget about school for another month or so. It rained a few drops one afternoon, but that did nothing more than settle the dust. It felt hotter than ever after the rain ended.

Daddy still had Mr. Joe locked up and was waiting to hear from Richmond. They had promised to mail him a copy of a file on Joseph George Jenkins. Daddy hadn't told me the name of the person he had called in Richmond or what kind of file it was, but to me it didn't sound good. I wondered if they had a file on me somewhere in Richmond.

I was no longer responsible for milking Bessie Mae. Daddy found a man who would do it if he could have half of the milk as pay. Mr. Joe readily agreed and preferred that the man Daddy hired take all of the milk since Mr. Joe couldn't use any of it for the time being. I could now focus on my obligation to control the catfish population in the Staunton River.

Once a day I would go by and check on Bessie Mae just to be sure that she was getting the attention she required, and to be certain that the man Daddy found was doing his job correctly, now that I had become an expert on milking a cow. Scottie was once again his usual self, which is to say that his obnoxious level was compatible with his age.

"Where are you two going?" Mama said.

"Fishin'," I said.

"Don't want you dilly-dallying around Mr. Joe's place, you hear?"

"What exactly does that mean, Mama?" Scottie asked. One of the features of his obnoxious nature was the continued attempts to prove that he was more cunning than our mother. Despite the innocent tone of his questions, I was always aware of the true sarcasm which lived behind the majority of his questions. I had a strong sensation that our mother was aware as well.

"It means if I find out that you two were snooping around Mr. Joe's place, then I'll wear your bottoms out so that you won't be able to sit down for a month and then realize that there is no point in asking me questions like that!"

It was one of her milder threats, but we understood the consequences if we broke that commandment. It didn't stop us usually, but sometimes it did slow us down just thinking about what she would do if she caught us. One thing I could say about Mama -- she was good on her promises and threats. If she told you she would do something, you could lay bets on it. I never could accuse my mother of duplicity. Once in a while she would be given to hyperbole, but not often. More than once I had felt the wrath of her belt on my bottom, and she could hurt a body. Scottie was still learning that his failures to fool the boss lady had serious consequences.

Still, I had some things to check out and Scottie was always willing to be dragged into my schemes without too much coaxing. One thing that bothered me about the manner in which we found the bodies of Buster and Micah was that Daddy never could find their clothes.

One of the chief differences, my father informed me, between the criminals created by Sir Arthur Conan Doyle and the real-life ones my father encountered, was that the ones who actually existed in the real world were not altogether an intelligent lot. The ones from fiction were a good deal smarter than those from reality. Since I believed my father's point, those clothes were probably not destroyed.

"We're not gonna catch many fish, sister dear."

"Don't call me that. Pray tell, why are we not going to catch many fish?"

"We have rods and reels, hooks and sinkers and floats, but no bait."

"Yeah, I know. I ain't planning to catch any fish. We've got investigating to do."

"But Mama will really be suspicious if we come home without fish. She knows that we always come back with fish. With Mr. Joe in jail, we ain't got nobody to say we give 'em to."

"Gave them," I corrected him.

"Whatever. You get my point?"

"I get your point. We'll stop at Moon's Grocery and get some worms."

"Catfish don't like Moon's worms," Scottie said.

"Boy, you sure are hard to get along with this morning."

"You ain't thinkin' straight. If we're gonna cover our tracks, then we got to use our heads, or Mama will use our bottoms. I was in the hospital last week. I don't want to go back."

Scottie grinned a little at me and I gave him a gentle shove. He was right. I wasn't thinking clearly about covering our trail, or our tails. We stopped at Moon's Grocery and I charged some chicken livers and permitted Scottie to carry them. It was the least I could do for him.

"Now, we're cookin'," Scottie said as we were leaving Moon's Grocery. It took so little to please my baby brother when he was trying to be obnoxious.

Once we were at Mr. Joe's place, I found a shady spot behind his house to put our fishing gear and store the chicken livers away from the hot sun. We might get to fish later. We needed to explore first.

"Come on. I want to show you something special."

I led Scottie toward my discovery earlier that week. We walked through the tall grass, the broken fence, and into the small grove of trees before we entered the kingdom of the butterflies. There was a well-worn path that twisted and turned through the wildflowers.

They were still there. Our entrance stirred them and they fluttered skyward.

"Wow! There must be zillions," Scottie said.

"Close enough. Aren't they beautiful?"

"Let's catch some."

"No. If you grab them you might kill them. Let them come to you, Scott," I used his given name and my official tone so he would know that I was serious.

We stood where the path abruptly ended, surrounded by flowers and bushes. It would have given fear to anyone who was claustrophobic. After several minutes the butterflies began to land on us as if we were wildflowers.

"They won't hurt us, will they?" he said.

"Don't be silly. They're just making friends. Relax."

"How can I relax when I have a million butterflies all over me?"

A transition began. Some would fly away from us, some new ones would come and take their places. They must have been investigating us. I knew that we were in no danger, but I did wonder what the creatures were doing. Maybe they were checking our fragrance. I decided then that I needed to engage in some studying of butterflies.

"What's over there?" Scottie moved slowly away from me and most of the butterflies abandoned him.

"I don't know. This is as far as I have ever come."

"There's an opening in these bushes," he said. I watched him push his way through the shrubbery and disappear.

"Yuck!" I heard him call out.

"What's the matter?"

"It's a swamp over here. There's a cow in this junk."

"Just one cow?" I said.

"Only one."

"That must be Bessie Mae, Mr. Joe's cow."

"The one we milked?"

"He's only got one."

"She's knee-deep in gunk."

I passed through the same opening my brother had just taken. The terrain changed drastically. One minute we had been surrounded by flowers, bushes, and beautiful butterflies. The next minute we were surrounded by manure, flies and a horrible smell, to say nothing of the dark, murky swamp-like substance at least two feet deep.

"This is probably where Mr. Joe gets his manure for his grass."

Bessie Mae was standing across from us on the far side of the swamp, munching on some of the tall grasses which were prolific in that section. She looked in my direction as I came through the opening, but she didn't stop grazing. She seemed undisturbed by our arrival.

"I'll bet she doesn't get many visitors back here," Scottie said.

He moved slowly over towards her because that was the only way you could walk in the swamp. The swamp seemed to be a mixture of mud, manure, and water. I suppose that *swamp* wasn't a good name for what to call this place. Mr. Joe must have spent years walking over here and collecting his so-called fertilizer in a bucket and then carrying it back to spread on his yard. I couldn't imagine doing that. But then, I couldn't imagine having a yard full of luscious green grass like Mr. Joe's either. It was not a high priority for me.

Scottie walked around to the other side of Bessie Mae, continually rubbing her as he moved along slowly. She was a healthy-looking cow and seemed to be content with life. I judged her more of a pet than a farm animal, despite her milk production. Scottie was talking to her as he rubbed her.

"Are you standin' in the swamp?" I asked.

"Not now. There's a little dirt mound, or path over here that forms a short, semi-circle part-way 'round this gunk. I'm standing on the edge, in the path," he informed me.

I waded through the murky mess toward my brother. I stopped when I came to Bessie Mae. She ignored me. I rubbed her side and then looked over at Scottie to be sure that he had found what he claimed to find. There was a short stretch of dry land that formed a semi-circle on that side of the swamp. To the right of where I was standing with Bessie Mae, the dry land path covered a few yards in length, but then ended abruptly turning into a long stretch of weeds and grasses. More stuff for Bessie Mae to eat as the occasion might provide.

Since I had now been standing in that black liquid for several minutes and had suffered no loss of either of my legs thus far, I decided it was time to plunge one of my hands into the black morass to see what I might find. Compared to putting my hand into my brother's vomit the other day, this was a piece of cake. I felt a mild sensation much like the imaginary *bees* in a baseball bat when you hit the ball on a cold day. I removed my hand and wiped my fingers on my pants leg.

I looked over at Scottie and he was following suit. Scottie was many things, but he was no coward when it came to doing stupid and unusual stuff. Of course I led him into some stupid and unusual stuff, so he didn't have what you would call a good role model.

"It some kind of glob," he said bringing up a dark lump of something strange.

I maneuvered my way around Bessie Mae and approached his position close to that short path of dry land. Scottie dropped his newly found treasure onto the dry path. I took a stick, scratching and pulling at the blackened mass until I had it stretched out in a recognizable shape.

"It's a shirt," I said. "It looks like a— ... oh, my God," I said without thinking. "Show me where you put your hand in that gunk."

"You used God's name in vain," he said, attempting to chastise me.

"Oh, get a life, Scottie. I did no such thing. It's an expression, nothing more."

"Now, show me where you put your hand in that black stuff," I demanded, using my official sisterly voice.

"I ain't stickin' my hand back in there," he said.

"Didn't ask you to stick your hand back in."

"You think I'm scared?"

"No, but you ought to be. We have no idea what this stuff really is. Just show me the spot."

"You put your hand in it! I saw you!" he claimed, as if my deed made it okay to do.

"Just show me the spot where you put your hand into the black swamp."

He pointed to a place in the swamp about two feet from the bank. I prodded the area back and forth with my stick. It broke in half and I had to find another short branch. I found a longer and sturdier tree limb and continued my search. Bessie Mae was undaunted in her cud routine despite the presence of two kids poking a stick in the thick, black water close to her. I stopped and looked around.

"What is it, Clancy? Whose shirt is that?" he pointed to the muddy glob I had tossed on the dry ground nearby.

I was silent and ignored his question. I was looking for another place to search.

Scottie found a smaller tree limb about three feet long and began dragging it through the water as he walked around the edge of the swamp, moving towards the place where both of us had entered when we first arrived.

I changed positions. I poked around directly under Bessie Mae. Nothing seemed to bother her. My stronger tree branch found another glob of something. I successfully speared it and used both hands to bring it up out of the quagmire. It was a pair of pants. They appeared small enough to fit Micah, who was several inches shorter than his older brother.

"You reckon these dirty things belonged to Buster and Micah?" he asked.

"That's what I'm thinking. Daddy has been searching all over for this stuff. Maybe we had better go get him and bring him here."

Using my stronger tree branch, I moved the blackened pants from the murky water close to where I had laid the blackened shirt.

"But he would bring other people and that might disturb Bessie Mae," Scottie said.

"This is more important than disturbing a cow. Besides, she probably wanders in and out all the time."

"Why can't we look for the rest of the clothes?" he said.

"It'll take us too long. We ought to let Daddy do that. They're probably here. But, as you can see, this is a pretty good sized swamp-ish place. It'll take us longer than we can allow ourselves. Better go get our daddy and bring 'im back."

"Do we take these with us?" he held up the shirt on the end of his skinny tree branch.

I hesitated in answering because I really didn't know what to do. Daddy had always said that evidence needs to remain where it is found until after it has been documented or something like that. It was part of being official with the investigation. That meant we had touched some evidence, moved it from its original place, and our daddy wasn't going to be too happy with us. However, he most likely would be happy that we had found it. I was hoping for that.

"We can't leave them here," I finally said. "I'd rather Daddy get upset with us for moving some evidence than for leaving them and returning later to find them gone."

"Who would want these dirty clothes?"

"How about the person who killed Buster and Micah? He might remember that he left them behind, and might want to find them in order to get rid of them. Make sense?"

"No, it does not," he said emphatically. "Why would they bury them here in the first place if they planned to return later and remove them? That's just stupid."

"Criminals sometimes do stupid things. Don't you ever read?"

"No. I just follow you around."

"Come on. We need Daddy. Let's get out of here and get cleaned up."

As soon as we began our exit, Scottie's zillions of butterflies entered the swamp area, circling around us in their haphazard flight patterns, constantly moving in all directions. Some of them landed on Bessie Mae who seemed to be as undisturbed with them as she was with us. A few perched on me and then on Scottie. However, to my surprise, the vast majority of them landed atop the black morass in which we were still standing.

"What are they doing?" Scottie asked.

"I have no idea," I said, pleading ignorance. "But we need to go. Now."

I managed to secure both garments onto the end of my rather sturdy stick so that they wouldn't fall off. Then we slowly trudged through the thick marsh-like composition, making our way through the butterflies, back through the bushes, and returning to the ordinary world.

By the time we had returned to Mr. Joe's house we were having a hard time deciding whether to go fishing or get back to town and find Daddy. Scottie's argument was that Mama would skin us alive if she knew we hadn't gone fishing and had gone exploring instead. He thought we ought to at least give fishing a try for an hour or so. His logic was that it would make no difference in this evidence whether it was found today or tomorrow.

My argument was that this was evidence that was important to our father and we needed to protect it. We needed to get it to Daddy as soon as possible. I figured that Mama could have a tirade and life would go on a few hours after that.

We decided to compromise.

I left Scottie at the river fishing. I also left the clothes there with him. I really didn't want to touch them anymore than I had to, to say nothing of dragging them all over Clancyville while I searched for my daddy. I could travel faster if I was traveling light. That meant traveling without those filthy clothes and my little brother.

It also meant that I had to take off my dirty wet sneakers and my socks, and roll up my jeans to at least mid-calf so I could hide the black residue which remained steadfast to the lower part of my clothing.

I ran most of the way to town, but now and then I walked to catch my breath and do some thinking. I wasn't sure how this new discovery would help Mr. Joe. In fact, the closer I got to town, the more I realized that this wouldn't help Mr. Joe at all, unless there was something Daddy might find on or in the clothing. The fact that the clothes were found on Mr. Joe's property didn't look good at all to me. Here I was bringing more evidence to my daddy that pointed directly at the man I was trying to help prove innocent.

It crossed my mind to not say anything, to turn around and head back to the river. We could hide the clothes out there where nobody would find them. Something told me that wasn't the thing to do. As much as I believed in Mr. Joe's innocence, I also believed in my daddy. I had to trust him on his investigative method. You follow the clues. You let the evidence talk to you, at least that's what he told me.

# Chapter Twelve

Daddy and I got to the river a little more than an hour after I had left Scottie. It only took me ten minutes to hustle back to town, but much longer to find the Sheriff. Scottie already had a string of catfish Mama would be pleased with. There were not too many things at which my little brother could best me. Fishing was one of them.

I told Daddy about the butterfly haven and Bessie Mae's manure swamp. He wanted to see what we had found first.

"Why are you barefooted with your jeans rolled up?" he asked as he drove us towards Mossie's Point.

"Better let me answer that after we get to where we are going," I said, hoping that my delaying tactic would grant me sufficient pardon to live to fight another day, so to speak.

He didn't appear to be too upset with me when all was finally revealed to him. I think he was just glad that somebody had found those clothes. That had been bothering him almost from the beginning, although he had never said much about it. Some details like that just nag at you until you get some relief by finding or uncovering or figuring out. Sometimes you just get lucky and stumble into something.

Scottie had hung the shirt and pants on a low tree branch so that they could be drying. I had told him not to wash them out. They were nowhere close to dry by the time Daddy and I arrived. In addition to their dampness, they also maintained their horrible odor quite well.

"Did you check the pockets?" Daddy said.

"No, sir. We just pulled them out of the muddy gunk and walked over here with them. Did I do the right thing by not leaving them where we found them?" I said.

"Probably. Since you didn't wash them or try to rinse them off with water, they might still help us. But the fact that they have been in that mud and manure for so long means that they won't be much good to us. The location is most likely the one relevant thing."

"You mean the fact that we found them on Mr. Joe's farm," I began, "… that won't hurt Mr. Joe?"

He knew how I felt about Mr. Joe's situation. I also believed that in his heart he had similar feelings. I sensed that he was not happy about this development. He nodded, frowned a little, and basically ignored my question.

"Come on," he said, "you two show me Bessie Mae's hideout."

Bessie Mae was gone by the time we returned to the swamp. So were the zillion and one butterflies.

"Scottie found the shirt over in that area," I pointed to about where Bessie Mae had been standing in the black, gooey stuff and chewing her cud. "The pants were in the same area but closer in to the bushes."

"I'm gonna need some help for this," Daddy said as he looked around at the large, muddy area. He then removed his shoes and socks before he rolled up his pants legs.

"You've got some help," I said proudly. "We found the first set. We'll find the other clothes, too. If they're here."

"Right you are," he said. "But, a good investigator never assumes anything."

"What did I assume?" I asked.

"You're thinking that those other clothes are here as well."

"Well, I did allow that they might not be here."

"Yes, you did, Miss Clancy. I just didn't want you to get your hopes up. So, let's get started. It doesn't appear that there's an easy way to do this," he said as he stared at the black, murky substance near our feet.

Scottie and I found the tree branches we had left and began searching while Daddy went in search of his own tree branch. When he returned, Scottie laughed and said that Daddy was using a whole tree. It was certainly long enough to reach out into the middle section of the swamp from almost any reference point, which is what we needed to search—the entire swamp.

Scottie and I stayed close to the bank as long as we could, and searched that area. Daddy poked and prodded his way from the middle towards the land, continually encircling the dark, murky, quagmire. It seemed like forever before we found another piece of clothing. It turned out to be another shirt. It was a T-shirt, or what was left of it. It had been torn in several places, but the shreds were still hanging onto each other as if for dear life. It appeared to have been in a major battle. It was larger than the other shirt, so I guessed it belonged to Buster.

A few minutes later Scottie found a pair of underwear and then the other pair of pants. I found nothing my second time through the mess. I figured that the boys were barefooted, and then concluded that we had found everything except the second pair of underwear. I made my observation known to my daddy.

"Boys don't always wear underwear, Clancy," he said.

"I always wear underwear," Scottie said.

"That's because of your upbringing, young man," Daddy said.

I shook my head in amazement. I apparently had a lot to learn about the male of the species.

We used the outside hydrant at Mr. Joe's house to wash up. We were careful, but we still managed to get some of the black gunk on our clothing. We washed carefully. Daddy made sure of that. Scottie was one of those lick-and-a-promise type people, so you had to watch him closely.

It was almost one o'clock by the time we arrived at home. Daddy put each of the garments in a separate, black, plastic trash bag and labeled it as to first shirt, first pants, etc., and he wrote down a rough location according to the layout of Bessie Mae's mud pond. Daddy was good at drawing maps and diagrams, so it was easy for him to figure out where things were originally by creating a drawing. He then charted each item we had discovered by placing a dot on his drawing with his own annotation describing the article found at that spot.

On the way home he told us that it wouldn't be a good idea to mention to Mama that we had been investigating on our own at Mr. Joe's place prior to his arrival. We could tell her, he said, that we helped him after he arrived and found the place. He said it would be our secret. Scottie and I liked that idea a whole lot. Nothing like having inside help in dealing with our determined mother.

After lunch we helped Daddy inspect the garments. The first set was completely dry and had an iridescent sheen on them. He used disposable latex gloves to handle the items.

"Wonder what that is on those clothes?" Scottie said pointing to the first shirt and pants we had found.

"I'll have it analyzed over in Roanoke. The lab can figure out what it is."

"Do you have any idea, Daddy?" I said.

"Not the foggiest, Clance. Could be anything out there in woods."

He put each piece back into its own bag and tied them shut. He put them in the trunk of his car and headed off towards town leaving us to wonder what we could do next to help him.

I watched Scottie clean the fish he had caught. We had a rule in our house with which no one could argue. You catch a fish, you clean that fish. No exceptions. It was most enjoyable for me to watch Scottie work because usually I was right there with him cleaning and stripping the catfish. Mama never ventured out to watch this less-than-delicate operation because she couldn't stand the smell of raw fish or the sight of fish guts. I knew that I was safe sitting on the picnic table smiling at my brother and thinking of my next move in the investigation.

"What you plannin'?" he said finally.

"I'm going back to Hines' place to get some evidence on him."

"You're crazy, you know. You're gonna get caught one of these days. He's gonna walk in on ya, and then you'll be up to your ears in trouble.

Real trouble. Creek without a paddle, as the old sayin' is. That kinda trouble. And he's mean, you know."

"Yeah, I know. But I'll be careful."

"Heard that before."

"Yeah, yeah."

"What kind of evidence you need?" he asked.

"It's called leverage."

"What's that?"

"In school this last year we studied basic machines in science. It was interesting. There's a machine called a lever. It helps a person move something larger or heavier than the person is capable of moving alone. It is accomplished by a person using his brain and using it with some simple object with the aid of a fulcrum."

"You're over my head."

"Well, I need to move Ralph Hines, who's a lot bigger than I am. All I need to do is find something that shows what he's been up to with those pictures he has."

"But he'll just deny it."

"That's why I need leverage. I need something which is obviously his, but also connects him to those horrible pictures in some way."

"Oh. So, whataya looking for?"

"I have no idea."

"Sounds like a Clancy plan. You want my help?"

"Yeah, but it'll be more dangerous tonight. We need to do this after it gets really dark. So, we have to slip out past Mama after dark."

"Boy, you are livin' dangerously. If she catches us, it'll be … Well, you know it won't be healthy for us."

"We'll be careful. Daddy is working late tonight so this is a perfect time."

"What about Hines?" he asked.

"Daddy said he gets off at ten o'clock, so we have about an hour to work. It'll be dark enough for what I intend if we wait to slip out around 8:45."

"That's your plan?"

"Except for finding what it is that I don't know I'm looking for."

It was close to nine before we escaped the house and were halfway to Ralph Hines' place. It was dark enough for us to walk in the shadows and dodge the street lights. We cut through the yards where we knew we could. Some folks had fences and dogs that we avoided at all costs.

Hines' place was dark so we proceeded with my plan.

Scottie knocked on the front door just to be sure no one was home.

Silence prevailed after Scottie's knocking, so I headed to the backdoor. It was like before. Turn the knob, open the door, and walk inside. My life of crime.

I went straight for the closet in the bedroom. This time I had remembered my earlier failure to bring along the needed surveillance tool. I had borrowed Mama's flashlight.

I searched carefully each shelf in front of me. Finally, on the top shelf I found a box engraved with Ralph Hines' name and the year *1968*. Inside the box was a collection of nude photos of young boys. Even with my limited experience in this sort of thing I could see that these were actual photographs and not pictures cut from magazines. I shuffled through them until I discovered one of Buster Scruggs. There was another person in the photo with him. That other person resembled Hines, but since his face was turned away from the camera it was impossible to be sure. I continued shuffling through the contents of the box. I found another photo of Hines by himself. The clothes he had on seemed to match the clothes of the unidentified person in the earlier photo with Buster. I figured they were a match. To my reasoning, this was the leverage I needed. At the last moment I decided to keep the whole box. It was risky, but the charges against Mr. Joe demanded some risks.

Once outside I showed Scottie the box but didn't show him the contents. We were walking towards the maples when some car lights drove into the driveway and someone got out and entered the house through the back door. We hid in the bushes until the lights came on inside. We figured it was Hines, but we couldn't be for certain. A little fear helped us to run all the way home.

This burglary stuff was getting to be too easy, or so I thought.

That night after I took off my jeans and had put on my shorty pajamas, I noticed some shiny stuff below the knees and concentrated around the cuffs of my jeans. I smelled it. It definitely came from Bessie Mae's swamp. I hoped that Mama wouldn't note the slight sheen nor the smell of my jeans before she tossed them into the washer.

It was overcast on Sunday morning. There was a threat of rain, but it hadn't started yet. Church was a regular routine for us in those days. Mama and Daddy made sure that we didn't miss Sunday school, although occasionally we did miss the preaching service. Some Sundays Daddy had to work, but we still went with Mama. There were no valid excuses for missing church unless you were dead, or sick and feeling like you were going to die.

She never had any special job in the church, but she always went. I don't recall her holding any kind of official position or even doing some routine task. Still, I think it was important for her to show up there each week. It was a like a badge or something. She was a member and had to go. That meant her children had to go, too.

Scottie and I did okay in church. We liked Sunday school but didn't care much for the other. Most of the time the preacher talked about things that either didn't interest us or that were beyond our understanding. Once in a while I listened to what he said and wanted to know more. Mama didn't discuss anything that pertained to religion with us on any regular basis. If I wanted to know something about God or church, I always talked it over with Daddy. He generally had more to say about a given subject.

We were all in church that Sunday. Daddy said that he needed a break from the investigation. I wanted to use the time to pray. I figured I ought to do everything I could to help Mr. Joe. I wasn't above praying, but I wasn't too sure about how effective it was. I spent most of the time thanking God for stuff, but this was different. This was something I wanted God to do for Mr. Joe, and I was not used to that kind of praying.

Scottie fell asleep during the sermon and Mama had a hissy-fit on the way home.

"There's no excuse for you going to sleep in church. You get plenty of sleep during the night."

"I'm sorry, Mama. I'll try to do better next time."

I felt sorry for him, but only when our mother would go on a tirade for some unjustifiable offense. At other times I figured he got what he deserved.

"Betty Greesome surely did wave her arms a lot this morning," Mama said.

"It's her job," Daddy answered.

"Well, she could just wave at the choir. She doesn't have to wave at the congregation."

"It helps with the timing, I think. Most folks don't mind."

"Well, I mind. I don't like it. It's not necessary. She's just trying to flaunt her position, that's all there is to it. I wish someone would tell her to stop."

"Why don't you tell her, Mama?" I said.

She turned sideways in her car seat no doubt thinking that I was trying to be smart. I was actually being sincere and had the look on my face to prove it. Thank God I wasn't being cute. She would have killed me right there in the car. Murder on a Sunday afternoon. After church.

"I wouldn't dare do such a thing. Why would you suggest that, young lady?"

"Well, if you feel that strongly about it … perhaps you are correct and you should say something to the preacher."

She was momentarily speechless. I had finally made a valid point with my mother. It didn't happen often. If I had kept a journal, I would have certainly made an entry about this conversation, on this particular day in my life. Milestone moment.

"I just wish that Betty Greesome would not be so flamboyant about her job."

"That's her personality, dear. She's a lively woman," Daddy said.

"What do you mean by that?" Her tone did not sound pleasant. I figured Daddy was headed for trouble.

"She's full of life. She loves music and people. She's always laughing and talking with people, especially with the children," I chimed in to help my father. Actually Daddy could take care of himself with her, but I knew what he meant this time so I thought I'd help.

Mama stared at Daddy as if what I had said was foreign to her ears and that my father was hiding behind his little girl's words.

"Thank you, Clancy. That's exactly what I meant by 'lively.' Don't give Betty such a hard time."

"Well, I don't like all that hand waving stuff. It looks phony. Put on. We can sing perfectly well without all that."

"Probably so, dear, but we have to learn to accept the changes which come. She's been waving her hands for nearly three years. Why are you just now complaining about it?"

I could tell that Mama was frustrated with Daddy's reasoning. He was right, too. There must have been something else stuck in Mama's craw or else she would have said something a long time before now. Our choir director had been in our church for a number of years but only recently had started directing the congregation in singing. The translation of that for my mother was that the song leader waved her hands at us.

"Mrs. Frank Satterfield made an official complaint to the deacons about her," Mama said.

"Oh, for cryin' out loud, Rachel! Why are folks always stirring up trouble over nothing?"

"This wasn't about nothing."

"Mary Jo Satterfield is complaining to the Deacon Board about Betty Ann Greesome directing the congregational singing, and you think that's something important?" Daddy's question was not rhetorical.

I could tell that my daddy was beginning to lose patience with Mama. Scottie and I just looked at each other without offering a gesture or saying a word. At least we knew when to be quiet and listen. Their conversation was turning toward the serious.

"It wasn't about that, Bill. It was about her daughter, Elizabeth. Mary Jo thought that Elizabeth was spending too much time with Betty after school, after the children's choir rehearsal."

"What?" Daddy's voice sounded as if he couldn't believe what Mama was saying.

"So, she asked Elizabeth about it. That's when Elizabeth broke down and cried."

"Cried about what?" he asked.

"Not in front of the children," Mama lowered her voice. "I'll tell you later. But it's not good."

"But is it true?" he asked.

"Mary Jo doesn't lie. If she said it happened to Elizabeth, then it did, as far as I'm concerned. I'll give you the details when we get home."

We rode on in silence. I could tell that my daddy was not happy about this. He hated conflicts inside the church and he despised gossip. Mama knew better than to pass along idle gossip to him, so this must have been something about which she was fairly certain.

I had little to do with Betty Greesome, the church's director of music. I knew her, but I wasn't in the choir for children. I had my share of talents, but I couldn't sing. I liked to listen to music, but that was the extent of my musical interest. When I sang at all, it was usually in the shower when I felt really good about something. Besides that, I didn't like the songs Miss Greesome chose for the choirs. I was still hooked on *Rainy Night in Georgia*, but Betty Ann Greesome would never have her little cherubs singing Brook Benton's song in church or anywhere else.

I was more than a little curious about my mother's concerns, but there was no way she would permit me to be a part of that conversation she was planning to have with my father once we were home. More to point, I was more concerned about my future confrontation with Ralph Hines and what Ralph Hines had to say in answer to my newly discovered leverage against him.

# Chapter Thirteen

Growing up in the sixties and seventies, I was different than most of the kids my age. I fished more than I played sports. I studied people more than I played with friends. I read more than I watched television. I did have a few favorite shows. One was *The F.B.I.* which came on Sunday nights after church. We almost always went to church, but we were usually home before eight o'clock so that church never interfered with my program.

That Sunday night Scottie and I were in my room waiting for the program to come on our television that was located downstairs in the living room. Whatever happened at our church that evening was over with earlier than usual. Mama and Daddy were downstairs talking, probably about Mrs. Satterfield and her precious Elizabeth. If I had thought that stuff was important I would have been listening in on their conversation, which I did from time to time just to see what was happening in our little world of Clancyville according to some adults whom I trusted.

Despite the fact that I was waiting on some entertainment to provide a little diversion for me, I was actually more focused on finding some way to aid Mr. Joe. Scottie was on my bed examining the ring that I had found. I was at my desk plotting an imaginary conversation with Ralph Hines. Just planning ahead.

"What was Buster's real name?" Scottie said.

"I don't know. We called him Buster."

"That's a nickname, Clancy. Can't you tell a nickname?"

"Look it up in my school annual. It's over there on the shelf next to the Sherlock Holmes' book."

Scottie retrieved the book and plopped back on my bed. In a few minutes he announced his findings.

"Lydell. His name was Lydell Scruggs. Boy, I'm glad I wasn't born into his family."

"Probably a family name, like Clancy," I said.

"Yeah, but Ly-dell. No wonder he liked being called Buster."

He rolled the ring around with his fingers while he sang softly one of the hymns we had sung at church that evening. Unlike me, Scottie could sing well.

"*Shall we gather at the river, la da, da de da, de da-ah--* Holy Cow, Clancy! Look at this," he said. He sat straight up and threw both of his legs over the side of the bed.

Before I could move the three steps from my desk to the bed, he was standing beside me holding out the ring for me to examine.

"Look, the initials there ... *L. S.* That could be Lydell Scruggs."

"Could be," I said. "But I doubt it."

"He could have been wearing the ring and it fell off his finger."

"Maybe," I said. "Still, it's a large ring and his hands were most likely too small for it to fit. And another thing, it's an old ring, from back in the 1950's."

I then remembered what Mr. Goldsmith had told me about the tape residue.

"But that doesn't mean that Buster wasn't wearing it. Maybe he found it or somebody gave it to him. Who knows?"

"Okay," I said changing my thinking about Scottie's idea regarding the initials, "but the tape was not on the ring when we found it."

"What tape?"

I explained what Mr. Goldsmith had told me a few days earlier.

"We need to find that tape," I said.

"What if it's in the swamp?" he said.

"Well, if the tape came off while they were at the swamp, then why was the ring dropped in the barn?"

"Maybe the ring wasn't dropped in the barn," Scottie said. "At least not dropped by Buster. Maybe it didn't slip off of his finger in the barn because it wasn't on his finger in the barn. Maybe the person that killed him had the ring and dropped it."

It was plausible.

"What about someone taking it away from Buster and then losing it?" I asked.

"Or maybe it wasn't Buster's ring," he suggested.

I had to consider the real possibility of his last statement.

"It's time for your show!" Mama called to us from downstairs.

We forgot our investigation for an hour and enjoyed *The F. B. I.*

It was raining by the time we went to bed that night. We needed the rain, but I could only imagine what it would do to Bessie Mae's mud-swamp. Maybe I would take Monday off and go fishing. Fish always bite better after a rain. That's what all the old fishermen who sit and gossip at Moon's Grocery say. I fell asleep that night thinking of the initials *L. S.*, tape residue, engraved boxes, Deputy Hines' dirty secret, and Mr. Joe confined in a small cell in our jail downtown.

The sun was out bright and hot by the time I had finished breakfast. Scottie and I were on the back steps plotting our day. I wanted to go fishing badly, but I knew that I first had to check the library for that book I was expecting. I also wanted to get Deputy Hines alone and talk with him, but I needed more time to plan that. Going fishing would give me some time to think through my various activities and review my plan of action with the stupid deputy.

I left Scottie on the front steps of our house as I headed towards the library.

"Give me half an hour, then we'll head towards the river," I said as I walked towards downtown Clancyville.

It took less than five minutes to discover that the book had not come in as yet, so I had time to go by the jail and say hello to Mr. Joe.

Hines was drinking coffee when I entered. He was pretending to work on something at his desk, but he never could fool me. I walked past him without saying a word. I had nothing good to say to him, not even a pleasant greeting in the morning.

"Where do you think you're going?" he said.

He deserved a really nasty response, but I refrained from the temptation. He was too easily riled, so I thought better of upsetting him this early in the day. I didn't have time to banter with the man.

"I'm just goin' in to say hello to Mr. Joe."

"He's eating breakfast and doesn't want to be disturbed."

"He'll see me," and I walked on inside the cell area without waiting for Hines' approval.

I figured I would have a few minutes before Hines would get his dander up and come strutting in acting like God Almighty with a badge.

Mr. Joe had finished his food and was walking back and forth in his cell.

"How are you?" I said.

"I'm doing okay, Miss Clancy." He used the voice I liked best.

"We found the clothes."

"Your father was in earlier and told me. Is that a good thing?"

"I don't know. Just another piece of evidence, I reckon." I sounded like my daddy.

"So, you and Mr. Scott are taking some time to fish Miss Clancy?"

"Always. Scottie caught a mess, but I've been investigating mostly."

"What are you investigating?"

"Well, exploring might be a better word. I found those butterflies I told you about."

"Oh, good. That's really something special in nature when we are permitted to see it firsthand."

"Yeah, it really is. There must millions of them."

"Could be. They love that spot back there with Bessie Mae."

"Or Bessie Mae loves that spot back there with them," I said and laughed.

"True. Could work both directions. I imagine you put two and two together and now know the secret for my green grass."

"You said it was Bessie Mae's manure, right?"

"I did, in fact. It's really that mud that Bessie Mae stands in while she enjoys life among those butterflies."

"Then why doesn't your yard smell like that place?"

"I mix that mud with water to thin it some. I imagine that when I water it down a little, the odor goes away, at least for the most part."

"Is that the reason you water it down ... to control that odor?" I asked.

"Not really, but, well, it's part of it, I suppose. I have to water it down because I couldn't put that mixture on my yard as it is. It's much too thick and too caustic. If I put it on my grass just like it is, the grass would burn up in a few hours. So, I water it down to keep from destroying the grass. Thinning it out helps the grass as opposed to killing it. So far, so good. Seems to work pretty well. You've seen the grass, so you know."

"Yeah, it sure is green. Must be something good in that stuff, whatever it is. Have you ever thought about having it checked?"

"Checked?" he said.

"You know, analyzed. They do that at Virginia Tech, or so Daddy said."

"I consider it a blessing and I really don't need to know what the composition is that makes it effective. I accept it as it is. It works, that's what I care about. The only drawback is that the stuff smells horrible when it gets on your hands and clothes."

He stuck his right hand through the cell bars close to my nose to permit me a sniff.

I grabbed his hand and placed it next to my nose and inhaled deeply. I could detect the faint odor of Bessie Mae's manure swamp. It wasn't nearly as powerful as what we had smelled two days ago while searching for those clothes.

"Okay, you two been at it long enough. Time's up. You need to git on outta here, little girl." Hines came in as predicted to interrupt us. I bit my tongue because I knew that one of these days he was going to get his comeuppance.

I squeezed Mr. Joe's hand and told him not to give up hope as I was ushered from the back room towards the front door. Daddy was coming in as I was going out the front door.

"Come on with me. I want to show you something."

I followed him to his car and he gestured for me to get in. I figured we were going to ride somewhere.

"I got the report from Richmond here. Just came in. I wanted you to know straight from me. Mr. Joe's got a record. It's bad, Clancy. It's really bad."

I made myself dizzy watching a monarch flutter from flower to flower. It was a nice distraction while it lasted. The only trouble was that it didn't last long enough. My heart was aching because of the information Daddy had received regarding Mr. Joe. I hated what that report contained.

Joseph George Jenkins was born in Sandston, Virginia sometime in May of 1901. The exact date was not provided. He was the youngest of seven children. He graduated from Shaw University in 1921. In 1922 Joseph George Jenkins brutally murdered two white men by strangling them to death. He was found guilty of manslaughter, sentenced to fifty years, and was paroled after serving thirty-five years of that sentence. He was twice denied parole. There was a note attached to the file that stated both denials came because the authorities did not find sufficient rehabilitation to merit parole.

I asked Daddy what that meant and he said that meant the parole board was not convinced that Joseph George Jenkins was safe to return to society. It meant that he had not demonstrated sufficient remorse to be considered for parole. He still posed a serious danger to society if he was granted a parole.

My daddy told me that it probably meant that since Joseph George Jenkins was a black man, the parole board was not going to give him any leeway or leniency.

I couldn't understand it. I did some quick math. He got out of prison in 1957. He had been out for sixteen years. What reason would there be for a seventy-two year old man to kill two small boys, even allowing the fact that he had murdered two men back in 1922? Why would Mr. Joe kill somebody after so many years? It was not logical to me. I simply couldn't understand it, but I had to face the facts. Daddy had the file to prove what Mr. Joe had once done. I was beginning to think that I had been wrong about my friend.

# Chapter Fourteen

By the time I got home from my what-to-do-next planning and scheming, Mama was waiting for me on the back steps. She didn't look too happy at my arrival.

"And just where have you been, young miss?"

"Thinking."

"Thinking. That's all? Just thinking?"

"Yes, ma'am."

"Couldn't you have done that at home?"

"It's easier away from people. Fewer interruptions."

"Interruptions? We interrupt you? We bother you, Queen Clancy?"

"I didn't mean it that way, Mama. I just like to get away when I have to think. That's all."

"Well, Queenie, you forgot about your little brother. He's been waiting here all morning for you. And just where were you? Off somewhere thinking. How nice for you. How painful for Scottie."

She was right in a way. I owed Scottie an explanation and an apology.

I found him pouting in his room.

"May I come in?" I asked.

"No!"

"I need to talk with you."

"I don't want to talk with you."

"I'm sorry I didn't come back for you. Something bad came up."

"I don't want to hear your lame excuses. Go away and leave me alone."

I decided it wasn't a good time. I could wait until later. I couldn't blame him. I deserved the cold shoulder, and he was giving it to me pretty good. I didn't really want to tell him about Mr. Joe, but I didn't have much choice. He would find our sooner or later, and it would hurt. I was still hurting.

I sat in my room and listened to the radio. I turned it down really low so it wouldn't bother Mama. I didn't want the hassle of her coming upstairs and yelling at me about my music. Ray Price was just beginning to sing *For the Good Times* when Scottie knocked on the door.

"Come in."

He opened the door but didn't say anything. He just stood there staring at me.

"Come in and close the door. Mama doesn't like my music."

He shut the door and stood by the bed. I was lying down on my right side facing the door with my right hand and elbow propping my head up. I pretended to be reading a book, but I couldn't concentrate on the words. I kept reading the same line over and over.

*"Don't look so sad, I know it's over,"* Ray Price sang.

"What came up?" he said at last.

"Pardon me?"

"You said something bad came up. I want to know what it was."

Scottie moved slowly to my desk and sat down.

"Yeah. I figured you would. Daddy got the report on Mr. Joe from Richmond."

"And?"

"And it ain't good."

"Don't say ain't. You sound funny when you say it," he chided me.

I forced a smile. I closed the book and swung around to sit upright on the bed. I could feel a cool breeze coming in through my window.

"Feels nice, doesn't it," I said to him.

Scottie moved from the desk and sat down on the floor close to my dangling legs. He was waiting for me to tell him what I knew. I was stalling. He knew my tactics well, better than my parents. He knew that I would tell him in due time, and I did. I told him everything I had learned. I also told him what I thought, which was that maybe Mr. Joe had killed Buster and Micah.

He didn't say anything. He just stared at the floor and listened.

When Mama called us to lunch, I jumped off the bed and unplugged the radio. The off and on switch was broken. I touched Scottie on the shoulder when I passed him. He was still sitting on the floor.

"Let's go eat."

"I ain't hungry." It sounded natural when he used that word. I think it just fit him better.

"I'll tell Mama but she won't be happy. You know she'll come up here to get you."

"Tell her I don't feel well." He got up and walked past me. I could tell then see that he was crying.

It was a minor miracle but I talked Mama out of going upstairs and checking on Scottie. I told her enough about what had happened and she seemed to understand.

"I knew that … man was no good."

"Mama, please. Mr. Joe is our friend. This is hard on Scottie and me."

She frowned fiercely, but held back whatever it was she wanted to say to me.

Daddy came in and joined us for lunch. We were having tomato sandwiches and milk. Mack Creasy grew the best tomatoes in town and usually gave Mama more than we could ever eat in a year. Mama hated waste, so tomato sandwiches were the only menu item for lunch almost every day but Sunday. We ate fried chicken on Sundays. Tomatoes were merely a side dish on holy days.

"Where's Scottie?" Daddy said.

"He's not feeling well," Mama said.

"Comin' down with something?"

"No. He's grieving about that colored man."

"Oh," Daddy said.

"Why he likes that old man, I will never for the life of me under-stand. I wish you'd go talk with him," Mama addressed her comment to Daddy.

"I'll talk with him before I go back to the office. How are you, Clancy?"

"I'll manage. Have you talked with Mr. Joe?"

"A little. I told him what I learned."

"What'd he say?"

"Nothing. Just turned away from me with his head down and lay down on his bunk. He surprised me. I thought for sure he would defend himself, or tell me that the report was wrong, or something. He didn't even look surprised. He just got on that bunk, faced the wall, and said nothing."

"He's guilty. What could he say?" Mama offered.

"Maybe he's sick, too," I said.

"Tell me, young lady, just what did you and your brother get into the other day when you came home all wet and dirty?" Mama asked.

"What do you mean, Mama?" I looked at Daddy trying to catch his eyes. I already knew where this conversation was likely to be going.

"I mean the clothes you wore home are practically ruined. I had Sarah wash them in two different kinds of detergent. She even added bleach to one washing. When that failed, I had her scrub them by hand, and still she couldn't get that stuff out of them. It's all over the bottom of the legs. I even washed them once myself," she added.

I knew this was serious if my mother washed clothes. She never washed clothes. She only cooked and washed dishes sometimes. Sarah did all the other household tasks.

"I was at Mr. Joe's farm searching for the missing clothing. You know, those boys' clothes. I guess it's my fault. I asked Clancy and Scottie to help me," Daddy said just in time to thwart my execution.

"Well, I don't know what it is. It shines when it dries on the fabric. It will not come out. I might as well throw your jeans away."

"Let her wear them to fish in, honey. At least she'll get some more wear out of 'em."

Mama said nothing to Daddy's suggestion. Her silence indicated consent.

"Mama, I'm gonna take Scottie to the library with me this afternoon. Maybe that would help him feel better."

"Yeah, that'll make him feel better," her voice was full of sarcasm. "That's just what your brother needs—an afternoon reading down at the library."

"Well, I didn't mean that he would read. He likes to look at *National Geographic*."

"He likes to look at all those naked African women in the magazine. He's not foolin' me," she said. I was glad that my little brother did not hear Mama's accusation.

For some reason that got Mama started off on some article she had read in *National Geographic* back when she was a girl. I listened reluctantly while Daddy finished eating, excused himself, and went upstairs to talk with Scottie. He was gone about fifteen minutes, but when he returned Mama was still talking about those aboriginal people she found so interesting back in 1952.

Daddy kissed me on top of my head and left. Mama paused long enough to watch him leave. She stood at the screen door for a minute longer than I thought necessary as he got into his old black-and-white and drove off. She looked like she wanted to say something, but there was no one to say it to besides me. She walked over to the sink and began washing our dirty glasses. We were served our tomato sandwiches on paper towels, so there no plates to wash. She didn't say anymore about those people in *National Geographic*.

Scottie and I raced to the library, and he almost beat me. He was getting too fast. I couldn't stand it if my baby brother ever beat me. I planned to spend some time running to stay ahead of him. I could outrun the boys in my school class, so it was a surprise that my little brother could come so close to outrunning me.

He didn't say anything about Mr. Joe. Whatever Daddy said to him must have helped. I was glad. I wished that Daddy would talk to me and make me feel better.

Scottie found some issues of his preferred magazine from the 1960's and settled into a private corner-table while I walked through the stacks. I wasn't really in the mood to read, I just wanted to get out of the house. Besides, I still was curious about that ring I had found and I needed that inter-library loan book to help me.

Fred Andrews was not at the main desk. One of the twins, Elba or Melba, was there. I had no idea which one, nor did I care. I wanted to avoid them both. Every few minutes I checked the large clock on the wall behind the main desk. I must have walked through the stacks forty times before I finally decided that I couldn't wait any longer on Fred Andrews to return from wherever he had gone.

"Yes," one of the twins droned out at me. She was not wearing her name badge.

"I am expecting a book from North Carolina. Would you check to see if it has arrived?"

"What's the name of the book?" she demanded.

"I don't know."

"Then how can I check on it?"

"I don't know. I'm not the librarian," I said before I thought. Her face flushed a bit at my remark and then she sucked in half of the air in the library.

"Listen here, Clancy Evans, if you want my help then I would suggest that you change your attitude this very minute!"

I waited a moment before replying. I halfway expected her to stomp her foot at me as she finished her sentence. There was no stomp. She simply gave me a blank stare as she waited on my apology. She would have to wait a lot longer.

"Mr. Andrews helped me order the book. It's a high school annual from Greensboro, North Carolina … Freemont High School. That's all I can remem— wait, it's 1956. The year is 1956."

"Well, I would certainly remember a book like that. But I haven't seen it. So, it's not in yet. Check by again next week."

"Next week? I could be dead by next week! When is Mr. Andrews coming back?"

"You are certainly impudent today. I ought to call your father and tell him how you are behaving. He needs to take you over his knee and teach you some manners."

I started to ask a question about how I would learn proper manners over his knee, but I decided against it. I decided my current attitude was not getting me anywhere with this villainous woman. She obviously had the upper hand and I had to bow to her authority.

"I don't mean to be disrespectful, but I really do need that book. Mr. Andrews might be able to tell me where it is."

"Well, he's not here. He won't be back for at least another hour. So, if you don't mind, I have work to do." She turned away from me with some type of sound and seated herself behind a stack of books that required her immediate attention. It could have been worse. The other sister could have been there to help her. Then I would have had to deal with both of them. Twin villainous sisters. Too much to consider even for me.

I grabbed Scottie and forced him out of the library against his will. He was engrossed with a *National Geographic* profile of women along the Amazon. We didn't get far down the street before we had the good fortune to run into Fred Andrews.

"Afternoon, Mr. Andrews," I said.

"Good afternoon, Clancy. Say, your book came in and I have it in my office. If you'll walk back with me I'll let you see it."

"Well, I'd rather not go back in there just now, Mr. Andrews. I sort of made one of your twins upset and she needs some time to cool off, if you know what I mean."

"Why, Clancy," he chuckled, "whatever did you say to her?"

"Well, I sort of hinted at her incompetence, you know. She's not real thrilled with me at the moment."

"Oh, my. I see. Well, maybe I could go in and process the book. You could stay out here on the steps. Scottie could go in with me and bring it out to you. You can look at it out here, but you can't take it home."

"Why not?"

"Well, it's not the kind of book that you can check out. It's a reference book. It has to stay in the library. I'm bending the rules a bit by letting you look at it out here. But, under the circumstances … well, I like to keep peace in the library, especially with Elba and Melba."

"I see. Tell me, Mr. Andrews, how do you keep those two separated?"

"Separated?"

"How do you tell one from the other?"

"Oh, that. I never bother. Since they dress alike, think alike and act alike, I figure, what difference does it make? I just call them Miss Winkle and go on."

"Elba and Melba Winkle?" I said in disbelief. It was the first time I could recall hearing their last name.

"Yes, those are their names."

Scottie and Fred Andrews disappeared through the double doors and I waited alone on the steps. The library was not a busy place in the summertime in Clancyville, so I sat alone while I waited for my brother to return with the book. It took about ten minutes.

Finally he emerged and we sat together under the large oak in front of the library leafing through that 1956 Freemont High School yearbook. It was boring to look at pictures of people I didn't know and probably never would. Scottie lost interest after a few pages and began humming some hymn from church. I continued my vigilance, hoping to find some clue, some lead, anything that might help in the investigation.

Not only was my task boring, it was also tedious, to say the least. The tedium came from searching every name under every photograph. I was trying to locate a name that matched the initials which Mr. Goldsmith had identified using his magnifying glass—*B A C* or *B A G*, and *L S.* It was methodical. It was laborious. It was like watching paint dry, maybe worse. It was the longest hour of my life.

# Chapter Fifteen

It was mid-afternoon by the time Scottie and I stopped by the jail to see if Daddy was doing anything exciting. I had given the yearbook back to Mr. Andrews and had thanked him for his help, but I hadn't found anything useful in my initial search. I was weary of looking at pictures of strangers from a past unfamiliar to me. The year 1956 seemed like a long time ago and I would imagine that most of the people in those photographs had changed to some degree.

Ralph Hines was in the back of the jail cleaning up, and Daddy was shuffling through some papers at his file cabinet when we entered.

"I hear that the funeral will be in a day or so," Daddy said.

"Why has it taken so long?" I asked.

"Well, they had some kind of delay in Roanoke. In fact, they're still working on the autopsies today, or so they told me this morning when they called."

"Does an autopsy take a long time?"

"Depends on lots of things. It could take several hours, or weeks. Believe it or not, we're not the only folks requiring an autopsy."

"Have you ever seen one?" I said.

"Once. It's not a pretty thing. I wouldn't want the job," Daddy said.

"What is it you two are talking about?" Scottie finally asked.

"Well, son, it's when you ask a doctor to cut open a human body and examine everything inside to determine what caused the death. We call that an autopsy."

"I thought we already knew what caused the death," Scottie said.

"Well, we have to be absolutely certain. We think we know, in fact, we're almost sure. But the law says that in deaths like these, we have to have a doctor examine the bodies and report what he finds after his thorough autopsy. He then lists a cause of death on his report."

"Oh," Scottie said.

"Well, we'll be off. Maybe we can get some fishing in before supper," I said.

"Don't you want to go back and speak to Mr. Joe?"

"No, sir. I have nothing to say to him."

We walked out the door and Daddy followed us outside.

"Clancy, I know that you are upset about what I told you yesterday. I understand that. And I think that information on Mr. Joe certainly makes him capable of killing. The truth is it does not make him any guiltier of this crime than he already was. Nor does it make him any less guilty than he already was. But he is still your friend. Our friend. People make mistakes. We can't just abandon those who make errors of judgment. It's some of that church stuff we're supposed to practice during the week, you know."

"What are you talkin' about?" I asked, having no clue as to what my father referred to when he said church stuff.

"Forgiveness, Clancy. Forgiving people of past mistakes, errors, or that churchy word sin. We all land there, sooner or later, I suspect. Forgiveness, you know, some of that stuff we're told to live. One of those hard words."

"But, Daddy, if he killed Buster and Micah, how can I be friends now with him? He might kill me."

"You honestly think that Mr. Joe would hurt you?"

"I don't know, Daddy. I don't know what to think," I said.

"Those iron bars are awfully thick. Besides, he's never made a movement towards you to hurt you or anything else, has he? He's had many opportunities."

"No, sir. But, well, I guess I'm a little scared."

"I understand. You scared, too, Scottie?"

"No, sir. I don't think he did it. Mr. Joe wouldn't kill children. He might have killed some men once, but I'll bet you he had reason. I think he's innocent, Daddy."

We all stood there staring at each other wondering. It was one of those moments when you had the feeling deep in your gut that what was just said was the truth, but you couldn't prove it. Scottie had reminded me of what I was feeling inside. However, the evidence was against us, against Mr. Joe, and so was the opinion of most of the town.

By the time we had settled into our favorite fishing hole on the Staunton River, the sun was just above the top of one of the big locusts trees which lined the river on the west side. Scottie was already getting a nibble as I was relaxing with my rod and reel, watching my red and white bobber bounce around in the swirls of the deep water.

"I hate fishin' with chicken livers," I said to break the silence.

Scottie reeled in his first catch of the day. It probably weighed close to a pound. It looked like a good one. I watched him put it on the stringer tied to one of the thousand roots that shared our favorite spot with us, below us, running out into the water from a lower portion of ground. There was just enough root showing that allowed us to attach our stringers to it and plop the fish into the water to preserve them for the rest of the time we would be there.

He bated his hook and cast out again to the exact spot of his initial catch. I marveled at the skill of my nine-year-old brother. It was a rule between us that we would not steal each other's spot as long as that person was catching fish there. Honor among fishermen or something like that.

He smelled his hands and looked at me.

"I don't know which is worse, the smell of chicken livers or that manure stuff Mr. Joe puts on his yard."

"I vote for the manure," I said.

"I suppose that black yuck wins out, but they're both powerful strong."

A notion hit me while Scottie was fussing about the odors. I turned it over a few times internally and then decided that I had better do something about it quickly.

I told Scottie to stay put and catch all the fish he could. I would be back for him later. I told him I had to get to Daddy's office before he left.

"You okay with staying out here by yourself?" I asked as I stood to leave.

"Of course. Why wouldn't I be?"

"Just checking, nothing more," I said, not willing to explain why I would ask such a question.

"What's the matter with you?" he asked.

"Nothing. I have an idea. I'll tell you later."

I ran as hard as I ever ran in my life. I finally had a clue that might just prove Mr. Joe innocent. I was hoping as I ran. I was really hoping.

It was nearly four thirty when I entered the Sheriff's Office. I was breathing heavily. Daddy was alone at his desk. Hines was nowhere in sight. Thank goodness.

"Can you call Roanoke?"

"I beg your pardon," he said, surprised at my intrusion and abrupt question.

"Can you call those people who are doing the autopsy?"

"Why?"

"Tell them to smell the necks of those boys."

"Do what?"

"Smell their necks. If Mr. Joe strangled those boys, then their necks will smell bad. They'll smell like manure! Good old cowshit mixed with mud and water and that globby stuff out there in Bessie Mae's secret spot!" I was so thrilled I laughed aloud.

Daddy was not amused. He seldom used nonstandard words which did not suit for mixed company, and certainly didn't tolerate his children using any. I crossed the line and he was about to lecture me over my first public indiscretion.

"I'm sorry," I offered the apology before he could go on the offensive. "I didn't mean to say that. Manure. Mr. Joe puts manure on his lawn to make the grass stay green. Mr. Joe's hands smell like manure most of the time. Sometimes it is rather faint, but it's still there. Don't you think that if he strangled those boys with his hands that the smell would be on their necks?" I was yelling by that point and it was hard for Daddy to get me to quiet down.

"Slow down, Clancy. You're not making too much sense here."

"Daddy, don't you see? If Mr. Joe killed those boys, he had to put his hands on their necks and leave his hands there for several minutes, long enough to suffocate them. Some of that odor would rub off on them. It's a strong odor. Their necks would smell like manure. I was talking to him the other day and there was still a slight odor on his hands after he had spent several days in jail. He's been away from that manure mixture for a while, and yet, I could still smell it on his hands. It was faint, but it was definitely there. You can't wash it off completely. It has to slowly wear off along with frequent washings."

It made perfect sense to me. I could see that he was slowly coming around to my reasoning. Daddy was always a cautious man when it came to outlandish stuff. He could be convinced of strange things, but he had to arrive on his own timetable.

"You haven't smelled it?" I asked.

"I don't always pay attention to odors. The people I arrest sometimes smell bad. They're either drunk or they haven't bathed in a while or both. I usually ignore odors. Have to."

"But Mr. Joe's not drunk or sick. He works with manure each week, I think, putting it around his yard. Or, he's mixing up a new batch to use whenever it is time."

"He puts his hands down in that mixture?" he asked.

"I don't know about that, but he must since his hands smell so bad."

"Does he use gloves?" Daddy asked.

"I don't know. I've never seen him use gloves for any of his chores, but I really can't answer that. I would doubt it, but I have no proof of that. But what I do know for sure is that gunk he uses on his grass, that mixture of manure, water, and whatever else is out there, smells to high heaven. He told me that stuff would kill his grass if he put it on without watering it down. And the other day, he let me smell his hands. The odor was present. So, even if he does not plunge his hands into that gunk he mixes, some of that liquid does get on his hands ... just from him messing with it."

"And doesn't wash it off?" he asked.

"The odor remains even after washing."

"Okay, so what? I pick up the phone and call this respected medical examiner in Roanoke, Virginia and tell him to walk over to those two corpses and smell their necks. Is that what you want me to do?"

It sounded absurd the way he put it.

"Yes, sir. That's it." I smiled at him. "Please hurry. I have a bad feeling about all this."

"Okay, Clancy. I will humor you on this one. But why the bad feeling?" he asked as he reached for the phone, flipped to the last page of his phone book, and then dialed the number. "You should be having a good feeling, if you think you have an idea which might help Mr. Joe."

"It's the bad feeling you get when you think you're too late." I listened as he talked to the person on the other end. We both waited as the doctor was called to the phone. It took longer than I thought necessary for the doctor to begin a conversation with my father. I was pacing in front of Daddy's desk.

"Yes, doctor. This is Sheriff Evans in Clancyville. I have a strange request to ask you regarding those two cadavers, the Scruggs brothers." Finally, the doctor was listening.

"Oh, I see," Daddy said and I didn't like the way his voice trailed off. "Well, it doesn't matter, I suppose..... No, nothing like that.... No, sir, I was simply following up on a clue from this end. ... I wanted you to check their neck regions to see if you could detect an unusual odor. ... Yes, I understand that. ... I see. ... Oh, you did? ... Could you tell what it was? ... I see. ... No. ... Well, it was a hunch we had here. ... No, sir. Sorry to have bothered you. ... Thank you. Yes, sir. Goodbye."

Daddy hung up and just looked at me.

"Your bad feeling was justified."

My heart sank.

"What'd he say?"

"He finished the autopsies around three o'clock this afternoon. They've already been sent to Carson-Grant Funeral Home here in town. There was nothing he could do. He did find some unusual liquid in their lungs and stomach. He said the liquid smelled bad. He had to send it off to have it analyzed. He didn't say anything about odors around the neck region."

"Do they wear masks?"

"The medical examiners?" he said.

"Yeah, the doctors who cut people open like that."

"I believe so."

"Well, then, there's no way he could have smelled manure on their necks, not unless he got really close and knew where to smell."

"I don't think that the masks protect the doctors from the odors. But you said yourself that the odor on Mr. Joe's hands was faint. Surely the odor around the neck region, if it exists at all, would be faint," he explained.

"Rats! This is not working out well."

I felt horrible.

"You were on the right track. It was a good idea. I'm sorry we were too late."

"I wish I had thought of it earlier."

"You still want to prove him innocent, don't you?" Daddy said.

"It could have gone either way."

"Not if he used gloves to strangle those boys."

"I'm goin' to get Scottie," I said.

"Wait a minute and you can ride with me."

"No, thanks. I'd rather walk. I want to think about this."

I left his office under a cloud. I heard him say okay in a surprised tone. I needed time to process what I had just learned. I really thought I had something with that manure smell. I decided then that I was just being too passive with my investigation. I would have to change my strategy and become a bit more aggressive. If I wanted to help Mr. Joe, I couldn't afford to come up with ideas that were too late. In my heart I wanted to believe him to be innocent, despite what my mind was being fed by the facts in evidence.

# CHAPTER SIXTEEN

Mama fixed our favorite meal that night. It was the first time since this whole tragedy began that something good had happened. But then, good is such a relative idea. Mama loved to nag us, but she could cook whenever she put her mind to it. Scottie and I both loved meatloaf and mashed potatoes. She threw in string beans from Aunt Mildred's garden but that didn't matter too much. It was the meatloaf and potatoes that made the day. However, Scottie and I were both compelled to eat the green beans.

I was completely lost in my self-indulgence with the food when Scottie committed what should have been a major faux pas by bringing up a taboo subject at the supper table.

"Mama, do we have guts inside of us like fish do?"

I have seen the time when Mama would have hit him for asking such a thing. For some reason she didn't even bat an eye or drop her fork. She continued to chew the bite of food in her mouth. Then she paused, looked him in the eye, and spoke directly to him.

"We do."

Daddy paused from his eating and watched her closely. He must have figured that it was some kind of delayed reaction on her part. I thought that maybe she would explode any minute now, but nothing happened. She just kept talking after she swallowed another bite of food.

"Of course we have more than a fish has, but it is similar. The whole system is complicated, but vital to both fish and humans."

"Do human guts smell as bad as fish guts?" Scottie asked.

"That's enough talk about fish and humans, young man. Eat your supper," she said as she took another bite of her meatloaf.

There was silence, but only for a moment. Mama picked up her explanation of human anatomy where she had left off. She was very careful with it and avoided any improper words or images.

Daddy and I quietly waited for the thunder bolt that never came. Scottie never missed a beat. He kept on shoveling the food in and listening to her enlightened soliloquy. After a few minutes, when I could tell that something strange was happening in our family and no one was going to get smacked or insulted, or die, I started enjoying my meatloaf again. I think the food tasted better after that, although that's hard to say for sure. It was good before Scottie's indiscretion and Mama's strange response.

After we finished our apple pie and ice cream, I pulled Scottie up to his room and shut the door.

"You've got to help me," I said.

"Do what?"

"I have to check out something downtown. I need a lookout."

"Gimme a break. You always need a lookout."

"No, I don't. At least not every time. But this time I do."

"Get someone else."

"Look, I'm going down to the funeral home and see if I can get a closer look at those bodies."

"You're what? Are you crazy? I'm having nothing to do with that. It ain't ..." he didn't know how to finish his thought.

"Ain't what?"

"Ain't ... uh, it's wrong. I can't do that."

"You don't have to do anything. I'll do the doing. You just stay outside and guard."

"I always guard. I'm always the lookout. One of these days this lookout is goin' to get caught looking out and really be in trouble."

"You won't be in half the trouble I'll be in," I explained.

"Big deal! I'll still be in trouble. Little me. Myself. I'm just a little boy."

"Oh, gimme a break. You sound pathetic. That crap doesn't work on me and you know it. I've never made you do anything you didn't want to do."

"That's not true," he said.

It wasn't true, but I was desperate. I needed him to help me pull this off. The next-to-last thing I wanted to do was to get caught in the Carson-Grant Funeral Home on Main Street. The very last thing I wanted to do was to smell some dead bodies. Still, I felt as if I had no choice in the matter.

It was after 9:30 when I crawled through one of the rear windows of the Carson-Grant establishment. I left Scottie guarding my entry point and looking out over the empty parking lot partially hidden from Main Street. He was well protected unless someone came around a corner with a flashlight and a lot of suspicion. He didn't think much of his protection.

"You hurry, ya hear?"

"I'll hurry. Don't get cold feet."

"What's that mean?"

"You know, that's what the stronger bad guy tells the weaker bad guy when they are just about to pull off a job or something."

"You mean do something stupid, don't you?"

"That would be one explanation," I offered as I began my climb into the building. I didn't want to tell him exactly what *cold feet* meant. It would be like giving him an option, as in something to think about doing to me.

I left the window open in case I needed a fast exit. I had no idea what to expect once I was inside the place. I had only visited it once with Mama and Daddy when one of our old, faithful church members had died. As I climbed through the window I could hear Scottie muttering something about it being summertime and that his feet were not cold at all.

It was an old two-story building that had been renovated a few years back. I roamed around downstairs but could find only rooms filled with chairs and paintings hanging on the walls. The office doors were locked.

I finally discovered what I was after upstairs. I noticed that the room was very cold. The floor was wooden except right in the middle where this strange table sat. The floor underneath that strange table was tiled, sloped downward, and had a drain where the tiles ended. I had an idea what that was used for, but I didn't want to think about it. I had the feeling that I was close to what I wanted to find. I opened every door and drawer I could see. They had to be here somewhere.

After several minutes of exploration, I finally discovered the refrigeration unit where Buster and Micah were being kept. It took all of my strength to open the steel doors and pull out the long tray-like bed. I guessed wrong on the first three doors. I was greatly relieved that they were all three empty, too. My fourth guess was correct and I rolled out Buster.

"Oh, my God," my voice echoed in the chamber and it scared me just before I realized what the sounds were doing in the chamber-room.

Buster looked awful. But of course he had just been through an autopsy so I suppose I shouldn't have expected much. I had never seen a body after an autopsy. It was quite a shock. I held back my tears.

I didn't like Buster much because he was one of those bullies whom you loved to hate. He was forever getting into trouble at school. He wasn't a bad boy or anything like that, but he was one to pick a fight at the drop of the proverbial hat. He even tried to pick a fight with me once. Only once.

Buster was stupid when it came to fighting and knowing who to fight and who to leave alone. He should have left me alone. I had a good reputation around school and town for being able to take care of myself, much to my mother's chagrin and my daddy's pride, but Buster was a Scruggs and had to see for himself. He learned the hard way.

One day during a late afternoon recess when he had more courage than sense, he shoved me from behind, no doubt thinking that I would run away crying and would permit his surprise attack to go unmolested. He thought wrong. I slowly picked myself up from the dirt, dusted my hands with my back to him, and then maneuvered myself into a position between the sun and my opponent. The sun was behind me so that he had to look in the direction of the sun to keep an eye on me. My daddy taught me that trick.

I saw him squint at me and then raise his hand to cover his eyes in an effort to see more clearly. That was the move I was waiting on. When his hand went up, so did my foot, right into his groin. I can still see him bending over holding himself and turning blue. That's when I punched him in the nose with my left hand. I didn't use my right because I had to write with it during the rest of my classes that day. I was always thinking, even under stress. Besides, I wanted to give him a chance by hitting him with my left. It was my weaker hand. And he was already on his knees.

I misjudged my strength just a little. Or, I misjudged the ability of his nose to withstand my close-range jab. Blood went everywhere. There was more on him than me, but I caught enough to know that I was going to be in trouble when I got home later that day.

I broke his nose. He never bullied me again. We did have one other run-in, but he was simply seeking verification the second time we disagreed. In fact, we almost became friends after that. Nothing close, but I think he respected me for standing up to him. He wasn't too keen about the embarrassment of having a girl whip him, but after a few guys called him some unfriendly names a week later and he pulverized them for their verbal slips, all was right with his world. He was the king bully again over the entire fourth grade, except for one unrelenting female. He never bothered me again.

As I thought back on that whole episode, I was sorry he was dead. He wasn't as mean as he made out, nor as tough. Most of the kids were afraid of him because he always could talk a good fight. Fear is a great weapon to use on lesser opponents. That could be why he was lying dead in front me. Somebody used fear on him at some point.

His body smelled funny. I couldn't believe that I was intending to get closer than I already was to smell him. I leaned over and smelled his neck. I didn't want to touch him.

Nothing. I checked both sides of his neck. When I moved the covering back over him, I caught a whiff of something like manure. It was mixed with the other odors and made it difficult to detect exactly what it was. Maybe it was simply my imagination.

It was the same with Micah. I had to check just to be sure. There could have been two killers. One could have killed Buster and the other could have killed Micah. There was nothing on his little neck. I was relieved for Mr. Joe's sake. It was enough for me to know. It didn't prove Mr. Joe's complete innocence, but it did make me feel better. Perhaps this was some verification of my theory about the odor and Mr. Joe's hands.

As we were walking down Henry Street towards our house, Scott finally spoke to me.

"You know, you get me to do some stupid things, Clancy. One day I'm gonna have a heart attack and die, just because of you. Goin' out with you is worse than watching a Frankenstein movie."

"I know," I said. "I owe you for this."

"You always say that, but you never pay up."

# Chapter Seventeen

I had dubious proof that Mr. Joe didn't strangle those boys—a box full of pornographic materials stolen from the home of Ralph Hines, a class ring from 1956 with the initials of *B A G* or *B A C* and *L S*, and my own nose-testimony that there was no manure odor on either of the necks I had inspected. I also had a yearbook from Freemont High School in Greensboro that had lots of wonderful pictures of folks I never knew. I was heavy laden with nothing much at all.

Discouragement was casting a long shadow over me. I needed a break or some encouragement or both.

I decided to go visit Mr. Joe. I figured he needed some encouragement, too.

Scottie stayed home and played with his toy soldiers. I wandered into the jail, hoping that I wouldn't have to do battle with Deputy Hines. I was in luck there. Hines was out with Daddy on some call.

Mary Lee Nottingham was sitting at the desk. She was the part time secretary who controlled the local jail whenever my father and his force of one were out on a call. She was lost somewhere in her fifties and carried an attitude of utter superiority to all people, but especially towards children and men.

"And what do you want?" she asked.

"Are you kin to the secretary at the high school?"

I figured she must be related somehow, or they both had been trained at the same school of office-graces.

"What did you say?"

"Are you any relation to Mrs. Vance Hilmar, the secretary at the high school?"

"Why on earth would you ask such a question? Of course not! I'm a Dalton by birth before I married Harvey Stonewall Nottingham, God rest his dear soul. She's a Peacock, or some such name. A foreigner. I think from Georgia."

"A foreigner from Georgia?" I said.

"What is it you want, Clancy? I have loads of work to do here, and I don't have all day to sit around talkin' to you."

"Well, Mrs. Nottingham, I came to see Mr. Joe."

"I don't think that's a safe thing to do, young lady."

"He's still behind bars, correct?"

She knew where I was headed and tried to cut me off.

"That's not the point. That man might have killed those two little boys, God rest their souls. You want to be number three?"

"I'm a higher draw than that. Look, he's my friend. He's not going to kill me through those bars. You stay here with your loads of work, and I'll go talk with him."

I moved faster than Mary Lee Nottingham could mount an objection. I walked past her desk and let myself into the back room before she could clear her throat. I figured that I might catch some wrath on the way out. It was always like this getting past her, no matter what I wanted. My singular ace in the hole was that I knew she would never come back in the jail area to get me. Unlike my nemesis the stupid deputy, she was deathly afraid of prisoners, especially those accused of murder. We hadn't had many of those during my young life, but I do recall one other time when my daddy was holding a man on suspicion of murder for another county. At any rate, I knew Mrs. Nottingham's fear of coming into this area. She didn't trust the iron bars and the locked doors. She must have thought that she would be next on some hit list.

Mr. Joe was sitting on his bunk with his eyes closed. I stood at his door for several minutes. I could tell that he was mumbling to himself.

"Excuse me, Mr. Joe."

"Oh, my, oh my, Miss Clancy. Good to see you, young lady."

"Did I interrupt your prayers?"

"Can't interrupt prayers, child. I'm always talking to God. I do a right smart amount of listening too, or try to, most of the time. Doesn't pay high dividends to ask God for something and then not listen for the answer."

It made sense to me, but I wasn't into much praying. I prayed on Sundays and on nights when folks I knew were sick or in trouble. I also prayed when Mama stood over my bed like a sergeant-at-arms and forced me to talk with God. And I had prayed recently for Mr. Joe. It wasn't much of a prayer, as prayers go, but at least I acknowledged him with words addressed heavenward.

"I'm sorry I doubted you the other day."

"What do you mean?"

"Daddy told me about the file he got on you from Richmond."

"Oh, that," he said. His voice was lower now. It had a wonderfully smooth quality to it, like silk.

"Why'd you kill those men, Mr. Joe?"

"Do you know what rage is, Miss Clancy?" His voice was as calm as the river some days.

"Is it when you blow your top?"

"That's pretty close, pretty close. I think all the hatred in the world came over me at that time. It consumed me, child."

"What caused it?"

"Well, I've been thinking about that for a long time. Long time. I thought about it while I was in jail and I've thought about it since I've been out of jail. I guess it was hatred."

"Did they hate you?"

"Yes and no. I think they first hated the color of my skin. They didn't even know me. They just hated who they thought I was. And they hated what they saw."

"Did they hurt you?"

"They killed my heart, child."

"I don't understand."

"They never laid a finger on me. They killed Lucy and Rebecca."

"Who are Lucy and Rebecca?"

"Lucy was my wife. We were married fourteen months. The most beautiful woman in the whole world. Beautiful inside and out. She was everything. Everything, Clancy. Do you understand what that means to another person?" He got up from the bunk and moved around in his cell. I could tell that he had great feelings for the Lucy he had mentioned.

"A little," I said softly.

"And then in May she gave birth to our beautiful little daughter, Rebecca. Oh, my, we were so happy. I had a good job, a good wife, and a child. I was the happiest man on earth, I tell you. Everything was right."

I could feel his passion as he spoke of his family. Mr. Joe was a special kind of man. He had great feelings for the people he loved. That in itself made him different from a lot of the white people I knew.

"What happened, Mr. Joe?"

"Sometime in late summer of that same year I had to go on a trip for my company. I left my wife and daughter at home. We lived just outside of Raleigh. Nice little house, green shutters, you know, like the American dream. It was our perfect dream, Clancy. It was our house. Our first house. Our only house...."

He walked back over to the bunk and sank back into it. I probably should have stopped him at this point, but my curiosity was too much for me to mind my manners and end his painful explanation. I felt like I had to know the facts concerning what he had done to deserve so many years in jail.

"While I was gone, two drunk white men came into my house and raped my wife, then they strangled her and my baby girl, Rebecca. They tried to burn my house down, but they were too drunk to think straight. The fire burned part of the house, but they left some of their clothes behind in their blind ritual of murder and rape. Those clothes helped to identify them. But that didn't matter because they bragged about doing it. They told some people what they had done and that they wouldn't go to jail for killing no niggers. They called me an uppity nigger when I went to see them."

"That's why they did that to your family?"

"That's why, Clancy. They stood in the doorway of their clapboard shack and called me an uppity nigger. Told me how much they enjoyed raping and killing my wife. Told me that they had to kill that nigger child so that she wouldn't grow up and have more nigger babies. Said we had enough niggers on the earth already. Enough. So, I killed them."

"The rage," I said.

Mr. Joe looked up at me, and then nodded slowly.

"It was wrong, Clancy. But it was the rage that came over me. I felt more hatred at that moment than I ever thought I could ever feel. I have felt nothing like it since then. It was horrible."

"You strangled them?"

"Yes."

"With your hands?"

"Yes." He looked at his hands as he spoke.

"How could you strangle two grown men at the same time? You don't look that strong, Mr. Joe."

Our eyes met. He was silent. I could tell that something was on his mind, but he didn't answer me. His head dropped a little and he stared at the floor.

"Mr. Joe? How'd you do it?"

"Better let it drop, Miss Clancy. It all happened a long time ago. Details are hard to explain now. I'm an old man. Prison did a job on me, child. I'm too tired to think right now. And, you're asking a question to which you do not need to know the answer."

I knew it was time for me to go. Mr. Joe was a different person to me now. I still liked him, in fact, I liked him better because I knew him better. In one way I was sorry that I had asked all the questions. In another way, I was glad. But I hated to see all that pain come back to him. Maybe the pain had never really left him.

"I'll come back tomorrow. Do you need anything, Mr. Joe?"

"My Bible," he said softly in that beautiful, resonant voice.

"I'll get it. Anything else?"

"That's sufficient."

I walked towards the door that separated the cells from the office area.

"Thank you for believing in me, Miss Clancy. You just might be the only friend I have."

"No, sir," I said. "Scottie's your friend, too. And my daddy wants to believe, but the facts are hard on him right now. Still, I think he wants you to be innocent."

Mr. Joe smiled and I left. Mrs. Attila-the-Hun Nottingham was still guarding the office. She grunted in my direction as I departed. I wanted to give her a parting gesture of my feelings about her, but I thought better of that idea. Daddy always said that a man better learn to control his impulses. I knew he meant girls too.

# Chapter Eighteen

Mama fixed tomato sandwiches again for lunch, but this time she side-dressed them with potato chips. They went down a lot better with the chips. I actually liked tomatoes, but I would have preferred the addition of hamburger meat sitting atop that slice of tomato between my two pieces of bread. Scottie hated tomatoes. He ate peanut butter and grape jelly sandwiches for the most part.

Daddy came in late and was in a hurry to leave when he had finished his sandwich. I caught up with him as he closed the door to the black-and-white. His window was down.

"I need to talk with you when you have time," I said.

"Okay. Is this going to be a long conversation or short?"

"Depends on you. I have some stuff to show you. You might have some questions about it."

"What kind of stuff?"

"I'd rather not say until you're ready to talk."

"Fair enough. How about I come home early tonight? Say, four thirty or so? Will that give us enough time before supper?"

"It might, if we're alone. Maybe we could go somewhere private in your car."

"Good idea. It's a date then, okay?"

"Okay. Thanks, Daddy."

He drove off and I knew he would be fair with me about some of my collected evidence, but he would also ask me some very hard questions about a few items. My hope was that some of what I had discovered might give him some clues or some ideas about where to go next. I was beginning to run out of trails to follow. I needed to bring him in on all that I had found, learned, and considered.

Scottie was ready for some serious fishing when I returned to the house. He was tired of playing with his soldiers all morning and needed some energy-releasing activity. The fishing was fine with me. He could fish and I could contemplate Mr. Joe's predicament and my upcoming, later-that-day meeting with the sheriff. I felt uneasy about showing my father the little pile of evidence I had. Still, I was at a crossroads. I had to do something to get my juices flowing again. Confessing my sins of commission was not exactly what I wanted to be doing with my father the sheriff, but Mr. Joe's life was more valuable than my fear of parental retribution. I was also gambling that my father would not tell his wife what I had done.

By the time Scottie and I returned with our six measly catfish of no real size, it was a little past four. We had just enough time to clean the fish, clean up our mess, and put our latest fish-additions in the outside freezer for a later meal before Daddy pulled into the driveway at the time he had promised.

I gathered up all of my evidence, threw it into my book satchel and jumped into his car. I was ready for business. I was also ready for a lecture. I had the feeling that the lecture was going to be a good one, too.

"Where to, boss?" he said.

"Let's drive out past Mr. Joe's place, near the river. That's private enough for us to talk."

He drove, and I sat in silence rethinking my rehearsed speech and some of the defensive comments I knew I would have to make at the appropriate times. This whole revelation was a big gamble. I might have something of value or I might have a bag full of nothing more than fanciful ideas. I had no way of knowing. This was all a new experience for me. I had never been this much involved in a crime case. I had always watched Daddy from a distance because I had never thought too much about doing stuff like I had done. But after I started reading the famous cases of Mr. Sherlock Holmes, well, that's when I started thinking that maybe I could help some. Then all of a sudden I was in the middle of a murder, a double murder, and I really couldn't help myself. At any rate, I didn't want to stop now.

He found a shady spot near our fishing hole and parked. The river looked inviting, but I had no time for such summer pleasures. I suppose all fishermen feel the beckoning of the water when they sit this close to it on a shady afternoon in early August.

"What's in the bag?" he said.

"Evidence, I hope."

"Evidence of what?"

"The case you're on," I opened my satchel and pulled out the ring. I wanted to start with the first item and go along in order. It might make more sense to him that way.

He took the ring and examined it closely. I watched him study it carefully as he moved it around so that the sunlight might reveal some hidden mystery.

"Where did you find this?"

"At the crime scene, sort of."

"What do you mean 'sort of'?" His body language was telling me that he was keenly interested.

I was becoming more anxious by the minute. My daddy was not a violent man, so I was not afraid of him. Still, I had to move cautiously about revealing my clandestine exploits. I had no idea as to how he would react.

"Well, you remember that I commented on how clean the area was near to where we found the bodies?"

He nodded and I continued: "So I figured that Hines had thrown out Scottie's vomit nearby. Hines wouldn't walk too far carrying that stuff. I also had a hunch that Hines wasn't too careful with what he cleaned up and threw out. I found the vomit in a trash bag inside a barrel behind the barn. The ring was in the vomit."

"You went through that stuff?"

"No other way I could think of. Investigating is dirty work."

He smiled. I could tell that I had won some brownie points with my disgusting confession. I figured I would need them in a few minutes.

"Why didn't you bring me this earlier?"

"Didn't know it was important enough until I checked it out."

"Checked it out?"

"Yeah, I took it—excuse me, yessir, I took it to Mr. Goldsmith and he used his large magnifying glass to read the writing on the inside of the ring—*B A C* or *B A G.* That last letter is hard to make out. I'm guessing it is a *G* because of that little mark just to the right. I've studied it a lot since Mr. Goldsmith looked at it. I use my stamp magnifying glass. That other writing is easier to read: a heart and *L S.*"

"What do you make of it?"

"Nothing yet, except Scottie thinks that *L S* probably means Lydell Scruggs."

"Buster?" he said.

"Yessir. That's what we figure. I agree with Scottie. Somebody gave this ring to Buster and had it inscribed with that heart and Buster's initials. According to Mr. Goldsmith, that *L S* and heart inscription is a lot more recent than the other initials."

"Why didn't they use *B S*?"

"Don't know, maybe… to hide. Fewer people would know *L S.*"

"And what does *B A G* represent?"

"Wish I knew. I'm still searching for that one."

"Searching where?"

"I had Fred Andrews send for the 1956 Freemont High School yearbook, and I looked through it to see if I could recognize a face. Nothing so far." Daddy gave me a strange look and a slight smile.

"You've been busy," he said.

"Yessir, but that ain't all."

"There's more?"

I pulled out the box I had taken from Ralph Hines' place and handed it to him without opening it. I wanted him to open it. It was more dramatic that way.

He saw Ralph's name immediately, looked back at me with a slight frown, then opened the box. His expression never changed. My daddy had one of those poker faces that would have been impossible to read while playing him in five card stud.

"Where did you get this?"

"Do I have to answer that?" I knew this was going to be a delicate part of my presentation-confession.

"Yes, ma'am, you do." His voice was firm but not yet the fatherly scold I had anticipated before all this started. I figured that was coming really soon now.

"Hines' place."

"His house? You entered his house?" His voice was changing ever so slightly.

"Yes."

"Alone?"

"Yes. Scottie was the lookout."

"The lookout?" he was calmer, almost as if he were questioning a witness or a suspect.

"Yessir. I didn't want him to get caught inside and I needed him more outside to let me know if somebody… like Hines, was coming into the driveway or whatever."

"I see. You do this often? Breaking and entering?"

"No breaking, just entering. The backdoor was open."

"Why on earth did you go to Ralph Hines' place? What gave you the idea to go to his house?"

"The idea came from Scottie. He said that the scuttlebutt around town was that Hines was queer."

"You broke into a man's house because of rumors around town?"

"I entered a man's house because Scottie told me that his friend Billy Bob Doss had been warned to stay clear of Hines by Billy Bob's father. Rufus also said the same thing to Scottie."

"Rufus Worley and Billy Bob Doss were your sources on this?"

"Not directly. I didn't question them. I took Scottie's word for it."

"Oh. Why didn't you go directly to Rufus and Billy Bob?"

"Just in case it was a rumor. All I had to do was to find something in Hines' house that would support Scottie's rumor. And, as you can see, I did. I found more than I was looking for."

"I can see that. But you broke the law. We can't use this in a trial."

"None of it?" I said.

"No, ma'am. Hines could sue you … us. Unlawful entry, stealing, whatever."

"But you can see what kind of person he is."

"Yes, I can see that. But we acquired the information illegally. We cannot use it. Understand?"

"Yessir. I understand, but I don't like it."

"I don't like it either. I don't like you running around town breaking into people's homes. I don't like you putting yourself and your brother into dangerous situations. This is not a game, Clancy. What you did was very dangerous. Extremely dangerous. Are you listening to me, young lady?"

Finally, the tone I had been expecting surfaced. It wasn't as bad as I had figured, but I knew that it might get worse. He was still being extraordinarily calm about all of this. But I hadn't told him everything yet. I hope he could control himself when he knew it all.

"Yes, sir. I hear you," I answered dutifully.

"Have you broken into any other home in the community?"

"I don't break. I enter. I find a way inside without breaking. I don't like to do damage to other folks' property, even if they are bad people."

"Don't mince words with me, Clancy. Whose house have you been inside illegally besides Ralph Hines'?" His voice was flat and firm. It was the Sheriff of Pitt County talking to me now. I was a little uncomfortable, but I had to tell him.

"No one's house. The Carson-Grant Funeral Home."

He was either too shocked to say anything, or too angry, or very curious. I decided to keep talking until he found his voice.

"A window was left unlocked and I climbed in. I was hoping to find Buster and Micah's bodies before they were embalmed. And I did! I found them on the second floor in the refrigeration closet, I guess you would call it that."

"What were you looking for?" Daddy was back.

"I wanted to smell their necks."

"Oh, my Lord. Have you lost your mind completely? You're something, you know that?"

I figured that wasn't a question to answer so I let it pass. Having a smart-mouth with my father was not something I ever intentionally did. We sat in silence for a few minutes. He was thinking, I'm sure, of what to say next. I was wondering how I was going to get out of this alive and with my dignity still intact.

"And?" he said finally.

"Sir?"

"Did you smell anything?"

"Plenty, but no manure around the necks. I think Mr. Joe's innocent. I don't think he killed those boys."

"I didn't tell you everything the Medical Examiner told me. That dark liquid he found in the lungs and stomachs of both boys had a strong manure odor. It means that those boys were probably drowned before they were choked. Mr. Joe still could have killed them."

"But why, Daddy? What was his reason for killing them? It just doesn't make any sense to me. If he wanted to kill some kids, he could have killed me and Scottie. He had plenty of chances to do that."

"Yes, I know. I've been thinking about that. It doesn't make any sense to me either."

We were silent for several minutes. He was looking at the two photographs I had placed on top of the pile inside the box. He was comparing the two pictures. He was also rolling the ring around his right index finger with his thumb.

"And you think Ralph Hines killed those boys?"

"Not necessarily. I don't know what Hines has to do with this. I have nothing to connect him to Buster and Micah, except those photographs. It is a possibility, but I can't find a connection. I'm at a roadblock. That's why I came to you with the stuff. I thought together—"

"Together?" his question interrupted.

"Yes, sir," I said meekly.

He was thinking again.

"Your mother know any of this? Never mind. Of course she doesn't know anything. She would have locked you in your room and interrogated me for hours. Besides, I know you well enough to know that you would never tell your mother this kind of stuff. Does she suspect anything?"

"I don't think so."

I waited several seconds to see if he had more questions. I didn't want to interrupt his thinking. Maybe he was developing a plan of action. Then again, maybe he was thinking about what he was going to do to me now that I had confessed my transgressions.

"So, what do you think about all this?" I broke the silence first.

"Well, Clancy," he was calm again and I was relieved, "most of it is useless in court. Everything except the ring. But, the rest of it is useful for … us."

He looked sideways at me and smiled, sort of.

"You've got to promise me," he continued, "no more breaking and entering—no more entering period! If you get caught, I would have to lock you up. Then I would be asked to explain your actions since I am your father and somewhat responsible for you. You could put yourself and me in a very bad position. So, promise me. No more of this!"

"Yessir."

"Is that a promise?"

"Yessir. That's a promise."

I didn't like to make promises, especially ones like this. But I decided I didn't have much choice at the moment. He was still my daddy, and I had to mind him. It was a tough position for a budding detective to find herself.

"Let's go to the library. I want to see that yearbook," he said.

# Chapter Nineteen

Daddy and I sat at a long table thumbing through the 1955-56 Freemont High School annual under the ever watchful eyes of the twin dragons who were perched at the Circulation Desk. I was worried that Mr. Andrews might have already sent the book back to North Carolina. He said that he had been busy and hadn't gotten around to it. Besides, he told us, he usually kept things like that for at least two weeks before returning them.

"Do you see anybody you know?" I asked, ever hopeful.

"Not yet," he said.

He took his time looking at the photos. He seemed to be much more cautious about his search than I was. I guess I was just too impatient with the thing. I figured the picture in the book would simply jump up and call my name. I had no idea that detective work could be so tedious. I had already learned that it could be gross—Mama would say *indelicate*—but tedium was a new revelation. My knowledge was increasing.

After twenty minutes or so he closed the book and stared at the cover for a few seconds. He seemed lost in some thoughts about something. I wasn't into mind reading so I was lost too.

"Whataya thinking about?" I said.

"I was trying to think of who I would know that had come here to Clancyville from Greensboro. No one comes to mind. That must mean that either I don't know as much as I should about these people, or that the person didn't come here directly from Greensboro."

"Do you know anyone who came here from North Carolina?"

"Good question. Let me think…" He was silent for several minutes. I looked around to see if the dragons were lurking nearby in an attempt to feed their curiosity. I knew that they were dying to know what Daddy and I were up to. I couldn't spot them immediately. Fred Andrews was back at the Circulation Desk at this point, and the dragons must have been off in the stacks re-shelving books.

"Fred Andrews came from North Carolina," he said finally.

"I didn't know that. He might know some other Tarheel, right?"

"It's worth asking," he said.

I was up and moving towards the Circulation Desk before he could suggest that I do that. Fred was the kind of man who was very pensive whenever someone would ask him a question. I got the kind of answer from him that I expected. He told me to give him until tomorrow and that he would make a list of the names that came to mind.

Daddy and I were pleased with this, so we returned the book, asked him to hold on to it a few more days, and then left. I waved at one of the dragons on the way out. She made a hissing sound at me and didn't wave back.

After a supper of black-eyed peas, home-made biscuits, mashed potatoes, gravy, and country-style steak, we were all fat and sassy with contentment. It was at those times of pure pleasure in my childhood that I had to be especially careful not to get myself into trouble with my mouth. I usually tried to allow Scottie more opportunities to talk so he would be the one in touch with our mother's darker side.

"How long has it been since you have been to see Aunt Nona?" Mama was speaking to both my brother and me. Scottie groaned before I thought about it.

"I beg your pardon, young man. Did you say something?"

"No, ma'am. That was just my stomach growling," he lied.

"Well, you'd better not. I have you know that your Aunt Nona was a fine woman in her day, and she helped me a lot when I was growing up. The least we can do is visit her."

"She's crazy," Scottie said. He was really fat and sassy with food tonight. I never would have publicly said such a thing to my mother. I might have said it to Daddy, but not to Mama. Aunt Nona was blood kin to Scottie and me through our mother.

"You want a whipping?"

I never knew why Mama asked us that kind of question. Only a fool would say yes to it, and neither one of us was fool enough to say that. I decided that it was some kind of rhetorical question which parents often ask their children from lack of originality on their part.

"I'm sorry, Mama," he said, "but you know it is hard to talk with her. And she talks crazy sometimes."

"You can still show respect for old people, young man," Mama was still bent out of shape with his remark. "And, she's family."

Aunt Nona was Mama's oldest living aunt on her father's side of the family. That made her, of course, our great aunt. She was almost ninety. Besides being crazy, she was deaf. But as far as I knew, those were the only two deficits she had. Family tradition and town gossip had it that she had been crazy most of her life. Deafness came on her during the last eleven years, my lifetime.

Nona Clancy was a long time widow, the last living sibling of my grandfather on my mother's side. My Grandpa Clancy was the most famous member of the family. He was the most famous person in Clancyville. Even though they had named the town after his grandfather, my grandfather had done more for the town than any living man or woman. He was Mr. Clancyville. While nearly everyone in the family, as well as in the town, shied away from dear Aunt Nona, my grandfather treated her with the utmost respect and courtesy. He visited her in her home every week of his life, no exceptions. The family fiction had it that she would tell him things that she would say to no one else. There was also the story that he sought advice from her, but no one in my family believed such a tale, and certainly not my mother. She believed that her father needed advice from no one. That little tidbit was a major part of his history, or legend, as it became after his death.

I decided it was time for me to rescue Scottie from his very deep mud hole with Mama. He was slipping fast into a mess he wouldn't escape without great assistance. There was a time when I enjoyed hearing him yell whenever Mama would whip him. But those days had passed. I hated for anybody to get a whipping, especially Scottie and me. However, I was not above inflicting pain upon my brother when the need arose.

"Let's go right now, Scottie," I said.

"Go where?" he said.

"Go visit Aunt Nona. This is a great time. She'll love to see us, won't she Mama?"

I was plotting here and hoping to win out.

I think that my mama was so shocked at my offer to visit my great Aunt Nona that she completely forgot about our chores after the evening meal. I am sure that she would remember later and lecture us when we returned. For the moment, we escaped and were on our way down the street to visit our batty old aunt who was at best half-baked. I loved her, but she was crazy. Scottie got that part correct.

As we walked, Scottie complained.

"Well, I got you out of clearing off the table," I reminded him.

"Oh, yeah, you did."

"Stick with me, kid. You've got to use good judgment sometimes. Mama's family is sacred, you know. And especially those on grandpa's side. Founding fathers and mothers, remember?"

"What'd they found?"

"Started the town way back when," I corrected. "Grandpa's grandpa settled here and provided the town with a name."

"How do you know all that?" he asked.

"I listen, sometimes. But I really don't know the whole story. He was wealthy and owned most of the land around Clancyville. I think it was only natural that the folks who moved in later would name the place after him."

"Was he crazy as well?"

"You mean grandpa's grandpa? Or, do you mean grandpa himself?"

"I'm getting confused with all this. I 'spose I mean my grandfather," he decided.

"You mean like Aunt Nona?"

"Exactly. Was grandpa like her?"

"No one has ever said anything about that. If he was, it must have been a dark secret. Maybe we should ask Aunt Nona if her brother, our grandpa, was crazy like she is."

Scottie turned his head slightly and gave me one of his incredulous stares. Then he rolled his eyes heavenward and shook his head at me.

"The problem with crazy people is that they make me feel uncomfortable talking with them. And her stories! I can't make sense of them. You do the talking, okay?" he said.

"Just listen and act like you're interested."

"Easier said than done."

He was right. Her stories could go on for what seemed like hours at a time. No end. No point. No substance. It was a child's nightmare. Now I was volunteering us to go and actually visit this notorious, ancient geezer without adult supervision. Maybe I was the one who was half-baked.

Her oversized white house on Washington Street made our large white house look small. It was only two stories, but it looked taller. She had those small attic windows at the top that gave the impression of a third floor. The porch covered all four sides of her house. There were three swings and numerous wicker chairs conveniently placed for people to sit, talk, and drink sweet tea in the summertime. Of course no one had done that in years, but the furniture was still available for such behavior.

She had more money than the rest of the town combined, so her house was always in beautiful condition. Somebody was usually there painting some part of it, either inside or out. This summer they were painting the upstairs parlor, the guest bedrooms, the downstairs library, and a backyard gazebo that was about the size of my bedroom. They were nearly finished with everything except the library and the gazebo. She had required them to move every volume from the shelves and store them in boxes before they could even think of walking into her library with a paintbrush. The painting of the gazebo had been added at the last minute, so it undoubtedly would be the last project for her estate that summer.

Matilda Franklin was the lady who stayed with her in the evenings. The family had agreed to keep an eye on her during the daylight hours, but had wanted someone to sleep over each night. Matilda was paid handsomely for her care. Aunt Nona fussed non-stop whenever Matilda was out of ear-shot. She fussed about Matilda having to stay with her at nights. But she would never fuss in front of Matilda. She said it wasn't lady-like or dignified to fuss in front of the servants. We never could convince her that Matilda wasn't one of the servants. Aunt Nona's advanced age and history made it difficult for anyone to convince her of that.

It did no good to ring the doorbell, so we promenaded into her house unannounced. She usually stayed in the downstairs parlor or in her upstairs bedroom. She wasn't an invalid nor did she have trouble climbing the stairs. In fact, for a person of her advanced age, she was in remarkably good condition. There were no known illnesses, except deafness. She walked upright, straight as an arrow and had no need of a cane. Sturdy and batty. Despite her deafness, she didn't yell at us when we talked. We had to yell at her, which was always unsettling to my mother. I couldn't understand why that bothered her so much. She had plenty of experience with yelling at her children.

"Hello, Aunt Nona. It's Clancy and Scottie," I yelled out as loud as I could.

The sound ricocheted off the high walls and throughout the house. I waited an appropriate time before I yelled again.

No response.

"Aunt Nona!" I yelled once more. This time I found some more volume and it got through.

"Oh, my, my," came the reply from somewhere upstairs. "Come in, come in, Clancy, my love. Are you alone? Did that precious little Scottie come too? Please come up and visit with me. It's been ages since you were here. I'm up here, child. Come up here and join us. I am having the most delightful conversation with Captain Mortimer. He's just in from a trip around the Keys and through the Bermuda Triangle. I must tell you ...."

She continued talking incessantly. Scottie and I followed the sound of her voice until we found her sitting on her bed in her bedroom on the backside of the house. It was a small miracle that my voice had carried that far. We entered and sat down while she was still talking and greeting us as if we had not heard anything she had said. There was no Captain Mortimer visible to our eyes.

I stopped my search for a man in uniform after a quick scan of the entire room upon entering. Scottie continued turning, first he looked around, moving his head left to right. Then, when his first scanning produced no visible person, he began moving his head right to left. When that failed, he turned around in circles. Brothers can be rather obnoxious when challenged.

I punched him hard in the shoulder and whispered, "Stop it!"

"So good to see you both. And such a wonderful surprise after supper. You know that Matilda is downstairs cleaning up the dishes. She's such a wonderful cook. Do you know Matilda my housekeeper? She's such a fine acquisition. I don't know what I would do without her, but you know I don't need her as much as my nieces and nephews think. I can actually get along quite well without much assistance. Tell me how your parents are. I can't remember when I last saw your mother."

She took a breath and I spoke.

"Two days ago, I think, Aunt Nona. She came by to check and you were doing fine. The painting seems to be going well. They're almost finished."

I was yelling and I hated it. Scottie covered his ears with his hands and I yanked at them while I was still talking. There were times that I could kill him and feel good about it.

"Oh, my yes, child. I love the paint job those wonderful painters are doing for me. They're such nice men, but they smoke too much. I hate tobacco. It leaves an awful smell wherever it is and seems to hover in the air, especially in the summertime. Except that I do love that wonderful tobacco smell on the Captain. He smokes a pipe and some rich South American blend of the finest leaves, he tells me. Hasn't it been so horribly hot this summer and no rain, and those murders, my oh my, I hate it so much when something tragic happens to young people. Are you okay, Clancy?"

She actually stopped chattering and asked me a question. I was caught completely off guard. It wasn't often that Aunt Nona asked questions to give folks an opportunity to provide an answer. It was rare indeed. She waited on me to answer. Scottie was still looking around the room, probably for Captain Mortimer. She was actually pausing in her speech pattern to permit me time to say something.

"Yes, ma'am," I yelled at her. "I'm fine."

"Why do you yell at me, Clancy? Is your voice changing?"

"I don't think so, Aunt Nona. I thought you were hard of hearing," I softened my voice considerably. I was using my normal volume now. I waited to see if she would respond.

"I have a new hearing aid, dear. It's wonderful. I can hear everything you say. You have such a sweet voice and it is so unbecoming for young ladies to yell, don't you think? Tell me, Scottie, what mischief are you into this summer?"

Again, another pause and the wait. She was actually engaging us in conversation. This was totally unheard of in the annals of Clancyville lore regarding our Great Aunt Nona, at least in my lifetime. Nona could actually hear and talk much like normal folks. Wonder of wonders. Modern technology had finally caught up with her.

"Where's this captain person you were talking to?" Scottie asked.

Aunt Nona looked around the room. She seemed to be searching for the missing man.

"I don't know. He must have stepped out for a moment. If he doesn't return soon, I will have Matilda check on him. I want you to meet him. You will like him immediately. Now, where were we? Oh, yes, Scottie, tell me all about the mischief you've been into so far this summer."

# Chapter Twenty

We sipped sweet iced tea and talked about the residents of Clancyville most of the evening. Aunt Nona wanted to talk about everything. Now and then she would add some unrelated comment about Captain Mortimer as if we knew him personally. I decided somewhere near the end of our two hour conversation that she must not get much company for her to enjoy talking with two children for so long.

"Anything interesting happening at the church?" she asked in the middle of our chatting about the county fair, crooked politicians, the price of coffee, and the new nursing home that had just been completed on the west side of town.

"Nothing I know of," Scottie said without hesitation.

"Yeah, Mama's upset with Miss Greesome," I offered.

"What's your mother got stuck in her craw this time?" she said.

"I don't think she likes Miss Greesome at all. She was fussing last Sunday about her directing the congregational music. She doesn't like all that hand waving."

"Not much to fuss about, if you ask me. But that Betty Greesome is a real trick, she is. At least your mother is showing good judgment to question that woman. Personally, I don't trust the lady. No, ma'am. I don't trust her at all."

"Why not?" I said.

"Because she's sneaky, that's why. She puts on airs. She pretends to be something she's not. We used to call that being two-faced."

"How do you know this?"

"Clancy, I only stopped going to church about a year ago. She's been directing the music in that church for almost ... what is it now ... eight, no, nine years? Yes, I believe it was 1963 that she came to town. Sometime later that year, I think it was. So I know what I know, Clancy. She smiles and says nice things when there are lots of people around, but when it's just her and someone she knows well or some child, well, let me tell you she talks rather differently then. I heard her once and I know what I heard."

"What did you hear?" I was curious even though I generally found no reason to dislike Miss Greesome.

"Old man Thomas Craddock was speaking to her and, oh, I forget who it was standing there with her, but Mr. Craddock said something about the music. There were three of them. I think he was joking with her, but she took it the wrong way and became defensive. When he told her he was kidding, she didn't say anymore to him. But then just as soon as he walked away, she called him an SOB. Do you know what that is, child?"

"Yes, ma'am."

"I do, too, Aunt Nona. Sonofabitch!" Scottie said proudly.

Aunt Nona laughed aloud. It was a good, hearty laugh, one I had never heard from her. She smiled a lot, but seldom laughed like that. It sounded like a laugh that had come from a long way off in her past.

"Scottie, you're too much. Captain Mortimer makes me laugh aloud at times. My, my, my. Simply too much. What am I going to do with you, young man?"

She paused briefly to get her breath before she continued.

"I first thought she was just mad at what Mr. Craddock had said, but then she started speaking ill of other people who were not present, and she referred to them using every vulgar and disgusting term you can imagine. My, my, my, what language that religious lady could use. You should have heard her. No, no! On second thought, you should not have heard it. It would burn your ears. I heard every word. I was standing around the corner from her, just out of sight. I heard every word she said. So, you see, I don't trust her. She pretends to be so good and holy, but in reality she's nothing but a gutter-mouth. Why, the Captain is a sailor and he doesn't talk like that, at least he doesn't use language like that in front of me. I don't think ladies should be vulgar, Clancy. Firm, but not vulgar. Nor should gentlemen talk that way, Scottie."

"I've heard Mama say things about her, but I figured that Mama was just fussing at somebody besides me for a change. I really didn't pay any attention to it," I interjected.

"That's not all. I've heard rumors about her, rumors that aren't very nice. Now mind you, they're just rumors so I can't be for certain, but where there's smoke, often there's fire. I've heard the Captain say that many a time. You've heard that before haven't you?"

"Yes, ma'am," I said.

"And it's true, Clancy. But whether these rumors are true, I can't say. Horrible things to say about a person."

"What did they say about her?"

"You're just a child, Miss Clancy. I don't know that I should be talking like this to you. But if you promise not to repeat this rumor, then I'll tell you. Promise? You, too, Scottie?"

We both nodded as if we had taken some secret vow to keep silent until death.

"Well, I heard Priscilla Dalton say that—"

The phone rang and interrupted Aunt Nona's gossip report. I was just as glad because I really didn't care one whit what Priscilla Dalton said about anybody. She was an old maid who sat around and talked about the whole town, whoever happened to pop into her mind. She was a real mischief maker and I didn't take much stock in what she said about anybody. She even told some people that my daddy was stealing from the town fund once. Daddy had to pay her a visit just to get her to stop spreading the untruth.

Mama was calling to tell us that it was past time to come home. It was after nine-thirty and she was worried that maybe we had gotten lost the two blocks between our house and Aunt Nona's. I think the truth was that she couldn't believe that we were still talking with Aunt Nona since she knew how much we usually dreaded visiting relatives, especially the old ones.

"Will y'all come back and visit me again real soon?"

Aunt Nona had apparently forgotten all about that nasty, tasty rumor she was about to divulge to us.

"Sure, Aunt Nona. Maybe we can come next week," Scottie said, with some excitement.

I was shocked at my brother's response.

"Tell you what. I'll have Matilda make you a pound cake and I'll get some of that delicious ice cream from Moon's store and we'll have us a party! Maybe Captain Mortimer will be here by then and we can all have a good time listening to his sea stories."

I could tell that she was more excited about the idea than my brother. However, once she had mentioned the pound cake, she had his attention completely. He loved pound cake and ice cream. I liked pound cake okay, but my favorite was Boston Cream Pie. I always thought that it was funny to name a cake Boston Cream Pie. Never made any sense to me. But I still liked the way it tasted even if the name had little resemblance to fact.

That night as we were saying goodnight to our parents, Mama told us that she had a surprise for us, but that we would have to wait until morning to find out what it was.

"Is this because we were good and visited with Aunt Nona?" Scottie asked.

"No, it is not, young man. Do you think you ought to be rewarded when you do a good deed?"

"I guess not," Scottie replied. "But if not then, when do you get rewarded?"

"Don't get smart with me, Scott Evans. I'll take a belt to you and—"

"Mama, he's tired. Aunt Nona talked for nearly two hours. He didn't mean anything by it," I said, holding off her threat.

I figured the least I could do was to bail him out once more. He still hadn't caught on exactly how it was that one could talk with our mother, and not put a foot in one's mouth. Most of the time, Scottie was simply changing feet whenever he opened his mouth with Mama. I hoped Aunt Nona would never find out that I had stretched the truth about her talking that evening. The truth was that Scottie and I loved every minute of our time with her because it was an honest-to-good-ness give and take conversation—she could hear us and we actually understood most of what she was telling us. It had been a fun evening and went by rather quickly. At least now we had another diversion in the summer. It would help pass the time in a fun sort of way. I was also curious about Aunt Nona's Captain Mortimer.

I thought it strange that Mama didn't threaten to take away whatever surprise she had in store for us come tomorrow. That made me suspicious. She usually threatened that whenever something was planned for us and then we behaved in some disapproving way. She passed up an opportunity and I figured that our surprise must have been something that was coming whether we controlled our tongues our not. It appeared that our mother had no control over this particular surprise.

I just hoped that it was going to be a good one.

Samuel Walters Clancy was the surprise that Mama could not control. He was her older brother who lived in Boston and did as he pleased. He was unmarried with no children, but considered Scottie and me his own. At least that was the way he treated us. It felt good to be spoiled rotten by a doting uncle who had the means to do whatever he wanted and whenever he took a notion.

Uncle Walters was a photographer by profession and a philanthropist by desire. I was never sure how he made money from simply taking pictures. I know that he inherited some money from his mother and father, just like my mother did. She put hers in the bank. Said it was for a rainy day. Uncle Walters put his in the stock market and must have done very well there. Daddy once said that Walters Clancy did not have to work for a living unless he wanted to work. I took that to mean that he had a lot of money.

But for all his money, he was a likable fellow. He never allowed his wealth to interfere with his being a genuine human being. The world was a better place because of him.

I was the first one down the morning he arrived. There he was, sitting at the breakfast table just like he belonged there. His presence created a positive mood for the whole house, even for my mother. That was one of the reasons it was so nice to have him around. Mama was a nicer person when he was with us. It used to concern me that she could be so nice with Walters around, and yet so contrary when he wasn't, but I finally got used to it and haven't wasted much time pondering that in recent years. His visits were therapeutic.

"Good morning, my little chickadee," he said when I entered the kitchen.

I ran and hugged him without saying a word. It was simply great to have him so close.

"I was in the neighborhood and thought I'd drop by. Is that okay with you?" he said.

"Okay? I reckon! How long can you stay?"

"Clancy, that's rude to ask someone how long they're going to stay."

"But I didn't ask him how long he was going to stay. I asked how long he *could* stay. Big difference, Mama."

Normally she would have given me one of her classic Boris Karloff stares, and then spoken harshly to me about smarting off to her. But with Uncle Walters in the house, she let it slide. She probably was curious as to how long he *could* stay as well.

"She's right, Rachel. And Clancy, I wish I *could* stay a month with you. But, alas, I cannot. I am here only for a night or two, and then I'm bound for Boston. I have some items to attend to, a few appointments to keep, and some photographs to take."

The way Uncle Walters said it made it sound more like an adventure instead of work. Daddy told me once that Walters Clancy worked at his own pace and no one ever pushed him into any kind of tight situation unless he permitted it. He said that his brother-in-law was the freest person he knew.

"Can you go fishing with us?"

"Clancy, I don't think my brother wants to spend his time fishing when he is only going to be here for two days."

"Well, let me think about that invitation, my dear. It sounds absolutely appealing, but my sister may be right in that time is an enemy and I have to watch it closely this visit. But, we'll see. I cannot, for the life of me, categorically refuse such an invitation from such a wonderful young lady. I might work in an hour or two. That would be okay, wouldn't it?" he spoke with his usual flair.

I honestly think my uncle could have talked his way out of jail if he had to. He could have been a politician except that he wasn't much into politics. At least I never heard him mention much about that. He talked about people and beautiful scenery. He never talked about the government or war or any other stressful subject. He never talked money either.

"Where's Scottie?"

"Still asleep, I think," I said.

"Why don't you go wake him, Clancy? I think he'll want to see Uncle Walters," Mama suggested.

By the time I returned with Scottie, Daddy and Walters were in some kind of discussion in the living room. Mama suggested that we leave them alone for the time being. She said it was man-talk, whatever that meant.

She fixed a great breakfast that morning—you name something, we had it. We all sat around laughing and talking and eating, and the morning passed by like a refreshing breeze. It always felt that way whenever our uncle was around.

After Daddy had gone to work close to 10:30, and Mama was busy cleaning the kitchen, Scottie and I had Uncle Walters all to ourselves. We sat in the front porch swing and told him about our investigation and whatever we could think of that he might find interesting. No matter what we talked about, he mirrored our excitement.

Sometime before lunch, we happened to mention the butterfly herd and with little effort he convinced us to take him to the place where the butterflies swarmed over the flowers and created their magic. Mama would have normally objected to a trip so close to lunch, but since it was Uncle Walters' idea, how could she say no? We were really enjoying this. Life was so much easier and so much more fun with Samuel Walters Clancy around.

# Chapter Twenty-one

"Why do you have so many cameras, Uncle Walters?" Scottie asked. I considered asking that very question.

"Well, one's a 35 millimeter with color film, the other's a twin-lens reflex for close-ups and portraits, and the third one is a 35 millimeter with black and white film. I like to take a variety of photos, utilizing multiple cameras, Scottie. Sometimes a picture is enhanced quite a lot by using black and white film instead of color. Other times, well, color is obviously more popular, and most people like it, so I try to capture the colors of whatever form I photograph. And then, there are the negatives created by the film I use as well as the camera type. The answer, I think, Mr. Scottie, is that I like options. That means I have to have more than one camera in order to fulfill my desires."

He laughed and walked on at a brisk pace. He covered more ground than we could. I noticed that I had to take nearly three steps to his one. Scottie was trotting to keep up. Uncle Walters was taller than our father, somewhere over six feet, I would guess. Daddy was somewhere under Uncle Walters' height. Walters was tall and lean. Our daddy was nearly tall and muscular.

"Where is it you two thieves are taking me?" he asked.

I cringed a little at his endearing title. I was wondering if Daddy had told him about some of our most recent exploits.

"It's magical!" Scottie said.

"How so?"

"You'll see," I teased.

It was hotter than usual but the temperature didn't seem to bother me. I was walking along my favorite road with my favorite uncle with my heart and head full of great anticipation. We were going to see the butterflies.

"Now, you might want to get your cameras ready. We're just about to the spot," I said to him as soon as we passed through the high grass behind Mr. Joe's barn. "We need to move a little slower now, so as not to disturb Mother Nature too much."

He paused and readied his cameras for our surprise. He was always a good sport and a willing subject in our adventures. But I don't think even my dear uncle was prepared for what he saw when we led him into the flower garden hidden by the bushes and trees on the backside of the farm.

For some reason it was an even more beautiful scene that day than any other time I had visited. Maybe it was because I hadn't been there in a few days and had somehow forgotten the gorgeous array of colors that the butterflies mixed with the wildflowers offered to any person with half a vision. The sunlight coming in almost directly overhead flooded the area with all the light imaginable, and it was breathtaking.

"Wow!" Scottie said.

Uncle Walters and I were speechless for a few moments. I waited to see if he was going to start photographing. He just stood there with his mouth open and his cameras hanging around his neck. I nudged him gently in the ribs and pointed to the cameras.

"Wow, indeed, my young nephew," he said.

He grabbed his cameras one at a time and began shooting. It was nonstop for him for at least fifteen or twenty minutes. Scottie and I stood out of the way initially until he motioned for us to walk out into the flowers amid the few thousand butterflies. We laughed and seemed to float along with the staggering beauty around us, but no one said a word. It was perhaps the most tranquil moment of my young life. It was as close to ecstasy as I had ever been, without knowing much about ecstasy.

I think time stood still that day, at least for an hour or so. It was as though we three creatures were at one with nature and all of her unspeakable beauty. Our laughter, mixed with the sunshine, flowers and butterflies, carried us further into some trance-like state. Speaking was not necessary. It was simply too wonderful for words.

When Uncle Walters had finally stopped clicking his cameras and we all had moved in and through the multi-colored festival of lights, my common sense returned and I motioned to Scottie and Uncle Walters to follow me. I wanted to show him Bessie Mae's secret swamp.

Within moments we were standing on this side of Bessie Mae's mud pile. She was all the way across the quagmire, chewing her cud and minding her own business. Our intrusion did nothing to upset her. She turned her head slightly in our direction as if to acknowledge our presence and continued chewing, making no sound save the familiar chomping. She remained all but oblivious to our visit. This seemed to be normal behavior for Mr. Joe's cow.

"What is this?" Uncle Walters said.

"Wish I could tell you."

"She seems to enjoy being in it, huh?" Uncle Walters said.

"I think it cools her toes," Scottie laughed.

"It looks a bit unusual," our uncle said. "It's more than mud, I think. Do you know what it is?"

"No sir. Mr. Joe's not sure what it is exactly. He occasionally puts it on the grass around his farm house to make it stay green while the rest of the Clancyville grass turns an ugly brown and dies."

"How did he know it would work on his grass?" Uncle Walters said.

"I don't know," I said. "I never thought about that. Maybe it was an accident. It contains manure; in fact, it smells horrible. Test it yourself."

Uncle Walters leaned down closer and smelled it from a safe distance without touching it.

"Yes, ma'am. It does smell horrible. Smells a little like manure, but there's more to it than that."

"It stays on your clothes, too," Scottie added. "Mama is still fussing at us for dirtying our clothes in it last week. No matter what she does, they won't come clean."

"Were you out here playing in this?"

"Not exactly. We were looking for stuff. We found the clothes of those two boys who were killed. They were scattered in here everywhere."

"Oh," Uncle Walters said. "This is the spot. Dirty business, huh?"

"In more ways than one," I said.

"You did wash down quickly after you were in this stuff, right?"

"Yes, sir. Is it dangerous?" I asked.

"Probably not. Its location here in the open air and the fact that only one cow contributes to its fertilizing qualities make it relatively safe. Still, manure that is breaking down gives off some gases that could be dangerous. You wouldn't want to spend a long time in this quagmire."

"Quagmire?" Scottie said. "I've heard that word. What's it mean?"

"Slushy mud," Uncle Walters translated.

"How come you know so much about manure?" Scottie asked him.

"I know a little about a lot of things, Scott. It pays to read and keep your eyes open, even if all you do is take pictures. In fact, I think that's precisely what photographers are supposed to do—keep their eyes open. And detectives as well," he said, looking at me out of the corner of his eye. "You still working on those murders, unofficially, of course?"

"Yessir. Against my daddy's druthers. Daddy thinks that a lot of evidence points to Mr. Joe as the one, but Scottie and I believe him to be innocent. Daddy says he has to follow the evidence. We're following our hearts, I suppose. Big difference."

"Yes 'im, big difference. Keep up the good work. Details. Look at the details. The same as in photography. Never take your eyes off your subject. Sometimes you can stare for hours at the same scene, the same photo, the same whatever, and then presto! You see something brand new, something you missed. Amazing, huh?"

"Sounds like it. You do that?"

"With my pictures as well as with life. I am always looking for the unseen. Same as you detectives, right? I believe that every crime is solvable. Every criminal makes a mistake. Sometimes criminals don't even know they've made a mistake. You have to be smart enough to catch the mistake. Simple as that. The secret is to keep looking. The answers are there. You have to find them. And, never forget that there is always more than one right answer."

He moved slightly to the right and found just the angle he wanted for a photo of Bessie Mae in her slush. I was wondering if the smell of the area would be captured in his photograph. I certainly hoped not.

It was well after four o'clock when we returned to the house. Mama was a little concerned, but hid her true anxiety from her brother. Scottie and I read her like a book. We had phoned Mama from downtown to tell her that Uncle Walters was treating us to lunch, and not to worry about us.

"I was just about ready to call the sheriff on you. Where have you allowed these children to take you?"

"Nowhere I didn't willingly go, sister dear. We had the most delightful time out at Mr. Joe's place, then we dropped some hooks into the water for a spell, then I treated my favorite niece and nephew to a hamburger lunch at Spoonie's Grill downtown."

"Oh, I see. And what on earth did they show you at that farm out there?"

"Rachel love, you should take time out from your life to enjoy living. There's a world of goodness and wonder out there, just for the looking. You should try it sometime. You might become engaged."

"Engaged? What on earth are you babbling about? I've more work than twenty black folks right here in my own home, and you think I should go playing with you and the children down by the river?"

It was the first time I ever recall hearing my mother raise her voice to her older brother. She simply never did it before now. We were all stunned, except for her brother. He simply smiled and then sighed.

"Of course I do, Rachel Jo. I expect you to live, to enjoy life. To stop being so serious all the time. You're missing a great deal of goodness."

"Somebody has to be serious around this family! If I left it up to you all," she turned her back and entered the house still fussing at us, "nothing important would ever get done around this place. Clancy, go get cleaned up and come help me with supper. Your daddy will be home in about an hour. Scottie, you show your uncle where he can clean up. You all look like street urchins. Walters, you have mud all over your shoes. I expect the children to come home looking like tramps, but not you."

She was out of sight by this point but still jabbering on about our looks, her life and her work load around the house. Uncle Walters stifled a laugh with a hand over his mouth. I got tickled at him for laughing at Mama, so I quickly covered my mouth as well to prevent a sound escaping and landing near my mother's hearing. Scottie giggled aloud at both of us without using any restraints.

"What was that? Did you say something young man?" Mama directed her thrust at Scottie from behind the screen door on the back porch.

"No, ma'am. Just clearing my throat. I'll show Uncle Walters where he can get the mud off his shoes."

Scottie led Uncle Walters to the side of the garage where we kept a garden hose attached to a spigot for washing the river off after fishing. I don't think that's exactly what Mama had in mind for her brother, but it didn't bother our uncle a bit. I went on inside and hurried through my washing so I could help Mama prepare supper. She didn't let me do that often enough to suit me, so when she offered I usually jumped at the chance.

Supper was ready by the time Daddy drove in the driveway, a few minutes after five. Mama had his schedule, except for emergencies, down pretty well after fifteen years of marriage. She never did like the emergencies which often caused delays. The rule was that we had to wait an hour if he didn't come home at five o'clock. We couldn't eat, we'd just sit and wait, hunger mounting, patience thinning. Then after an hour, she'd fuss for a few minutes, and then we'd sit down and eat supper. Clancyville was usually a quiet place so we didn't have too many emergencies until that summer of 1973. There seemed to be an epidemic of emergencies that summer.

Mama outdid herself for our evening meal. We had a regular Sunday fare that night with fried chicken, green beans, corn on the cob, boiled potatoes, fresh butter beans, some kind of fancy congealed salad, and fresh homemade biscuits. She also forced us to indulge in eating a newly baked apple pie after we had finished behaving like gluttons from the main fare. We sat around for at least two hours enjoying the great food and the stimulating conversation. Scottie and I mainly listened to Uncle Walters talk about the many projects he had ongoing in Boston as well as a few other cities.

After the dishes were cleared and cleaned, everyone retired to the den or the television room, as we called it, to continue the lively conversation. I decided that this would be an excellent opportunity to check on some things about Mr. Joe's case without being bothered or missed. Our uncle could easily keep the family occupied for hours with his stories, and Scottie's presence would keep them from asking about the children. I wanted to hear what my uncle said, of course, but I also had to steal every opportunity to get away from my parents in order to investigate. I didn't tell Scottie where I was going in case my absence from the house was discovered. That way he would be out of harm's way—if they believed him.

"I'm going upstairs for a few minutes," I told my daddy.

That was true. I did go upstairs for a few minutes. But that was about it. I left through my bedroom window, climbed down the lattice work beside the front porch, and set off into the early darkness of the evening.

# CHAPTER TWENTY-TWO

I hated to break a promise to my daddy so soon after making it, but I didn't think I had much choice. A man's life was at stake. Deep down I really believed that Mr. Joe was innocent despite his past. That made my decision easier. I loved my daddy, but it was wrong for a good man to be convicted of a crime he didn't do.

It was something that Uncle Walters had said that had me thinking about all that evidence I had found. Daddy said it wasn't useful because it was discovered illegally. But maybe it still had some value to it. Uncle Walters mentioned details, paying close attention to the details.

There were two things I needed to concentrate on that evening. One was that high school annual, but it was at the library and the library was closed until tomorrow morning. The other was that closet of Ralph Hines filled with all those dirty pictures that he collected. That was open as far as I was concerned.

Since Daddy was home, I headed straight for Hines' place. With only two law enforcement officers in town, it was easy to decide who was working and who was not. I use the term *working* loosely, since I was absolutely certain that Hines was not home and that he was downtown sitting at his desk not working. The not-home part of that certainty was vital for me.

It was dark in Hines' house when I crawled through the bushes at the back. There was a blue light on in one of the windows so I crept up to the house to check out that room in case someone was inside the house. Nothing was moving. I figured it to be a night light of some variety. It had not been there on my prior visits.

I had remembered the need of a flashlight once more, and this time I managed to procure my father's larger variety.

The back door was not only unlocked, but the door itself was not fully shut. That should have made me suspicious, but I figured that Hines was just consistently stupid. I went straight for the closet full of pornography and let my flashlight slowly move from shelf to shelf searching for something I might have missed. I had no idea what it was I was looking for, but I knew that I was looking for details this time. Uncle Walters told me that details were important. I believed that if I stood there long enough I would discover a clue that would answer some of my questions. I had nothing that linked Ralph Hines directly to those boys except that one photograph. Well, it was that one clear, obvious photograph of Hines compared to that other photograph of Buster and, more than likely, Hines as well. Those two pictures were important, but not enough.

That's what I was doing when I realized a shadow was over me from my backside, and I felt a strong hand cover my mouth. Whoever it was removed their hand long enough to force what turned out to be a handkerchief into my mouth to keep me from screaming. My surprise mingled with fear kept me from reacting fast enough so as to scream or protest loudly. I was held tightly against someone's body with one hand so I couldn't turn around and see them. They used their other hand to tape my mouth with that handkerchief inside. I gagged until I was able to cope with my restriction.

I fought as hard as I could, but the strength of my adversary was significant. In the struggle, I dropped my daddy's flashlight.

With my mouth taped, I was forced to breathe through my nose. Then suddenly some type of hood was thrust over my head, and immediately it was truly dark. Since screaming was futile in my present situation, I decided to conserve my energy considering that I might need that energy later in order to escape. The person who immobilized me didn't say a word. He or she just worked quickly and efficiently at what they had to do to restrain my movements. My guess was that it had been a man, taller, and a little stronger. I was the weaker one in that skirmish.

My hands were tied behind my back, and my entire torso was wrapped in some kind of cord so that I couldn't wiggle much or walk at all. They picked me up and carried me out of the house. I could feel the night air against my legs and arms.

Whoever it was that was carrying me walked on gravel for a few steps, then I detected the sound of a car trunk being opened, squeaking loudly in the nighttime air. I was thrown inside. The squeaks returned as the lid was shut. Whoever it was that had bound me was strong enough to carry me without help. I estimated that we rode for about ten minutes. When the car was moving it created a horrible burning smell, like an old car that someone hadn't cared for properly. Even after the car stopped, that smell hung around for a few minutes.

The squeaky trunk was opened, I was removed and dumped onto the ground, and then I was lifted and carried once again. I didn't hear any gravel underfoot this time. There was a distinct sound of grass rustling and then yet another squeaky door was either opened or closed. It wasn't the same sound that the car trunk had made.

Some familiar smells came through to me and then I heard another door open or close just before I was tossed unkindly onto some hay or straw. It was prickly and hard in some places, much harder than I would have preferred. Then someone spoke to me in a muffled voice. I could only assume it was the person who had bound and brought me to this place, since I heard no other voices since arriving.

"Stay out of this. If you continue to snoop around, you could end up like Buster and Micah. This is your only warning," the muffled voice said. The person must have been speaking through some type of device, either a box or some cloth. There was no way of knowing whether it was male or female. The voice tried to sound dramatic.

The door shut and I heard what I thought was a padlock closing.

I was at least relieved at this point to know that whoever had taken me didn't intend to harm me, at least that was my guess. I was safe for the time being. My thinking was that I was located outside of town, but not too far away. It would be later in the evening before anyone would begin searching for me. At the moment, my family probably still thought I was upstairs in my room.

As soon as my heart stopped beating so rapidly, I relaxed a little and fell asleep. I had no idea how long I slept.

When I awoke, I lay there considering what had happened. Uncle Walters' suggestion about details had come none too soon for me. I went through my entire ordeal, from the hand over my mouth, to the point where I was thrown onto the hay, my present condition. I relived every thing I could recall.

The hands that had bound me were strong and quick. They didn't feel rough, however. I tried to recall what it felt like to be held up against another human being and tied up at the same time. I was struggling so much then that I couldn't remember what it felt like. Then I remembered the smell. There was a strange odor that had accompanied my capture. It had been some kind of sweet odor, but not the kind of sweetness that was appealing to me. It had been one of those nauseatingly sweet fragrances that some people wear after shaving or when dabbing on perfume. That smell was striking. I believed that I could remember it well enough to identify it if I encountered it again. It was that bad.

I was grateful that the hay was soft. I finally decided that I was in a barn or out-building. I had to be near Clancyville because of the brief time it took to arrive here once I was placed inside the trunk. I could hear birds outside, so there was a likelihood of trees around, maybe some bushes as well. Except for the hood over my head and my body being bound by that small cord, I wasn't too warm, even when I figured that the daylight had finally come around. I reasoned that darkness, as well as daylight, has a feel to it.

I was hungry. That was another detail that informed me of a large block of time having passed. I wasn't too concerned about food at the moment. I was more concerned about my parents. I knew that they would be worried sick. But I relaxed a little in that regard when I remembered that Uncle Walters was there and he would definitely have a calming effect on my mother. Daddy would stay calm regardless. Scottie would figure that I could get myself out of my new mess.

I'm not sure when it was that I finally decided that wherever I was, it felt familiar. I suppose that it was what they call a sixth sense that gave me that impression. Maybe it was just intuition. I don't really know which. The smell, maybe the birds outside, or the hay and the short drive from town—all of that probably filtered through my senses and gave me the strong impression that I was locked in a familiar place. I had no rational reason to believe such, but it was a strong inkling.

That revived my hopes rapidly.

It had to be hours later that I heard some kind of animal walking around outside of where I was. The steps were heavy, giving me the rather clear idea that it had to be a large animal. I narrowed it down to a cow because of the slow step movement as well as the cud-chewing sounds I could discern. It was not a herd of cows. It was a singular beast outside and close to my position.

I couldn't talk to the cow, so I just lay there, listening to the slow, methodical heavy movements, and the rhythmic chewing.

I dozed off again because I remember waking up. I was not tired, but I was very hungry by this point. I had slept, but I had not eaten. It felt like I was well into my first full day of captivity. With the hood over my head I had no way of telling how much time passed except for my stomach. The emptiness was gnawing at me.

I was bored and angry as well as hungry. At some point I decided to see if I could get the rope loose from my body and my hands. Mentally, I journeyed back to my capture and relived that so I could recall whether they had tied me top to bottom or vice versa. They had secured my hands first and then bound my whole body. They had finished near the back of my knees. I deduced top to bottom.

I rolled around on the hay hoping to discover something in my predicament that might help me get free. It was hard on my hands to do that, but I had a better chance of escape if I could free myself. When I bumped into one of the walls, I felt a sharp object much like a nail. With a great deal of effort and newly acquired joy, I maneuvered my legs so that they would hook the cord around the object and allow it to pull the binding when I moved away from the wall. It seemed like forever that I did this. Finally, one hard pull brought release. More joy.

I wiggled my entire body, rolling over and over in the hay until my legs were free from bondage. I then stood up and did some kind of hula hoop dance trying to make the rope continue its circular motion away from my chest and upper torso. I probably would have been embarrassed to watch myself do this unraveling dance. Minutes later I could tell that the cord or rope was hanging down from my hands behind me. My hands were still secured tightly, but the rest of my body was free now. The feeling of accomplishment is significant when one finds herself in captivity.

I then leaned against the board-wall behind me and slowly slid my bound-hands lower and lower until I was able to pass them under my butt. I then bent over forward, assuming a kind of crouching position as I lifted my legs, one at a time, and then put each of them through my bound-hands. This little procedure allowed me to now have my hands in front of me so that I could free myself completely from my body restrictions.

Quickly I removed the hood, the tape over my mouth, and the handkerchief. Unless you have spent many hours with a wadded up piece of cloth in your mouth, you have no idea the supreme feeling of relief that comes when it is excavated. It felt so much better to be able to open my mouth, take a deep breath, and scream if I wanted to. It was a lot cooler too.

My prison cell was probably a barn, or at least a very large shed used as an out building. I couldn't tell at the moment. My impression was that this place was familiar. Again, my intuition was aiding me. With my limited experience with barns recently, I had a hunch I had been placed in Mr. Joe's barn, but I had little way to verify my guessing on that location. The strong impression was that I had been in this place prior to this moment.

Now that I could see, I easily found the nail on the wall and sat down next to it. I picked and gouged myself several times in my attempt to free my hands. They were sore and showed some minor bleeding by now. At some point during this painful ritual, the rope stretched and I was able to slide one hand through. Pain and joy mixed together with that achievement.

It was still light outside when I had finally freed myself. The self-inflicted scratches and gashes hurt like the dickens, but I was no longer tied. It was a grand moment for me. The person who had done this to me had not harmed me. I was frightened, of course, but there were no marks on me from my abductor.

I sat down after removing the ropes. I had expended much energy. That, plus the lack of food, made me shaky. It felt good to sit and lean against the wall of the barn. I was free but I was still a prisoner. As I was beginning to wallow a bit in self-pity for my plight, Mother Nature sent me a nearly silent word of encouragement. A small, delightful orange and black monarch fluttered into my cell and danced around the room in the late afternoon sunlight which penetrated my plight with tiny shafts of light. The butterfly had somehow crawled through a tiny gap in the planks of wood and flickered before my eyes. It was the most beautiful word-picture I had seen or heard in quite some time.

I knew where I was. At least I must say that now my hunch was almost completely verified, at least to my own satisfaction.

I found a few cracks between the boards of the barn and peered through them until I could finally see Mr. Joe's house in the distance. Now with my newly found encouragement and renewed hope, I tried the more obvious escape route. The door to my hay-filled prison cell would not budge. I shook it vigorously for several minutes; however, my strength was not up to its usual level, so I simply sat down where I was to regain energy. I was exhausted.

The locked door of my hay-filled chamber came as no great surprise to me. I couldn't imagine that my captor would have been dumb enough to leave the door open, unless of course my captor had been Ralph Hines who left his own backdoor unlocked. The amount of time I had been imprisoned was of concern to me because I knew that my family would be worried sick. They would also be angry.

When actual darkness finally surrounded me my encouragement from the afternoon was shaken a little. The butterfly had long since left me alone in my cell, the sun was gone, and I could no longer see Mr. Joe's house. I had no way of knowing how much time had passed. I was still hungry and worried. That's all that mattered at the moment.

The car lights coming down the road raised my spirits considerably. As soon as I heard the car door open and then shut, I began screaming at the top of my lungs. I was weak, but strong enough to make plenty of racket. The car lights permitted me to see my daddy running towards the barn with a flashlight. Uncle Walters was with him, as was Ralph Hines.

When they finally freed me from my barn cell, I hugged Daddy and Uncle Walters. I looked in the direction of Ralph Hines who made no comment. He stared at me with contempt.

"Is this the extent of the rescue party looking for me?"

Uncle Walters laughed. Hines frowned and kept his mouth shut. Daddy wanted to know the whole story of how I got to this place. I did the best I could with details since time was not clear to me. I omitted some of the more damaging details since Hines was present. I didn't out and out lie to the sheriff, but I didn't exactly come clean with him either.

"How did you find me?" I asked, hoping to shift the conversation in another direction.

"We received two anonymous phone tips. The first one said you were last seen headed towards Dan River. We searched that end of the county most of the day. Then Hines was at the office while I grabbed a bite to eat, and he reported the second anonymous phone tip that said you were out here at Mr. Joe's place."

I had been a prisoner in Mr. Joe's barn for about twenty-four hours. I was really happy it hadn't been any longer than that. It was good to be found again. Hunger had been my biggest issue with the captivity.

As far as Clancyville was concerned, I hadn't missed much excitement on my day away.

# Chapter Twenty-three

I waited until we were home and Hines had left before I filled in the gaps about my kidnapping. Mama had gone upstairs to help Scottie get ready for bed. Daddy and I were alone in the kitchen. He looked tired, almost as tired as I felt.

"I bent the truth a little earlier, Daddy."

"You mean you lied?"

"Not exactly, I just let you think I was walking down one of the streets in town when I was captured."

"So, where were you?"

"Standing in Ralph Hines' closet."

"I see."

He showed little emotion. He was too calm to suit me, but then I didn't want the full force of the law of my father to come down on me at the moment. Or even later.

"And what were you doing in Hines' closet?"

"Looking for details."

"Find any?"

"Not in the closet."

"Then where?"

"The person who kidnapped me wore some sick smelling after shave stuff. They were physically strong, at least stronger than their victim, and they smelled nauseatingly sweet."

"After shave, you say?"

"It could have been perfume. Hard to tell. Just a sickening, sweet smell."

"Any other details?"

"One. The car smelled like oil. You know when a car burns oil and smells horrific. That's what it was like. It was as bad as the perfume, just in the other direction, you know, opposite of sweet. I was glad I had that hood on to help filter the odors. But that was the only time I was glad for that hood."

"You broke your word to me, you know," he said.

"Yessir. I am sorry about that. But Mr. Joe's life is at stake as you know. I had to go back and look for something I might have missed the first time. You would have said no if I had asked."

"You're right about that."

He was still in absolute control of whatever I figured were his genuine feelings about me at that moment. A part of me keep waiting for him to explode.

"What's next?" I asked.

"Your mother is going to need some cooling off time. I will not let her know where you were when apprehended. We'll just let the misleading version stand for now."

"Don't you think it is significant that I was at Hines' house when I was kidnapped, and that I was told by whoever grabbed me, that I needed to stop snooping around?"

"Yes, ma'am. And I also think it is significant that Deputy Hines was the one who reported that second phone tip as to your exact location," he added as he got up from his chair.

I was surprised, maybe even a little shocked, that my daddy had chosen to grant me one of his insights into this ordeal. He had already told me about Hines being the one who received the anonymous phone message. Even though I had lied to my father and had disobeyed a clear directive from the man I loved more than anything, here he was discussing the case with me. I was feeling lousy and rather stupid from my escapade. He was no doubt trying to help me to feel better.

He said nothing else as he left the room. I knew what he was thinking. I was good at reading my daddy some of the time.

When Scottie wandered into my room just before bedtime to check on me, I asked him what he had been doing while I was a captive in Mr. Joe's barn.

"I have that 'two-nition' stuff. Same as you."

"What on earth are you talking about?"

"Ah, Clancy, you know. When you can read minds or get a strong feeling about something."

"Oh, you mean intuition. Like Sherlock Holmes has. The word is in-tuition. You left off a tiny syllable."

"Oh. What's a syllable?"

"Never mind that. Sherlock Holmes is the only male I know of who has ever had that."

"That 'two-nition'?"

"Yeah, that," I said, without bothering to correct him this time.

"That makes me the second one," he said and walked out of the room.

"Wait a minute!" I called out to him.

He was already in the hallway. He poked his head back into my room.

"What?" he asked.

"What was your intuition regarding?"

"Regarding?" he seemed puzzled with my question.

"You said you had some intuition while I was away. What were you thinking?"

"Oh, that. I just thought that maybe you were at Mr. Joe's place."

"Did you tell anybody what you thought?" I asked.

"Of course not. I'm a little kid … who's gonna believe me?"

One good thing about my captivity was that it forced Uncle Walters to delay his leaving. We were all glad about that, including my mother. However, she wasn't too happy about my adventure; in fact, she managed to inform me quite succinctly that she worried herself sick while I was missing. She asked a lot of questions. I avoided answering most by telling her that I had told Daddy everything. She wanted to vent more than she wanted to know where it was I was going at that time of night when I had been taken. Besides that, we had company at home, she had said succinctly to me. Mama was like that most of the time. I let her vent without giving away too much valuable information. I was also endeavoring to keep my scalp.

Uncle Walters stayed for the weekend and went to church with us on Saturday and Sunday. It wasn't that we were so religious or anything. The double funeral for Buster and Micah Scruggs was held on Saturday afternoon at our church. They were not members, but I heard that our pastor was kind enough to offer our large sanctuary because most of the town wanted to come. I think that kind of thing happens whenever little kids die or are killed. We were the largest church in Clancyville, so I imagine that our preacher would have been asked if he had not volunteered our building.

Most of the town did come, as a matter of fact. Mama said it was the largest funeral she had ever attended. I think it made her a little upset that it was larger even than her father's funeral, the town notable. Mama kept mental records of stuff like that and it was vital to her well being that not too many folks from other families got the best of her and her family. I thought it was nice that so many people wanted to pay their respects to the Scruggs' family, since the Scruggs' were not as well thought of by the general public. I think everyone felt sorry for the parents of those two boys, even for Mr. Scruggs who was often referred to as "low-life white trash." I heard some folks call him that once and even though I didn't understand it, I didn't much care for the description. Seemed unkind.

The pulpit was shared by two preachers that day. I thought that funeral service would never end. My pastor went first and said some flowery, untrue things about Buster and Micah. He didn't know them like I did, so I couldn't blame him too much. Still, he could have done his homework and found some more truthful things to say about them.

Then their preacher got up and railed at the town for not taking care of its children. He seemed to think that all of us were at fault in the death of these two precious commodities—his words, not mine. I doubted the truth of either their preciousness or their capacity as commodities. They were simply two wild boys who had a horrible ending to a very difficult life. They should have asked me to say a few words. I wouldn't have called them commodities or precious. Still, I felt bad that they had been killed.

Sunday's worship was a whole lot better than Saturday's funeral. I almost cried once at the funeral. They made all of us sing *Amazing Grace* and that song about did me in. The only thing that saved me was that I stopped singing after the second verse.

The best part of Sunday's church service for me was having my uncle there. It was great to be able to sit with him. Sometimes it's nice to have family come to church with you so you can show them off to the people. It's especially nice when they're a rich, eccentric uncle from Boston. When the preacher recognized Uncle Walters from the pulpit at the beginning, he asked him to stand. Scottie and I stood with him. We were that proud. I wanted everyone to know that this man was my kin. I think it embarrassed Mama because she pulled on the back of my dress in an effort to make me sit down. But it was too late. I was standing as close to royalty as I believed I would ever be.

Daddy thought it was funny and appropriate. He said so on the way home.

Mama didn't fuss about Miss Greesome waving her arms at the congregation as we drove the short distance home. I guess she was trying to put on her best behavior for Uncle Walters.

"Enjoyed the worship this morning, if that's an appropriate thing to say," Uncle Walters said.

"It was a good service," Daddy agreed.

"I liked the part where he welcomed Clancy back to the community," Scottie added.

"I thought that was totally uncalled for," Mama said.

"Well, it was done in a light-hearted manner, but I know Reverend Flowers meant every word of it. He was truly worried about you, Clancy," Daddy said.

"I was worried about me, too."

"You had us all worried," Mama said.

"So, why was the preacher so worried about me?" I asked my daddy by poking him in the back shoulder as he drove along slowly.

"Hard to say, Clancy," he answered. "Reckon it's something that preachers are supposed to do."

"You two," Mama said. "It has nothing to do with what's expected. He's a kind man, and I'll have you two know that he was organizing a prayer vigil to focus on your safe return when you were found."

"What's a prayer vigil?" I asked. Scottie leaned over and whispered that he had thought of that question as well.

"It's when all the church members or the community, I suppose, are asked to come pray over a period of time and offer their prayers for someone or something," Mama explained. "People are given specific times to be at the church, say, and … well, it's like a prayer-chain."

"Was this church-wide or town-wide?" I asked.

"I don't know," she said. "What difference does it make?"

"I just wondered if people from the whole town would come out and pray for me."

"Were you scared the whole time?" Scottie asked.

"No, I think more at first that at the last. After that butterfly found me and I knew where I was, I was okay. It was like playing hide and seek, except for the hunger."

"Speaking of hunger, why don't we go out to eat lunch today? We'll give Rachel a break from kitchen duties for a change," Uncle Walters said. "It'll be my treat."

"Walters, you've done enough for us these past few days. You're our guest as long as you are staying in our home."

"Thank you, sister, but I insist. Let me take you to some place you all enjoy eating. Please let me do this."

Reluctantly Mama and Daddy allowed him to take us to Rudy's Restaurant over in Dan River. It was a short drive and nice to get away from Clancyville for even a few hours. The food was pretty good, not nearly as good as Mama's, but edible. Uncle Walters made the meal enjoyable with his stories and questions. The one good thing about going out to eat was that I was able to order something that my mother either never fixed, or that she made infrequently for us. Since Uncle Walters was paying for this meal, I ordered a T-bone steak, a baked potato, and a soft drink. My mother made sure that I also added some green beans to that feast.

Late Sunday afternoon I visited Mr. Joe at the jail and told him about my ordeal in his barn. He had been worried something awful, so I was glad to let him know that I was okay. Not much harm done, all things considered. My wrists were healing nicely and I was safe. He warned me to stop snooping around, that the people who killed those boys were still out there. That was an eye-opening moment that grabbed my attention suddenly. That thought had neglected to register with me until he had said it. I was so focused on helping him that I had forgotten to consider the fact that if he was innocent, then whoever was guilty was roaming our town free and able to strike again.

We said a tearful good-bye to Uncle Walters on Monday morning. I hated to see him go. On the way to the bus station he told me about a new gadget which was going to take the world by storm in the next few years. He called it a personal computer. He said that it was coming along quickly, and that he expected great things from it soon. He thought that it might be something I would be interested in as I continued with my education. He suggested that I keep up with its development and learn all I could about it. He said he would help to keep me up to date on the progress of its development. He also said he wanted me to know how it worked. He told Scottie the same thing, but Scottie wasn't much interested in machines. Fishing was more on his mind than some yet-to-be-fully-developed personal computer that might change our lives. I wondered just how personal a machine could become.

As the bus moved off from our location, Scottie nudged me when our parents were getting into the car to take us all back home.

"Why do you think Uncle Walters rides a bus when he's supposed to be rich and all?"

"What does rich and all have to do with taking the bus back to Boston?" I asked.

"Why doesn't he own a car, or maybe take an airplane? Isn't there an airport in Boston?" Scottie asked.

"First, he doesn't like to drive cars. Second, yes, there is an airport in Boston. Uncle Walters prefers to travel by bus."

"So, my question … Why?"

"Maybe he's eccentric," I said.

"What does that mean?"

"Strange."

"Everybody in this family is strange," he concluded. "I still don't get the idea of a bus."

After we watched the bus disappear from view, I walked to the library to see if I could reexamine that 1956 Freemont High School annual. I was hoping that if I leafed through it long enough, or slow enough, I would discover some valuable detail I had missed earlier. There had to be something in that book which would help me in this investigation. I was determined this time.

Scottie rode back home with Daddy and Mama. I walked to the library with my questions swirling around. I had no answers swirling with them.

One of the twin dragons watched me suspiciously the whole time I was there. On my third time through the book I finally noticed a name I recognized. It was listed at the end of the senior class in a section marked "Not Pictured." I had a lead. A bonafide clue.

I wanted to take the book with me to the jail to show Daddy, but I wasn't about to ask that dragon at the desk if I could. I already knew her answer. I didn't want to turn the book in and then have to go through the same rigmarole again just to retrieve it in a few minutes. I waited until Elba the dragon, or maybe Melba, wasn't looking intently in my direction, and I eased into the stacks to hide my volume. I shelved it between two of Arthur Conan Doyle's collections of Holmes and left the library without the dragon lady seeing me.

Daddy usually stayed in the jail office on Monday mornings, so I was fairly certain that he would be available to come right back with me and see my discovery for himself. I would tell him, of course, but he would want to see it in black and white. It goes to his nature.

"I can't leave the jail unoccupied when I have prisoner, Clancy. You know that," he said in answer to my request.

"Okay, I'll stay and you go to the library."

He smiled.

"You really mean that, don't you?"

"Of course I mean it. You think Mr. Joe's gonna harm me? I'm the only chance he's got! He's my friend. I'm as safe here as I am at home. Maybe safer."

I smiled.

"That's not the point. I can't leave an eleven-year-old in charge of the jail."

"Bad press, huh?"

"Very."

"Well, call Mrs. Nottingham. She can come and guard the violent prisoner."

"Don't get smart, young lady. Rules are rules. The community wouldn't like it much if I was all the time leaving the jail without someone here."

"So, Mrs. Nottingham is a guard?"

"That's enough, Clancy. I have to stay for now. Mrs. Nottingham will be in at lunch. I'll meet you at the library a little after twelve. That's the best I can do."

"Then it will have to do," I said and departed.

I walked home kicking rocks all the way. Rocks were bad for the shoes, but good for the spirit. I had to get rid of my built-up aggression against life and rules. Everything moved too slowly to suit me. Adults especially. That is, all the adults I knew except for Uncle Walters. He had the right pace. Sometimes Daddy had it, but too many times he was restricted by what other people expected of him. I suspect all those rules he talked about also restricted him. I hated that about his job. I didn't think it was fair at all.

We were having leftovers for lunch because of Uncle Walters' visit. It was another good reason I liked it when he came around. I was in need of a break from tomato sandwiches.

"Mama, I'm meeting Daddy a little after twelve at the library. Is it okay if I eat a late lunch, say 12:30 or so?"

"Is this official government business?" It was as close as she had ever come to making a joke. My mama didn't say funny things intentionally, at least not that I ever heard.

"Yes, ma'am. Very official."

"I thought you were off of the case."

"I'm constrained as to what I can do and where I can go."

"Constrained, huh? That sounds like your daddy's word."

"Yes, ma'am. To be sure, that's a Daddy-word."

"Well, I'll believe you are *constrained* when I see it. Okay, 12:30 p.m. sharp. No later or you'll go hungry until supper."

I bolted upstairs and yelled "thank you" over my shoulder as I jumped the steps two by two. Scottie was playing with his soldiers when I entered his room.

"We finally have a name for that ring," I began.

He immediately dropped his fighting men and lost all interest in his toy war at hand.

"Who is it?"

"Betty Ann Greesome's name was listed in the senior class of 1956 at Freemont High School of Greensboro, North Carolina. She wasn't pictured."

"Miss Greesome? Are you sure?"

"Absolutely."

"How come you didn't see her name those other times you looked at that annual?" he asked.

"I have no idea, except that her name was listed on the page following all of the photographs of the people in her class. Her name was listed along with other names of people who did not have their picture in the annual. She was lost in the midst of the names given. I think I focused too much on the pictures and not on those pages that just had names."

"Wow! So what does it mean?"

"What does what mean?"

"Her initials are inside the ring. What does that prove?"

"Well, I would like to know why her ring was found in the barn."

"You mean in the trash can?"

"Hines cleaned up the barn and put it in the trash can along with your vomit."

"You don't know that."

"About Hines? I do, too."

"No, you don't know that Hines cleaned it out of the barn. What if Hines didn't put the ring in the trash can when he was dumping all that junk from the barn? What if the ring was never in the barn, but with Hines the whole time? Or what if someone else put that ring in that trash can, before Hines put the vomit stuff in there?"

"No one else could've placed that ring in the trash can because I found that ring inside the plastic bag buried in your vomit. That vomit was dumped there by Deputy Ralph Hines when he cleaned up that area from inside the barn. Daddy told me that he used a trash bag. So, if someone had dropped that ring in the barrel behind the barn, it would have been under that trash bag, not in it. But, you raise an excellent point about that ring possibly being with Hines and he lost it somehow when he dropped the plastic bag down into the barrel. Maybe."

"See, I got good ideas," Scottie said. "But, it doesn't explain the *L S* initials on that ring if those initials represent Lydell Scruggs. Why would Hines have such a ring?"

I was pleased that my little brother had made some careful considerations. Usually I was not pleased when he had an idea before I did, especially something as important as this. I had only been guessing that the ring had been inside the barn to begin with, near the boys' bodies. It was still a plausible notion that Hines didn't even know that the ring was there in the barn when he gathered up globs of vomit and hay and whatever, and tossed all that gunk into the trash bag, then into barrel. Too many options. Too many possibilities.

"You're right, but I need to think about it for a while. It doesn't make any sense for Hines to throw away that ring. Or the question becomes, if he did throw it away, why there? And it doesn't even have to be Hines, does it? I can't make any sense out of this," I said, exasperated.

"No sense that we can make of it," Scottie added, "but it might make sense to him since he's an idiot." He was proud of himself for his conclusion. That was my little brother. One minute he could offer a helpful insight, the next moment he would say something utterly ridiculous.

"Oh, go back to your play war. I've got things to do and so much to consider."

# Chapter Twenty-four

Daddy was sitting in his official sheriff's car outside of the library when I sauntered up. I led him inside and told him to follow me into the stacks to where I had stashed the book for us to view without the dragon ladies observing. I didn't refer to the twins as the dragon ladies when I said it.

"It's gone. The book's not here. It's not where I hid it."

"You're sure?" he said.

I just looked at him without answering, and then promenaded myself to the main desk with some attitude. I believed that one of the dragon ladies had taken it. More than believed it, I was mostly certain of it. They had been the ones watching me, or trying to keep their eyes on me. Maybe I had only thought that I had eluded their vision upon leaving the library earlier. This was not going to be a pleasant scene. It had all of the makings of a disaster.

I tried to be nice and innocent. Both virtues were pushing my limits.

"You gave me a book earlier and I was over there at the table reading it, and now the book is gone. Did you happen to take the book when I left the library?" It was my nicest voice.

"I have no idea what you are talking about," Elba or Melba said.

"You saw me sitting at the table?"

"Yes."

"You saw me with the book which you had given to me, right?"

"Yes."

"And you saw me leave the library?"

"No. I did not."

"You weren't watching me?"

"I was helping my sister with another patron. I left the desk and when I got back, you were gone."

"You never saw the book?"

"I saw the book with you while you were sitting at the table over there, young lady. And you, by the way, are responsible for that book. So, just where is the book?"

"That's what I'd like to know," my voice became a little sarcastic. This twin was taxing my effort toward niceness.

"Sheriff Evans, you know that the book will have to be replaced."

"Yes, ma'am, I understand that. We'll take care of it. Just let us know how much we owe you."

Daddy turned me around and guided me out through the exit. He pointed to his car and I got inside.

"Now what was that all about?"

"Somebody took the book. If the dragon lady didn't do it, then somebody must have been watching me and took that book after I left. I hid it in the middle of some other books. Someone had to have been watching me the whole time. I did not leave that book out on the table where I had been sitting. I shelved it in the wrong place so that only I would know where it was."

"Okay, so tell me what you found."

I sighed, hoping to expel my anger over the missing book.

"Betty Ann Greesome graduated from Freemont High School in 1956. She was not pictured in the book, but her name is listed at the end of her class among the other names of the people not pictured. The ring belongs to her," I said emphatically.

"Oh."

Daddy sat in silence for a few minutes. I was angry with myself for leaving the book. I should have been more careful. I should have taken it with me. It's what I get for trying to do the right thing within the rules of the library. I'd file this episode for later reconsideration.

"What are you thinking?" I finally said to him.

"I was thinking that maybe I ought to go pay Miss Greesome a visit."

"But we don't have the book. It's my word against hers."

"Not entirely. There are bound to be other copies of that book. That fact would be easy enough to check out. I would just like to know what her answer would be when I ask her about that ring being found at Mr. Joe's barn."

"Can I go with you?"

I knew what his answer would be, but I asked anyway.

He shook his head and we headed towards home.

I stood by the curb and watched him drive away. He was going to the First Baptist Church to meet with Miss Betty Greesome, the Minister of Music. Some days she kept office hours and he was hoping to find her on neutral ground, or so he said. He told me that he expected some type of evasive behavior from her, the usual fare from guilty people. But, he also had told me, at least she would know that he knew, and that he had the ring. He would tell her that the ring was evidence, and that might shake her a bit. He said that it was worth a try. I kinda liked his strategy, and I did want to see him at work first hand. I also wanted to see Miss Greesome squirm a little.

I had asked again if I could go with him, but he advised against it.

I was deep in thought when I entered the back door. It slammed behind me. "Clancy!"

"I'm sorry, Mama."

"If I have told you once, I've told you a million times, don't slam the back door!"

"Mama, is there any door in this house that I can slam?"

"What?" her raised pitch level was coming from the living room. I was standing in the kitchen, a good safe distance away. If I had to, I could make a break for it. The only trouble with running was that I always had to come back. Home was like that. You had to come back to it sooner or later. At least that was my understanding at the time.

"I was just wondering if there is another door in the house I could slam."

"Are you trying to be cute with me?" her pitch was not quite to the level of a yell.

I decided that it would be in my best interest not to answer that question. Either way I would have been in trouble since she already knew the answer to her question.

"You and your brother are always making too much racket. I need some peace and quiet around here. And I can do without your cuteness and sarcasm, young lady!"

I ran up the stairs as she continued to fuss. Scottie must have been in his room, but I didn't see him when I passed. Sometimes he hid under the bed to read or play silently or talk to himself. He felt safe under there, I think. I closed the door to my room and sat on the bed to do some serious pondering. I required my own peace and quiet now and then. I had made it home in time for my lunch, but at the moment I was not hungry. I decided to let a meal pass. I could easily make up my hunger at suppertime.

Later that afternoon the brilliant idea came to me to go visit the Scruggs family. I didn't have much of a chance to offer my condolences to the family at the funeral. Since our two families did not socialize, it was awkward for me at the funeral. Besides that, Mrs. Scruggs was so emotional that it was nearly impossible for anyone to say anything to her while she was involved with so much emotional grief. I heard my mother whisper to my daddy that it was heart-rending watching her during that funeral.

I decided that maybe I ought to offer my respects now, two days later. Buster and I were more than just casual acquaintances. We had actually exchanged blows and harsh words. He wasn't a friend or any-thing, but after several encounters, we had an understanding. He left me alone so I didn't have to beat him up on a regular basis. I didn't know his little brother Micah except to see him now and then around town. I also knew both of them by their dubious reputation.

Mama thought it was a good idea for me to visit them. She had made two apple pies during Uncle Walters' visit, and we still had a third of the first pie left over. She wrapped up the uncut second pie for me, and I set out in the mid-afternoon to visit Mr. and Mrs. Donald Scruggs.

The Scruggs were a large family, so I expected a lot of people to be hanging around the house. Some folks did that in our town whenever there was a funeral, and afterwards. They would come a day or so before the funeral and remain several days following the main event. They'd just sit and eat and talk for several days. It seemed like a waste of time to me, but what did I know? When I said something to Sarah about that societal tradition, she said it was cheap therapy. "Sometimes, Miss Clancy, peoples need peoples," she said.

It took me less than ten minutes by bike. I had one of those ten speed marvels with hand brakes. It was a great bike. I loved it as much as Daddy loved the motorcycle he kept locked up in the garage. He didn't ride his bike much because Mama was so deathly afraid of the thing. Every now and then he would take it out and go for a long ride. Occasionally he would use it in his work, but not too often. He referred to it as his Hog whenever Mama was not around. She despised that terminology. His Hog was so clean you could have used nearly any part of it as a plate for your food. It was a Harley-Davidson Sportster. My bicycle was a Schwinn Roadster and nobody in his right mind would have eaten off of it. Once in a while Daddy would take me for a ride on his Hog. That and fishing were the only two things better than riding my bicycle. A likely exception to my favorite things to do was the satisfaction I was having by helping my daddy with the investigation that summer. That was quickly becoming a priority over everything, including fishing as well as riding my bike.

I hadn't ridden my bike since June of that summer. After school was out, I took it on some long rides all over Clancyville. But once Scottie and I began our serious fishing, I stopped riding and began walking. I had a wire-basket mounted to the handlebars for carrying stuff, but it wasn't sufficient for my fishing tackle. On the occasion of visiting folks after a funeral, it was quite sufficient for carrying a homemade apple pie.

Donald Scruggs and his wife Ruby had a small, dark gray, framed house on the edge of town. Once upon a time it was white, I suppose.

That was my best guess. There were some trees in the yard but not much grass. The dirt seemed to be plentiful. The Scruggs ordinarily had two or three cars parked in the yard in the dirt. Their yard was their driveway, it seemed to me. The day I arrived to pay my respects there must have been fourteen cars parked in their dirt in the front and on both sides of the house. It looked like a used car lot, except the cars were not lined up in rows. They were parked at odd angles with one another.

A radio was playing some loud country music and the porch was full of men sitting around talking. I saw no children anywhere. I remembered that Buster and Micah had an older brother named Randall, and maybe one or two younger sisters. I couldn't remember for certain. Randall was sixteen and in high school, but he was only a freshman. He had failed a couple of grades. Formal education was not his strong suit, or so the rumors of the town had it.

"Wut you want here?" a voice spoke to me out of the shadows of the porch. I couldn't tell who it was, but it sounded like an older man. I approached the front step cautiously with my mother's apple pie held out in front of me as if it were an offering of some sort.

"I came to see Mr. & Mrs. Scruggs. I am sorry about Buster and Micah." I was a little scared in this environment, despite my fearless approach to the house and porch. I didn't know these people, and it took all of my courage to get me this far. Curiosity also helped me. I stopped my approach at the step and waited.

"My wife don't want to be bothered. She's a grievin'. You've said yor piece, now git," the man said as he sat down in a plastic porch chair surrounded by his fraternity. I was talking to Donald Scruggs himself, I figured.

"Daddy, that's no way to treat a friend of Buster's," Randall said from behind me.

I turned to see this tall, ugly teenager staring at me with his hideous eyes. Neither eye focused on the same spot, and it was creepy to look him, especially his eyes. I chose to look at a pimple on his forehead instead.

"This here's the one who give old Buster, God rest his soul, a beatin'," Randall continued.

"Wut?" Donald Scruggs got up from his plastic throne and moved closer. He stood on the porch and looked down at me. That singular step was now between us.

"A girl, a damn girl beat up my boy? I don't believe it!" he said to no one in particular.

I remembered the pie in my hand and decided I would try to change the direction of the conversation.

"My mother sent this pie for you folks," I tried to sound as polite as I knew how.

Randall reached out and took the pie from my hands without a word of thanks or anything. He handed it to a man seated and then continued to stare at me. That man who took the pie from Randall stood up from his wooden chair and carried my gift into the house.

"You beat up my boy, little girl?" Donald said as if the gift of the pie and its transferral never actually happened. It seemed to be of no importance to him.

"Well, I didn't exactly beat him up, Mr. Scruggs —" I began my explanation.

"That's not wut I heard," Randall chimed back in before I could finish. "One of Buster's friends told me all 'bout it, said you clobbered him a good 'un. Sent that sucker flyin'." He was starting to laugh as he told his almost true version of one of our two physical encounters. Buster was a lot like Randall. He had been a slow learner and I had been forced to engage him in a second round of education. There were no witnesses for this performance, I had thought. By the time our little repeat skirmish was over and done, I had poor old bad-boy Buster begging for mercy as I was exerting pressure on his arm and shoulder in a half-nelson. It was one of my finest hours. But, no blows were exchanged in that second round.

"You got a lot'a guts comin' round cheer after whipin' up on Buster," Randall said.

"Buster and I had an understanding," I offered, "we respected each other." I was stretching the truth a little, but I felt my predicament called for some negotiation tactics.

"Wut kind of understandin'?" Donald Scruggs said.

"He wouldn't beat up me or my family if I would leave his family alone."

"That's a stupid understandin' 'tween a boy and a girl," Randall offered.

"It worked for us," I said.

"Stupid kid," Randall said, "he don't even know how to handle women. Didn't ... I mean didn't," he corrected himself. "I'd show you a thing or two. You just try something on me, little Miss Big Mouth. I tried to tell Buster how to take care of hisself, but he knew so much, he wuz so smart. Dumbass kid, had to go and get hisself kilt."

I thought for a second that Randall was going to cry. Everything got really quiet after he had finished his brief soliloquy. Donald Scruggs walked over to his teenage son and put his hand on his shoulder. Scruggs the elder was still on the porch as he reached down to touch his tall eldest son.

"Go on in the house. I'll take ker of this here," Donald said to Randall.

He moved across in front of me, jumped up onto the porch, and slammed the screen door hard as he entered. I thought I heard some sobbing coming from inside the house after that.

"I don't like your daddy, you know that, little miss?"

I shook my head, as if his statement was news to me.

"Know why?"

I had several answers but none of them seemed particularly relevant at that moment. I let his question pass as if it were rhetorical.

"I'll tell ya' why. It's that nigger Joe he done got in his jail house down there. That man done kilt my boys and he should die fur it. I mean die a horrible death, little girl. Do you know wut I'm a'talkin' 'bout?"

"Mr. Joe didn't kill your sons."

"Mister? Mister? You call that cold blooded killer a mister? He's a damn killer-nigger and nothin' more! Do you hear me?"

I could hear him too well. He was nearly screaming by this time and I thought that maybe my mother could have heard what he was saying, and she was two miles away.

"Wut makes you think he didn't do it? You ain't nothin' but a nigger-lover anyhow." He turned his back to me and walked towards his chair. He obviously didn't expect me to answer his question. He remained standing in front of the chair.

"I think the person who kidnapped me and locked me in the barn killed your sons. Mr. Joe was in jail when that happened."

Donald Scruggs turned quickly and frowned at me.

"I figured that was just somebody in town who didn't like you and wanted you out of the way. If it'd been me that dun it, you'd still be tied up and waitin' fer help."

Donald Scruggs laughed at his hypothetical threat, and then everybody on the porch joined him in laughter. I didn't think it was funny.

"Who said I was tied up?"

He stopped his grinning and the laughter on the porch died down slowly. I waited a few seconds before I spoke again.

"I was getting too close and I scared somebody. They told me to stay away and stop snooping around."

"I'll bet they did. You otta listen to that advice and stay out'a it. None of your damn business. The murderer is already in jail. Let's jest kill 'im and be done with it. That's wut I say," he spoke as if he had authority, and then he turned to the men seated on the porch around him.

"Then you'd be guilty of murder, Mr. Scruggs," I said.

"I'd be a hero," he said, "I'd be a damn hero if I killed that …." his voice trailed off. He was way beyond being angry. He sat down and said nothing more to me.

"Better go now, kid," a new voice from among the men said, "Donald gets mighty upset when he thinks 'bout those youngins' of his."

I was turning my bicycle around to leave when I heard the squeaky screen door open and then slam shut. I looked in the direction of the porch and saw a woman come out and lean against one of the dirty white square columns that supported the porch roof. It was Ruby, Buster and Micah's mother. I remembered her from all the wailing she did on Saturday. She looked as if she had been crying for a long time. She was wearing a sleeveless, dingy yellow print dress. There was some kind of small design on it, but I was too far away from her to figure out what it was exactly. Undersized, red flip-flops were on her dirty feet. One of them had a broken strap. Her hair was matted and she had a smudge of dirt on her face. She looked pitiful.

"Who are you?" she asked me.

"Clancy Evans."

"What you doin' here, Clancy Evans?"

"I came to tell you—"

"She came to tell us that Joe the nigger didn't kill yor babies, Maw. Can you beat it? She's got gall, I'll give her that. By gosh, gall!" Donald said from his perch.

"I came to tell you that I was sorry about Buster and Micah."

She began to moan. She wasn't exactly crying, at least not tears, but the sobs were deep and mournful. She wrapped her arms around the square porch support. The full weight of her small body was now leaning against that wooden column. She hugged it like it was a person. It hurt to listen to that poor woman wail as she groped the support, now hugging it tightly.

The men got silent, but no one moved to comfort her. Everything was still. She slid slowly down the support until she finally collapsed on the porch floor, all the while still hugging the dirty white wood. She just sat there in her pile of misery, hugging and weeping and softly wailing.

"He killed my babies," she sobbed and gripped tighter to the wood. "He killed my babies. Oh, God, he hurt my babies so bad, sooooooo bad."

No one knew what to do or say. Someone should have tried to comfort her, or at least take her back inside. No one moved. No one was looking at her except for me. They all just sat there like statues—unfeeling, unmoving, perhaps not knowing what to do for her. No one offered comfort to the grieving mother. It was all I could do to keep myself from dropping the bicycle and running to her. I knew that would be a mistake. Something told me to stay put, so I did.

Ruby suddenly spoke again.

"You go tell that no count, gawd awful—…why did he do such a thing to them? They never did nothin' to him. Do you think that's right? Why in God's name—…wut was he a'doin' to my babies? Oh, … poor little babies. God took 'em, you know. That's wut the preacher said at the funeral. God took 'em. Said we had 'em long e'nuff. Said God wanted them now. They wuz precious in his sight and God wanted 'em."

Finally Donald got up again and came to her. He gave me a hard look and motioned with his head in the direction of the road. I read it as my invitation to leave. He tried to direct her back inside the house.

"Wut would God want with my children, child?" she asked in a soft voice, not hysterical nor sobbing now. It was a child-like voice that seemed to be asking an honest question. "Didn't God know that I needed my boys? Why would God take my sons from me? It don't seem fair … does it seem fair to you? Maybe God sent that …."

Her voice trailed off after Donald took her inside. I could still hear her as she began to sob once again. It was past time for me to go. Besides that, I wanted to leave and I was extremely relieved to be on the road headed home. My heart was breaking for Ruby. I wished she had somebody other than Donald Scruggs to help her through her misery.

# CHAPTER TWENTY-FIVE

After supper I spent a long time alone in my room. I didn't tell anyone about my experience with the Scruggs family. Mama asked me about it after I returned home, but I just told her that they seemed to appreciate the pie and my coming, which is pretty much what my mother wanted to hear. Chalk up another lie to my ethically-challenged behavior. I was beginning to think I was moving in the wrong direction, and much too quickly. Is this the way detectives operated?

Daddy wasn't around and I was glad. He wouldn't have bought my version of what happened there. He knew Donald Scruggs better than that. Mama's ignorance helped me from telling her exactly what had taken place.

It was a while after supper, but before dark, that I happened to look out my back bedroom window and see my mother throwing away some clothes. I recalled what she had said to me about my things, so I put two and two together. I climbed down the lattice work and retrieved my old jeans from the metal trash can. I returned to my room by the same route with my goods in tow.

Scottie was waiting for me, relaxing on my bed, when I climbed through the window.

"What's up?" he said.

"Mama. She's throwin' away my stuff. She tossed my jeans in the outside trash can," I answered.

"They ain't no good. They got that sh—… ah, manure all over them," he caught himself before he let loose a word that was absolutely forbidden in our house.

"You better say manure. Daddy will get you good if he hears you using words like that."

"I know. Sometimes I can't help myself."

"Try real hard. The effort may save your life."

"What you gonna do with those old jeans?"

"Keep 'em to go fishing in," I said as I stuffed them in my out-of-the-way-place inside of the walk-in closet where I thought my mother would never look. I had multiple hiding places in the closet. In fact, I had so many that sometimes I forgot where I put the things I hid.

"Better not put them where you have something else or you'll regret it. They still smell a little. And that shiny stuff might move from one item to another."

I retrieved them quickly from the hiding spot, smelled them, and then put them back in the same safe place. There was nothing extraordinary about their odor. I decided that my mother simply liked to fuss, and that she was making too much out of my jeans getting a little manure on them.

Scottie left me alone to ponder for another hour or so. I was planning my next move with Betty Ann Greesome. Daddy had told me before supper that she acted surprised to see the ring and that she had no idea how it came to be at that barn. She at least claimed the ring to be hers. I would have asked her about those *L S* initials and that heart. Daddy didn't push her. He just wanted her to be aware that he had the ring and was keeping it as part of an ongoing investigation. He also was hoping that if she was guilty of something, she might be foolish enough to make a stupid move. He had told me more than once that you have to get close enough to your suspects to force them to worry about what you may or may not know, as well as what you may or may not do. That way, he reasoned, they will think too much and ultimately do something not in their best interest.

Now that Daddy had finished questioning her, I figured it was my turn. I would try to find a way to force her to do something stupid.

I told my parents that I was going walking and that I'd be back in a while. That didn't set too well with them since my most recent escapade forced me to spend a night tied up in Mr. Joe's barn, so Scottie was appointed to go with me. That made little sense, but who was I to question the wisdom of adults. My valiant protector was my nine-year-old brother. I could only imagine how useful he would be against an armed committee of desperate people who might want to put me out of commission permanently. I told them that much. Daddy smiled and said nothing, but Mama's face turned dark in her frowning routine while holding her composure extremely well. She rarely enjoyed my humor. I wondered about that on this occasion.

I think I must have made my point too well because I was told to be back within an hour and stay on our block of the town. I could circle our block in less than fifteen minutes. With those restrictions, I might as well stay home. However, the need for fresh air was too strong. And Scottie wanted to walk with me.

It was a good hour and some change before darkness would descend upon our tiny village. The katydids were in full song among the trees along our street. It was a wonderful summer evening that allowed folks to gather themselves from the heat of a long day and feel the cool breezes in the twilight. It was summertime in the South. Folks were sitting on their porches. Some kids were playing in the front yard at one house. Jessica Thompson was out walking as usual. She walked twice a day, early morning, and late evening. She walked the entire circumference of the town, about three miles the way she did it. I think she was the very first walker Clancyville ever had. Most folks thought she was crazy to be out twice a day walking and not going anywhere. She began this routine back at the end of the sixties. When she was asked why she did it, she always gave the same answer—exercise. It hadn't caught on yet. She was still pretty much the lone walker of our town. One day the craze would hit, and there would be many crazy people out walking and jogging and doing their best to shed some pounds and tone up. Our little town would one day owe Miss Jessica a debt of gratitude. At the moment, she was simply "Old Weird Jessica" as she galloped along all by her lonesome. It didn't help her cause any that she wore black and white high-top tennis shoes.

I spoke to her when we passed. She nodded and kept moving.

"Is she crazy?" Scottie asked.

"I don't think so."

"Then why does she walk like that?"

"Like what?"

"Fast."

"Good exercise, I suppose. Good for the body."

"But no one else does that."

"So," I said.

"So, she's crazy."

"We're walking. Are we crazy?"

"Yeah," he said. "We definitely are crazy."

By the time we arrived at the farthest corner from our house, still on our block, so to speak, I stopped and looked in the direction of the Baptist church. It was simply a diagonal block away from our present location. Miss Greesome lived next door to the church. She roomed there with a sweet little lady named Barbara Bingham who was a retired school teacher. She had a huge house and enjoyed having boarders. Greesome had lived there from the first day she had arrived in Clancyville. It was an ideal location for her work, and it saved her money. Our church didn't pay her a great salary, so every little savings helped. In fact, like most churches, there had been some debate over hiring a person for that job back in the sixties when she arrived. Daddy was in favor of it, and Mama said no.

I had to admit that she had done a good job with the music program, especially with the children. The adult choir still sounded flat on most pieces, but the kids had managed to form a solid choral group and were permitted to perform more often. I always enjoyed them. I didn't sing, but I enjoyed hearing the music.

"What are you planning?" Scottie interrupted my thoughts.

"Nothing."

"You're lying."

"No, I really have no plans. I just have a disposition."

"What does that mean?" he said.

"It means I have a deep desire to go visit someone, or at least go check out their present location, and see if an idea comes to me en route or while I'm there."

"Sounds weird and dangerous to me."

"Which, the visit or developing the plan as I go?"

"In your case, both. Haven't you had enough excitement this summer? Gee whiz, Clancy. You could've been killed, you know. Did you think of that?"

"No. I guess I didn't."

"Why don't you let Daddy do his work and you stay out of it?"

"Because he needs more brain power than Ralph Hines. Besides, I suspect that Ralph Hines had something to do with it. If he's part of it, then how much help could he be? And, as you already know, Daddy believes the evidence so far suggests that Mr. Joe is guilty."

"Even if Hines wasn't part of it, he still wouldn't be much good," Scottie added truthfully.

"See? We've got to help Daddy. I think this whole thing is complicated."

"What does that mean?"

"That means it's not a simple killing. Those two boys weren't killed because they walked up to the wrong place at the wrong time."

"Pre-medicated?" he asked, using the wrong word. It sounded funny.

"Yeah, something like that. That's a big word for you," I smiled at him.

"I heard Daddy use it. What does it mean?"

"Well, premeditated means that whoever killed those kids planned it. They thought about it ahead of time."

"What other kind of murder is there?"

"Anger. Revenge. Passion."

"Passion? I thought that was for love in the movies."

"You can hate someone so much that you want to kill them. I reckon that hatred causes passion or a passionate killing or something like that."

"How come you know so much about this stuff?"

"I read Sherlock Holmes."

"You find this stuff in books?" he said.

"Some books. Some of it. Some of the time."

"Does Mama know you read this kind of junk?"

"I don't think she's ever read about Mr. Holmes. She read all the classics. She was educated in the finer stuff."

"I'll bet she wouldn't let you read this junk if she knew what you were learning."

I shrugged and had to agree with him. If she had her way, she'd try to make a well-bred lady out of me. For my money, it was like trying to make a silk purse out of sow's ear. I was refined in my own way, not hers.

"We'll let it be our secret, okay?" I said.

"Yeah. Sure thing. I'll use it as a lever."

"A what? What are you talking about?"

"Remember you talked about having a lever on Hines?"

"Oh, that. Leverage."

"Yeah, that's it. I'll use it as leverage against you. I think it'll come in handy since you're my sister and all."

He began walking in the direction of our house, away from the corner.

"Wait a minute. I think I want to go this way."

"You can't."

I gave him an exasperated look.

"Come on, Sis. You just can't go off looking for trouble. Whoever killed Buster and Micah is still out there."

"I'll be careful. Promise. You stay here and guard."

"Guard what? There's nothing to guard. There's not even a street lamp."

"All the better. You sit in the shadows and wait for me. I'll be back in a few minutes. We'll be home before the hour is up."

I looked at my watch.

"We still have a good forty minutes to prowl," I said.

"*You* have forty minutes to prowl, whatever that means for you. I ain't prowling. I'm sitting and guarding the darkness right here."

He didn't sound too happy, but then he never did when I forced him to aid my wild schemes. I crossed the street and headed towards the church building and Mrs. Bingham's boarding house. Forty minutes wasn't nearly long enough to suit me, but it would have to do on this night.

# CHAPTER TWENTY-SIX

The house was dark except for a back room downstairs. There were three table lamps all on and I could easily see most aspects of the entire room.

I eased up to the window and looked in through the sheers. The television was blaring and I could see the back of a head in a chair. It had to be Mrs. Bingham because of the size of the head and the gray hair. Betty Ann Greesome was an oversized short woman with a large head full of short, brown hair.

I figured I could wait a few minutes to see if anything developed before I would have to scram. I knew that my parents weren't up to any late arrivals at this point. I figured that they'd ask too many questions, and I would get deeper into trouble. Sometimes I knew my limitations with my parents. Sometimes.

After a few minutes I was tired of craning my neck to look into the window and tired of standing on tiptoes. I eased down behind some bushes and rested while listening to the television. I had no idea what I was waiting for, but I decided to stay put for another few minutes. I had a few minutes to kill.

Just as I had given up hope that anything productive was going to occur, a human voice came into the room and began talking with Mrs. Bingham. I thought I recognized the female voice belonging to the one who had entered the room.

"Did I get any calls?"

"What?" Mrs. Bingham said.

"Did I get any calls?" the other voice was louder now.

"Calls? No, I don't think so. I took a bath late this afternoon, but I don't remember hearing the phone ring."

"I'm going out for a while. I'll see you later."

"I doubt it, dear. I'll be going to bed as soon as my show is over. You know I don't like to stay up late."

"Have a restful sleep. Goodnight."

"Well, I ain't going to bed now, dear. But thanks just the same."

I heard a door shut and then there was nothing but the sound of the television dialogue and canned laughter.

I eased myself to the edge of the house and looked down the driveway. I could see Miss Greesome pulling out in her old Ford. I could smell oil burning. It reminded me of that night I was imprisoned and riding in the trunk of a car. I walked to the edge of Mrs. Bingham's driveway and watched Betty Ann Greesome's car moving slowly down the street to some unknown destination. More and more pieces were fitting together for me.

"Well, you took your own sweet time gettin' back here," Scottie was a little upset when I returned to his post. "Did you learn anything?"

"Yeah, Mrs. Bingham likes to watch comedies on television."

"Oh, that should be valuable information. You should tell Daddy when we get back."

My brother was surely developing a taste for sarcasm. Perhaps I was more of an influence than I had imagined.

"There's more," I offered.

"Tell me."

"Betty Ann Greesome drives an old beat-up Ford that burns oil. I could smell the fumes at a distance. I think her car was used in my kidnapping. She may even have been the one who took me."

"That oil smell doesn't prove anything," he said.

"Probably not," I said as he and I walked home together, "but it drives another nail in her coffin as far as I'm concerned. It places her in the pool of suspects."

"How's that?" he asked.

"It makes me more suspicious of her."

We made it home just under the hour's time limit and no questions were asked. I went to bed early. The summer heat was finally getting to me.

Mr. Joe was just finishing his breakfast when I arrived at the jail the next morning.

"Well, Miss Clancy. What have you been up to lately?"

"Checking out clues, Mr. Joe. I guess you would call it investigating."

"And?"

"Not much is helping. Well, not much I can prove, anyhow."

"I appreciate your efforts, young lady. Have I told you that?"

"Yes, sir. You have. And you're welcome. I'm glad to help you."

"Well, don't give up. It'll come together. So, what have you learned?"

"I think that Betty Ann Greesome's car was used in my kidnapping, and it was definitely her ring I found at your place. She told Daddy that she had no idea how the ring got there."

"How'd you know it was her ring to begin with?"

"I had Fred Andrews use the library loan thing, and I finally found her name under the section of people not photographed in a yearbook from a high school in another state. But someone removed the annual from my hiding place in the library before I could show Daddy. I hid it in the stacks while I went to get Daddy to come look at it, and when I got back … I'm rambling on and on."

"That's okay. Sometimes when a body's got a lot to say, the mouth just lets go and you can't stop. Sometimes I get that way myself. Although it has been a long time since I had that much to say."

"Well, truth is, I think that she's in on it, but I don't believe that she killed those boys alone. Somebody else is involved in this. There have to be others besides Miss Greesome."

"Any ideas?" he said.

"You mean about who else might be in on it?"

"Well, that, yes, ma'am, or anything else you're working on?"

"Just Ralph Hines, but Ralph's so stupid, it's hard to believe that he could do something like that and not leave a clearer trail. I'm suspicious of him. If I could just connect…."

I stopped and had a thought. I knew just what I had to do.

"Something's going on inside that devilish mind of yours. I can smell the smoke," he said as he smiled.

"Yes, sir," I said and grinned. "I'm getting an idea."

"I thought so. Probably dangerous, too."

"Some might figure it that way. But, I'll be careful."

"Don't be foolish, Clancy. Please, child. They killed two, they'll kill again if they have to. You have to remember your age and all," he spoke in earnest, that much I could tell.

"What's my age got to do with it?"

"Oh, my, Miss Clancy. I do say, you are quite something else."

"I know. I'll be real careful."

"Your family all right?" Mr. Joe asked.

"'Bout the same, thanks. Mama fusses a lot and Daddy works most of the time. Scottie plays and fishes. I do some fishing, but mainly for thinking purposes."

He smiled and nodded. He understood me pretty well.

"My mama used to fuss a lot, too. But she had so many kids, she had reason to fuss. What's your mama fussing about these days?"

"Mostly about me and my brother. You know that time we got all that manure on us and found those clothes in Bessie Mae's hiding spot? She fusses mostly about me getting a little of that manure water on the cuffs of my jeans. It didn't do that much damage, but my mama likes to fuss about it anyway. She says I have ruined my jeans. She threw them away, but I saw her do it, so I retrieved them. Then I hid them."

"That stuff is pretty powerful. It might be good for grass, but it's hard on clothes. Have you noticed the shine?"

"Daddy said something about that to me."

"Truly, that manure has a glow to it in the night when it is exposed to light. Like a bright sheen or something. I think it's the butterflies."

"The butterflies?"

"Yeah, that place where Bessie Mae hides out is like a burial ground for all of those beautiful butterflies. Some of them die there. And all that butterfly pollen sort of collects in that manure. It could be the cause for the shine, but I'm guessing. Those butterflies and their pollen may even be the secret of that mixture for the grass."

"I never heard of butterfly pollen. I thought bees had pollen."

"They do. Butterflies pollinate the same as bees, they just don't make honey with their pollen. And, the butterflies have a substance on them that is really scales. Tiny scales. It's a lot like pollen, in a way. Rubs off on things—people, flowers, manure. It gets all mixed up in that black, swamp water and works magic on my grass. That's my theory, Miss Clancy."

"And trouble on my clothes, or so my mama thinks. Say, Mr. Joe, how do you know all of this?"

"I pay attention to the butterflies. Have for years. I learn by watching."

"You learned about the scales by watching?"

"Oh, that. No, ma'am. I studied that in college."

"You studied butterflies in college?"

"Well, some. I majored in a part of agriculture, called horticulture. I studied gardens and flowers and plants and the animals and insects which are connected to all of that."

"You wanted to become a gardener?"

"I suppose you could say it that way. I love to grow things. I love to watch things grow. I liked the beauty in nature and have always enjoyed being a small part of it. I still watch nature. I pay close attention to what's happening around me."

"And you grow beautiful grass."

"Well, I help it all I can. I better not take too much credit for that growth. After all, I still pray and that never hurts."

I didn't say anything more to him at that point. I wasn't much into praying, and I had little first hand experience to offer. I seldom saw results from my requests. I said a quick good-bye and left. Mr. Joe was still being my teacher.

"Let's ride," my daddy said to me. That was all the encouragement I needed to jump inside his black-and-white. I would have gone anywhere on earth with my father. I suddenly felt important as the two of us were heading down one of the streets of our small village.

"Where're we goin'?"

"That cow's swamp."

"Bessie Mae's favorite spot."

"Yeah, Bessie Mae's swamp," he confirmed.

"Why?"

"Well, it seems that the medical examiner wanted to visit that sight, so I took him out there and showed him the swamp. I left him there."

"Left him there?"

"Yeah, he said he wanted to snoop around and get some samples."

"Why?"

"He believes that black liquid he found inside the lungs of Micah and Buster came from that swamp. If he's right, it means that they were drowned there."

"Drowned."

"Yes, ma'am. That's what he said. Remember, I told you a few days ago that he had found some black liquid in their lungs and stomach."

"But you didn't say that they had drowned!"

"My oversight. Sorry. Perhaps I halfway expected my chief investigator to come up with that all on her own. But, to the point, the Medical Examiner now knows that they were drowned and then they were strangled, post mortem."

"Can I assume that post mortem means after they were already dead?"

"Precisely, my dear."

"Somebody wanted to make sure that they were dead, don't you think?"

"I'd call it overkill. Somebody probably drowned them, strangled them, and then hung Buster, for some reason, just to make sure."

"Wonder why they didn't hang Micah, too?"

"Can't say, but it might be as simple as they didn't have enough rope or they thought Micah was already dead, or Buster saw or knew something which his little brother did not. Could be anything."

"Couldn't have been the rope, Daddy. Mr. Joe had plenty of rope in his barn. Had to be some other reason, perhaps something you just offered. Maybe Micah was dead and they knew it. Or maybe Micah didn't know what Buster knew."

"What does that mean to you?"

"I don't know, I was just playing Sherlock Holmes and speculating."

He grinned, and then laughed.

"Speculating, huh? My daughter, the detective. You speculate all you want to, but just don't let it go any further than speculation. I don't need the wrath of your mother coming down on me because you put yourself in harm's way … again."

When we pulled close to the barn and exited the car, the M.E. was coming around the corner toward us.

"Did you find what you were looking for?" Daddy said.

"I think so. I just have to check these samples with what I took from the two corpses. I'll let you know after I compare them. I think it's the same, but I don't like to guess."

"Can you tell me what you're looking for?"

"I want to know exactly what's in this substance."

"It's mostly manure," Daddy said.

"True enough, Sheriff, but I have to be more specific than that. I think there's more here than just manure and water."

"Possibly caustic, maybe even deathly poisonous?" Daddy asked.

"You bet, Sheriff. They definitely could have been poisoned."

"So, you're thinking that drowning may not have been the cause of death?"

"No, I'm not saying that. They definitely drowned. No question in my mind. My autopsy was thorough. They drowned. But, that black substance could definitely be a poison, maybe even contributing to their deaths," the M.E. said.

"So how do you figure they drowned? Swamp's not that deep," Daddy said.

"Correct. My theory of the crime is that someone pushed their faces into it, held them there—" he stopped and looked at me. I could tell that he was wondering whether he should talk like that in front of a little girl.

"She's heard worse, doc. Go ahead."

"They were held face down until they stopped breathing. They inhaled that junk. Like I said, I found enough in their lungs to make my call. That was a relatively easy call for me. Plus, there were bruises on their necks and shoulders which would support my belief that they were held firmly down in that murky substance until they drowned."

"Horrible way to die. Hanging would have been more merciful," Daddy said.

"Maybe, maybe not, Sheriff. If I'm correct about that black substance being deadly poison, then for my way of considering, drowning would have been more merciful. Hanging them was nothing more than a show. Their little bodies didn't have sufficient weight to cause any damage to their throat region. All in all, horrible business, Sheriff. Some mean folks are responsible for this."

# Chapter Twenty-seven

I rode home in silence with Daddy. Neither of us felt much like talking. "Rough way to go," he said simply. He said it more than once.

"Yes, sir," I finally answered him.

That was it. There wasn't much else to say. I thought that just plain death was bad, but their way of dying had to be horrible. I could only imagine the fear that those two boys went through before they died. I tried not to think of it too long. I could feel some tears welling up in me, and I thought I might explode. Life could be downright nasty sometimes. I was having a hard time figuring out how a person could hate another person enough to do such a thing. It was beyond cruel.

After a lunch of tomato sandwiches, I told Scottie what we had learned from the Medical Examiner. He handled it better than I did, at least he didn't look like he was going to be sick or cry. He made a face, but that was about it.

His way of handling almost any crisis was to suggest that we go fishing to think it over and to forget it. I always thought that such a notion was contradictory, but it seemed reasonable enough to him. Maybe it was more about forgetting it by distraction than it was mulling it over. I was more into mulling stuff over and over.

When we asked Mama about the fishing idea, she vetoed it quickly and informed us that we were all three headed to visit Aunt Mildred, Uncle Tom, and Aunt Nona that afternoon. It was a bimonthly ritual for my mama to visit her only living relatives in town. Scottie and I did not always have to go along with her.

I understood why she visited Aunt Nona, or at least I thought I did. Aunt Nona was old, mildly crazy, and needed family to check in on her. Despite the fact that she had a paid caretaker and housekeeper, and had hired workmen for the summer, she was still lonely. So said my mother. I suppose that the imaginary sea captain was proof enough of that. That's what Mama thought as well. She also said that Aunt Nona was probably going to die soon. She was certainly old enough to die to my way of thinking.

Aunt Mildred was another case. Mildred's disposition was more like Uncle Walters' than it was my mother's. She was an active lady, but she was restricted somewhat because of her wheelchair-bound husband, Uncle Tom. He had fallen from a ladder while painting their house. He broke his back and had been paralyzed from the waist down since he was thirty-five. That had been five years ago. Aunt Mildred took care of him constantly; nevertheless, her multiple activities in the community caused her to be always on the go. She did restrict her travel to the city limits of Clancyville.

Uncle Tom had a great attitude about his accident and his life since, but it was tough to see a man so young just sit there, unable to get up and walk. He taught himself how to paint landscapes and portraits, so at least he was involved in something he loved to do. He was becoming a good artist, too. At least I thought so. I liked his Norman Rockwell style of painting. It was interesting the way he painted people. He seemed to show their character flaws as well as their good points. Mama didn't like the way he portrayed her. He only painted her once since she made such a ruckus. My guess was that he didn't want to offend his sister-in-law. For my money, he drew a perfect likeness of her. She took exception to the reality of the painting.

"Now, both of you mind your manners this afternoon. Don't act like little children."

I wanted to say something really bad whenever Mama said something stupid like that, but I figured that I had had enough trouble with her this summer. I let the opportunity pass.

"Scottie, talk about something besides fishing, please," she continued.

"But that's what I know. Why can't I talk about fishin'?"

"Because your aunts and uncle get tired of hearing about how many fish you catch, and how to clean them, and what their entrails look like. It's revolting."

"Their what?" he asked.

"Guts," I said.

"That's enough, Clancy. Let's not be gross."

Some words my mama didn't like very much, and she usually made it clear we were not to use such words in her presence, or whenever polite conversation was dictated. Whenever she was around, we generally learned a lot of vocabulary because she used words we didn't know. Daddy talked the way we talked, but not her. Now and then my father would offer up a new word, but that was mostly for my edification. So, I am mostly in debt to my mother for my good vocabulary.

"What do I talk about, Mama?" Scottie said.

"Talk about the weather. Talk about school. Talk about church. Talk about anything but fishing."

"Won't be much talk. Weather is hot. School is yucky. Church is boring," he said under his breath as he finished his argument.

She heard him anyway.

"Find something to talk about besides your fishing exploits," her tone was firm.

"But that's what I do the best."

"I know," she said in a disgusting tone. "Stretch your young mind and find other subjects. Am I clear?"

"Yes, ma'am," he sounded reluctant, but he was in a bind.

"May I talk about fishing?" I asked, smiling a little.

Her look was stern. She made no reply to my bit of humor.

"I suppose the murders are out of our jurisdiction as well?" I said.

"Absolutely!"

We walked on in silence wondering what there was to talk about with these people who knew us better than our mother seemed to know us. Looked like a lot of silence was heading our way for the afternoon. We'd have to do a lot of sitting and listening. Suddenly a thought came to me. While we were restricted in what we could talk about, she failed to restrict any answers we might offer up to questions posed to us. I felt as if I had an out to my mother's imposed constraints.

We stopped at Aunt Mildred's and Uncle Tom's house first. It was actually the farthest away from our house, but Mama always correctly reasoned that it was easier to leave their house than it was Aunt Nona's. Aunt Nona had a passion for talk. Mama called it *idle talk*.

"Come in, come in!" Aunt Mildred greeted us at the door. "Good to see you. How are you? How's Bill?"

"We're fine, thank you, sis. Bill's working too hard, as usual. He's always working more than they pay him for, but you know Bill." Mama sounded different whenever she spoke to her sister. She sounded friendly, not the way she sounded when she spoke to us.

"Come on back in the kitchen. I'm doing some canning and I have to keep an eye on the stove." She led the way as if we didn't know the house by heart.

"How's Tom?" Mama said.

"Oh, the usual. He's in the back painting. Clancy, you and Scottie go on back. He'd love to see you both."

"We won't disturb him?" I asked.

"Naw. He loves for you two to visit. Go on back."

I was relieved to be separated for a few moments from women's talk. Uncle Tom was really a neat guy who handled his adversity really well.

"Hey! Scottie and Clancy! Good to see you. Come on in and join me. I'm just painting a little ditty you might like."

We walked around to his side of the easel and stared in disbelief at his latest creation. He seldom left the house, except for visits to the doctors. He painted what he saw, he said, from his mind's eye. Sometimes he would dream things and then paint them the next day. He loved watercolors, but he also used pastels. His painting room was a complete disaster, but it was his life and he seemed to love it. Most of his creations hung on the walls of his work area except for two or three of his better pieces he placed on easels around the room. Aunt Mildred displayed some of his art in various rooms of their house.

"What do you think? Colorful, huh?"

Scottie and I were spellbound. It was our secret butterfly world right there on his canvas. He had painted hundreds of flowers and that many more butterflies. It was the most colorful painting he had ever created. The variety of colors seem to explode right in front of our eyes. It was a moment for both Scottie and me.

"Where did you get an idea like this?" I said.

"Dreamed it. Had the same dream two or three nights in a row. Had to draw it to get the image out of my head. I like it, don't you?"

"I love it," I said.

"Me, too," Scottie quickly added.

"Good. Makes me feel better knowing people appreciate my work. Especially such fine art critics like you two. I know it's fantasy and all, but still, it has a lot of color, and that's important to life."

"It's not fantasy, Uncle Tom," Scottie corrected him.

"Say what?"

"There is a place just like that. Out at Mr. Joe's farm."

"Don't kid me like that, guys."

"No kidding," I said. "It's almost exactly as you have drawn it. Millions of flowers and millions of butterflies, at least it seems so when I am standing there in the midst of it. Well, maybe a few less than a million of each, but … wow, there are literally hundreds, if not more. It's a magical world. It's special to at least four people … well," I corrected myself, "three people and one cow."

"You'd better sit down and explain all that to me."

We told him the whole story and he loved it. It was as exciting to watch his eyes dance as it was for us to tell about our discovery of the world he had painted.

"So, you two and Mr. Joe are the only ones who know about this spot."

"Don't forget Bessie Mae!" Scottie said.

"No, we're not the only ones. Daddy, Uncle Walters, and that doctor from Roanoke have been out there, and...," I hesitated, remembering what Mama had said to me earlier."

"And what, Clancy?" Tom said.

"The killers know about it, too."

"Killers?" Uncle Tom seemed to be more than mildly curious.

"The ones who killed Buster and Micah Scruggs."

"I thought Mr. Joe had been accused of that."

"Haven't proved it. I think he's innocent. Daddy thinks that the case against him is weak, but because he's black and because of his past—" I stopped my sentence abruptly, then finished, "Well, it doesn't look too good for Mr. Joe."

"I see. So, who's working to help clear Mr. Joe in this mess?"

"I am."

"We are," Scottie corrected me.

"We are," I said reluctantly, rolling my eyes at my brother.

"Well, I'll say this for Mr. Joe. He's has two smart people on his side, not counting the Sheriff of the county. And, does Mr. Joe have a lawyer?"

"Yeah, but he ain't much. Mr. Joe can't afford a good lawyer, so he got Talbert Young to do it, or rather the judge appointed Talbert Young to handle the case. Nothing like having a part-time preacher and a part-time lawyer on your side."

Uncle Tom laughed at my comment.

"You don't mince words, Clancy, that's for sure."

We spent about an hour with Aunt Mildred and Uncle Tom that afternoon. It was nice to see him working and especially on something so beautiful. When we were leaving, he whispered to us to be careful and to keep up the good work for Mr. Joe. We promised that we would. He also winked at me and told me not to give Talbert Young such a hard time. Tom told us that he thought Mr. Young was a decent enough lawyer.

Our next stop was Nona's.

"Aren't you proud of us, Mama? We never once mentioned fishing." Scottie said.

"But I bet you talked about those two boys who were murdered," she said.

"No, ma'am," Scottie said quickly. "We did not talk about those two boys." He smiled at me, quite pleased with himself at offering the truth of the matter.

However, my mother's point was that we had, in fact, talked to Uncle Tom about the crime of that summer. She knew us only too well.

# Chapter Twenty-eight

"Oh, I am so glad to see you folks I can't stand it. How is everyone on your end of the block? You look so good today, Rachel. How do you keep yourself so young? And these children are so handsome. What ever do you feed them to make them so strong and beautiful? Oh, please sit down and stay with me for a while. I'm so lonely in this big old house. You know I feel so empty here sometimes. It's like I live here alone."

She paused just enough for Mama to answer and tell her how glad we were to be there. Mama was yelling because she forgot that I had told her Aunt Nona had a hearing aid that worked now.

"No need to yell at me, Rachel. I can hear you just fine. In fact, I hear everything nowadays. It's so wonderful to hear again. I have missed so much. All that gossip was just passing me by and, well, now I know so much of what is happening around town, you know. I hear it from Matilda Franklin. She's such a good servant and all. I don't know what I would do without her. She really takes good care of me and tells me everything that is happening in town and in church. But she doesn't live here anymore for some reason. She's got her own place now, and I just guess she's happier living there rather than staying with me. Uncle Herbert must have allowed her to do that before he died. Have you been to church much this summer?"

Uncle Herbert has been dead for nearly forty years, and he arranged nothing for Matilda Franklin who was a little girl when he died. Aunt

Nona was so confused about most things, it was hard to separate truth from fiction with her. Most people just assumed she was crazy and let it go at that. She lived in a fantasy world, and none of us tried to talk her out of whatever dimension she entered before she spoke. It was better for her, we reasoned. Besides, reality wasn't that much fun as I was quickly learning that summer.

"We go every Sunday, Aunt Nona," Mama said.

"Well, that's good. I'm so proud of you and the way you are raising your family. Your mother would be proud of you too, God rest her soul. How is Bill? I think he works too much, don't you? I think he ought to take some time off now and again, just to be with his family. You never know how long you're going to have them. He might not live as long as I have lived. But, he seems like such a dedicated young man. It's so hard to find fault with him about his work habits. Tell me, Scottie, what have you been up to this summer?"

She actually paused and waited for Scottie to answer. I did, too. I could feel that Mama was holding her breath, waiting for the inevitable answer.

"I've spent a lot of time in my room, reflecting, Aunt Nona."

"Reflecting? I see. What have you been reflecting on, young man?"

"Life and death, Aunt Nona."

I cringed a little. He was moving in a wrong direction.

"My, oh my. Such heavy subjects for one so young. Have you reached any conclusions, Scottie?"

"Yes, ma'am. I would rather be out fishin' than helping Clancy investigate those murders."

I closed my eyes and could feel my mother boiling. Her temperature had to be rising quickly. Aunt Nona was oblivious to our family tension.

"Oh, yes. So much nicer, I think, to be fishing and enjoying life outside. Have you caught many fish this summer? I used to fish a lot in my younger days. I would bait my hook with the best of them. Never bothered me any. Worms, chicken livers, guts, you name it, we used it! Caught fish! That's what counts, you know. Caught hundreds of catfish. Is that what you catch, or do you fish for something else?"

"Catfish is the only fish for me. We've caught tons of fish this summer, Aunt Nona. We try to go as much as we can because once school starts, it interrupts the fishing."

"Aunt Nona, we brought you some jelly and pickles. I hope you like them," Mama interjected herself into the conversation about fishing. For whatever reason, she did not want it to continue.

"Oh, you are so sweet, dear. It's no wonder that you have such beautiful and sweet children. I don't know how you do it all. Bringing me foods that you fix and taking care of your home. You're such a special person."

"Thank you, Aunt Nona. You're special, too."

"Oh, no. Not me, child. I'm an old scalawag from way back. I stayed in more trouble than you've ever thought about. I used to get expelled from school at least every month. And some days I didn't even bother to go. Those were the times I went fishing instead, until I was in high school."

She winked at Scottie and at me. I could tell that Mama wasn't really happy about what Aunt Nona was revealing to us regarding her early life.

"Is there anything we can do for you, Aunt Nona?"

"Yes, there is, dear. Stay here with me and talk. I want to know what's happening in Clancyville. I heard all sorts of sordid gossip, you know. Matilda tells me all manner of things that are going on at the church or in town, and I need some verification."

I was laughing inside. My mother was absolutely the last person in Clancyville to know anything about anything, to say nothing concerning verification.

"Well, Aunt Nona, I can't tell you much. I stay so busy with my family and all."

"Oh, I know, dear. You're such a wonderful housekeeper and all. And good cook, too. I know that your children appreciate that good food you give them, and Bill as well. I know that he loves you very much. So, tell me, Clancy, how is the murder investigation going?"

I cut my eyes hurriedly to my mother and saw her cringe slightly. I didn't know what to say. I was caught completely off guard. I just stared at Aunt Nona for a few seconds waiting for some inspiration to hit me. I needed a way out of this present dilemma. My mother was simply too close for me to answer Aunt Nona's question as I desired.

"Well," Mama said finally, "I think that I will go downstairs and see if Matilda needs anything. I'll be back in a few minutes."

She left the room. She excused herself and simply walked away from our conversation. I was bewildered. It was like she had taken her cue to exit stage right. Scottie looked at me in his own bewildering manner. Aunt Nona had won the first round.

"So, tell me, Clancy dear, what's happening?" she said with a wicked smile.

Between the two of us, Scottie and I filled her in on what had happened while our crazy old Great Aunt Nona asked questions about every aspect. I refrained from telling her too much for fear that some of it might get back to the wrong people, since she liked to talk. I certainly didn't tell her the names of our suspects or from where exactly I had gotten my clues. I was relieved that she didn't ask me directly who my suspects were.

"So you believe that Mr. Joe is innocent?" she said.

"Yes, ma'am. We both do. Daddy does, too, but the evidence is against Mr. Joe at the moment."

"What about Betty Ann Greesome?"

"I beg your pardon," I said.

"Betty Ann Greesome, you know, the Minister of Music at our church. What about her?"

"What do you mean, what about her?" I said. My heart was sinking fast. I was trying to hold onto my information about Miss Greesome.

"I mean, is she a suspect? Those could be her initials in that ring you found. And you know she has this thing for children."

"What thing?" Scottie asked.

"Well, this is hard for you two youngins' to understand, but some folks have this thing for children, a sort of sexual thing, if you know what I mean. Well, whatever it is, either a sexual thing or some fascination. Some folks … I don't really know how to put it delicately."

"You mean that they prefer children to adults?" I finally asked.

"Yes, that's exactly what I mean. And she's one of 'em, or so I have heard from Matilda Franklin, who knows everything about everything going on in that church."

"One of them?"

"Oh, yes. I have heard rumors that there's a club. They meet and exchange information and other things. I hear tell that there are men and women in this group."

"You have any names of the people in this club?" I said.

"Well, if you promise not to tell anyone … Ralph Hines, your daddy's deputy. His name's been mentioned."

"Anyone else?"

"That's all I can recall at the moment. No, wait. Some fellow named Barker, but I don't recall his first name. Didn't know the man. And, seems like there's another woman, maybe two. I can't remember, Clancy. Sorry. If I hear any other names, I'll be glad to pass them along to you. So, what's your next move?"

"Same thing we've been doing, trying to discover more clues and follow our suspects around until they make a mistake. We just don't have enough on them. Say, Aunt Nona, you didn't happen to hear where this club meets did you?"

"Matilda didn't know. But you know what I think?"

"What?" Scottie said.

"I think that they meet in the church."

"Oh, they wouldn't do that, would they?" I said.

"Why not? Who would suspect such a thing? Think about it. What better place to carry on the Devil's work than in the Lord's house. You see them meeting there, but who would guess what they were up to? Great place to hide out. I used to hide out in the church, but back then I would hide out with the boys. That was more fun. And more normal, if you understand my drift. But you check that out, okay? I think you might find it interesting. But, Clancy, my dear, do be careful. You were lucky once. Be extremely careful, child. The forces of evil do dark deeds, and they don't care who they hurt."

"Yes, ma'am. I'll be careful," I said, as my mind was racing with this revelation and possibility.

When we left her, Aunt Nona seemed to be in good spirits. I was in remarkably good spirits as well. I had some new leads to check.

"She's crazy, you know," Scottie said.

"Yeah, I know. But, I have to check it out."

"You mean the church?"

"Yes."

"How are you going to check it out?"

"I don't know yet. I'm thinking. I figure that they would be smart enough to avoid the normal flow of people, like on Sundays and Wednesdays. That leaves five days. I could begin by getting a bulletin from Mama and seeing what's scheduled, you know, like meetings and things. I'll just have to do a hit-and-miss stake-out."

"You're crazy. You don't even know if Aunt Nona is right. She could be making it up."

"It's the best lead I've had in a while."

"You don't seriously think that this club would put some announcement in the church bulletin, do you? That's plain stupid."

"No, you're right. They wouldn't advertise their intentions. Still, I might find something suspicious. They could be hiding in plain sight."

"I think you're wasting time. And Mama's gonna get suspicious if you're out every night."

"I thought about that. You'll have to help cover for me."

"Doin' what?"

"We'll start the evening out by playing in your room with the door closed. Then I can slip out, and you stay in your room with the door closed. When she comes up to check on us, you can simply say that we're playing and everything is all right."

"What if she asks you a question through the door, and you're not there?"

"You answer. Short answers. One words. Yes, ma'am. No, ma'am. That sort of stuff. It'll be enough."

"You and Aunt Nona are both crazy. This ain't gonna work, I tell you. I don't like it."

"You don't have to like it; you just have to do it."

Scottie winced.

Mama was walking home in front of us, and we were making our plans several feet behind her. She stopped at one point and waited for us to catch up.

"What mischief are you two planning now?" she began. "How do you think your Aunt Nona was?" she changed the subject abruptly, which meant that she really wasn't interested in our schemes since she believed that we were mostly harmless children. Maybe we were. Then again, maybe not so much. Well, perhaps harmless, but still children full of schemes and notions.

"Crazy as ever," Scottie said before he thought.

"I don't like you talking about your Aunt Nona that way. She can't help the way she is. It's a disease that all old people get. She has hardening of the arteries or something like that."

Scottie gave me a puzzling look. He had no idea what Mama was talking about, and I was wondering a little myself.

"I think she just has a problem with her memory, Mama. She's a little confused sometimes, but she also remembers lots of things clearly, accurately. Better than some folks."

"She's getting senile, too," she continued, ignoring my opinion, "and I just worry about her. We're gonna find her dead one of these days."

That didn't strike me as bad, but then that was my philosophy. I figured we'd all wind up dead *one of these days*, and Aunt Nona had lived a good, long life. I was hoping for a few more years myself, but Aunt Nona had no illusions about living forever. At least she had said as much to us. Besides, I had the feeling she was lonely for her dead husband, Uncle Herbert. I never knew him, but I had been looking at the pictures all over her house of the two of them together as long as I had been visiting her. The pictures showed them standing close together, hugging or holding hands, and always smiling.

"Well, you children don't pay any attention to what she says, you hear? She's disturbed, and I don't want you thinking that she knows what she is talking about."

Mama walked on in front of us, and we slowed down a little in order to continue to make some plans in private.

"I don't agree with her very often," Scottie lowered his voice, "but I do this time. She's right about Aunt Nona and you'd better listen to our mama for a change."

"She may be right, but it's the best lead I've had, and I have to check it out."

"You're gonna get both of us in trouble," he said, shaking his head in absolute disagreement.

# CHAPTER TWENTY-NINE

Daddy was mowing the grass when we got home from visiting our relatives. The house sat in the middle of our property so that he had to cut as much in the front as he did in the back. Still, our allotted grass crop was not that much. I think he enjoyed this weekly summer ritual. He would take his shirt off and walk briskly back and forth cutting our grass in perfect rows. I loved to watch my daddy do hard work. He had such a trim, fit body that it was enjoyable for me to see him sweating in the afternoon sun with what he referred to as *good exercise.*

Sometimes he would let me help him cut the grass by giving me a turn at the old power mower for fifteen minutes or so. I never did like it that much, but I enjoyed doing stuff with Daddy. Scottie liked to help, too. Daddy would give him a much shorter time mowing with that old mower while keeping a steady eye on him.

Mama would simply remain in the house and worry while we were outside working with Daddy. She would always tell him to be careful with us, that one of us was going to cut a foot off with that old mower. She had a good imagination.

Scottie and I only got to mow a few rows that afternoon. We had stayed a long time at Aunt Nona's so there wasn't much grass left for us to help cut. Mama gave us the usual warning before she hurried inside to start supper. After the yard had been cut, Daddy turned the mower up to make some adjustments and change the oil. Scottie went inside to play and I stayed to watch Daddy finish his work on the mower.

"How are the relatives?" he said.

"They're fine. Uncle Tom had a dream and then painted a picture of it. Guess what it is?"

"I can't imagine," he said, still focused on his mower adjustments.

"Butterflies. Thousands of butterflies and flowers in a field! Can you believe that?"

"Well, that is something. Did he know anything about those butterflies out at Mr. Joe's?"

"No, sir. Not a thing. Said he had a dream and was so happy with his dream that he had to paint it. He said he painted it to get it out of his mind, but I know better than that. It's quite good, Daddy."

"Oh, I'm sure it is. Tom's a good artist. He's learned a lot, but he also had a lot of talent to begin with."

"What do you mean?"

"He studied art in college. He was quite good."

"But he wasn't an artist when he got sick, was he?"

"No. His parents wouldn't allow him to major in art in college. He took a few courses, but they insisted that he study law."

"He was a lawyer? I never knew that."

"Pretty good lawyer, too, but he didn't like it. Too much stress, he said. I think that's why he had that stroke. It was just too much for him. He should have been an artist."

"What do you mean by *stroke*?" I asked.

"You know, the accident he had. We've talked about that before."

"I thought he fell from a ladder and broke his back."

"Oh, he did fall, but it was the stroke that caused the fall. A stroke is when you have a blood clot in the brain, for the most part, and then lots of different things can happen to you. It caused your uncle to fall from a ladder, and ... well, you basically know the rest."

"So, what you are telling me is that he was an artist early in his life, didn't get to study it as much as he wished while in college, and then had a stroke, fell from a ladder, injured himself, and finally got to be an artist in the end. Doesn't that mean that he finally got to do what he always wanted to do?"

"Yeah, you're correct, my darling daughter. Quite correct. It just happened for him a few years later."

"It's never too late to do what you love to do, is it?"

He stopped working on the mower and looked in my direction. His eyes were fixed, but they were not looking at me. He was looking at something a long way off. I had never seen that look in his eyes before that moment. Something was on his mind, but it didn't last for long. He finally released that far-off stare, noticed me, smiled, and then went back to work on the lawn mower.

"Are you doing what you love to do, Daddy?"

"Yeah, this mower and I are really old friends."

"I mean being Sheriff and all."

"Oh, that. I suppose."

"Do you love your job?" I asked.

"I like helping people, Clancy. But I don't like dealing with the sordid side."

"Sordid?"

"Dirty. Nasty. Mean. I meet all kinds of people. Most of them are good, decent folk. But there's an element of folk out there that are just … well, evil is the only word which makes any sense to me."

"All criminals are evil?"

"No, but some are. Many are, I suppose. Anyway, that's the part of my job I don't like at all. It makes me mean myself. I have to be mean in order to deal with some of them. I fight it, that is, I fight against becoming mean. It's getting harder and harder."

"Daddy, you're not mean. You could never be mean."

I wanted to hug him but he had his hands full with the lawn mower, and he was sitting in a awkward position. Besides that, he had grease on his hands and splotches of that yucky stuff in a variety of places on his chest. I didn't want to hug the grease. Well, maybe a part of me wanting to hug him despite the grease.

Mama called from the back door and I ran inside to help her set the table for supper.

"Clancy, have you thought any more about joining the church?" Mama said.

It was one of those bolts from the blue. Earlier in the year Mama had said something to me about joining the First Baptist Church of Clancyville, but I hadn't given it any thought since she had mentioned it. I guess the time wasn't right for me, or the interest or the inclination. I was content with the way things were as far as my relationship with the church was concerned. I never could get straight in my mind what difference it made for kids like me to join the church. As long as my parents were members, and I went when they went, why should I have to be a member? If I became a member, then I could go to the long, boring business meetings of the church and vote. Big deal.

"Not really," I said.

"Well, you should. You believe in Jesus, don't you?"

"What's Jesus got to do with joining the church?"

"Why, everything! That's what membership is all about."

"I thought it was about voting in long, boring meetings."

"Don't get smart, young lady. When you join the church, you are saying that you have accepted Jesus in your heart and you want to be a Christian. So, you join the church and are baptized."

It sounded simple enough, but I knew there had to be some catch to it. Adults didn't usually make a big deal out of something that simple.

"Why do you want me to do it?" I said.

Mama was shocked. She couldn't answer at first. She nearly choked on her piece of cornbread. She drank some tea and slowly regained her composure. She stared at me for a long time. I was beginning to get uncomfortable. It was like I had used profanity, except that she wasn't angry. I detected some measure of disappointment in her face. "I want you to go to heaven, Clancy. If you're a Christian, you'll go to heaven when you die. If you're not a Christian, then … Well, it's not a happy thought. It's hard for me to answer. I, … I think you should go talk to the pastor. He can help you with all this. But you need to be interested in making that decision."

I hated it when adults told me what I needed to be interested in doing. It was mostly frustrating to have others try to live your life for you. I already knew that church was important, or why else would we go every week? I knew that Jesus was important, but I had never felt the desire to do what Mama was asking me to do.

I didn't know what to say to her. She had me cornered and I was trapped.

"Would you like to talk with Pastor Flowers?" Daddy said.

Daddy usually stayed out of these religious discussions unless our chatter became heated. He was one of those quietly effective Christians who said very little about church and God. But when he did say something, it was usually important.

Suddenly, a superior idea came to me. It was a revelation, I suppose.

"Okay, I'll go talk with Pastor Flowers," I said it with too much enthusiasm. As soon as the words came out, I knew I had overstated my prior position regarding church membership.

"Now don't go because we want you to go. You should go because you want to learn something about the church," Mama instructed.

"I want to learn something about the church," I said, this time without the added enthusiasm from the idea bubbling inside my brain. This was too good to be true.

I was proud of myself. I actually said it with a straight face. It even sounded sincere. The only trouble was that my words didn't mean what Mama and Daddy likely thought they meant. I wanted to learn something about the church, but not about joining. I wanted to learn whether there was a club that met there during the week. If I could get the pastor to tell me, then I wouldn't have to camp out in the church every night of the week, and my little brother wouldn't get caught in the crossfire between Mama and me.

"I'll call him tonight and try to make an appointment for you as soon as possible."

I nodded and continued eating. This was working out better than I had expected.

After Scottie cleared the table and I had washed the dishes, I wandered out to the front porch to sit in the swing and listen to the sounds of the summer night. There was hardly any traffic on our street, so it was usually quiet except for the normal hum of katydids, crickets, tree frogs, and cicadas. When it came to thinking, our front porch swing on a summer night was almost as good as our fishing hole at the river once you became accustomed to the chorus of critters. I found it both relaxing and stimulating.

Mother Nature was in full chorus on this night. The only unnatural sound was the squeaking of our porch swing as I swayed back and forth. In a matter of minutes I was deep in thought. I wasn't concentrating on anything in particular, but my mind was full of random things dancing around and making me wonder about life, about myself, about people in general, and about my family. Now and then I would mentally shift to a tangential thought regarding Betty Ann Greesome, Ralph Hines, and the poor Scruggs family.

"Little miss troublemaker," it was voice from the dark shadows, and it startled me. I jumped ever so slightly at the sound of it. It belonged to Ralph Hines.

I turned quickly and met the eyes of that despicable man standing on the ground behind my swing. The only thing between us were the railings of our porch. He was standing in a gap of our bushes, not more than four feet away.

"You had better stay out of this Clancy Evans, if you know what's good for you. Mind your own business, little girl. Bad things have happened to children in this town. It's not safe, you know. Bad things often happen at night."

"Why isn't it safe at night?" I said just as the front door opened and Daddy walked out. I turned in his direction as he approached me.

"Who are you talking to?"

I pointed with my thumb over my shoulder toward the gap in the bushes behind me.

I looked back to where Hines had been standing and he was gone. He disappeared as quickly as he had come.

"I was just talking to myself," I said, once I realized that Hines was no longer there.

"What was that thumb signal over your shoulder?" he asked as he sat down next to me.

"Oh, I was just swatting at some gnats bothering me," I said, unconvincingly.

"Nighttime gnats, huh?"

"Maybe it was a pestering lightning bug, you know," I quickly changed to another species of night critters.

"That's generally a sign of old age. Adults do that, but I didn't think that children did it." He made the swing go a little higher and faster.

"Swatting lightning bugs? That a sign of old age?"

"Talking to yourself," he said, laughing at me.

"I talk to myself a lot. It helps, sometimes."

"Yeah, me too. Have you ever argued with yourself?" he said.

"Yes, sir. I argue with myself a lot, as a matter of fact. But I can't tell who wins and who loses."

"That's a tough one. Maybe when you get older you'll be able to distinguish the voices inside your head, and name them. That way you can tell who wins the argument, and who loses it."

"But it's all the same voice, isn't it?" I asked.

"No, ma'am. Different voices. Most of the time only two. One is usually good, and the other is usually looking for trouble."

"How can you tell the difference between them?"

"The good one doesn't talk as much as the one looking for trouble."

He patted my knee and then we sat there swinging for a good while without talking. We listened to the leaves rustling, the squeaking swing, and a dog barking off in the distance. The katydids' song was drowning out the other night critters.

"Your mama's right, you know. You're getting to the age where you need to be making some important decisions."

"You mean about church and all?" I stopped pushing the swing but it kept moving. Daddy was the force behind that.

"That's right. Being a Christian is a serious matter, Clancy. You either accept the teachings of Jesus or you don't. You either decide to live by them, or you don't. As far as I am concerned it has little to do with going to heaven or going to hell. It has to do with living now."

"Well, what I've heard so far is okay. But some of Jesus' teachings are hard or strange sounding."

"Yeah, that's true. Some of them are difficult to practice as well. And they do sound strange to us. But most of the time they work, at least that's the way it's been in my life."

"How long have you been a member of that church?" I asked.

"Oh, my, let's see... maybe fifteen, no ... less than twenty years, Clancy. I'd have to stop and figure it up. But it's a number of years."

"So you were older when you joined. Older than eleven."

"I was. It took me a long time to make that decision. But I thought about it for several years. I guess I was slow."

"Or thoughtful," I suggested. "So, you'll be patient with me, huh?"

"You bet. But," he got up out of the swing and walked to the front door, "I still think that it's a good idea to go talk with the preacher. He should know how to help you."

He went inside and I felt badly about deceiving my parents as to the reason why I wanted to talk with Pastor Flowers. Maybe I could work the discussion with him in such a way that I could do both. I wondered which voice that was.

# CHAPTER THIRTY

The Reverend Mr. Homer Flowers wasn't as busy as I had figured he would be. I actually wondered if I had made the right decision to talk with him since I had a hidden agenda. Still, it was easier for me to get the information from the pastor than to spend five nights hiding out either at the church house, or lurking close-by. So here I was about to face a religious relic in our community, a holy man, someone who might have the ability to see straight through me. He had been the pastor of our Baptist church longer than I had been alive, something like fifteen or so years. I wasn't really in awe of the man, but I did feel the need to tread lightly.

I had never spoken to him privately in all my years. I had never had a reason before now. For all I knew the man had supernatural powers, after all, he was a *man of God*, whatever that meant. I had no way of knowing if I could pull this off. This could be a serious test for me.

My session was scheduled for ten thirty and by nine o'clock I was anything but calm.

"You're like a cat walking around a room full of dogs. Can't you be still?" Scottie said. "What's wrong with you? I've never seen you like this. You'd think you were going to visit some of our weird kinfolks at Thanksgiving or Christmas."

"It's a lot worse than that. I've never had to sit down one on one with a preacher. What if he reads me like a book and knows exactly what I am up to?"

"Run away."

"Run away? Is that your game plan for me?"

"Yeah, get out of town."

"Oh, you're a great help! I can't get out of town, you silly bumpkin."

"Well, you could at least run out of his office."

"That would do no good either. I'd just have to do some major explaining when I got home. You know he'd call Mama."

"Yeah, I suppose he would. Adults are like that. Well, just tell him the truth."

"I can't do that."

"Why not? This is a preacher you're gonna talk to. You can tell him the truth."

"What? Tell him that I don't really want to join the church, and that I only want to know the church schedule of meetings so I can spy on Miss Greesome? I don't think he would be too happy with my deceit, nor delighted with my honesty."

"What's deceit?"

"Lying."

"Oh, that. But if you are telling the truth, then why is that lying?"

"Okay, false pretenses."

"I don't understand."

"I got the meeting with him under false pretenses. In short, I lied in order to meet with him. He wouldn't be too happy with that."

"So what'll you do?"

"Don't know. That's why I'm worried."

We spent forty-five minutes talking and it did absolutely no good. Occasionally my little brother could make some reasonable observations as well as some reasonable suggestions in specific situations, but not this time. By the time I left the house for my meeting, I was a nervous wreck.

The walk calmed me a little. I entered the side door to the large building and followed the signs directing me to the Church Office. The door to the office was mostly glass so it was easy for me to see the lady sitting behind the desk. She was typing something and stopped when I opened the door. There was a name plate on the desk that read

Marjorie Foster. She smiled and told me to have a seat. She said that Reverend Flowers would be with me in a few minutes. She said that the pastor was on the phone with someone and that he would see me when he finished. I nodded, sat down, and said nothing to her.

I don't know how long I sat there, but I was there long enough to start thinking and worrying about what might happen to me in the next few minutes of my life. It was not a happy time. I would rather be out somewhere breaking and entering, even against my father's expressed desires.

"Good morning, Clancy," Pastor Flowers said, interrupting my worrisome internal monologue. "Please come in. Hold my calls, Mrs. Foster. We don't want to be interrupted."

I sat down in the only chair in front of his large desk. It was comfortable enough, but it was much too close to his desk to suit me. I wanted to move it, but I didn't dare since I was already seated and he began talking right away.

"Have you been fishing a lot this summer?" he asked. His voice sounded friendly, maybe even approachable.

He had a soft voice, but not a deep mellow one like Mr. Joe had. It sounded more like the deep voice of a woman to me.

"Yes, sir."

"Successful?"

"I beg your pardon?"

"Have you caught many fish?" he clarified.

"Oh, yes sir. My brother and I have a secret hole at the river and we nearly always catch fish. Must be a big school that lives there."

"Sounds like it. Do you think you might show me where that secret spot is?"

I hesitated just before I was about to answer. My usual response to someone asking me for information about our secret fishing hole was that it wouldn't remain a secret if I told. I didn't want to say that to the pastor. He must have read my mind.

"Oh, I'm sorry, Clancy. Forgive me for asking such a thing. I shouldn't be asking you to give away your secret spot. Wouldn't be a secret long if you told, right?"

"Oh, that's okay. Never hurts to ask," I said, trying hard to control my ever-present fears. At least he bailed me out on that one.

"No, I was wrong to ask you. Please forgive me."

"Oh, no, sir. There's nothing wrong with asking. I just couldn't tell you without first checking with Scottie. It's his secret spot as well. It wouldn't be fair, you know."

"I understand. Now, how may I help you?"

"Well, I've given this a whole lot of thought and I can only conclude that I ought to be honest with you about what I want."

"By all means. I would want you to be honest with me."

"Even if it means that I came here under false pretenses?"

"Well, I don't know about that, but why don't you tell me what your visit concerns. Maybe I can help. Is that fair?"

"Sounds fair. Try to keep an open mind about this, please."

"I'll try, Clancy."

I began to tell him the whole story. I started with the murders, which, of course, he already had heard about, but I wanted to fill him in with some of the details which I knew. If I was going to come clean, I wanted to do it right.

Pastor Flowers listened to the entire sordid mess, plus all of my extra details added to spice up the story. Somehow I believed I could trust him. He never interrupted, he just listened. I figured that he must be okay since he began this so-called religious discussion by asking me about fishing. A fellow like that couldn't be too bad.

I told him about Mr. Joe and all the clues that I had found. I stopped short of telling him the names of the suspects. I wasn't sure exactly how to approach the subject of Betty Ann Greesome. I thought that naming the suspects might be a little tricky, so I stopped at that point to see if he had any questions.

"Well, I must say you have a first rate investigation ongoing here, young lady. You must know that I am quite proud of you for forging ahead in this effort to prove the innocence of Joe Jenkins. That's quite admirable. However, I do think you have been altogether a bit careless when it comes to subjecting yourself to danger. You are aware of the danger, aren't you?"

"Yes, sir. I guess I figured that I could depend upon my daddy, or that I would get out of whatever I got into."

"Like you handled your overnight in the barn?"

"Yeah, like that. I never worried about being killed or anything."

"But you could have been, correct?"

"I suppose so. But the person who kidnapped me never threatened to kill me or hurt me. They just told me to keep my nose out of it."

"Well, Miss Clancy, you might want to remember that if Joe is innocent—"

"Now you're starting to sound like my daddy," I said, interrupting his sentence.

"Well, there are some of us who care about you, believe it not. So, be cautious when you are checking into things. This is really not the sort of thing that a young girl your age should be doing. It's dangerous enough for adults."

"So you're not gonna tell me to stay out of it?"

"Would that do any good if I did?"

"No, sir, not much. I mean, I respect you and all, but—"

"And I believe you respect your parents, too, but I am positive that even if they told you to stay out of it, you wouldn't, would you?"

I was beginning to like him more and more. Maybe I was right about him being able to see through me.

"Mama told me to leave it alone, but that hasn't stopped me yet. You see, I am sure that Mr. Joe didn't kill those boys. Some evidence is still out there that proves him innocent. I simply have to find it, or find something which ties it all together. I already think that I have some clues that point in a good direction. I just need some answers to my questions. I need to find something that proves Mr. Joe innocent."

"Yes, you have some clues, I believe, from what you have told me. But, tell me, why did you come to see me? You didn't come here to confess high treason against your parents," he said and smiled.

"Not exactly. But I need your help. I need to know the monthly schedule for all of the groups that meet here at the church."

He looked a little puzzled, but he didn't flinch at my strange request.

"I think we can do that," he said, after pondering a bit. "But if I tell you that, you will have to promise to tell me something in exchange for such valuable information."

I thought that was a strange request. Something told me that perhaps he was belittling my investigation into this whole thing.

"Like what?" I said.

"Like who are your main suspects and what is the connection between your murder investigation and our church schedule? You conveniently left the names out of your story."

This was unexpected, but it had come down to a major decision. I was either going to trust him or leave without my information. I figured the time had come for me to trust someone besides my father. Pastor Flowers had some information that I needed, and I was curious as to why he wanted to know more. We both had been honest with each other, so it was now time for me to take a chance with him.

"Wait," he said before I could answer, "let me see if I can guess. With what you have told me about your evidence, I think you probably suspect Miss Greesome in some way. But that one is easy. The initials give it away. However, the other one is harder. I am assuming that you have at least two strong suspects."

"Yes, sir." He was doing really well, so I let him talk.

"Am I warm yet?"

"So far so good."

"Good," he said, and he sounded excited. "The other one is much harder. It could be Ralph Hines because of the way he's been acting towards you, but the evidence, unless it is directly related to him—"

"It is," I said, not being able to contain myself. "I think that Ralph Hines is in it somehow with Miss Greesome. That's why I need the church schedule."

"Oh, my. That's very interesting," he said as he stood and looked out of the window behind his desk. "Indeed, Clancy Evans, this is all very interesting."

# Chapter Thirty-one

Pastor Homer Flowers just stood there with his back to me gazing out his study window. I waited for him to explain his mild surprise at the mention of Ralph Hines and Betty Ann Greesome together. It took him a few minutes of contemplation. I don't believe that his problem was that he didn't know what to say. I think the problem was that he was drawing conclusions in his mind while he was thinking of how to respond.

"It has to be Hines and Greesome," he said finally. "If your clues are correct, then it fits."

"Do they meet here together?"

"They came to me a few years ago and asked if a therapy group could meet on Thursday nights. It was for divorced people, they said. At the time it sounded like a good idea. They're still meeting, as far as I know."

"Have you ever attended one of their meetings?"

"No, but I sanctioned it. I trusted Betty. I took the idea to the deacons and they approved it, of course. It sounded like something that would benefit some folks in our community. Maybe I should go to one of the meetings."

"I don't think that would do any good, Reverend Flowers. You show up and they're not going to do anything they usually do. We need to be there, but without them knowing we're there."

"You're a sneaky little girl, aren't you?" He winked at me.

"Sometimes I have to be sneaky."

"Okay, what's your plan?"

"Uh …," I hesitated just long enough for him to take note.

"You don't think I'd let you hide out in this church building alone with the chance that those two are behind the murders, do you? What kind of pastor would do that? We'll do this together."

He winked again, and smiled. At that moment I knew that I could trust him. It's a funny thing about intuition, or whatever it is you call it. I had the gift of knowing people even at the age of eleven. I wish I knew how it worked, or even what it was. But I didn't know back then, and I don't know much more about it now. I just believed that there were some folks I could trust simply by the way they looked.

Pastor Flowers and I planned our strategy. We agreed to meet thirty minutes earlier than the scheduled Thursday night therapy session. He said that he wasn't positive about the room they used for their meeting, so we would have to hide somewhere in the building and then do a search. For an eleven year old it sounded like great fun. Judging from the way his eyes danced when we planned our secret mission, it must have sounded like fun to a fifty-plus year-old minister, too.

When I told Scottie about my meeting with Pastor Flowers, he first thought that I was pulling his leg. He just knew that it was going to be my downfall since I had originally planned to lie to the preacher. He couldn't believe that I actually leveled with him, telling him nearly everything about our investigation. But he was also relieved to know that he wouldn't have to risk life and limb by coming down either to the church house on Thursday night to help me spy on Hines and Greesome, or be a lookout close to the building to alert me if danger approached.

"Are you scared?" Scottie asked.

"No, I don't think so, but that's easy to say since Thursday's not here yet. I'll probably get butterflies in my stomach by the time I'm hiding out in the church waiting for that therapy session to get started. But, I won't be alone."

"Maybe that'll be a good sign—the butterflies, I mean."

"Yeah," I said, "maybe it will be."

I told Mama that the preacher and I had a good meeting, and that we talked about lots of different things. That was the truth. I just didn't tell her everything we had talked about, nor was I specific about any of it. Fortunately, we did talk about religion and about me joining the church and what that meant before I left his office. He explained it rather well for an adult, and I understood better what it was that everybody wanted me to do. My mama had failed to mention anything about baptism being connected with joining the church. That was the one shock that Pastor Flowers mentioned to me. I definitely was not ready to take the plunge, but I told him we ought to talk about it some more and that I would think about it. He advised me to pray about it. I didn't mention anything about my inept prayer life.

I did mention to him that he could help me a great deal to get out of my house on the upcoming Thursday night. All he would need to do would be to set up another session for the two of us to discuss my religious experience. At least that would be what I could announce to my parents. He agreed, but he insisted that at least part of our time together ought to be discussing church membership some more. I gave him that concession since he was willing to help me in chasing down a lead.

Thankfully, Mama didn't ask any questions. Her only comment was that she thought that meeting a child at 6:30 in the evening was questionable, and that he ought to meet with me earlier in the day. I first said that it was summertime and was still light at that time, and then I mumbled something about the pastor's busy schedule. That seemed to satisfy her, but she still wasn't too happy about the idea of a meeting at that hour of the day, summer or not.

By the time I arrived at the church house promptly at 6:30 on Thursday, some butterflies were dancing a jig inside me. I wasn't as pleased with their presence as Scottie had suggested I would be. But I felt a whole lot better when I encountered Pastor Flowers and the two of us went to his favorite hiding place—the baptistry, that special place in some churches where folks are baptized. I had seen several people baptized in my young life; one of them was especially noteworthy. Billy Ray Anderson drank half of the water while he was under, then he surfaced with coughing and spitting before he was able to readjust himself to normal breathing. I was laughing so hard that Daddy made me leave the church.

"Why do you like this place?" I whispered.

"Special place for many folks, and for me as well. This is where it all starts. Besides, no one would ever think of looking for us here. The danger is that someone might hear us if they enter the sanctuary. We just have to speak very softly and not make any abrupt movement. This fiberglass underneath us tends to squeak and groan unless you are careful when you move around."

"You have hidden here before?" I asked him, wondering why an adult would hide out in the baptistry, or any other place in this building.

"Not exactly hiding, Clancy. I come here to be alone. It is quiet. Safe. It's an unexpected spot for a minister to be found when there is no water in it."

He chuckled to himself. He must have been thinking of his position as pastor. Still, I had to wonder why he might choose to come here, of all places in the building. There were no chairs. We sat on the steps.

"But what if someone did find you here?"

"Wouldn't bother me any. I most always bring my Bible or some prayer book to read. It's a good place to talk with God."

"But what if someone finds the two of us here?"

"Well, we'll just tell them I am showing you how baptism works. You don't know how baptism works, do you?" His eyes twinkled at me.

"Don't think so. Never had it done to me, but I've seen you do a few. I just stand here like a statue and you dunk me, correct?"

"Close enough. But there are a few things I can show you when the time comes."

"Can't wait. But for the matter at hand … how are we going to know when the therapy group is all settled in and doing therapy?"

"Good question. You'd be surprised what you can hear in this building when all is quiet and you're sitting here meditating in silence."

"Is that what we're doing, Pastor Flowers?"

"You mean listening for what we can hear in this building?" he asked.

"No, sir. I mean what you said about meditating?"

"Oh, that. Well, no, not exactly what we're doing at the moment."

It crossed my mind to wonder what we were doing at the moment. Despite my appreciation for his help in this, I felt a little odd sitting there in that empty, fiberglass chamber, waiting on some sounds to emerge that would indicate a meeting was beginning, or about to begin.

He must have noticed my apprehension, so he began talking about his own religious experience. He whispered, mostly. Much of what he said to me did not connect simply because I was on another train of thought. I was too much focused on discovering all that I could regarding the therapy group.

After several minutes of listening to him whisper about his experience as a young man, he suddenly stopped talking. We sat there in the quiet. It was mostly awkward for me. I tried hard to remain focused on the mission at hand.

He looked at his watch and then seemed to be pondering something difficult. We sat there in silence for what seemed a long time. Finally I heard some noise coming from another part of the building. Voices. I couldn't make out what they were saying, but it was definitely people gathering somewhere near us.

Pastor Flowers put his right index finger up to the front of his lips just to be sure that I didn't say anything. I complied. We sat there in silence for several more minutes. The voices died down until finally we could hear nothing but ourselves breathing.

"Okay," he whispered, "I think we can leave now. We just need to be careful. It's about ten minutes after seven and I would think that whoever is going to gather is already there."

"Where?"

"I don't know, but we'll find them. I have a hunch."

I followed him out of his secret hiding place as we slowly ascended the steps, then just as quickly, descended the adjoining steps. The wooden floor in the room adjacent to the baptistry began to creak, so we slowed our pace even more.

"I think," he whispered, "that this group might be meeting downstairs in one of the back rooms on the lower level. There would be plenty of privacy there and you could only see the lights from the alley side of the building. Let's try there first."

This building was his territory and not mine. Still, I felt as if I could trust him, so I followed along behind. I thought it was dangerous for us to be walking down the hallway in the open, but there was really no other way to approach the rooms as far as I could tell. As we neared a closed door on the left side of the hall, I could hear some muffled voices. He nodded in the direction of that door and then put his index finger against his lips once again.

We were close.

Pastor Flowers led me into a room on the left next to the closed door room. He pointed to a wall and carefully closed the door to our room. I could hear the voices coming from the other side of the wall. He motioned for me to sit down in one of the cane-bottom chairs lined against the wall. All was quiet except for the sound of the talking. I put my ear against the wall, and, surprisingly, could hear reasonably well. Pastor Flowers did the same after he sat down.

"But what are we going to do?" one voice said. It was a woman speaking, but I didn't recognize the voice.

"No more meetings for a while," came the answer from another female voice. That one sounded familiar. It could have been Miss Greesome, but I couldn't be certain.

"You think anyone suspects us?" a male voice asked.

"Not you," responded a familiar voice. "They know some things, they just don't know much, and besides, they can't prove a thing. There ain't no cause for alarm. We just have to be careful."

The last voice belonged to Ralph Hines. I would have known it anywhere.

"So, we'll stop our negotiations for a while. This is merely a precaution, or … are you holding something back from us?"

"No, I'm not hiding anything. This is just temporary. We'll be back in business in no time. You can count on it. We're just being careful." The voice that sounded like Greesome had an anxious level to it.

"It's that kid, isn't it?" a new male voice said. "I think we ought to just take care of her and our problems would go away. Right Hines?"

"Yeah, I 'spec so," he answered.

"Well, you can bet she's told her daddy a lot, but whether he believes her, we don't know. So, we'll just lay low and stop production."

"I don't like it a little," the husky voice said.

"Our whole business could collapse and we could all go to jail for a very long time if we are not careful," the Greesome-like voice said. "We have to use our heads here. We have to curtail our activities for a while, at least until after that nigger is convicted. We have to have patience now."

"But there is no guarantee that he will be found guilty," another female voice said.

"No jury in this county is gonna set him free on the evidence. He'll die for the murder of those kids. Just watch," Hines said.

"He better," said a voice that sounded familiar, but I couldn't place it right away. I had heard it before, but at that moment I couldn't decide who the speaker was. Detecting the voices, and who they belonged to, was much harder than I had suspected.

"Okay, we'll contact all of you when we need to meet again. In the meantime, don't expect any activity or production. Our contact in Richmond understands the situation. And, be careful leaving here. You two leave first, and then you. Hines and I will wait," the Greesome voice was giving directions. She seemed to be the one in charge of the meeting.

Pastor Flowers eased over to the door of our room and opened it just enough to permit him to look through the crack. I guessed that he wanted to see the people as they walked by. I was still leaning against the wall with my ear pressed against it. I was hoping to catch another word or two, something that might help me to identify someone in that group. Suddenly, my cane-bottom chair slipped on the tile floor. I came crashing down and landed on the hard tiles with a thud. The fall jarred me.

Pastor Flowers quickly shut the door and locked it. He gave me the quiet sign. I froze in my undignified position on the floor. I was embarrassed and frightened at the same time.

Someone tried to open the door. Whoever it was, shook the door-knob and the door violently. Fortunately, the lock held and the door remained attached to the hinges.

"Let's get out of here," Hines said.

No one else spoke, but we could hear people running down the hall-way. We waited a long time before we said anything to each other. I didn't know what to say to Pastor Flowers. I was humiliated by falling and making so much noise, while at the same time relieved that we had not been discovered. We had come dangerously close, but had man-aged to escape detection. At least the therapy group could not identify who we were. They only could guess that something fell in the adjoin-ing room and made a loud racket.

I started to believe that I was like a cat with nine lives, but I was using them up quickly.

# CHAPTER THIRTY-TWO

"Are you okay?" he asked me.

"Yes, sir. Just angry with myself."

"No need for that. It could have just as easily been me that fell. I'm relieved that it wasn't me, maybe even a little surprised. I'm such a klutz sometimes. I stumbled and fell just the other day climbing some stairs. I think I was born with two left feet."

"Nice of you to say so, but I'm the one who fell."

"No harm done, Clancy. They never knew for sure that we were even here. At the very least, they didn't see us. They're the ones who are sweating."

"Well, maybe you're safe and unsuspected. But, considering what I heard through the wall, I don't know how safe I am. Did you see anybody before I blew our cover?"

"I saw Sally Johnson and Rita Anderson leaving."

"Who are they?" I asked.

"A couple of women from the Java community, part of the so-called therapy group. I don't know much about them."

"No one else?" I asked.

"Afraid not. What about the voices you heard? Recognize any?" Pastor Flowers asked.

"Yes, sir, Hines and Greesome were there, I'm pretty sure. Another voice was familiar, but I can't place it now. I know it, but it just won't come to me. Any voices familiar to you?"

"Greesome for sure, but I don't know Hines as well as you do. I think that Greesome is the only one from our church here, at least in terms of voice recognition."

"So we know that Hines and Greesome are doing something, but what? What do you think they were talking about?"

"Detective work is a little out of my field; however, with the clues you told me you had, and with some working knowledge of the sinful side of the human race, I'd say that our little therapy group is into some type of business that uses children. Could be child pornography business," he said. "They didn't talk specifics."

"How do the murders fit in?" I said.

"That is a little harder to say. It could be almost anything. Maybe the two children were involved somehow with these adults ... I don't know, Clancy. That's really difficult to piece together. We need somebody with more expertise than I have for solving that. I wish I could be of more help."

"You can. I need you to talk with my daddy. If you will confirm to him what you and I heard this evening, then that will go a long way toward backing up what I will tell him."

"I'll be glad to speak to your parents on your behalf in this matter. Maybe this will help your father's investigation."

"Thanks," I said, somewhat relieved at having his word on the matter.

We left the building through the front doors. That was Pastor Flowers' suggestion. He said that no one ever used those doors during the week, and that if any of that therapy group had been hanging around watching, they most likely wouldn't be watching the front doors. It was dark outside by the time we left, so it was easy enough for us to slip away into the hot summer night.

Pastor Flowers and I took a back way to my house. I hid in the floor of the backseat of his 1967 Fairlane. He didn't think it would be a good idea for us to be seen together. He said he didn't want to take any unnecessary chances for my sake.

Both Daddy and Mama were surprised when I entered with the pastor. They hadn't expected a visit from Reverend Flowers that time of the night. I told Mama a general idea of the reason for his call, and she surprised me by not scolding me in front of him. She excused herself to go make some coffee and slice a few pieces of her latest apple pie. She always was a slave to domestication and Southern politeness, but I must admit that her Southern hospitality tasted quite good.

Daddy listened carefully to what we had learned from our snooping. We gave him the names, of course, but couldn't identify all the principal players. Pastor Flowers also suggested what could be a possible rationale behind the so-called therapy group, considering all of the evidence we had so far. Pastor Flowers quickly added that he was only guessing, but I thought his guess had some credibility.

My daddy was non-committal, but he listened. When Mama returned with the pie and coffee, the conversation immediately changed, and I excused myself from the adults.

Once upstairs I told Scottie about our adventure, and what we had learned. He was equally impressed with the preacher's savvy. I had a difficult time explaining child pornography as a business worth killing someone over to my little brother. It's hard to explain something you have a hard time understanding yourself. I told him that some people will apparently buy anything, and if money is involved, then murder can easily be added to the crime. My daddy said that business, greed, and murder form an all-too-common trilogy in law enforcement work. Scottie didn't seem too impressed when I told him that.

Some time after the minister had left, Daddy called me back downstairs. I wasn't sure what direction this conversation between us was going to take. We sat on the front steps where we both could see the stars. That was a good start, as far as I was concerned.

"Why did you involve Mr. Flowers in this?" he said.

"He involved himself. I simply told him the truth about why I wanted to see him."

"The truth? What truth?"

I had momentarily forgotten that my daddy was not part of my little scheme to get inside the church, nor a party to my deceit.

"I pretended with Mama to want to know more about joining the church, when actually I wanted to know which night Betty Ann Greesome had a meeting at the church which involved Ralph Hines."

"And why would you want to know that?"

"Because I suspected that both of them are somehow involved in this murder."

"What's that got to do with church?" Daddy asked.

"Aunt Nona told us there was some sort of club or group that meets at the church. Greesome and Hines belong to it. It raised my suspicions enough to check it out. I know that those two are involved in the death of those kids. I don't know how yet, but I believe they're part of it."

"And the preacher just volunteered to help you when you told him all of this?"

"Yes, sir. He said he didn't want me hiding out alone in the church, just in case I might be right about Hines and Greesome. And I was right about them being involved in something. They didn't say enough to use as evidence against them, but they said enough to make me suspicious. Reverend Flowers is also suspicious of them. Didn't he tell you all of that?"

"Some. I guess I have no right to be upset with you since you had someone like the minister helping you, or should I say aiding and abetting you?"

"Both, I reckon. Not sure what *abetting* means," I said.

"Basically means about the same thing as aiding."

"So it's redundant."

He shook his head. The shadows were too dark for me to tell if he was smiling.

"Now where did you learn that word?"

"What, redundant? Oh, from reading, I 'spose. Who knows? I pick up words all the time. Like *abetting*, just now. I'm a growing, learning girl."

"Yes, you are. But I think you're so much more than that."

"You know, Daddy, the preacher's actually a fairly good detective for an amateur."

"You should know."

I smiled to myself, but said nothing. I could tell by the tone of his voice that I wasn't going to get a whipping for doing this semi-dangerous research. But I could also tell that he wasn't really happy about what he had learned from both Pastor Flowers and me.

"Don't you think you owe your mama an explanation?"

I thought, *yikes.* I had not considered that he would come to such a conclusion.

"Well, the truth is we did talk about becoming a member of the church. I learned a lot about all that, so I guess I did what I told Mama I was going to do. I just did a little bit more."

"Little bit more, huh? And the pastor helped you out, huh?" he asked.

"You could say that."

"Come on, time for bed. We'll talk tomorrow morning after breakfast. I'm tired of all this cloak and dagger stuff you love so much."

Next morning after one of Mama's hearty breakfasts, I sat in the black-and-white waiting for Daddy to come out and go to work. He finally emerged some ten minutes later than usual.

"I thought you might be taking the day off," I said.

"Funny, I was hoping the same thing about you."

"No, sir. I don't have time to take any days off."

"Well, do me a favor. I want you and me to do some hard thinking about this messy investigation. We can't just stumble into something, we need to do some planning. Let's consider all of the evidence we have which supports Mr. Joe's claim of innocence."

"Okay, sounds good to me. Let's go."

"No, I want you and Scottie to go fishing. Let Scottie fish and you think. I'll be at the office all morning studying this myself. We'll meet here for a late lunch. Let's say, after one. We'll compare notes then. Okay?"

It was easy enough to agree with my father since he was treating me almost as an equal. I was quite flabbergasted and thrilled to think that he would actually want to discuss the case with me, and to give me the benefit of his wisdom and experience on police matters. I found it quite satisfying that my daddy would want to have a think-session with his daughter.

I suppose the truth was that he figured it would be easier to look after me by having us join forces than for me to continue with my solo efforts. After Pastor Flowers had talked with him the night before, Daddy now knew that the danger for me was increasing with all the snooping I had done.

Mama was considerably less excited about us going fishing than Scottie was. It took practically no time for Scottie to gather up his fishing gear. Mama was torn between having us out of her hair all morning, and being worried about us alone at the river. It was a good thing that Mama didn't know everything that had happened since Scottie and I had stumbled onto those bodies in the barn. She probably would have locked us in our rooms for the remainder of the summer. Check that— she would have kept us locked up until Christmas, or until Daddy had discovered who was behind the whole thing.

After listening to Mama's do's and don'ts about Mr. Joe's place, we headed toward the river for a little fishing and some serious contemplation.

Some time around mid-morning when Scottie was reeling in number eight or nine, I was completely lost in my thoughts about how to proceed with the information we had on Greesome, Hines and their dirty business. The real issue for me was that we had lots of stringy evidence, but we had nothing that tied all of those strings together. I passed the time ignoring the tugs on my line while I was struggling to devise a plan to bind all of our loose-ends. I wanted to develop a scheme to trap my suspects.

"Hey, sis! This one is the biggest yet, don't you think?" Scottie said as he held up what appeared to be a real keeper, as we fishermen say.

I nodded but refused to release my mental focus on the matter at hand—what we knew and what we didn't know. Progress on that was horribly slow.

"The least you could do would be to say something about this beauty," he insisted.

"Great fish, now leave me alone," I said, without looking.

"Hey, did you come out here to fish or what?"

"Or what! Now leave me alone. I have to think."

"Okay, but you're letting the best part of life pass you by. Girls are sure hard—hey, do you smell smoke?"

His abrupt change of subject caught my attention, and I suddenly realized that I did smell smoke. I began to turn in a circle, searching the tops of the trees for some signs… there it was, a large, black cloud rising rapidly from the direction of Mr. Joe's place. My heart sank. I immediately thought that someone had set fire to his house out of a sheer hatred.

"Come on! We've no time to lose," I said as I ran in the direction of Mr. Joe's place.

I reached the opening in the woods where you could first see his place. It wasn't the house; it was the barn on fire. I tried to get close to the barn, but the intense heat forced me to stay back. Scottie joined me seconds later.

The fire was now leaping over into the bushes and the trees to the right and to the back of the barn. Scottie and I moved around toward the front of the barn, easing along the tree line. It was hotter than I would have preferred, but we were still a safe distance away from the flames.

"The butterflies!" Scottie yelled and ran in that direction.

I caught him before he could get too close to the intense heat. I held on to him.

"You can't do anything!" I yelled. "Let's move."

He fought to free himself for a few seconds, and then finally gave up. He was trying to hold back the tears. I moved us back away from the heat to a safer distance across the road where we could watch the burning structure with our own private agonies. I hated the helpless feeling which both of us had at that moment. We just stood there and watched the fire destroy the barn, the woods, and those beautiful flowers hidden behind the barn. The fire was probably killing the butterflies as well. I hoped that some of the butterflies might escape, but I had no way of verifying that hope. Too much smoke, too much heat for me to see any hopeful evidence that those beautiful insects could survive. It was horrible to watch, and horrible to think about those beautiful creatures dying.

"Shouldn't we go get help from town?" he said.

"They'll see the smoke in town. This is huge. They'll be here faster than we could go get them. It's best to wait."

"But there won't be much left," he said. His observation was on target.

"Yeah, I know."

Just then there was a loud explosion and the flames shot skyward in a giant rush. The sudden flash of fire and blistering hot air knocked us both down. The heat had intensified dramatically with that explosion. My heart was pounding faster now. I saw real fear in the eyes of my brother. I helped him up and moved us further down the road towards Mr. Joe's house, away from what was now left of the barn.

In a matter of minutes, it was completely destroyed. The barn fire had nearly burned itself out. However, the fire behind the barn in the woods was still blazing; in fact, it seemed to me that the forest fire was now bigger, more intense.

The noise from the explosion had been deafening. We were both scared. The whole scene was chaotic. I wanted to do something, but it was nearly impossible to think at that moment.

"Where's Bessie Mae?" Scottie said.

I had forgotten about Mr. Joe's cow. My heart sank. She could have been inside the barn or she could have been trapped in the mud hole behind the barn. I expected the worst and tried to prepare myself for it. It was bad enough for Mr. Joe to lose his barn, and for the flowers and butterflies to be destroyed, but it would break his heart if Bessie Mae died in the fire. Scottie and I felt the same way.

I had no idea what to do. I just stood there next to Scottie, holding his hand, watching the black smoke soar from what was left of the blaze.

I said nothing. I refused to give him any false words of encouragement. I could see little that encouraged me.

# Chapter Thirty-three

The firemen worked frantically to subdue the fire in the woods around the barn. The volunteer fire departments from Java, Tightsqueeze, Climax, Sandy Level, and Tagman's Grill showed up that day to aid Clancyville's finest in subduing the forest blaze. The biggest fear was that the fire would consume all of the forests between Mr. Joe's place and the river. It took several hours to finally get the fire under control. It must have been after four by the time most of the departments were closing up shop and heading back to their fire stations.

The Clancyville volunteers were the last to leave. The Chief left a few men on hand to watch for the possibility of a breeze carrying some embers to an untouched section of the forest.

It was a nightmare. It was the first forest fire I had ever witnessed first-hand. After Daddy arrived he made us move even further away. We watched from Mr. Joe's front porch most of the afternoon, after the Climax volunteers had soaked the outside of Mr. Joe's house as a precaution. Scottie and I sat on the wet steps and watched all of the activity.

The fire had such intense heat that the house was nearly dry by the time the firemen had controlled the wooded areas. I was thankful that none of the firemen were injured badly, except for one or two who had inhaled too much smoke and had to be taken to the hospital in Dan River.

Daddy helped the firefighters even though he wasn't a regular volunteer. When the fire was over, he looked as exhausted and as dirty as the rest of the workers.

After the majority of the fire trucks and volunteers had left, Daddy and the Chief of the Clancyville unit came over to the front porch to talk with us.

"How'd it start?" Daddy asked.

"Don't know," I said, shaking my head as if to be more emphatic with my ignorance. "Scottie noticed the smell of smoke while we were at the river. I noticed that the smoke was coming from this direction, and then we ran here as fast as we could. I was scared that it was Mr. Joe's house. Then when I saw that it was the barn, I stopped there. Over there," I pointed to the spot where we had first paused to watch.

"Then what happened?" the Chief said as he lit a cigarette.

"There was an explosion. The heat from the force of it knocked us down and scared us bad. I grabbed Scottie and we ran down this direction several yards, somewhere over there. That's where we were standing when you arrived." I pointed again.

"Any other explosions?" the Chief asked, before he took a long drag on his cigarette.

"No, sir. Just the one. It was like the fire hit something which caused it to increase all of sudden."

"Did you see where the fire increased after the explosion?" the Chief asked.

"In that direction," I said and pointed to the forest behind what was left of the barn, which was practically nothing more than a few black timbers. "Over where Bessie Mae usually hides out."

"Bessie Mae?" the Chief said.

"Mr. Joe's cow. She likes to hide over in the mud near all of the butterflies. I hope she wasn't over there today."

"She wasn't," the Chief said and took another drag. "One of the firemen found a cow way back at the far end of those fences. Didn't know her name, but it must be the Bessie Mae you're talking about. She's the only cow we found. She's safe."

"Oh, that's great," Scottie said.

We were both relieved.

"Sheriff, is it okay if all of us walk over in that direction where Clancy pointed to that sudden burst? I'd like to check out that area. It sounds suspicious, you know. You don't mind if the kids walk along?"

"Sure, as long you think it's safe enough, let's go. Come on kids."

Scottie hesitated.

"I don't want to go, Daddy," he said.

Our daddy looked a little surprised, but he seemed to understand.

"Sure, Scott. You stay here with…" he looked around for one of the firemen who was still on duty, "…Charlie, keep an eye on Scott here. We're gonna walk a bit."

Charlie Rowland nodded and moved closer to the porch. Scottie sat down in the rocker without saying anything. Charlie sat down on the steps of the porch.

"Clancy, you know the way to Bessie Mae's spot. You mind leading us?" the Chief said.

"No, sir." I headed off slowly. I had no idea what to expect from all the fire damage. I figured it wouldn't be good. It was like walking in the woods after a heavy rainstorm. Everything was soaked. The chief difference was that everything was also charred, leafless, and dead.

Finding the trail was not as easy as I had thought. With the barn mostly gone, and the heavy underbrush turned into ashes, I had no markers to guide me. I used my instincts along with what I could remember. It was still smoking in some places, but for the most part it was an easy walk. Just painful to see the natural beauty destroyed.

Of course, all of the flowers were gone, as were the butterflies. It was sad to walk through that area and see the destruction, but the absence of the butterflies was particularly painful. It made me feel heavy, like I was carrying someone else's burden. Maybe this was why Scottie didn't want to come with us. He was sensitive like that.

I stopped at a spot that I thought should have been the edge of Bessie Mae's mud hole. Everything around us was the same black color as the fire-damaged places we had just walked through, so it was difficult to tell precisely where the black mud-hole had been. Something told me that this was the spot.

"Is this the place you referred to earlier?" the Chief said.

"I think so, but I can't be for certain. I can't tell if that is mud there or something left over from the fire."

I started to take a step to test my suspicion when the Chief and Daddy stopped me.

"Whoa, Clancy," Daddy said. Let the Chief test the area."

I watched the Chief put on some heavy gloves and take some kind of rod from his canvas bag he had carried on our trek. He began poking the ground until he could decide what it was.

"Yeah, this is likely the spot."

He spoke to no one in particular. He lifted the rod to his nose and sniffed it several times. This was Clancyville science at work in the twentieth century. I said nothing.

"Sheriff, smell this."

Daddy took the rod and sniffed.

"Gasoline?" he asked.

"That's what I think."

The Chief walked to another spot some fifteen feet away and stuck the other end of the rod into the ground. He lifted it and smelled again.

"Same thing over here, Sheriff. This place has had gasoline poured all over it. Somebody wanted this section to burn. Clancy, you say you saw the barn on fire before the trees caught fire?"

"Yes, sir."

"But the explosion came from this direction?"

"I'm pretty sure it did."

"I think I'll go back and check for gasoline at the barn. I have an idea we'll find some evidence there unless they just lit a match to whatever was inside it."

"It had hay as well as some odd pieces of lumber on the inside," Daddy recalled and relayed to the Fire Chief. "There was a lot of kindling in that old structure."

"Oh, yeah. That was where you had found ... the two bodies," the Chief said.

Daddy nodded without answering.

"I'll go check for some accelerant. I'm already thinking gasoline, since it was used out here."

"We'll be along directly, Chief," Daddy said as we both watched the Chief walk back through the charred forest until he finally disappeared.

"Don't you think it's strange that our Fire Chief smokes cigarettes?" I said.

"Lots of people smoke."

"Yeah, but the Fire Chief?"

"Be kind, Clancy."

"I just think it's stupid or something."

"Probably, but get used to it. People don't always think about their actions or habits. We're all guilty to some extent."

"Well, I think and you think. What's so hard about that?"

"You need to develop a little more understanding of the human condition. Most people don't think, and most people don't like to think, at least not about their habits, the things they do every day. I'm just lucky enough to have a daughter who uses her brain," he winked. "Now come on and help me, and stop worrying about the smoking Fire Chief. You walk around that way in the circle, and I'll walk around this way. You think that this is the spot where we found those clothes?"

"It's a guess, but, yes, I think it is. At least we're close right here. So what are we looking for?" I asked.

"A reason to set fire to this mud hole. Somebody went to a lot of trouble to pour gasoline in this spot. I figure someone's trying to hide something."

"Don't you think the fire probably destroyed whatever … you know, whoever wanted whatever to be destroyed got it done, don't you think?" I said.

"Maybe," he said as he moved along slowly, looking down and searching diligently.

We separated and walked in opposite directions. I went to the right. It was like the time we were searching for the clothes except that there wasn't much black, swampy mud this time around. I was lucky enough to find a solid stick that had miraculously survived the inferno without disintegrating into ashes. I used it to poke and prod what was left of the mud. It was not nearly as mushy and soft as it had been before the fire. Most of the water in the swamp had evaporated, I guessed.

When we were within twenty feet of meeting each other on the other side, I noticed a mound of something out from us a few feet, and just a little off center of what used to be the middle of the swamp.

"Daddy, look out there. Wonder what that is? I don't remember that."

"Think it's been added?" he asked.

"It wasn't there the last time we were here. Or we failed to notice it. You think it's safe to walk out there?"

We had not ventured out into what was the former swamp as yet, so neither of us were certain about the stability of the ground in the middle. Daddy held up his hand as if to hold me at bay and stepped out into the area we had carefully avoided.

"I think it is fairly solid. Come on, let's see what this mound is."

The ground was soft but firm enough to permit walking. I sank in a little as I walked, but what was left of the mud didn't come up too high on my tennis shoes. We were still waiting on the Medical Examiner to call with a report on the composition of the black swamp liquid.

I arrived at the mound first. I began poking with my stick. It was charred earth like most of the other land around us. There was just more of it in one location. The temptation to feel this strange burned earth was too much for me. Just as I was about to take a handful, I saw a human hand slightly unearthed on my side of the mound.

I gasped.

"What's wrong?" Daddy said, as he came up behind me.

"Someone's buried here," I said calmly.

"Stay where you are. Don't touch anything."

I pointed to the hand as he approached. I could now discern some other parts of a body mostly hidden under the blackened mound. It was lying face down. I watched my father gently begin to slowly scrape the dirt from around the body. He worked for several minutes while I watched.

"Do you think he died in the fire?" I said, finally.

As soon as I had asked the question, I realized that the body was that of a woman. It was the hips, at least that's where my mind ran to at the moment.

"Could be, but we can't tell from looking."

"Can we roll the body over?" I said.

"Ordinarily I would say no, but in this instance there's not much we could do here to destroy the crime scene unless we removed the body entirely."

"That mean yes?"

"Yes, ma'am. You mind helping me turn the body?"

I had never touched a dead body. I had considered touching Buster and Micah when I discovered their bodies in the barn, but I stopped short of actually doing it. I had been close to their bodies at the funeral home when I was there to smell them. But there had been no touching. I had been asked by my daddy, the Sheriff, to help him move the body. This was like some official request to actually touch a dead person.

We rolled the partially charred body over and I was amazed to discover that the underside had not been burned as much, probably due to the soft mud of the swamp now caked on the whole underside of the carcass. It was obvious that the body was a female. Her face was completely covered in soft, black mud. I watched Daddy wipe the gunk away from the face of the victim. After one or two swipes, we both knew who it was.

"Betty Ann Greesome," he said.

# CHAPTER THIRTY-FOUR

My bath that evening was one of those rare occasions when Mama actually helped me to bathe. I didn't mind that particular night, since my chief desire was to rid myself of the mud and whatever else was out there in that horrible place. I scrubbed and she scrubbed, and by the time I was finished, my entire lower body was red from our collective aggressive fierce cleaning ritual. I didn't object. I felt clean after the ordeal.

After I dried myself, Mama rubbed some skin cream on my legs, and that really felt good. It was the first time in my life that I could recall her doing anything like that for me. Of course, she could have done that when I was a baby and I wouldn't have remembered it. But for my waking years, my years of awareness, it was a first.

I went to bed early mainly because the events of the day had tired me completely. I suppose finding a dead body, even one suspected of being a participant in a crime, could easily have that effect on a person.

I slept late the next morning, and by the time I arrived downstairs, Daddy had been long gone. Scottie was up and playing with his cereal. Mama was fussing about something at the stove. I could hear humming coming from the ironing area. I knew that Sarah was busy with our clean laundry.

"Are you hungry?" Mama said.

"A little."

"I fixed some biscuits and bacon. Would you like anything else?" Her voice sounded extremely kind. Her tone was not the fussing one. She must have thought that I had been injured somehow in the fire. I wondered how long I would be able to milk this kindness.

"Biscuits and bacon sound good to me."

"Get your juice out of the refrigerator," she ordered.

Everything tasted especially good that morning.

Scottie asked to be excused from the table and said nothing to me, not even a good morning. Usually I got a grunt out of him or a slap on the back of the head. I got nothing.

While I was wolfing down my third biscuit filled with strawberry jelly and topped with bacon, the doorbell rang. A few seconds later Sarah led Pastor Flowers into the kitchen. He sat down at the table with me.

I scrambled around to find a napkin. I just knew I had food on my face coming from the enjoyment I had with that jelly biscuit.

"Good morning, Clancy. I hope you are feeling okay this morning."

Mama served him coffee with cream and sugar. I found a napkin and wiped my mouth vigorously with several passes.

"Yes, sir. I'm feeling fine."

"You had quite a day yesterday," he said.

"Every day seems to be going that way lately. It'd probably be real nice if I had one of those long, dull, boring days for a change."

Mama stared at me as if I had broken two of the Ten Commandments.

"I'll bet you do," he took a sip of his hot coffee. "Oh, my, this is good Rachel. Thank you. Hits the spot."

"Why, thank you, Reverend Flowers. Would you like something to go with it?"

"No, thank you, Rachel. This is perfect."

"Well, if you two will excuse me," Mama said, "I have work to do upstairs. Sarah and I have some jobs that require both of us."

She left the kitchen quickly. I couldn't imagine what task upstairs would require both my mother and Sarah since my mother expected Sarah to do everything but cook. The other thing was that Sarah remained downstairs in the laundry space, ironing and humming softly. Maybe it was some prearranged meeting that the two of them had planned earlier. Maybe not.

I was chewing my last bite of jelly-bacon biscuit, and Pastor Flowers was now drinking longer swallows of his coffee that had no doubt cooled a little.

"What do you make of this, Clancy? This is a real turn of events, huh?" he said.

I wondered how Pastor Flowers had learned what had happened yesterday. It was still morning and I knew that my daddy was not likely to be advertising our discovery of Greesome's body around town.

"Yes, sir, it is. Don't know what to make of it yet. A bit frustrating, you know. Just when we had a lead to follow, the trail dies."

"Or was killed," he said.

"Yeah. I don't think they'll find it was suicide. Somebody didn't like her very much."

"Or just wanted to get rid of her. Maybe you were right about her and someone believed it was necessary to remove her. Any ideas who did it?"

"No, sir. There wasn't too much to go on at the crime scene. But the autopsy ought to provide something. But I have no idea what that would be. I'm still new at this."

"What'd your daddy say?"

"Nothing to me. I slept late this morning and he was gone before I came downstairs to eat. I'm on my way to see him in a few minutes. You got any ideas?"

"Me? No, … hey, I'm just a clergyman. What do I know about crimes and murders?"

"Well, I'm just an eleven-year-old kid. What could I possibly know?"

I understated what I really thought, but I have learned that it's not a good idea to brag about my accomplishments in the presence of adults.

"You've a sharp mind, young lady. And you have a good sense about this … kind of stuff. Insights. Deductive skills. You also know people and their behavior better than many adults. You use what you have very well."

"Thanks. It's nice to know someone older appreciates my talents."

"You're welcome," he smiled and finished his coffee. "And I'm not alone in my opinion. Mr. Joe Jenkins thinks the same as I do."

"You've been to see Mr. Joe?" I said.

"A few times. Just to help keep his spirits up."

"Doesn't he have his own pastor?"

"I don't know. Perhaps he does, I suppose, but it never hurts to have people come to see you when things are going badly. I've never seen another preacher visiting him. He's never mentioned anything about attending a church to me. I visit lots of folks in the community, even people like Joe Jenkins."

I wasn't sure what he meant by that comment, and I really didn't want to know what he meant. I let it fall.

"I'm sure he appreciates you visiting," I said.

"He seems to."

He slid his coffee cup and saucer towards the middle of the table. The conversation seemed to die on its own. It was one of those awkward moments that sometimes occur between two people when there doesn't seem to be anything else to say. I waited for him to speak. He seemed to be waiting on something, too. After more awkward time passed, I decided to act. I couldn't stand the tension in the room.

"Would you like some more coffee, Reverend Flowers?"

"Oh, no, thank you, Clancy," he seemed to awaken from his private thoughts.

He tapped his fingers on the table a couple of times, and stood up.

"I'll show myself out. Just wanted to check on you and be sure that you were okay. We're sort of partners, I suppose."

"Thanks. I'm okay. Just worried about … well, you know."

"Yeah, me too," he said and walked out the back door.

The screen door slammed shut while he was walking down our back steps. I waited expectantly for my mother to appear and seek retribution on the culprit who had dared to slam a door in her house. I couldn't wait to tell her that it was the preacher.

I thought about that partner comment he made as we was leaving. I had no such thinking about him in that manner. Besides, I really didn't know him all that well. And, to note the obvious, he was a minister.

Hines was in his usual sitting position behind the desk when I arrived at the jail.

"Whataya want?" he snarled at me.

I ignored his question and started past him to the back of the building to visit with my friend. He jumped from his chair and grabbed my arm before I could get to the door. I tried to wrestle free from his hold, but his grip was too tight on my upper arm. I continued in vain to struggle against his strong hand. Finally, I resorted to my womanly wiles and kicked him in the shin as hard as I could kick. I figured that tennis shoes needed a lot more thrust than regular leather shoes. He quickly released my arm, grabbed his hurting ankle, and leaned against the wall to keep from falling. He yelped some non-discernible sound, clutched his wounded leg while raising it from the floor. I noticed some dried mud on his boots. The mud had some black specks embedded in it. It appeared to be the same type of mud that I had walked through yesterday.

After I entered the jail area, I closed the door and took a deep breath to gain my composure. I was both satisfied and relieved by the time I was able to speak to Mr. Joe.

"Good morning, Miss Clancy," he said. "And what have you been up to so bright and early today?"

"Oh, I was just dancing with the devil. How are you, Mr. Joe?"

"I be fine, Miss Clancy. And you be careful dancing with the devil. You could weave a tangled web with him, you know."

"Does that mean I would be working for the devil or against him?"

"It means that even you are not smart enough to outwit the devil when it comes down to it. Just a word to the wise, my good friend."

"I'll keep that in mind. I suppose you have heard about the fire?"

"Yes, ma'am. Your daddy came in last night and we talked a long time. I'm just glad that you and Scottie are safe."

"Sorry about your barn."

"It can be rebuilt. I've been needing to rebuild that old structure for a year or two. I'll start on it as soon as I can, provided that I get out of this place. Barns can be replaced. It's a bit harder with people."

"Bessie Mae's okay. That's some good news."

"Yes, ma'am. Glad to hear that, too. She's been good to me for a long time."

"I guess you know that Greesome's death is not a good thing."

"I know. I don't believe anyone's death is a good thing."

"She was a strong suspect on my short list."

"I understand."

"No, sir, I don't think you do. I'm running out of clues and suspects and possibilities and ideas … It's bad, Mr. Joe, really bad."

"Now, Miss Clancy, you can't go and give up on me."

"Oh, I'm not giving up on you. I'm giving up on me. I'm just a little girl way over her head in this mess. I can't seem to find the ends that fit together. And just when I find something or someone, that something or someone leads to nowhere."

"Oh, Miss Clancy, you can't give up on you either. No, no, no, no … a thousand times no. That'll never do, young lady. You're my only hope. Maybe you just need a break for a while. Rest some. Think some. Go fishin'. Do something enjoyable. Relax a little. I'll be okay in here. So far, so good."

"We don't have time for that, Mr. Joe. There'll be a trial any day now, and I just can't prove anything, although I know you're innocent. It's frustrating!"

"Yes, ma'am. I understand the pressure, but you can't give up. I have a strong feeling that something is bound to happen. Something in my bones is telling me that something good is just around the corner. I've been doin' a lot of thinking myself about all this. And you know what I've concluded?"

"What?" I said.

"I think that the people behind this whole mess are not too intelligent."

"You mean like stupid?"

"Yes, ma'am … like that."

"Then why can't I catch them?"

"Well, think about it. You have caught them, at least some of them. Maybe most of them. The leaders, that is."

"But one of them is now dead."

"That's my point. I think that she was killed by one of her own kind, a partner, somebody in it with her. And Clancy, that was, to use your word, stupid. Really, really stupid. Somebody made a mistake, and I think it's gonna hurt them sooner or later."

"Well, it better hurt them sooner than later, 'cause we're running out of time."

"Patience, child. You've got to have the patience of a black person."

"Whataya you mean?" I said.

"I've been waiting all of my life for acceptance by white folks. I've been waiting to be a part of the American family. Just because my skin is a different color, I'm treated as something less than whole. Sometimes, less than human. I'd love to change that right now, overnight. But it won't happen like that. So, I have to be patient. Long patience is required. You have to be patient, too. Trust yourself. Trust the belief within you that what you are waiting for is right, good, honest, and just. That's what I keep holding onto."

"I wish that I could … you know, have the faith you have, Mr. Joe."

"You can, child. You can. You pray much?"

"Pray? What's that got to do with any of this?"

"Maybe nothing. Maybe everything. I just asked a simple question."

"Every now and then I pray. I say a blessing at a meal, sometimes. Once in a while I say a prayer before I zonk out at night. Nothing regular."

"Well, then God knows your voice at least, right?"

"I guess so, but sometimes I wonder."

"You remember why my grass is so green, don't you?"

"Yeah, you put that manure-mud all over it."

"And I pray. I pray for green grass while I spread manure-mud all over it. One is just as important as the other is, for me. I ask and I do. You been doin' … a lot of doin'. Now maybe it's time for you to do some asking."

I didn't really have an answer for him, but before I could say anything at all, the door opened abruptly, and Hines shouted at me to get out. We exchanged hard looks, I rolled my eyes, and then sighed loudly. I decided it wasn't worth my time or energy to go at it with the imbecilic deputy.

I said goodbye to Mr. Joe, and then looked out the front window of the sheriff's office where Hines had been busy doing his usual nothing during my visit. There was a large crowd gathered in the street around the front door. They were angry and shouting.

"What's going on outside?" I said to Hines.

"Nothing I can't handle. You git outta here!" Hines said.

"Oh, I bet you can handle that crowd. What do they want?"

"This nigger here."

"What for?" I said.

"They're aiming to have a lynching party, at least that's what they're shouting. They seem to be working up a good froth towards it. I'd help 'em myself, but since I'm the law, I guess I'd better try 'n stop 'em. Now you go on and git outta here a'fore you get lynched yore self!"

He didn't sound too convincing to me about trying to stop them because he was the law. I decided it might be better if I stayed.

# CHAPTER THIRTY-FIVE

I figured that Daddy was out at Mr. Joe's investigating yesterday's fire and the death of Betty Ann Greesome, and there was no way he would get back to town anytime soon. I also figured there was no way that Ralph Hines would risk his life to protect the likes of Joe Jenkins, a black man accused of killing two white children. I had a strong hunch that even if Hines wasn't part of that lynch mob, he would at least behave kindly towards them, and maybe even let them have the prisoner without much fuss. He could always lie about it later.

Somebody had to do something, or Mr. Joe would be dead shortly.

It crossed my mind to run to the river and get Daddy back to town as fast as possible. I dismissed that idea quickly when I realized that it would take at least thirty minutes for me to run to the river, and then ride back in Daddy's car. That was more than enough time for the mob to lynch Mr. Joe.

I had read some about lynch mobs in history, but I had never seen one. This was 1973 and I didn't know any people who were still into lynching. My experiences were severely limited. I had watched a few cowboy flicks; however, I really didn't know all that could happen. I did decide that they wouldn't do a lot of jawing with Hines, nor would he want to engage them in very much conversation, since his sympathies were with them. There was no way I was going to trust the likes of Ralph Hines to do anything close to right.

Before Hines could usher me out of the front door, I made a quick and major decision. I turned and kicked him once more in the same shin. I tried to kick even harder this time. I must have been halfway successful since he grabbed his leg and fell to the floor almost simultaneously. He yelled even louder this time. He cursed his pain and me.

I retreated into the cell area. I was making up my last stand at the Alamo as I went along. This was all new for me, but I believed that if I left that jail I would never see my friend alive again. Something told me to stay and take my chances.

"What's going on, Clancy?" Mr. Joe asked as he moved to the front side of his cell close to me.

As I closed the door to the cell area, I noticed that Hines was on his feet again. He was still cussing and rubbing his shin. A bruise on top of another bruise is a painful experience. I was pleased.

I was hoping for a lock on the cell area door, but I had no such luck. No lock on the inside. I leaned against the door as if my weight could stop the likes of Hines or any other adult person who tried to enter.

"There's a crowd of folks outside coming to pay their last respects to you, Mr. Joe. Oh, man, I wish we could lock this door!"

"You can. See that long piece of wood there in the corner? Lay it across those iron hooks attached to the wall," Mr. Joe advised.

I obeyed his instruction and we were secure in our prison from the mob outside. It was a small miracle. Whoever had thought of that security measure maybe had a lynch mob in mind. Whatever the reason, that log-bolt was what we needed to remain safe inside the jail. There was no other way in or out except through a couple of barred windows high up on the walls. They would take a good deal more time to remove.

I felt better, even relieved a little.

"Open this damn door, Clancy!" Hines yelled at me.

He was shaking the old door something fierce while he screamed.

"Don't think so, Mr. Deputy. I'm going nowhere and neither is Mr. Joe. We'll just stay right here until the Sheriff returns, thank you."

"You're breaking the law, Clancy. You're gonna get in trouble over this."

"Really? What law is that? Is that one of those lynch laws?"

"Don't get smart with me, girl. It's not safe for a little girl like you to be inside there with a murderer," he shouted through the door.

"A sight safer in here than out there. I wouldn't want to change places with you. I'd say it's fairly dangerous for you on that side of the door."

I heard him cussing to himself as he shook the door another time. There was no way that man alone was going to knock down that door and get to us.

"Why don't you go talk to that crowd and get them to go home," I suggested to him.

"Why don't you go to hell, you smart-aleck kid. You're always meddling in things that don't concern you."

"Yes, sir, that seems to be my nature. But until they make a law against that, you'll just have to live with me and my wonderful personality."

He cussed some more, but didn't shake the door again. I think that even he knew it was futile for one man to break it down.

I could hear the crowd through the door now. The outer office sounded like it was full of people. I could hear angry voices, mostly loud ones, and impossible to distinguish. I could even hear some women's voices. That surprised me. Of course the men would be there, but I expected more intelligence from the women of the town.

"Women are out there, too, Mr. Joe," I said.

"Anger is no respecter of gender."

I leaned against the bar on the door, and then placed my ear against the wood, listening to the voices. Then I heard a familiar voice. It was one of the same voices I had heard the other night at the church. I still couldn't recognize who the speaker was, but it definitely was one of those voices.

Too many loud voices were speaking simultaneously for me to make sense of what they were saying. I continued to lean against the door trying to focus my attention on one speaker. I had no idea what I was going to do next. I had no idea what they were going to do next.

I had two things that I desperately wanted. I wanted to go find my daddy, and I wanted to let Mr. Joe out of his cell. Neither of those wants was going to happen anytime soon.

"Open this door now, little girl! We can't be responsible for what's gonna happen to you!" This was a new voice yelling at me. Hines had been replaced.

I decided that there was no point in yelling back anything to the people on the other side. I'd just save my energy and think. I figured that thinking would serve us better in this frightening situation.

"Have you any ideas, Mr. Joe?" I said.

"Nothing comes to mind, Miss Clancy, … except maybe praying."

"What are we going to pray for?" I said.

"Intervention."

"Does that mean my daddy, the Sheriff?" I said.

"Something like that, only bigger."

"You pray, and I'll sit over here and think some more. This could get a lot meaner, fast."

It must have been at least half an hour before anyone on the other side of the door yelled anything specifically at us again. The den of noise from the mob had been constant during that elapsed time, but nothing had been directed at us that I could tell. Mr. Joe was on his knees by his bunk with his head bowed. It appeared that he took his praying seriously. It was the first time in my life that I had ever seen a grown person on their knees praying, that is, any adult other than a preacher. Come to think of it, I had never seen Pastor Flowers praying on his knees. It wasn't something adults normally did in our church. We kids were taught to kneel by our beds, offer our prayers, and then climb inside the covers. Adults must have been excused from such practices, or so I thought. Maybe Mr. Joe's upbringing held onto him.

It had been a year, maybe two, since I had been on my knees beside my bed praying. I couldn't recall exactly when I had stopped that ritual.

I sat down in the corner by the door next to the wall opposite the cells. I wasn't about to turn my back on that door, and get on my knees. If that angry mob came busting into this room, I wanted to meet them face to face. I just hoped that God understood my predicament, and would tolerate my non-kneeling prayer-posture. That, or God would pay attention to whatever Mr. Joe was asking and ignore my lack of proper ritual position.

I could hear Mr. Joe's voice but I couldn't make out his words. He seemed to be engaging God in quite a conversation, but I couldn't discern specifics.

At some point, I decided to offer some words myself, but I kept my eyes open and my head up. I didn't have enough faith to close my eyes or bow my head in such a crisis.

"God," I began, "I hope you recognize who I am. This is Clancy. I apologize for not talking to you more often these last few years. I have plenty of excuses, but I won't go into that now. We've got a terrible situation, and we need some help. My daddy's out at Mr. Joe's place, and he doesn't know that these people have come here to lynch my friend. If they get inside this room there isn't much I could do to stop them. I hope you appreciate our difficulty here. I'm not so worried about me, to tell you the truth, but I surely would hate for Mr. Joe to die like this before we can prove his innocence. It would be really great if you could get word to my daddy and send him here quickly. One more thing, God, just to be sure you understand what is happening here … we're running out of time."

I stopped talking and waited in silence. It was then that I noticed Mr. Joe had stopped praying, and was looking at me. He must have been listening to my prayer because he was smiling. He went back to his conversation with God while I sat and waited on whatever was going to happen next.

When I told God that we were running out of time, I had no idea how accurate my words were. The moment after Mr. Joe returned to his prayers, there was a loud crash against the door. It shook me so hard that I fell forward. Within a few seconds there was another crash against the door.

"Hit it again, it's startin' to give some!" someone yelled.

"Bert, get over here and help us. This damn thing is heavy," another voice shouted.

Another hard blow landed against the wooden door. The whole door started to give a little, first cracking at the hinges, and then moving along a center line from top to bottom. I was standing next to Mr. Joe's cell by this point. I could have retreated further back down the single hallway, but there was no use to do that. I knew the mob wasn't after me.

It would only be a matter of time now before they would be in the room with us. Whatever it was that they were using to ram the door was working effectively. I figured that somebody on the other side must have been praying for them. Whoever it was appeared to be more effective than either Mr. Joe or myself in this prayer business.

The door began to split in larger cracks, both top to bottom and side to side. The large wooden beam that had kept us safe was beginning to crack as well. I moved to the front of Mr. Joe's cell door. He was still on his knees praying. I could feel the fear rising inside of me. It was horrible. I wondered if people who are about to die by some extreme method ever felt what I was feeling. No way to know, except for what I was experiencing at the moment.

More of the door was splitting now. It wouldn't take much more for the mob to get inside.

"A few more swings and we're in," someone said.

"Heave, boys!"

There was a loud thud. The door cracked enough for me to be able to see the lower part of some bodies at work on the other side. Large splinters of the wooden door were falling all around me.

"Again!"

Another thud was heard. The door was definitely not going to hold.

"Again!"

This time the bolt broke, the top hinge pulled out from the door jam and one of the men simply pushed over what was left of the door and several men climbed through. Some man pushed me away from the front of Mr. Joe's cell door, and another man unlocked it. It wouldn't have surprised me at all if Deputy Hines had given them the keys.

Mr. Joe was still praying. He seemed oblivious to all the commotion going on around us. I was amazed at his calmness.

My mind was racing. I was completely useless. I noticed that none of the men in the mob had weapons with them. If I had only been bigger and stronger, I could have engaged them in a fight. I would have lost, no doubt, but at least I could have tried to physically stop them.

As it was, I was too little, too weak, and too outnumbered to prevent anything that these desperate people wanted to do to my friend. Our situation was hopeless. I could only stand there in shock and watch.

They grabbed Mr. Joe from behind while he was still praying, and began to drag him out of the cell to wherever it was that they were intending to hang him. I sank down against the outside cell wall and began to cry. I hated my gender at that moment. I also hated my age and my size. I was a little girl who simply could do nothing to stop these angry people from killing a man I loved. I was powerless. I was a weakling.

It wasn't fair.

I normally wasn't a person who cried, at least not very much. The next few minutes changed all that. I made up for lost time in the crying department. I put my head between my legs and sobbed. I was furious, but I had no other way to release the tension. I was mad at the people who had come to take Mr. Joe away, and I was angry with myself for being so weak and so stupid. Then when I realized that God hadn't paid any attention to my prayer, so I was angry at God, too. The only thing I could do was cry.

I'm sure that it was the sound of the shotgun that brought me to my feet, and stopped the tears. While I waited for whatever sound might be next, I dried my eyes quickly with my hands. I heard no voices since the crowd had already moved out of the jail office into Main Street by this point. That shotgun blast suddenly made everything deathly quiet. My heart sank. The first clear thought I had was that they had shot Mr. Joe instead of lynching him.

My next thought was that it was my father. My heart was renewed. He owned a Harrington & Richardson 12 gauge slide action that could fire five rounds without reloading. He used to tell me that in his line of work he often needed more than two shots like many shotguns offered. He seldom used the gun, but he kept it clean and ready in case it was needed. It stayed in our kitchen closet next to the broom.

I moved in the direction of the sound of the shotgun.

As I was climbing through the broken door, I heard a familiar voice say, "Where is my daughter?"

I didn't hear anyone answer the question. I stumbled into the outer office and hurried toward the outside door so I could see what was happening in the street.

Before I could reach the door, there were two more shotgun blasts. I froze.

"She's inside the jail," someone finally said.

"Go get her," the voice said. It wasn't my daddy talking. It was my mother.

# CHAPTER THIRTY-SIX

I walked out of the jail building and into the street. The mob parted just enough for me to walk through a small opening. They were standing at the front of my daddy's office and facing the street. Mr. Joe was sitting inside of Aunt Nona's car, the one she had given my mother years ago. My mama was wielding my daddy's shotgun as Ma Barker had done in one of those old movies I had seen just after school was out. At least that's what I was reminded of at the moment.

She moved the barrel of the gun left to right, and then back again. There was no movement in that crowd. Nobody made a sound. All eyes were either on my mama, or the barrel of the gun. It was hard to tell which.

"Clancy, get in the car," she said.

I wasn't about to argue with her. It crossed my mind to say something stupid like "Where's Daddy?" but I didn't. We didn't need Daddy. My mama had complete control of the situation. She and the gun had control.

I climbed into the back seat with Mr. Joe.

Sarah was sitting behind the steering wheel of Mama's Studebaker Hawk. As soon as I was safely inside, Mama backed around to the rider's side, Sarah leaned over and opened the door for her, and then Mama climbed in slowly. She acted as if she had done that hundreds of times. It was reminiscent of a getaway scene from a bank robbery in yet another movie I had seen.

"Let's go," Mama said forcefully.

Sarah pushed down too hard on the accelerator so we burned rubber as we sped down Main Street of Clancyville leaving behind us what could have only been a stunned lynch mob.

I grinned broadly at Mr. Joe. He nodded back.

I was speechless. Mr. Joe leaned over and said, "Intervention."

"Are you okay?" Mama said.

"Yes, ma'am. I'm fine."

"You could have been killed," she said.

"They were after Mr. Joe, not me," I said in my defense.

Sarah ran a red light as if it was the most natural thing for her to do. We were going home as fast as Sarah could get us there. I had no idea that Mama's Hawk could go that fast.

"I know who they were after, but you still could have been killed! Don't you ever do anything so foolish again!"

I decided not to answer that. She was upset, and she was still holding onto that shotgun. Sarah was making excellent time through the streets of Clancyville. It didn't take us long to get home.

When we came to an abrupt halt in our driveway, Mr. Joe said, "Thank you, Lord."

Mama was sitting on the front porch in the swing with the shotgun across her lap when Daddy pulled into the driveway behind the house. Sarah was on the back steps with a rifle. Mr. Joe and I were safely in the kitchen drinking lemonade, sandwiched nicely between our two armed guards. All that danger had made me thirsty. Mr. Joe seemed to be calm, but I was still worked-up over the whole business.

Daddy walked into the kitchen and smiled.

"Well, I can see that the prisoner is still being closely guarded."

"Yes, sir. I'm under house arrest," Mr. Joe said.

"You okay, Clancy?"

I ran and hugged him. I didn't say anything at first. I just needed to have somebody hug me. It felt good to have my daddy hug me at that moment. I'm not sure I can explain why. Mama had been too busy from the time we had arrived till now to provide any hugging. Besides, I don't think that she was quite willing to lay down that shotgun just to hug her daughter.

"Another busy day, huh?" Daddy said.

"Yes, sir."

"Let's go check on your mama," he said.

"I'll stay here, if it's okay with you, Sheriff Evans," Mr. Joe said.

Daddy nodded at him.

We walked together, arm in arm, to the front porch. I stood by one of the columns while Daddy sat down in the chair closest to the swing. He took the shotgun gently from Mama's lap, opened it and checked the number of shells, then closed it and handed it back to her. That surprised me. I thought he might keep the weapon and return it to the closet.

"Hit anything?"

"Only what I was aiming at," she said.

"I'll bet you scared them pretty much."

"Hope so. They scared me."

"I was scared too," I added.

"Do you think they'll come here?" she asked.

"I don't think so. You took the air out of their balloon. And seeing you with a shotgun was probably enough excitement for most of them today." He smiled at Mama. She returned his smile as she relinquished the gun back to him.

"I heard that Sarah was driving the getaway car."

"News travels fast," Mama said.

"Didn't know Sarah had her license."

"She doesn't. This was her driving test. She passed," Mama said.

Several moments of silence passed between them and I thought the conversation was over. I moved towards the front door, opened it, and looked back at them. They were both standing at this point, and then Mama embraced Daddy. I hadn't seen them do that much in my life.

I left them to their hugging and went on back to the kitchen to check on Mr. Joe.

Sarah helped Mama with supper, and we had one huge meal. You name a vegetable, and we had it. Mama even got Sarah to fry some chicken for us. It was great. Sarah was as good a cook as my mother.

"Why are we eating like this in the middle of the week?" Scottie said.

"We have company, silly," Mama said.

I looked at Mr. Joe and smiled. Sarah was even sitting at our table, too. That was also a first for my family. It had turned into a rather good day after all.

"Can Joe stay here?" Scottie said to Daddy.

"Mr. Joe is welcome here tonight, but we'll have to make other arrangements tomorrow," Daddy said.

"Why can't he stay longer? It's safe here," I said.

"Relatively safe, as long as Sarah and Mama are sitting around with loaded weapons. But we can't live like that. Besides, Mr. Joe is still a prisoner of the state of Virginia and Pitt County, and I have a responsibility to see that he is locked up securely."

"So where's he going?" Scottie said.

"Probably Dan River. I put a call into the police over there and I expect to hear back soon."

"Thank you for this fine meal, Mrs. Evans. You and Mrs. Sarah make a good team no matter what you are doing."

"Why, you're welcome, Joe. And thank you for the compliment," Mama said, and smiled. Sarah nodded without speaking.

For the first time in my life I was proud of my mother. I couldn't remember her ever doing anything before now that had made me proud to be her daughter. This was big. I was not only proud of her, I was suddenly proud of the fact that one day I was going to be a woman. Maybe one day I could save someone like my mother had done on this day. She showed a lot of courage, and it made me feel safer just knowing that she was in the house with me.

I was sitting on the back steps when Daddy left for the jail house the next morning.

"Fishin' today?" he said.

"Doubt it. Need to stay around and keep an eye out for Mr. Joe," I said.

"Fishin' might help to get your mind off yesterday, and clarify some things still unknown."

"I've been thinking about it, Daddy. I'm not so sure I want to get my mind off the details of yesterday. Mama was something else, wasn't she?"

"Indeed, she was. You see why I married her?" he said as he hurried down the back steps and then stopped in the yard before reaching his official car.

I didn't answer his question. I figured he didn't need me to answer it.

"Try to stay out of trouble, okay?" he said.

"Yesterday wasn't my fault, you know."

"No, reckon not. But you did jump in without hesitation."

"The way I saw it, I didn't have a choice."

"Guess not," he said and turned to walk away. "Just like your mother, huh?"

He opened the car door.

"Anything on Betty Ann Greesome yet?" I said.

"Yes, ma'am. Seems she died of a heart attack."

"She wasn't murdered?"

"Well, funny thing about that. The back of her head was ... missing. It seems that someone was with her and put a weapon inside her mouth and shot her. But she died of a heart attack before the shot was fired. My guess would be profound fear at having that gun thrust into her throat just before someone pulled the trigger."

"Doctors can tell stuff like that?" I said.

"Apparently. It could have happened simultaneously, but the M.E. said he believed her heart stopped before the bullet took its toll."

"Wonder why she was out there?" I said.

"Don't know. I couldn't find anything yesterday when I was there. And just in case you get any ideas, you let me do the investigating out there, okay?"

"Have a good day, Daddy," I said as I moved hurriedly from the back porch to the car to hug him. "Dan River police coming after Mr. Joe?"

He climbed inside his vehicle, and then rolled the window down.

"Don't know. Haven't heard back yet."

"So, I'm in charge of the prisoner?"

He nodded without answering, and then drove away. It was good to have the Sheriff of Pitt County trust me.

I found Scottie playing with his soldiers. It took some coaxing, but he convinced me that fishing would be the best medicine for me. He argued that we could do some really fine thinking at the river. I told Mr. Joe that I would bring him some fish for supper. I was hoping that he would still be around at that time.

I checked with Mama to be sure it was okay for Scottie and me to head out. She said it was fine. That was the gist of her acknowledgement. It was fine.

As I was leaving, I noticed that Mama's shotgun was leaning against the wall between the back door and the kitchen cabinets. It was conveniently located so that she would be able to grab it quickly if she saw anything unusual from her kitchen window. I heard humming coming from the living room. It had to be Sarah, since she was the only one who hummed around our house. It would be years later that I would learn that Sarah had her rifle with her while she was busy doing her regular chores for as long as Mr. Joe was a guest in our home.

"Are we still investigating?" Scottie said as we walked along the dirt road toward the river.

"Yes."

"I'm fishin' and you're investigatin'?"

"Something like that. We have to bring home fish. I promised Mr. Joe some for supper. Besides that, Mama would be suspicious if we don't. Maybe this is the way she figures she can control us … you know, allowing us to fish but requiring actual fish when we return."

"Yeah, I know. I don't mind. I'd rather fish than go lookin'. I don't like detective work. It's too boring for me." He gave me a gentle shove and laughed.

"And waiting on fish to bite is not boring?" I said.

"I don't have to wait long for the fish to bite, as you know, sister-dear," he said, with sarcasm.

I stayed at the river with Scottie long enough to catch a few fish. He was bringing in one when I slipped away to go look around the mud-hole. If Betty Ann Greesome wasn't actually murdered, then she had to have a reason for being out here. Then I had a thought that maybe she wasn't out there of her own will. Someone may have taken her to that place, or coaxed her to come there, shot her without knowing that she was already dead from the heart attack, and then, just maybe, set fire to the woods to try to cover up what they had done. I was proud of myself for this extremely plausible theory of the crime. It then came to me that my theory was likely some obvious conclusion and I lost some enthusiasm for my discovery.

I stopped at the spot where Daddy and I had found her body. It seemed to be dryer than it was the day we dug her out. I circled the spot several times where her body had formed a sort of outline in the mud. I was hoping for some clue there to explain her presence. I found nothing.

As I was leaving to return to Scottie, I spotted a bank of dirt near what was left of a large tree that had been nearly destroyed in the fire. It appeared that someone had recently been working the soil. I used my hands to dig. There seemed to be more dirt above the ground than that dried mud concoction all around me.

In a minute or two, I unearthed a small wooden box. I carried my treasure to Joe's house to clean it some before opening it. I found an old rag on his wheelbarrow handle and I wiped down the box. I then washed my hands at the spigot and dried them on a clean spot of the same rag.

I sat down under one of the oaks in Mr. Joe's backyard to examine the contents. This was more exciting than reading one of Arthur Conan Doyle's mysteries with his master detective.

The box was about the size of the cigar boxes I had seen in my grandfather's house years ago. It had a lock on it, but I soon discovered that the box was so old that the large, singular top hinge slid right out of its hole. I pried opened the lid slowly to see if I could get inside the box without damaging the other hinge. I managed quite well.

The box belonged to Betty Ann Greesome, or so the contents suggested to me after several minutes of shuffling through the items inside. I found many old photographs of people I didn't know, several rings, some keys and a diary. The small diary had a faded red plastic backing with the barely legible imprinted words *My Diary* in the upper right section of the front cover. It was locked as well.

I studied the photos carefully. There were several pictures of children, fully clothed, and marked on the reverse side with one, two, or three drawn stars. There was a picture of Buster and Micah standing together with several trees around them. It could've been a setting in a forest. They looked frightened. Their photo had three stars on the back side.

I also discovered some photos of Betty Ann Greesome with Hines, along with several other people I didn't know. I thought that maybe these were shots of the therapy group. I shuffled through them, pausing at each photo to be certain that I either knew or did not know the people pictured.

Then the surprise photo of the box was in front of me. It was an older photograph of Ralph Hines and Donald Scruggs' wife, Ruby. They were standing close to each other, heads together, and they were holding hands. They were very young in the picture. If I had to guess, it appeared to be a photograph of two people who were very much in love, but then, my experience with that sort of thing was severely limited. It was dated 1960 on the back.

# Chapter Thirty-seven

By the time Scottie showed up with the largest stringer of fish I had seen in several weeks, I had gone through the entire contents of the box and was now simply studying the photo of Ralph and Ruby, the one that had captured my attention.

The more I looked at it, the more I was absolutely convinced that the two people in that picture were in love despite my lack of knowledge of such things. It looked like one of those photos you take on your honeymoon or some special date. I had seen some shots similar to that in my Aunt Nona's photo albums as well as my own parents' picture collection when they first were married. The date on the back of the picture is what puzzled me.

I had been piecing together the information which I had been discovering in my investigation. Somehow or other, I had concluded that Ruby and Donald Scruggs were already married in 1960. Perhaps I had assumed that through my naïveté. Buster and I had been born in 1961. Somewhere in the data-center of my brain I had filed the fact that I was a whole month older than Buster. I had been an August baby and Buster came along in September. I simply backtracked to conclude that Ruby and Donald were already married at least 9-10 months prior to his birth. My failure to comprehend and certainly to experience the ways of the world added to my confusion and questionable deductions on this point.

Maybe Ruby knew Ralph before she married Donald. Maybe Ruby knew Ralph at the same time she knew Donald. Maybe Ruby was seeing Ralph while she was married to Donald. It was all unsettling to me. I would have to check with Aunt Nona to see if she knew anything about this. I figured that Mama and Daddy would be of limited help.

"What'd ya find?" Scottie said.

"A locked box," I said.

"Where?"

"In the mud hole. Someone buried it. I think it belonged to Betty Ann Greesome. She may have buried it."

"Anything interesting in it?"

"At least one thing—a photograph of Ralph Hines and Ruby Scruggs," I said.

"What's so interesting about that?"

"They're standing rather close to each other."

"Close? What'd ya mean? Lettme see," he insisted. He laid his stringer of catfish on the grass and I handed him the photo.

"Close," I said again.

"They both have that same stupid grin on their face. They look like they just got married," he said.

I was suddenly gratified that my little brother agreed with me about one thing.

We cleaned fish for at least an hour when we got home. Mama seemed pleased that we had caught so many. There were green beans already cooking on the stove for supper. She said that we'd have cornbread and slaw to go with the green beans and the catfish. It all sounded good. In the meantime we ate tomato sandwiches for lunch, and then Scottie and I headed for Aunt Nona's soon after we finished eating.

Matilda let us in and told us that Miss Nona was upstairs in her room. We bounded up the steps and ushered ourselves quickly into her room unannounced. She was reading a large print version of the latest edition of some magazine.

"Well, to what do I owe this visit?" she said to us as we plopped on the floor in front of her wheelchair. Aunt Nona did not need a wheelchair. She managed to get around quite well for her age. She had told us that she sat in the wheelchair simply because it was comfortable enough and it gave her a faster mobility on this floor of the house.

Aunt Nona laid her small magazine face down on her lap as she waited for the answer to her question.

"We need information," I said.

"What kind of information would an old woman like me have that's any good for two youngsters like you?" she said sharply.

"Gossip," I said.

"Oh, that kind of information. Well, I have plenty of that. What can I do you for?"

"You mean, what can you do for us?" Scottie corrected her.

"I said it the way I meant it, now what do you need to know?" she laughed.

"Any old gossip about Ralph Hines and Ruby Scruggs?" I said.

"My, oh my, you two are into ancient history today, huh?"

"Not so ancient, Aunt Nona. I'm only eleven years old," I said.

"Not too long away from twelve, if memory serves," she quickly corrected me.

"I'm almost ten!" Scottie announced.

"Well, I see. Add the numbers together and you get 18, huh? I'm sitting here in the presence of age and wisdom. Now, let me see, what do I remember about Ralph Hines and Ruby Scruggs? Well, Ralph moved into our town when he was a scrawny young teenager. He and his family were from Richmond, I think. Some place near Richmond, some small, rural township ... can't recall the name. Sorry. He was a smart-alecky kid. Didn't have many friends. Didn't play sports as I recall. Not very popular. And Ruby, well, she was a looker in her day, but not now, I'm told. I haven't seen her in years. She was a Whittaker before she married that Scruggs guy."

She was silent for a moment and I thought she was thinking of more stuff to say.

"Well, what else do you need?" she asked finally.

"Oh," I said. "I thought you were thinking of more gossip. Don't you know any juicy tidbits about those two together?"

"Tidbits ... together? What are you talking about?"

"No rumors about them seeing each other or anything?"

"No rumors, child, just facts. Lots of facts."

"Tell us the facts," I said.

"You're not old enough to hear such things," Aunt Nona said.

"If I'm old enough to ask, I'm old enough to hear."

She laughed. I didn't think what I had said was all that funny. I was being serious.

"You sound like your old Aunt Nona with that logic of yours. But I don't know about Scottie here."

"He knows more than you think."

"I would not be surprised at that," she said. "Well, let's see how I can tell you what was going on back then. It seems that Ruby Whittaker took up with Ralph Hines in high school. Back in the late fifties. He was a year or two older than Ruby, I think. They got married on the sly one weekend, came back to town, announced their newly formed union, and within a month Old Man Whittaker, Ruby's daddy, had the thing annulled. He flat out called it off because she was underage. Only other thing I remember about all that was Ralph Hines being furious. He was so mad at Ruby's father that he went off someplace, got roaring drunk, then came back to Clancyville and destroyed some property."

"Does *annulled* mean something like a divorce?"

"Well, in a way, I guess. More like *let's pretend that it didn't happen.* When you annul a marriage, you terminate the thing as if you didn't do it in the first place. Rather stupid, if you ask me. You're either married or not. You can't go around saying you weren't married at all when you were. Stupid word, stupid idea."

"That was in the fifties, you say?" I asked.

"Yes, ma'am, somewhere between 1955 and the end of the decade. I don't remember dates so good anymore."

"When did Donald Scruggs come along?"

"Oh, yeah, him. Well, he was already out of school. He's a lot older than Ruby. He was working or doing something, I don't remember."

"Do you remember when they got married?"

"Well, it was, of course, after that annulment thing with Ralph Hines. I think, Clancy, it was around 1959 or 60. I can't say for sure.

That seems like a long time ago, even for an old woman like me who's lived nearly ... forever."

"Did Hines ever see Ruby again after their annulment?"

"Yeah, at least there was a rumor going around about that. But no proof. Just some hot gossip. I guess she still had the hots for him even after she was married to Scruggs. Oh, forgive me. I didn't mean to say that to you." Her face actually turned a shade of pink.

"Don't worry about it. I think I know what you mean; at least I know enough to know that if the gossip was true at that time, then Ruby Scruggs and Ralph Hines were more than just good friends."

"Yess'im, you could say that. In fact—no, no, no. I don't think you need to hear that."

"What?"

"Nothing, child. Say, why don't you two go downstairs and tell Matilda to fix you some cold lemonade. Taste mighty good on a hot day like this. And if you see the Captain, tell him I wish to speak with him."

"Great idea," Scottie jumped up and ran from the room before I could get my legs uncrossed.

I was a little worried about this Captain person she talked about. I didn't know if she was hallucinating or just doing some wishful thinking. I thought it best to ignore it for the moment.

"Tell me, Aunt Nona. I want to know all you know about Ruby and Ralph. It's important, or might be."

"Child, it was just gossip," she said in a more serious tone now that my little brother had left us. "Nobody had proof ... we just knew that something was going on. Nothing ever came out about it. If it was true, it was all hush-hush. I would imagine by now you know how folks can get. And back then, well, things were different."

"Aunt Nona, that's only thirteen or fourteen years ago. How different could things be now?"

"Oh, child, they were different. Seems like every decade is different. I sometimes sit here and wonder about the future: what on earth is it gonna be like in the nineties? Or beyond? But I won't be around then, so it won't be my problem. It'll belong to you, girl. It'll all be yours. The Captain and I will be long gone by then."

"Thanks, but I want to know about the past, especially what happened between Ralph Hines and Ruby Whittaker."

"Gossip was that she had both babies by Hines."

"Buster and Micah?"

"The same."

It was time for another long talk with Daddy. I still had two hours before supper, so I knew that Mama wouldn't need my help for a while. I called Daddy at his office. Luckily, I found him doing paper work.

"Can we meet and talk?"

"Whatcha got?"

"A small box with some clues inside."

"Wishful thinking, or do you really believe you have something?"

"I really believe we have something, but I don't know exactly what it means. That's why we need to do some together-thinking."

"Okay, let's do it. It's after three, so we should have time before our food is served. I'll meet you at the corner of Henry and Franklin. Be there in five minutes."

I was on time, and he was late. Nothing unusual in that. Daddy was late to most things unless Mama was in charge, and then he was always early.

He pulled up to the curb of Franklin Street and I got into his black-and-white. He drove around town as if he were doing his patrol work, which I guess he was. We talked.

"Here's the box," I opened it and he glanced down at the contents. "You might want to pull over and look at this photograph."

He stopped the car in front of Suzie and Cecil Jones' old two-story house about halfway down Franklin. I handed him the picture of Ralph Hines and Ruby Scruggs. I looked around to see if anyone was watching us.

"Won't they get suspicious that we're sittin' out here like this in your car talkin'?" I said.

"Yeah, they might, if they were home. Old Cecil is highly suspicious, and Suzie has issues with her nerves. But, since they're in Florida, I doubt it we'll draw a crowd."

"This time of year?"

"Doctor visit, I think. Suzie can't find any doctors in Virginia who suit her."

He studied the photo of the two young people.

"Interesting."

"If you add Aunt Nona's information, then it gets better."

"You mean Aunt Nona's gossip?"

"Yeah, that. But at least it's a start."

I told him all that Aunt Nona had said. He listened as usual without asking questions. He rolled his eyes a few times, but didn't make any comments.

"And Scottie heard all of this?" he asked.

"No, just some of it. He left the room for lemonade just before she told me the part about Buster and Micah being fathered by that fine and dandy deputy of yours."

"You mean the town gossip that alleges Ralph to be the father," he corrected.

"Yessir, the gossip makes that claim. Maybe some small truth there?"

"I've wondered, but I don't like to rely on gossip to make a case against somebody. And you say Scott was out of the room when Aunt Nona revealed this colorful data?"

"He was."

"Good. He doesn't need to hear all that. I would like for one of my children to have a long, healthy childhood."

"Hey, my childhood is healthy."

"What childhood? You're snooping around with me trying to solve a double murder … check that … it's now a triple murder we have on hand. You're eleven years old and you're investigating murder, incest, and pornography. Your aunt tells you about affairs, and people having babies out of wedlock. What kind of childhood is that?"

"Advanced?"

He cut his eyes at me, but didn't say anything. I took the picture out of his hands and studied it.

"It all causes me to wonder what kind of father I am to my two children," he lamented.

"I think you're a perfect father, Daddy. I like helping you in this investigation. Besides, I'm doing this for Mr. Joe."

"Since I allow you to do this, you would think I was perfect. Clancy, I'm a long, long way from perfect. Just ask your mother. And doing it for Mr. Joe? ... well, there is some truth in that, but I think a larger truth is that you relish this stuff. And here's another truth—you're good at it, but if you ever tell your mother I said that, I'll deny it."

"I think there's something here," I said, ignoring his comments for the moment. "My hunch is ... this is major. All we have to do is figure out what it means."

"Easy, huh? This is what detective work is all about. You have a clue, you know you have a clue, but you haven't a clue as to what the clue means."

"So we're clueless to the clue."

"One other thing, Clancy," he said.

"Sir?"

"I think we have more than one clue staring at us."

"From the contents of the box?"

"What about the box itself? I'd like to know who buried it ... and when."

# CHAPTER THIRTY-EIGHT

"I think she buried it," I said, pointing to the woman in the photo that he was now holding.

"Ruby?" he asked.

"No, Greesome," I said, correcting his question as I pointed to the photo in my father's hand in which Greesome appeared.

"Greesome," he said.

"Yes, sir," I spoke slowly, succinctly and rather determined to make my point. Somehow I knew that I was onto something. I just didn't know what. I continued, "I think she was hiding some evidence that she didn't want anyone to find. I do mean no one. She wasn't just hiding it from you, the law."

"Let me see that box again."

He took the box and dumped out the contents on the seat between us. I looked around, still being cautious of our small town even though Suzie and Cecil's house was on one of the back streets of Clancyville where there was little traffic. Likely half the town had never been on this street. However, there could be a curious person or two watching us, wondering what we were doing parked here.

"Look at that stuff," he said after he spread it around the seat.

I studied it for a minute or two.

"What made you think it belonged to Betty Ann Greesome?"

"Well," I looked at the contents on the seat and searched for an answer. "Rings and ..." I didn't know what else to say.

"Is Betty Ann in any of those pictures?"

"Yessir. She's in some of them."

"Is she the major subject?"

"What do you mean?"

"The focus, or the person in the center of the photograph?"

"Well, she's part of the group," I said, not really knowing where he was going with his question.

"She's one of many, correct?"

"Yessir."

"Anything in this box that has Betty Ann's name on it?"

I took my time studying the items on the car seat. I found nothing with her name or initials on it.

"No, sir. I guess not."

"But there are lots of pictures of Ralph Hines, right?"

"Yessir."

"And lots of photos of Buster and Micah."

"There are some photographs of other children," I said.

"Yes, but they all have their clothes on," he concluded.

"But what about the stars on the back of some of the photos?" I asked.

"Could mean anything," he said.

"So what's your point?" I asked.

"My point, daughter, is that you jumped to a conclusion about the owner of this box. You found it where Greesome's body was buried, or close to where, and you assumed that it was her box because of the proximity of her body and the buried treasure you unearthed. I didn't readily agree with you, but I had the same feeling at first. But the general contents don't prove that she was the owner of the box, nor do the specific photographs. We have nothing here to suggest that she buried the box."

"We need to open this diary," I said, picking up the small object and turning it over a few times to see if there might be another way to get inside it without the presence of the key.

He took out his penknife, pulled open a small blade, and began working on the lock. He was extremely careful as he inserted the point of the knife blade into the lock mechanism. I fumbled through the other items on the seat and found a small, plastic picture frame with two small photos of babies. The small frame was bulging slightly, so I turned it upside down and shook it. A small key fell into my lap.

"Try this," I said, and handed it to my daddy.

He closed his knife and returned it to his pocket. He used the small key I had discovered, and opened the locked diary. He read the first page or two slowly and then handed me the book.

"Humor me and read it aloud," he said.

I opened it to the first page in the book.

"This diary belongs to Ruby Jean Whittaker Hines Scruggs," I read the handwriting slowly. Each letter was large and round-shaped. It reminded me of a child's script.

I turned to the next page and began reading the first entry.

"*July 8, 1959. I felt the baby move inside me early this morning. I know that Ralph is going to be so happy about this. I know that it is our child and that Donald had nothing to do with it. I know. I wish that I could tell everybody that this baby is mine and Ralph's. Donald would kill all of us if he knew. I believe that with all my heart. It is our little secret. I want to share this little secret with everybody. It has to be our secret. We have to keep this secret maybe forever. That is funny. I don't laugh much, but some things are funny, really funny. I do not believe this is a little secret. This is big.*"

I flipped over several pages.

"Oh, listen to this: '*August 1, 1959. A butterfly landed on a flower outside my winder this morning. I tried to kill it, but it was gone when I got outside. I still hate them. They make me cry.*'"

"Strange, huh?" I said.

"Yes, ma'am. That's enough reading for you today," he said and gently removed the diary from my hands. "Let me read it first, and then, maybe, you can read it. Maybe. No promises."

I understood his tone clearly, so there was no need to ask questions. He wanted me to see that the diary clearly belonged to Ruby. That was his motivation for permitting me to read some. Despite my precociousness, I did know some of my limits, especially with him.

Scottie's catfish and Mama's extra fixings made for a great supper. We had more fish than we could eat over several suppers, even with Mr. Joe joining us for the feast. Scottie outdid himself with the catch, but we both took credit for it. Scottie didn't mind covering for me, since he was able to brag that he caught the most as well as the largest. I was not in a position to argue. He knew that.

Scottie leaned over after he had boasted about his accomplishments and whispered to me. "Leverage," he said.

My little brother was becoming a quick study.

Mr. Joe would be leaving us tomorrow. Daddy had made arrangements to keep him in the Dan River jail. The mayor had already paid a visit to my daddy and warned him about holding an accused murderer in his home. The town council was scheduled to meet later in the week, so Daddy was forced to bow to the power of the local government, and send Mr. Joe Jenkins to the big city for safe keeping. He would be out of harm's way. He would also be out of Clancyville.

I hated it and thought it was all nonsense, but I was only a child and had little power over the government. I was hoping that Mr. Joe wouldn't have to stay in Dan River for too long. I learned that his scheduled trial was only two weeks away.

The next morning, Daddy hung around the house until the two patrolmen from Dan River arrived. I decided to stay in my room until after they left with my friend. I didn't want to see them handcuff him and take him away. Scottie watched from my window while I did my best to ignore what was happening outside below in the driveway. Curiosity was killing me, but I dared not look. I didn't want to cry.

"They're leaving," Scottie said finally.

I ran downstairs and out the back door. I stopped and held the screen door open so it wouldn't slam. I really didn't want to get into it with my mama by violating one of her sacred cows on this particular day.

"You ready to go?" Daddy said to me, breaking my focus on the Dan River patrol car that was moving away from our house.

My favorite sheriff in all the world was standing next to the black-and-white and his driver's side door was opened.

"Yes, sir. Should I tell Mama?"

"I already told her you were going with me."

"Tell her where?"

"Nope. She didn't ask either."

Scottie waved from my window as we pulled away. He had planned a day with his toy soldiers. My brother and I would probably go fishing again tomorrow.

In light of our discovery of Ruby Scruggs' diary, my daddy had suggested that we go visit her and see what we might learn. I was guessing that he wanted me to go with him just to see what another kind of interrogation is like. He once said that all interrogations are different.

"Do you think she'll talk with you?" I asked.

"I don't know, Clancy. She's a strange woman. Even more so now since her boys died. I just hope that Donald is at work, or off somewhere. If he's home, it'll force us to come back later. I have a strong impression that he doesn't want us talking with Ruby."

"But you would come back later," I said.

"Oh, yes ma'am. I have to talk with her. It'll just be easier on her if he's not around. And, it'll be easier on me with my questions."

"Why are you taking me along?"

"Just a hunch. I think she likes children; at least that's what Sondra Richardson told me. She said that she visited Ruby the day after you had been out there. Ruby told her that she appreciated you *calling on her*, as she phrased it to Sondra. Said it took a lot of courage for you to come see them like that. She admired it, or something to that effect. So, I hope that when she sees you, she'll open up a little. Just a hunch."

"Yeah. I didn't feel so special that day. To tell you the truth, I was scared."

"Scared?"

"Donald Scruggs. He strikes me as a rather mean person."

"Hmm," he sounded. "Perhaps you're simply making a harsh judgment against him."

"Maybe, but I don't like the man. And I don't trust him. I can't tell you why. But, I can tell you that I'm glad he's not my father."

"Me, too," Daddy put his right hand on the back of my neck and squeezed gently.

I delighted in being a part of this adventure, this investigation with my father. I had no way of knowing just how formative this period in my life would be. What I did know was how much I loved my daddy and what it meant for me to be actually helping him in his work.

"Oh, I got a call from the M.E. He found a .22 slug encased in a part of Betty Ann Greesome's skull. He still maintains that she died of a heart attack and not from the damage inflicted by that .22 slug. Thought you might like to add that to your ever-growing knowledge regarding this case."

"So, it's not murder if she died from a heart attack?" I asked.

"Still could be murder. I believe the law allows the state to charge a person with murder if a threatening action leads to a person's death even though the person threatening does no bodily harm. Depending upon what type of threat is made, it could be ruled manslaughter instead of murder."

"But under some situations it could be ruled murder?" I asked for clarification.

"It could," he said.

The diary was lying on the seat between us. It brought me back to the matter at hand.

"You gonna show Ruby the diary?"

"Thought it might be a good discussion starter."

"What about Ralph Hines?"

"What about him?"

"You plannin' to ask her anything about your deputy?"

"Sure. I have to, it's in the diary, and that picture tells a lot, don't you think?"

"It's an old picture, you know. She could say that, in her defense. But, yessir, that picture and the fact she's held onto it all these years, do say something. But I don't think she'll talk about it. What could she say? We've got the diary, we've got the picture. Best thing she could do would be to keep her mouth shut."

"Say, whose side are you on? Glad you're not her lawyer," he said.

"I was just thinking … out loud, like you do sometimes. It won't be easy, Daddy."

"Yes, ma'am. I expect it'll be hard," he said. "But here's the thing that I often rely upon—folks don't always do or say what is in their best interest when answering questions."

Donald Scruggs was at work, so we didn't have that to deal with. We did, however, have to overcome four hound dogs and a few dozen cats. The dogs took exception to our arrival, but my daddy was good with animals, so we were able to talk our way onto the front porch despite their vocal objections. They weren't exactly aggressive, but they were loud. The cats were no real threat, even when we were invited inside the house and some of the cats came out to meow and investigate our presence. The cats were, quite literally, everywhere, outside and inside. This meant we had few options as to where we could sit. There was, quite simply, nowhere to go to avoid them.

"Git!" Ruby yelled at a yellow one.

The cat returned Ruby's command with an indignant stare, arched its back, and then finally moved away from us of its own volition when Daddy walked over and started to sit down in a cane-back chair next to Ruby. I found an empty spot on one end of the couch across the small room from Ruby and Daddy. Ruby half-smiled at me from her old tattered easy chair. It was a faded red, more pink now that it had some age to it.

"Yore name is Clancy, ain't it?" she said.

"Yes, ma'am."

"Oh, you don't need to say ma'am to me none, I ain't used to it. I git no respect like that 'round this here place. Donald don't even use my name, just calls me 'woman' most of the time."

"We need to ask you some questions, Ruby," Daddy began.

"Okay. I ain't too smart none since I didn't actually graduate. And I'm surrounded here by so much ignerance, but I'll do my best."

"Well, not those kinds of questions. These are questions you probably know the answers to."

Ruby was staring at me while Daddy was talking to her.

"You shore do have purdy red hair. Anybody ever tell ya that, Clancy?"

"Yes, ma'am. Sometimes."

"I told ya … ya don't need to say ma'am to me," her tone changed from pleasant to almost anger. She lost her half-smile.

"She can't help saying that, Ruby," Daddy said. "I brought her up to respect adults."

"Oh. I sure do like her hair. I wish my hair looked like that, but as you can see I got this old dirty-blond junk that ain't good for nothing," she tried to run her fingers through her matted hair. It looked as if she hadn't washed it in weeks.

"Ruby, is this your diary?" he asked.

Daddy held up the small book for her to see. Her eyes were still fixed on me and it took her a second or two to shift her focus to what Daddy was holding. When she finally saw the book, she reached for it. She began to cry softly and clutched the little red book to her chest. She rubbed the front cover gently as she looked up at the ceiling. She continued to cry softly.

I could tell that my daddy was as uneasy about all this as I was. It felt like we had violated Ruby's privacy. I felt sorry for her. I concluded that she had lived an unhappy life.

She continued to cry and began to rock back and forth in the chair, a chair that didn't rock. The diary was pressed against her chest as if it were her baby.

"Ruby, did you lose your diary?" Daddy asked.

"No, sir," she said sobbing gently, "I buried it."

"Where did you bury it?"

"Where no one would find it. Far away."

"But we found it, Ruby."

"Oh, God, I miss my boys. Sheriff, you don't know what it's like to lose yore sons, do you?"

"No, Ruby, I don't know that pain. I am sorry for you."

"Don't be sorry for me, Mr. Sheriff!" she screamed all of a sudden. The crying stopped, as did her rocking motion. "I don't need none of yore sympathy. Don't come out here feelin' sorry fur me none. Ya hear?"

"Ruby, why did you bury your diary?"

She was staring at me again, this time without smiling. I was glad that Daddy was present. Her eyes were terrible to look at, but I was afraid to stop watching her. I was afraid of what she might do. She was a pathetic sight.

"I didn't want Donald to find it. I got scared and buried it. I thought it wuz safe. I missed it something terrible, Sheriff. Terrible. Where did you find it?"

"Where did you bury it?"

"At that nigger's farm. Close to the butterflies."

"You mean Joe Jenkins' farm," Daddy said, for clarification.

"Yeah. Somewhere in the woods. It was a dark and muddy place. Muddy. The ground wuz so soft, it was a good spot to bury it. It all started with the butterflies. But, then they made me cry."

"Who made you cry?" Daddy said.

"The butterflies. They made me cry."

Daddy looked at me and I shrugged, not understanding where Ruby was going with that. I could see a few tears running down her cheeks as she slowly moved her gaze to the wall behind me, to my left.

"Ruby?" Daddy tried to get her attention.

"I found me a stick to dig with, and I buried my box. I couldn't use the …"

She stopped speaking and started to rock gently again. She didn't cry this time. She was humming some kind of lullaby unfamiliar to me.

"Ruby, I need to ask you about Ralph Hines," my daddy said.

She stared at me and continued to hum her lullaby.

"Ruby, was Ralph the father of your sons?"

Her humming was louder now. She seemed to be ignoring my father.

"Ruby, I need you to talk to me. It's important."

"Oh, my God, my boys are dead!" she yelled. "Both of them! Dead! They killed them. They were stupid, Sheriff. Stupid. They had no right to do that. They wuz mine. They wasn't his'in. I brought 'em into this damn world. It wuz wrong wut they did!"

# CHAPTER THIRTY-NINE

We both sat very still and watched Ruby Scruggs lose control as she clutched the diary, continually pressing it hard to her chest. At some point she screamed so loud that all of the cats cleared out of the living room, and we never saw them again during our visit.

She stood up as if she was planning to go somewhere, and then fell backwards into her chair. It was then that she dropped the diary and appeared to pass out.

"What's wrong with her, Daddy?"

"I think she's having a seizure. Go find a towel, dampen it and bring it back quickly."

"What about medicine?" I asked as I moved towards the bathroom.

"She can't swallow during a seizure," he said as he stretched out Ruby's body on the sofa.

I ran through a doorway searching for the bathroom. I found a hand towel on the floor.

"Is a hand towel okay?" I yelled.

"That'll be fine," Daddy called back.

I returned as quickly as I could with the dampened towel.

"What's that in her mouth?"

"My handkerchief. It'll protect her in case she tries to bite her tongue or the inside of her cheeks."

He had her head back at an angle, hanging off the edge of the sofa. He gently placed the towel on her forehead and rubbed her hands. I watched him for a few minutes, and then walked back towards the bathroom. I had spotted something in another room when I was searching for the towel, something I needed to investigate more thoroughly.

I walked into what appeared to be Ruby's bedroom. The object that had caught my eye earlier was an empty bottle of *Jack Daniels*®. There was a dirty glass sitting next to it on her bedside table. I studied the top of her dresser. It was cluttered with hairpins, papers, empty bottles of perfume, an unused hair brush, a dirty comb, a broken mirror, and some underwear. There were clothes scattered around the floor, along with paper and dirt. Housekeeping was not Ruby's strong suit.

Then I saw the rifle leaning against the wall in the corner by her bed. I started to touch it then thought better of the idea. There was black mud caked on the side of it and it was glowing. I knew exactly where that gun had been.

"What are you doing, Clancy?" my daddy called to me from the living room.

"Just lookin'," I said.

"Not touching, I hope," he answered back.

"No sir, just lookin'."

I returned to the living room to check on Ruby. She was still unconscious.

"How long will it take for her to come around?"

"Everybody's different when it comes to seizures. It might be a while before she comes to."

"How do you know she just didn't faint?" I asked.

"Fainting spells don't last this long, at least not usually. We'll just stay here with her until she awakens. We certainly can't leave her alone like this. She will need some reassurance when she comes to."

"How do you know so much about seizures?"

"I thought you knew that I knew everything about everything," he smiled at me.

"Well, even geniuses have limitations, right?"

"My father had epilepsy and I learned what to do from watching my mother take care of him."

"What causes the seizures?"

"Something to do with irregular brain activity, but I don't think doctors know for sure what it is in some cases. You just have to keep the person calm and comfortable. You protect their mouth, mainly their tongue, but never stick your fingers inside the mouth."

I don't know how long we stayed with Ruby, but it seemed like forever before she began to come around. She opened her eyes and glanced about the room.

"Everything's fine, Ruby. You're home and in your living room. You're lying on your couch. You passed out. Do you know who I am?" Daddy said.

Her eyes found me standing next to my father.

"Oh, my, child, you have such purdy red hair. I wish I had hair like that."

It appeared to me that Ruby was beginning our conversation over again.

"Are you okay, Ruby?" Daddy said.

She moved her head to see Daddy. One of her half-smiles appeared, then disappeared just as quickly.

"Why Sheriff, how good of you to ask. Wut are you doin' here?"

Daddy explained later that we would have to talk with her another day. He didn't need to explain that to me since I was convinced of it before I watched her body convulse. I figured he would have a hard time talking with Ruby on any day. This new revelation regarding her health might make it even more difficult.

"I saw a rifle in the bedroom," I said to him when we were alone in the car driving away.

"That's not uncommon, Clancy."

"It had mud on the side of it."

"And?"

"It was shiny mud, Daddy, like that mud in the swamp out near Mr. Joe's."

"Oh, that kind of mud."

"Yes, sir."

We drove by the jail so that Daddy could pick up some paper work he needed to do at home during lunch. Ralph Hines was just arriving when we were getting into the black-and-white to leave.

"Get in, Ralph. I need to talk with you," Daddy said.

Hines opened the front door on the passenger's side of the car as if to invite me to get out or move over. I wasn't about to move over and sit that close to the deputy. I moved to the backseat as Hines climbed into the front.

"Have you seen this before?" Daddy held up the diary for Hines to see, but it seemed that he kept his focus on his deputy's eyes.

To his credit, Ralph Hines never flinched. If Ralph Hines had a skill, it would be that he could lie. He might have been one of the best I had ever met, but I was still young.

"No, Sheriff. But it looks like a diary."

"It is. Belongs to Ruby Scruggs."

"Why would I have ever seen a diary of hers?" he said calmly, no flinching.

"Well, you knew her pretty well a few years ago, didn't you?"

"Ah, that was in high school. Just a fling. One nighter or so. Nothing between us since."

"Rumors tell a different story, Ralph."

"That's just small town gossip, Sheriff. Ain't no truth to it. Ruby's been married to Donald Scruggs for ... oh, gosh, how long is it now? Must be going on ten years."

"Moving close to twelve," Daddy corrected him with accuracy. "So you have never seen this diary?"

"Never. Why? What's in it?"

"Oh, the usual ... personal stuff. Mostly about Ruby. But, there were some entries about you."

"Well, if you know Ruby, Sheriff, then you know she's not all there. So, I can't be responsible for what a crazy woman might write about me. Where'd you find the diary?"

"Hidden."

"Humph ... wasn't hid too good, was it?"

"Guess not."

"Hidden where?" Hines asked.

"Buried in the ground," Daddy said.

"And you happened to come along and dig in the right spot," Hines was trying to be cute now.

"Clancy dug it out, as a matter of fact," Daddy said.

Hines jerked slightly when Daddy said that. I think he had forgotten that I was in the back seat. He turned quickly and looked at me. He forced a crooked smile, an unfriendly smile. I thought he looked evil, despite his feeble attempt at smiling.

"She's kind of handy in our work, huh?" Hines said.

"Sometimes," Daddy said. "Okay, Ralph. That's all for now. Just curious."

He slammed the car door and walked back into the jail. He glanced back in our direction when he reached the door, then turned and entered the building.

"What'd you do that for?" I said.

"Disturbing the tranquility, Clancy. I'm guessing here, but I bet you that Hines doesn't know who killed Betty Ann Greesome."

"What has the diary got to do with all that?"

"Not the diary, Clancy. The writer. She knows."

"She knows what?"

"She knows who killed her sons. All we have to do is find a way to get her to tell us."

"She'll go bonkers again."

"That's the trick, to keep her from going berserk, or *bonkers*, as you put it so indelicately. But it's buried somewhere in her mind. She's repressed it, but I can't tell for sure."

"Do you think that the killers know that she knows?"

"Regarding that, I have no certainty. It could be that if they did know that she knew who did it, then she might be the next target."

After lunch I had a strong desire to be alone. I told Mama that I was going walking; I just didn't tell her where I was going to walk. And she didn't ask, nor did she give me a directive.

I headed straight for Mr. Joe's place. Mama had told me, just after Mr. Joe had been transported to Dan River, that she wanted me to wait a few days before going back out there, but I wanted to look around some more. It could be that I wanted to grieve for the butterflies as much as anything. The sadness began to cover me before I arrived at the place where Scottie and I had first seen that congregation of loveliness.

All the way down the dirt road to Mr. Joe's house I kept thinking about him and what he might be doing in Dan River's city jail. I had never been there, so I had no mental image of what it was like to be a prisoner there. I felt sorry for Mr. Joe. I even caught myself praying for him at some point on my walk. That was a new experience for me. I wasn't used to lapsing into prayer, at least not before thinking about it long and hard. Maybe Mr. Joe's influence was rubbing off on me.

A feeling of sadness came over me as I passed by Mr. Joe's empty house. I figured it would be a long time before he returned. I looked in several of the windows just to make sure that everything was okay. Everything appeared to be in place, undisturbed, and looking lonely.

There was little left of what once was his barn. The grass was black all around the spot where the barn once stood. I took a stick and stirred some of the ashes. I wasn't looking for anything in particular, I just wanted to mull over the effects of the inferno. I didn't stay there for long. I had mixed feelings about the barn. While I was sorry that Mr. Joe had lost his building, I was glad that the place of such horror had been removed from the earth.

Moving closer to the burned-out flower section, I noticed a few butterflies flittering by me as I walked along. I could see absolutely no flowers anywhere. There were only the charred remains of what was once a grand forest.

Once again I encountered a couple of butterflies close to me. If they had come along in search of nectar, they were sure to be disappointed. Maybe they hadn't gotten the message about the fire as yet. I watched them flitter around in various places without finding anything upon which to land. Then, as if on cue, they moved off to continue their search in other directions.

I stopped to survey the area where once there had been such staggering beauty. It was a shame that someone had destroyed it. I kept asking myself why anyone would do that. I guess I was too young to understand such meaningless destruction. It was hard enough to understand how someone could kill another person. But the killing of the butterflies and the obliteration of the flowers and trees seemed utterly senseless.

Unless. Unless they were covering up something, or trying to destroy something left there.

# CHAPTER FORTY

I roamed around that scorched and blackened section of Mr. Joe's farm for at least two hours. I was looking for anything and everything. I decided simply to take in whatever was there.

My first serendipity came from a large old oak tree trunk. It has suffered minimal scorching from the fire and heat earlier in the week. A rather stately tree, if I do say so myself, since I don't know that much about trees in general or oaks in particular. Stately, I say, in that its shape was perfectly balanced, limbs jutting out equally on all sides. My guess would be that it's the kind of tree young artists might draw in art class. Too perfect for the canvas. But, there it was, seemingly out of place with no part of it out of place in reality. It called attention to itself, at least it called me to attend to it. I would definitely say that it was quite perfect.

That's what drew me to it. I walked around it several times before I spotted the carving, maybe a foot or more over my head. The initials on the top were *R* and *H*. The ones on the bottom were *R* and *W*. There was a heart between the two sets of letters.

I was no genius but I easily figured out who those initials represented. They had been carved on that tree several years back.

More walking in the burned out flower section revealed nothing important. I reluctantly moved into the former swamp. It was drying up little by little now. Bessie Mae was not permitted to roam into this section due primarily to the fire's devastation. The butterflies were all but gone, so they would not be contributing their magical ingredient that Mr. Joe had posited to me. The fire had taken out nearly all of the moisture.

I went back to the spot where I had found the wooden box. I had borrowed one of Daddy's old hunting knives which he kept in his workroom. I brought it just in case I found the need for some necessary digging.

I came to a spot that was enticing.

I began my search at the spot where I had discovered buried what turned out to be Ruby Scruggs' wooden box of treasures. From that original place, I began digging once more and gradually increasing my area of focus until I had unearthed a hole less than a foot deep with a circumference of maybe three feet. I didn't think that she was cunning enough to hide anything from my careful excavation. She was irrational, so I decided to try to think that way. Even for an eleven year old, that was tough. Besides that, I had inherited a methodical nature from my father. Nothing came from this digging endeavor.

I sat down on the rim of the former swamp. I studied the area looking for another place that Ruby, or anyone else, might have used to hide something. I had no reason to believe that Ruby had buried anything else here. I had no clue, no reason to be here, except the fact that my intuition had brought me to this place— and my desire to be alone and think and grieve. So, I sat there and thought about the entire drama as it had unfolded in my life during that summer of my youth.

I must have maintained the same position for some time. My legs started aching either from lack of movement or the fact that I had crouched without sitting at some point, perhaps to study something. With that positioning, I had lost all sense of time. When I stood to stretch, hoping to get the blood circulating once more, I fell forward into the hardened mud because my right foot had gone to sleep. The tingling sensation was irritating, to say the least. I was grateful that the ground was now hard. Prior to the fire, I would have had that black, muddy gunk covering me after my unplanned plunge. At any rate, I did get my hands black from the fire's aftermath.

When I stood up from my embarrassment, my eyes fell upon another old tree across from where I had been digging. This one wasn't an oak, and I had no idea what variety it was. What caught my eye was the hole in the bottom of it. I moved towards it slowly since my right foot was still trying to awaken from its slumber.

I knew better than to stick my hand inside a hole in a tree trunk, but curiosity overcame my fear, and I was forced to use my lesser judgment. I did decide to stick the knife in ahead of my fist. It was a good thing that I didn't have my mouth open, for no sooner had I poked that long knife blade inside of that hole, a frightened chipmunk scampered out. That rascal must have been running sixty miles an hour when he scurried past me.

It took a couple of minutes for me to stop shaking from the scare. If I had been expecting him, it wouldn't have been so bad. Surprise is usually the worst part of an encounter with a wild animal.

After I had relaxed and calmed myself back to some semblance of composure, I put my head down on the ground and tried to look into the hole before sticking the knife back inside. There was something brown in the hole. I used the knife to retrieve the object. I gently poked the point of the knife's largest blade into the brown object. It turned out to be a paper sack from Shelton's Grocery.

Shelton's Grocery had been a grocery store in Clancyville for more than forty years. Thirty-five of those years were before I was born. It burned to the ground when I was five. I had a vague memory of going into that store with my daddy, and he would buy me some candy out of a large barrel. Shelton's wasn't a traditional grocery store like we know these days. It was one of those stores that sold everything. It was a hardware, dime store, meat market, feed store, and grocery. It had a pot-bellied stove in the middle of the main floor where several old-timers would gather every day to play checkers and solve the world's problems. Shelton's also used paper sacks with their name printed on the side.

The sack was about medium size. I guessed that the sack had to be at least several years old. The chipmunk and his family had managed to nibble several tiny holes in the bag, but it was still intact enough for me to drag it out and open it. It contained a gingham dress and a pair of black patent leather flats. The dress was sleeveless with a pretty white collar. It looked like the kind of dress they used to wear to high school dances before everything became so formal. The dress was a long way from pretty by this point. It had splotches of mud on it and some stains. There was no way for me to know what contributed to the stains. I guessed that the dress had originally been some shade of white. Now, faded, it had become a dingy shade of yellow.

I took the dress out and held it up, letting it fall in front of me. It appeared to be about the right length for me. Of course, I naturally thought of Ruby Scruggs, since I was in this place because of her, and she was about my height. My guess that the Shelton's paper sack had to have some age to it helped my focus to be on Ruby.

I knew I was guessing as to the owner of the dress, but the circumstances of my being there, plus the initials I had discovered carved in that old oak, and the addition of my discovery of the wooden box buried by Ruby, mandated a safe direction for me to assume that the items stored in that tree were hers. I concluded that sometimes detective work is part imagination, part guesswork, and part location. Sometimes you simply have to be in the right place.

Mama fixed spaghetti for us that evening. It was delicious. If I ever learned how to cook like her, then I was going to make a great housewife. Even at that tender age, I had my doubts about ever becoming a great housewife. I enjoyed my mama's creations immensely. I just never took the time to learn how to duplicate them. I generally believed that I had more important things to do. I never quite shook that belief.

I took Daddy out to the woodshed after supper to show him my latest find. I had hidden the bag behind a loose board just above the spigot where we washed up after cleaning fish.

"What have you found now?" he said, holding up the dress.

I showed him the shoes and I told him about the initials and the heart.

"We certainly missed a lot out there, huh?"

"We weren't looking for this kind of stuff," I said.

"Oh, and so you were looking for this type of stuff this afternoon?"

"Not exactly. I was lucky. Just reflecting, and I sort of stumbled upon … this, and the other things … those initials and the heart."

"Clancy, my young sleuth, you are many things. Lucky is not one of the first words that come to my mind."

"You don't think it was luck that I accidentally found this stuff?" I asked.

"Coupled with your tenacity, your relentlessness, and your drive to get to the truth you believe is out there, luck is such a small part of your skills, my dear."

I wanted to hug him for saying all of that, but I had other things on my mind.

"You know what we need now?" I said.

"Besides a confession?"

"Yes, besides that. We need that rifle."

"Can't touch it. No probable cause."

"That means what?"

"Means that I need a reason to go ask Donald Scruggs to hand over that weapon from his bedroom. Besides, if we hadn't been there, and Ruby had not had a seizure, we wouldn't even know that there was a rifle in the house. No judge would give you a search warrant based on that."

"But Greesome was shot with a rifle."

"We don't know that," he said. "All we know from the M.E.'s report is that she was shot with a .22 caliber weapon. Could be a handgun."

"I'm betting it was the rifle. I saw mud and shiny stuff on it. That had to be the weapon someone used, someone like Donald Scruggs or maybe even Ruby."

"You don't know that either. You can't just guess because you don't like people. We have to have evidence that points specifically to a person, or persons. The best thing you can say is that there is a strong likelihood that the rifle you saw was at that swamp sometime in its life. Until you have more facts, that's just about all you can say with assurance."

"We can test that rifle, to see if it was the weapon, right?" I asked.

"Yes, ma'am. But now, we're back to that probable cause thing. You have no probable cause at the present to request that Donald Scruggs or Ruby hand over that gun. Sorry, we can't touch that rifle. But we do have more information about it."

He put the items back into the bag, opened his trunk, and dropped the bag. I leaned against his car as I watched him return to the house.

"Thanks for your newly found items. They might yet prove to be valuable," he said as he started up the back steps.

I had a lot to learn about the law and solving cases.

I remained outside, watching the daylight slowly slip away into dusk. I noticed that the days were getting a little shorter. That was always a sad realization for me. I had a sick feeling that school was not very far away once the daylight decreased. I was not ready to return to the rigors of study.

"Whataya doin'?" Scottie said.

"Just leaning and thinking. Nothing much."

"What was you and Daddy talkin' about?"

"Were."

"Thanks, Papa. Okay, what *were* you two gabbing about?"

"Same thing as usual."

"More clues?"

"Yeah, I found a dress and some shoes."

"Betty Ann Greesome's?"

"Don't think so. Too small for her. Suspect they belong to Ruby Scruggs. The dress was old and faded, with mud-spots and some unknown stains on it... say, I've got an idea. You want an adventure?"

"I refuse to answer that question. And since you know that my birthday is coming soon, you also know that I sure would like to be here for it."

"That's a week away," I said.

"Doesn't matter. I still want to be alive."

"Awh, come on. I need your help. You haven't done much the past few days. You weren't even with me for that riot at the jail house."

"And I'm glad of it, too. You could have been killed. If I had been with you, we could have been killed."

"Now you sound like Mama."

"Whataya want me to do?"

"Go inside and smuggle out a small container of Mama's spaghetti sauce. You can't let her see you do it. We're goin' huntin', Scottie."

Turby Rhinehart lived about four streets over from us. He had the laziest dog that I have ever known in my life. Turby would feed his dog once a day, at night. That dog would sleep all night long and not eat a bite of that fresh, dry dog food until the following morning. I know all of this because Turby told me about his dog, Butch, and his strange eating habits. Fed him at night, but the dog wouldn't touch it until the next morning.

Butch was also the worst watchdog in the whole town. You could sneak up on Butch, take off his collar, and he would never wake up. I knew that to be a fact because I did it once on a two dollar dare. I won the money.

We stopped by Butch's dog dish and borrowed about half of his freshly served supper as we were on our way to pay a nocturnal visit to Donald and Ruby Scruggs.

About two blocks before the Scruggs' house, I stopped and mixed the spaghetti sauce and the dry dog food, created two even portions, and placed them into two large plastic containers that I had taken from our pantry. My scheme was to occupy the hound dogs in the hopes that we could sneak up to that bedroom window, get inside, and retrieve that rifle without much fanfare. And without getting caught in the act.

I gambled on two things: one, that the hound dogs were hungry, and two, that I had brought enough food to keep them busy while I accomplished my cunning and beautifully designed scheme. The trick, of course, was for me to get in and get out before either being discovered by Donald Scruggs, or found by the dogs that likely would join together in a chorus and give us away, and then be found by Mr. Scruggs.

The dogs were hungry and greeted our food offering as if we were all old friends gathering for a picnic. Scottie stayed just out of sight close to the window while I was busy breaking another law in my investigation. I seemed to be good at violating the current regulations of our society. I hoped that my father would not finally arrest me. Of course, that would be my preferred comeuppance to being told to stop investigating altogether.

I was barely inside the house when the dogs ran to the window and began their unholy howling, warning folks at least two counties over about the break-in. Before I had a chance to even think about touching the rifle, Donald Scruggs flipped on the light switch and found me standing by the window without an excuse of any reasonable sort as to why I was inside his house.

To have said that I was scared to death at that moment would have been an exaggerated understatement. I was caught dead to rights.

# CHAPTER FORTY-ONE

It was the verbal abuse that bothered me the most at the outset of my confrontation with the man. He delivered tirades of words and phrases the likes of which I had never heard. I lost track of the names that he called me long before Ruby came into the room.

"Oh, my, it's that beautiful red-haired girl. Good to see ya, child."

"Good god, woman! She broke into my house for cryin' out loud. Don't ya have any sense a'tall?"

"Don't you just love the color of her hair?" Ruby said.

"Who gives a damn 'bout her hair? She's a criminal…broke into my house. I won't stand fur this. Ya hear me?"

He grabbed me and took me into the living room and threw me onto his couch.

Ruby didn't follow us into the living room immediately.

"You stay right there and don't move a muscle. I'm gonna git yore daddy over here right now. He needs to see for hisself wut you did … that I ain't making this up. I done caught you red-handed, you little red-headed bitch," he yelled.

Just as he concluded his verbal assault on me, Ruby came into the living room.

"Git me some rope. I'm gonna tie this little bitch up, and then git her daddy. Maybe he'll lock her up this time."

I wondered what he meant by *this time*. The only other time I had run into Donald Scruggs was my visit to bring some food and see his wife Ruby. He hadn't been around when Daddy and I came to see Ruby officially. Maybe Donald was in that mob at the jail a few days ago. Maybe that's what he meant. I was puzzled.

Ruby wandered out of the room. It appeared that she was meandering more than walking away with a purpose. Maybe she would find the rope, maybe not. I began to think that I might survive this ordeal as long as she was around.

"Whataya doin' in my house?" Donald Scruggs asked. There was a great deal of anger in his voice.

I decided that silence might be my best friend under the circumstances. I was scared. I usually held my own against adults, but this man was beyond my limits of engagement. I had the sense that he could be dangerous, and I certainly did not want to provoke him any more than I had already done by being caught in his bedroom. I was, after all, guilty of breaking and entering. That's what the County Sheriff would say, for sure.

"I asked you a question. Whataya doin' in my house?"

I had no lies that sounded plausible, even to me. Nothing I could say would help my predicament. In fact, if I had actually told him the whole truth, he would have lost the little control which he had at the moment. I held to my silence, hoping that something would happen soon to save me.

Ruby wandered back into the living room with some rope. He jerked it out of her hands and began tying me. First he bound my feet, and then he tied my hands together behind my back. It was a most uncomfortable position to lie in. I was glad that I was thrown back on the couch once he had bound me securely. I figured he would gag me next, but he evidently didn't have that in his repertoire.

"Woman, you stay right here and don't let this little bitch move. I want her here ... right here," he said, and pointed to my spot on the couch, "when I git back with the Sheriff. Ya hear?"

"I shore wish that I had red hair like that," Ruby said.

"Awh, you git crazier by the day. Just guard her and don't let her leave."

He grabbed Ruby and shook her violently. Suddenly, my fear for myself left. It was easy to transfer my self-concern to Ruby and all that she had endured with this man.

"Ya hear me?"

She nodded helplessly, with her head down. She was staring at her feet. It was as if she was in a trance. Wherever she was, she was a long way from Clancyville.

Scruggs stomped out of the house and was gone. I heard his old car start up after three attempts. It then sped away. I could hear some pieces of gravel hitting the front porch as he hurried off into the night to locate my daddy.

It was then that I remembered Scottie. Where was he?

The dogs were still barking outside, but not as much now. When Donald Scruggs left, so did most of the ruckus, for some reason. Ruby sat down in a chair close to the couch, the same chair she had been sitting in when we visited her yesterday. She appeared to be as faded as the chair.

"Can I touch it?" she said.

"What?" I asked.

"Yore hair. It's so purdy. I wanna touch it, pleaze."

"You can touch it," I said. I was in no position to refuse her request. My constraints were tight.

She moved quickly from her seat, got down on her knees and then gently stroked my long, red hair as if I were her little girl and she was my mother. If it hadn't been for the fact that I was hogtied and lying on the couch, it would have been a most endearing domestic scene. Instead, it played more like a farce without the laughter. I remembered reading about farce in school last year. I liked the word, so I kept it.

"Is that your rifle in the bedroom?" I said.

She smiled and continued stroking my hair without responding at first.

Time passed. I thought about Scottie, and wondered if he was safe somewhere outside.

"Yeah," she finally answered my question. "Donald give it to me fer protection. I use it to kill rats. And snakes," she said rather pleasantly, "and some stray dogs. Shot some old gray thang not long ago. Sume-times I shoots other things."

"Like people?" I said.

She stopped stroking my hair. Her eyes looked intently into mine, but I had the feeling she was not looking at my green eyes at all. She was seeing something other than my eyes.

"Sum peoples deserve killin'," she said.

"Who?"

"Peoples who take what belongs to others. Got no right to do that."

"Somebody take something from you?"

"Yeah. But she's dead. She won't take no more. Rats … snakes … and stray dogs … and folks who steal wut don't belong to 'em." She began gently stroking my hair once more.

"Did you shoot her?" I asked.

She paused from her methodical stroking of my hair, and smiled.

"I love yore hair. It's so purdy … so soft. Does yore mama brush yore hair?"

"Sometimes," I said. "Miss Ruby, did you shoot Betty Ann Greesome?"

"Her time to die," she said, matter-of-factly.

"Why?"

"She made me cry. Donald sed she helped that nigger kill my children."

"Was your husband with you?"

"We scared her bad. Donald helped to tie her up. She cried like a baby, like my babies cried, I guess. I didn't feel no sorrow fur her … none … not a bit. She made me cry and I wuz glad to see her cry. Cryin' can be bad, but not fur her. My babies cried, ya know. Oh, Lord, I know they cried so hard before they died. Donald said that they begged and pleaded, but she and that nigger weren't filled with no mercy a'tall. So he and that woman killed them. But she's dead now, and that old dar-kie's gonna die soon enough."

"Ruby, how did your husband know that your sons pleaded for their lives?"

"Wut?" she looked confused and stopped rubbing my hair. Her hand was resting on my head. "Wut did you say?"

"You said Donald told you that they begged and pleaded. How did he know that?"

She gasped and put both hands in front of her mouth. I just knew that she was going to have another seizure. I braced myself for the worst. Nothing happened for several moments. Then I saw the tears streaming down her cheeks as she stared at my bright red hair.

"Damn butterflies made me cry, too. I hate cryin', but I seem to do a lot of it. I lost everything out there. I lost myself. I lost my babies. So I had to kill them, don't you see?"

"You had to kill who?"

"The butterflies," she said innocently.

The sound of the car outside broke whatever trance we were both in at that moment. The sounds made by the car seemed to be coming at us, toward the house. I heard another car pull up right after the first one. Two car doors slammed, one at a time, in sequence, and Donald Scruggs came abruptly into his living room with my daddy close behind.

"There's the little thief, all secure for you, Sheriff. I want to press charges against her. And you gotta make 'em stick. Ya hear me?"

Daddy didn't say a word. He walked straight to the couch and began to untie me.

"She's okay, Sheriff Evans. I've been talkin' to her. She's a good girl, ya know. She didn't mean nothin' by comin' in here. I think she cum to see how I wuz doin'. I really do. She didn't steal nothin' that I know of."

"Shut up, woman. I caught her red-handed, right there by my window in the bedroom, afore she cud take anything. I been missin' stuff, so I reckon she's been here stealin' right along," Donald Scruggs' tone was different now that my daddy was in the room.

"You can come down to the office tomorrow morning and fill out some forms to press formal charges, Mr. Scruggs. I'll see to it that she won't bother you again."

"Ya damn right ya will. I'll be there at eight o'clock in the mornin'. Count on it! Ya make damn sure yore there, ya hear?"

"I'm sorry, Mrs. Scruggs. Please forgive my daughter."

"She didn't hurt nothin', Sheriff. I love her hair. Don't you think she has purdy hair? I wish I had —"

"Shut up, Ruby. Ya make me sick. We ain't forgivin' nobody, Sheriff. You take that little thief and git outta my house!" his voice seemed to find the strength to surge into some superior position with my father.

Daddy gently pushed me through the front door. As soon as we were out on the porch, Donald Scruggs followed and allowed the screen door to slam hard behind him. He stood on the porch watching us walk to the car. I turned and glimpsed him in all of his rage. One of the dogs came close to him and Scruggs kicked him in the side of the stomach. The dog ran off yelping around the side of the house.

Daddy didn't speak until we both got into the car.

"Are you okay?" he said.

"I'm fine. But before you lecture me good about all of this, I've got to tell you what Ruby told me while I was tied up on the couch."

He started the car and we drove towards home slowly.

"He's a mean person, Daddy."

"I know that. That's why I was worried about you."

I told my daddy everything. He listened intently. He never once looked in my direction. I knew he heard every word. I finished telling him what I had heard, and then told him what I thought. He stared straight ahead. He turned down a strange street and doubled back towards the Scruggs' house.

I had finished my story by then and waited for him to say something.

"Don't you have any questions?" I said.

"One. Where's Scottie?"

Daddy was gracious and trusting enough to let me go look for my brother since I was the one who had lost him. Actually, Scottie was supposed to be my lookout while I was pilfering the rifle. But a lot had happened since that plan had gone belly-up, so now I had to find him.

It was actually easier than I thought it would be. Scottie was still hiding behind the dogs' houses in the back of the Scruggs' place. He was leaning against one of the dog houses, petting a hound dog when I crawled through the bushes and found him.

"Where in god's name have you been?" he said.

"Don't talk like that. You're too young to be talkin' like that."

"What?"

"Mama will wash your mouth out with soap if she hears you talk like that," I said, knowing the truth of my statement.

"Shut up. Where have you been? I heard that old man yelling. Was he yelling at you?"

"As a matter of fact, he was."

"I ran and hid when the yelling started. So what happened inside the house?"

"Come on, I'll fill you in later, when we're alone."

"Where're we goin' now?" he asked.

"To the car."

"The car?" he said as he followed me back out through the bushes.

By the time we were both safely secured in Daddy's car, Scottie got the drift of what had happened to me without hearing all the specifics. He heard enough to know that I was in serious trouble, and that our daddy was so calm it frightened both of us.

"So do I go to jail tonight?" I asked him. I had the feeling I was addressing the Sheriff of Pitt County and not my father at that moment.

"Maybe," he replied.

# CHAPTER FORTY-TWO

The worst part about going home was telling Mama what had happened. I begged Daddy close to a hundred times in that short trip across town for him to tell her, but he would have none of it. I told him that I would be happy to serve a year of hard time if he would just do the talking and put in a good word for me now and again. I think now that telling my mother what I had done was my punishment, in lieu of jail time.

Scottie was trying without success to suppress his laughter in the back seat. I recognized the sounds he made in his feeble attempts to stifle his joy at my current discomfort.

It was close to ten o'clock when I entered the back door. Mama was sitting at the table with her hands folded in her lap. She looked unusually calm for a woman going through her daughter's current crisis. I was afraid to speak. I was certain that if I said anything, it would be the wrong thing.

"Are you okay?" she asked.

It was the same first question Daddy had asked earlier. Maybe there was a pattern here. Perhaps they had discussed my health already that evening. No doubt my mental health was on their minds as well.

"Yes, ma'am. I'm okay."

"What were you doing in their house?"

Ah, the question that could do me in if I told the truth.

"Do I have to tell you?"

"I think you better."

"I went there to steal the rifle that I had seen in the bedroom yesterday."

"Steal it?" she asked, as if to clarify the exactness of my words.

"Yes, ma'am."

"Don't we buy you enough stuff?"

"Oh, no, that rifle is not for me. The rifle is evidence. I believe it was used to shoot the back of Betty Ann Greesome's head off."

Mama gasped. This was her eleven year-old daughter speaking with words that she was most uncomfortable hearing concerning facts foreign to her.

"What on earth are you saying, child?"

Daddy walked in and pointed to a chair by Mama. I sat down. He followed suit next to me. Scottie came in and started to sit, but Daddy shook his head, and Scottie then moved off reluctantly, no doubt heading at least part-way up the steps. I would have paused to listen, too.

"You get ready for bed, young man. I'll be up to tuck you in shortly," Mama spoke to his backside. Scottie knew better than to turn around.

"Now, just what are you talking about Clancy Evans?" she asked.

"We visited Ruby Scruggs yesterday, dear," my daddy began. "While we were there, Ruby had a seizure. Clancy found me a wet hand towel to use on her head at my directive, and while Clancy was in the bedroom getting the towel, she spotted the rifle in a corner."

Daddy clarified the reason behind my clandestine thievery nicely, I thought.

"So you were a party to this burglary?" she said to him.

"Not quite. We talked about the rifle as evidence, but I told her that we could never get our hands on it legally."

"So you told her to go steal it?"

"I'm the Sheriff, dear. I don't tell people, especially my daughter, to break the law."

"I should hope not," Mama said.

Daddy was winning, but not by much. I was glad he was doing the explaining. Mama was a tough cookie when it came to interrogations like this.

"So, you took it upon yourself to go get that rifle?" her question was addressed to me.

"Yes, ma'am."

"How did you propose to get into their house without being seen?"

I told her my plan and I included my brother. I figured I'd better come clean on that as well. I was frightened when I mentioned Scottie by name. I think Daddy was a little uneasy at this point. He shifted his weight uncomfortably despite his years of familiarity with the kitchen chair. Mama's questions and judgments created not a little discomfort for all of us who lived in the realm of her rules.

"So, you involved your brother, broke into the Scruggs' house, and got caught. Donald Scruggs tied you up and … did he hit you?"

"No, ma'am. He pushed me on to the couch rather hard, but he never hit me. He called me a bitch a few times, but that's about it."

"Clancy! You know better than to use that kind of language in this house. Do you hear me?"

"I didn't say it, Mama. He said it."

"Well, we don't go around repeating it, young lady. I never," she sighed and frowned, while looking at my daddy. I suppose she didn't finish the sentence because of her exasperation. I think I had that type of influence on lots of folks.

"So what happens next?" she said. Her question was directed to the Sheriff.

"I guess we go down to the jail tomorrow morning and wait for Donald Scruggs to show up and make formal charges."

"And after that?"

"You don't want to know," he said.

"I most certainly do. This involves my daughter, and I want to know what's going to happen to her."

"I may have to lock her up, and then I'll call Judge Franklin in Dan River. He handles juvenile cases like this. He'll help us."

"Like this? You mean other eleven year old girls whose father is the sheriff of the county are out there breaking and entering, … and stealing rifles?"

"I never actually stole the rifle, Mama," I said, hoping that the truth would actually be some defense.

She cut her eyes to me, but words failed her at that moment. I was sort of glad she didn't say anything. If looks could kill, I would have been laid out for my funeral.

I looked at my father, seeking some solace from him. I could tell, despite his calmness, that he was not happy with me in light of what I had done.

He smiled, but I could tell that he got her point, so he didn't answer her question to him about other eleven-year-old girls in the county. I thought to myself how wise my father was at times. I wondered if I could ever attain that type of composure. I think I had too much of a mouth to simply hold back when the occasion called for it.

"Time for bed, Clancy," Daddy said finally after an unhealthy silence of several minutes. "I'll be up in a minute. You go on to bed now."

"Mama, I'm sorry."

"You mean you're sorry you got caught."

"Yes, ma'am, that too. But I am sorry if this is an embarrassment to you."

"I'm still living down my shotgun episode from last week, girl. This is not embarrassment."

I left the kitchen and headed upstairs. Her statement puzzled me, but I had no idea what she really meant by it.

I paused halfway up and heard Mama ask, "What are you really going to do?"

"I honestly don't know," Daddy answered.

Next morning when I awoke, I gradually became aware that my brother was sitting on the edge of my bed staring at some toy soldiers in his hands.

"Excuse me," I said sarcastically.

"We need to talk."

"Can't you wait until I wake up?"

"You are awake. You're talking. You don't do that if you're asleep."

"Well, I am now. So what's on your mind so early this morning?" I sat up in the bed, shifted my pillow, and leaned against the headboard.

"You."

"Me?"

"I think you need to run away."

"Are you crazy?"

"No, I heard Mama and Daddy talking this morning about old man Scruggs, and I think they're worried about what's gonna happen to you. So am I."

"So your solution is for me to run away?"

"Yeah. I think that's the best idea."

"Where do I go, Sherlock?" I asked in my best sarcastic tone.

"I'm not Sherlock. You're the Sherlock of this family. And, I have no idea where you could go. I haven't gotten that far in the plan. I thought you'd have an idea."

"I see. I could go hide out in Aunt Nona's house. It's big. She'd probably feed me and protect me for a few days. She has lots of rooms, so it might take them a long time to search everywhere in that huge house, right? But then, they'd find me eventually."

"Hey, that's a great idea. That way I could come see you and smuggle you in some of Mama's biscuits and junk."

"Right. I think your imagination is running wild. Aunt Nona could just as easily forget that I was there or that I was hiding out, and give me away to the first person who asked about me … 'Oh, yes, Clancy is here with me. She's up in the attic playing like she has run away from home. You can go on up and see her.' I don't think Aunt Nona's place would work too well."

"What about Aunt Mildred?"

"Scottie, I'm not running away. My daddy will think of something to get me out of this mess. Besides, we're close to the killers. We know some of them, or we suspect some, so I think it's just a matter of time. I wouldn't dare run off when we're this close."

"Run off?" Mama said. She was standing in the doorway of my room.

"Oh, nothing, Mama. We were just talkin," Scottie said unconvincingly.

"Didn't sound like nothing to me," she added.

"I forgot something in my room," Scottie said and left quickly. He was always bad at lying, especially when he became nervous. He'd have to work on that a great deal more in order to fool our mother.

"So, where are you going?" she asked me.

"I'm not going anywhere. Scottie thought I ought to run away."

"Oh. I wish you could. Where would you go?"

"That was the problem. On such short notice, I couldn't think of a place to hide out. Besides, the sheriff around here is such an outstanding lawman, he'd probably find me within a day or so."

"Probably so. I'm glad you're staying."

"I'm a little scared, Mama."

"Me, too. But we'll just have to trust your daddy on this one. We'll get through this. He's going to call that judge today and see what can be done. In the meantime, you'd better get up and prepare yourself to face whatever happens today. You don't have much time."

Up to this point in my life my mother and I had not had such a close relationship. You could even say that it was, for most of the time, adversarial. I discovered that word while reading about Sherlock Holmes. I knew that she was upset with me about all of this, but I had the feeling after our short little exchange that she was actually on my side for once, and seemed to understand. Maybe I had crossed the line too far, so that ranting and raving would actually do no good. Perhaps when all of this was settled, she would go back to ranting and raving. I was used to her ranting and raving. I was not quite adjusted to her being kind and understanding of my tendencies.

I ate a light breakfast. I wasn't hungry. Hard to eat when you are worried about facing jail time.

Daddy said nothing at all to me on the way downtown. I was silent as well. I had nothing to say, although I had plenty of questions about my fate.

He parked the car in his usual spot designated by the sign "County Sheriff." He sat there for a moment without moving.

"Are you going to have to lock me up?"

"Yeah," he smiled at me.

"I'm serious, Daddy. Do you think that the judge will say I will have to stand trial?"

"Let's just take one step at a time, Clancy. I'm not used to juvenile criminals. You're actually my first eleven year old B & E with intent to steal. You see, you actually confessed to me, so I know already that you did it. It's really up to Donald Scruggs just how far this will go."

"I'll be twelve in another week or so, you know. Will that play into this at all?" I asked.

"Aside from the fact that you should know better than to do what you did, I doubt if your advanced age will have any bearing on it."

"So my fate is up to Donald Scruggs?"

"Like I said. That man holds the cards for what might happen next to you."

I had a sinking feeling in the pit of my stomach. I knew it wasn't the little food I had just eaten. Toast didn't usually have that affect on me, but then I had never faced a probable jail term before now.

Ralph Hines was already in the office when we entered moments later.

"I'm expecting Donald Scruggs this morning, Hines."

Hines didn't say anything. He simply nodded in the direction of the corner bench where people sometimes sat. It was behind the front door and hidden from sight when you entered the office area. It was just under the cluttered bulletin board where the sheriff's collection of known felons was gathering dust and age.

Daddy closed the door and we both could now see that Ruby Scruggs was sitting quietly in the corner with a .22 rifle across her lap. I could see some shiny mud globbed on the side of the stock as well as the barrel. I figured it was her rifle lying across her legs. She had her right index finger resting on the trigger.

"Oh, you're that little girl with that purdy red hair who came to visit me, aren't you?"

"Yes, ma'am."

"Ruby, where's Donald?" my daddy asked.

She didn't answer. She stared at my red hair.

"Ruby? Your husband was supposed to meet me here this morning to press charges against Clancy for breaking into your house."

I heard Hines make some comment under his breath, but I couldn't tell what he was saying. I turned my head and looked at Hines. He seemed pleased with what was happening. I was confused about what was happening.

"Ruby?" my daddy said again.

She finally looked away from me, turning her gaze directly at my father.

"Yes?" she said.

"Where's your husband?"

"He won't be coming."

# CHAPTER FORTY-THREE

There was an awkward silence in the jail office that morning as the three of us stood watching this disheveled woman sitting on a bench in the corner with a rifle across her lap. Her right hand was resting on the rifle with her index finger on the trigger, as if she was prepared to use it. She had moved her index finger slightly at some point in our initial conversation with her so that now it was not holding the trigger, but it was close to it. One slight movement by that right hand and she could have that weapon raised to eye level and fired. Her left hand was resting comfortably on top of her right hand. Despite the fact that she was holding onto a rifle, she looked rather peaceful.

"Did you come to sign the paperwork and press charges, Ruby?" Daddy was still being the sheriff in charge of the situation. He was not willing to assume anything.

"No. I couldn't do that. This beautiful child was just comin' to see me. Why would I want to press charges, Sheriff?"

"Well, your husband was pretty upset last night."

"He changed his mind, Sheriff."

"I see. So may I ask why you're here, Ruby?"

"I came to tell y'all that we ain't gonna file no charges against this little red-haired girl. Donald wud want me to say that."

"Thank you, Ruby. We appreciate your kind consideration. Clancy was wrong to do what she did last night. It won't happen again."

"Ah, Sheriff. Kids will be kids, ya know that. Sometimes they's into mischief no matter wut we say or do as parents. Ain't that right?"

"Well, yes ma'am, you're right about that," Daddy said.

"I guess I'd better be goin' now."

She got up slowly and let the rifle barrel drop naturally to her side. She held it easily with her right hand, keeping her index finger close to the trigger.

"Ruby?" Daddy said just as she reached the door.

"Yeah, Sheriff?"

"Why are you carrying that rifle this morning?"

She stopped and looked at the firearm at her side. She appeared to be somewhat surprised, as if she had forgotten that she was holding it.

"Oh, Donald tried to take it away from me. I wouldn't let him have it. I guess I wuz jest holdin' on to it fur dear life. He sumtimes can be a mean person, ya know."

"You be careful with it, Ruby. It can be dangerous."

"Don't worry none, Sheriff. I knows how to use this thang."

She walked out the door and Hines released a loud sigh. Daddy was breathing a little easier too. I was relieved, but very suspicious.

I followed my father after he walked out the front door. He stopped on the sidewalk in front of his office. He was watching Ruby Scruggs walk down the street and climb into an old Ford truck. It backfired a couple of times and then pulled away from the curb faster than necessary. Ruby appeared to be heading in the direction of her house.

"Something's up," he said.

"Yeah, I think so too. Any ideas?" I said.

"I'm thinking that Donald Scruggs didn't change his mind about anything, and that maybe she did something to keep him from coming down here."

"Something permanent?" I asked.

"That's my fear," he said.

We jumped into his car and headed towards the Scruggs' house. When we pulled into the front yard, Daddy told me to stay in the car while he went inside to check on things.

"And, little lady, I am dead serious about you staying right here in that seat. Is that clear enough?" he said, without smiling a bit.

"Clear," I said.

I watched him enter the front door as he was calling out for Donald. I thought I heard someone answer. I waited impatiently in the car for at least fifteen minutes. I finally decided that I couldn't just keep sitting, that maybe something had happened to my daddy.

Just as I opened the car door and got out, Daddy came out the front door helping Donald Scruggs walk. Scruggs appeared to be injured, but obviously not dead. My thinking was that Ruby had actually killed him. I surprised myself by being relieved that he was still alive. I walked toward them and could see that Scruggs was limping badly. He was favoring his right foot. It was wrapped in what appeared to be a t-shirt and his wound was showing blood-soaked stains on top of his foot.

"Open the back door, Clancy."

I obeyed and waited by the car door as Daddy helped him down the two front steps. They had taken maybe three steps away from the porch when I heard the rifle cock. My eyes shifted quickly toward that ominous sound. Ruby was standing on her front porch, rifle in hard, aiming it in the general direction of her husband and my daddy.

I could see that her right index finger was clearly on the trigger this time.

"Put the gun down, Ruby," Daddy said.

"He tried to take my gun from me, Sheriff. He deserves to be locked up. Why'd ya let him out of the closet?"

"Stupid bitch. Put the damn gun down!" Scruggs yelled at his wife.

"Let me handle this, Scruggs," Daddy said. "Ruby, he's injured and I need to get him to a doctor. His foot is bleeding badly."

"I know. I shot 'im."

"You planning to shoot him again?" Daddy said.

"If he tries to take my gun," she answered calmly.

"Well, he's not going to take your gun, Ruby. Just put it down and let me get him into the car."

"No, Sheriff. I don't want him goin' to no doctor. I want ya to put him back into that closet."

"I can't do that, Ruby."

"Woman, I'm losing blood. I need to see a damn doctor. Now let the sheriff here git me in this here car so I can git to a doctor fast!"

She shook her head no, and kept the rifle pointed in the general direction of the two men. I decided it was time for me to intervene since this whole scene could easily turn ugly any second now. Part of me did not really care if Ruby shot her husband. But all of me did care that she might shoot my daddy, and that was absolutely no good.

"Ruby, would you let me have the rifle?" I said.

"What ya want this here gun fer? I need it right now, can't ya see that?"

"Evidence, Ruby. We need it for evidence."

"What? What ya talkin' 'bout?"

"I just want to look at the gun. You see that mud on the side?"

She rotated the rifle slightly as she dropped it down from her eye level.

"Wut mud? ... oh, this here mud-stuff on the wood?" she asked. The barrel was still aimed in the general direction of my daddy and Scruggs.

While holding onto the middle of the barrel with her left hand, Ruby tried to brush some of the shiny particles off the stock with her right hand, without much success. Once she realized the mud was not easily removed, she quickly returned her right hand to the trigger guard and her index finger to the trigger. She was fast, I'll give her that.

"What's this junk on my gun?"

"Mud, mostly. But there's another substance in that mud. We need to check it."

"It don't look like reg'lar mud."

"That's why I wanted to look at the rifle," I said. "It needs to be checked by the lab."

She slowly walked down the steps from her porch, moving purposefully towards me. I had no idea what she was going to do. The gun was still aimed in the direction of the two men.

She approached me, handed me the rifle, and said nothing.

I moved cautiously toward the driver's side of the vehicle, opened my daddy's door, removed the car keys, and then proceeded to walk to the trunk of the car.

Ruby followed me as I approached the trunk, like a child might do when handing over a broken toy for repairs. I glanced back at her a couple of times and noticed that she never took her eyes away from the rifle I was carrying.

I unlocked the trunk, placed the rifle inside, and then shut it. While I was busy handling the rifle, my daddy took the opportunity to put Scruggs into the backseat. His bandage was almost completely soaked in blood by now.

"Let's go, Clancy," Daddy said to me.

"I'm gonna stay here with Miss Ruby."

I could tell that my daddy didn't like my plan, but I had him in a bind. He wouldn't dare do anything to upset the delicate balance that we had just established. He chose not to argue. He would have questions and points to make later. At the moment, he decided that he had better trust me. I felt a little older at that moment.

"I'll be okay," I said to him, with some confidence. I knew that if he had Donald Scruggs, I had nothing much to fear from Ruby. I think he realized that was well.

He got in and drove off.

"He don't deserve no help," Ruby said, after the noise from the departing car had subsided.

"Can we sit on the porch?" I asked.

"Why, sure, child. Let's sit in the swing. That's my favorite thang to do when all the men ain't around."

We both sat down. A couple of the dogs came up to smell me.

"Git away from her, Spike! Jody, go on now. She's company," Ruby said to the ones who were curious about my presence. The dogs slowly changed their minds about whatever they had intended, and walked over to the front door and lay down in front of it.

"They're good watch dogs," I said.

"They're a damn nuisance. I like cats. Hate dogs. Dogs belong to Donald. He used to hunt, now he don't do nothin' with 'em. They jest eat and sleep and bark."

"Tell me what happened?"

"With wut, child? Ya know, yore hair's so beautiful in the daylight. It's shiny and all. I like that shiny look ya got there. Now, wut is it ya wanna talk about, pretty girl?"

"Why'd you shoot your husband?"

"I tol' all that. I thought I tol' that already. He tried to take my gun away. We wrestled and the gun went off. It jest happ'n'd to be pointin' at his foot. I wish it had been pointin' higher."

"So you didn't shoot him on purpose?"

"Not really. I hate him, but ... I don't know. He should've left my gun alone. It's my gun, not his. He's mean. Awful mean. He's mean most the time. Mean as a snake. I do hate that man. Maybe I should've kilt 'im."

"I don't think that would be such a good idea," I said.

"Yeah, that'd be a good idea. Maybe I will yet," she was speaking as if in a trance. Her eyes were focused on something far away.

"Why did he want your gun so badly?"

"That's wut I kept askin' 'im, 'Why ya want my gun?' But he didn't make no sense. He sed that was wut ya came for last night. That didn't make no sense to me. I thought ya came to see me."

I decided it would be in my best interest not to clarify what she was thinking.

She stroked my hair and then suddenly noticed my eyes, as if for the first time.

"Good Lord, ya got green eyes. My, oh my, green eyes and red hair. Where'd you git those green eyes, child?"

"Mama and Daddy, I guess."

She laughed. It was the first time I could remember ever hearing her laugh. She laughed hard, too hard, and I was worried. What I had said was not that funny.

"Mommy and Daddy, yes that's how it happens, I guess. Jest have to have the right mommy and daddy. Some of us are lucky, and some of us are cursed."

"Where'd you put your husband?"

"Wut?"

"After you shot him, where did you put him?"

"Oh, that. I dragged him into the large hall closet and locked the door. But he wuz a strong 'un and I knew that once he came to his senses he would be meaner than ever, so I took some wood and nailed it across the door to keep him inside."

"Why'd you do that?"

"Well, I guess to make sure that he didn't git out and git my gun, and go downtown to swear out that complaint against ya."

"Thank you," I said. It was the only thing I could think to say in response. I had the feeling it wasn't really appropriate, but then again maybe it was.

"Oh, you're welcome, Miss Clancy. You're a nice girl. And purdy. Sometimes I used to wish for a little girl. Now, well, I just wish for my boys to come back."

She stopped talking at that point and stared straight ahead. She began to cry softly as we both pushed the porch swing with our feet in unison.

"This is fun," I said to her. She smiled and nodded her head, still crying a little. Every few seconds, she would wipe the new tears from her face.

It was peaceful on her porch. Quiet, too. The only noise was coming from the rhythmic, squeaky porch swing as we pushed it back each time. No noise on the follow through, just the back-swing. And, there was some noise coming from the dogs. They were snoring quietly, tranquil-like. Ruby finally stopped crying.

"I need to ask you about something you said last night," I began.

"What is it, child?"

"You said something about killing the butterflies. You remember that?"

"I used to love butterflies. I figer'd butterflies and love went together, ya know. I went to that prom dance in high school years back. It wuz my first prom dance. Cum to think of it—my last prom dance as well. I had this frilly, pink gingham dress and all. Got me some new black shoes to go with it. Well, new fur me. Hand-me-downs, ya know. Older sister had sum. They nearly fit, well, almost. I think I wuz purdy back then. Maybe not as purdy as you are. At least I think I looked purdy that eve'ning. Had on sum makeup and all."

"You're still pretty," I lied.

"Naw. Not now. Donald done drove all the pretty outta me a long time ago. Once upon a time, I wuz pretty, I reckon. Some says I wuz a real looker, ya know. At that dance, child. I think I wuz a real looker at that dance."

"Who'd you go to that dance with?"

"That was Squirrel who took me to my first prom dance."

"Squirrel?" I repeated.

"Ever'body called him Squirrel. Weren't his real name or nothin'. He looked like a squirrel when he wuz a little kid ... that's where he got the name. He wuz handsome when he dated me."

"So how do butterflies and love fit into your story about the prom?"

"We danced that night ... Lordie, must have been past midnight before we stopped dancin'. That wuz fun. But we left and drove down towards the river, ya know, to be alone."

I nodded like I knew exactly what she was talking about. I had a hunch I knew what she meant, but I wasn't completely certain. My experiences as an eleven year old were limited in terms of dances and the like.

"Squirrel and I spent the whole night at the river. When I woke up the next morning there wuz butterflies all over me, all around me, they wuz everywhere!" She sounded genuinely excited at this point.

"So you thought that the butterflies were a good sign?"

"I reckon," she said. "We made love that night, girl, don't ya know. And the butterflies were all over me the next morning. I wuz naked as a jay-bird, except for those butterflies."

"So what made you cry?"

"Cry? I didn't cry, child. Why, I wuz in love for the first time in my life! I thought those butterflies wuz the sure sign of it. But I wuz wrong. Don't you see? Very, very wrong."

She stared off into the distance once again. Maybe she was focused upon something buried in her mind. The swing had come to a stop by this time. The only sound was the wind blowing some of the oak leaves in the trees in her front yard. Some clouds would block the sun now and again, drifting past it, permitting only an occasional shaft of sunlight to come through and allow a little brilliance in the dirt-yard. That brilliance never last long because of the next cloud that would come and block the light once again. The clouds and the sun played at this while Ruby and I sat in the swing on her porch.

Several minutes passed.

"So what made you change your mind about the butterflies?" I said after some moments of silence passed between us.

"Wut?" she seemed stunned when my question broke the silence. "Wut'd ya say, child?"

"You said you were wrong about the butterflies. How do you know you were wrong?"

"They wuz there when Squirrel said goodbye to me. They wuz flying and flitterin' all around, like they wuz happy or sum'thin'. I wuz hurtin' bad and those damn butterflies were jest flyin' about like ever'thang wuz lovely and all. I hated them fer that. They wuz like happy and all, and I wuz in misery 'cause he says bye to me. Says to me 'hits over, girl.'"

"This all happened the next morning after you woke up?"

"Naw, child. This wuz years later. Squirrel and I used to meet out there near the river to make love. One day he jest said we had to stop. He wuz worried and fearful."

"What was he afraid of?"

"My husband. Donald Scruggs hisself."

"You were in love with two men?"

"Naw, jest one. I never loved Donald Scruggs. My daddy forced me to marry that sonofabitch. No one cud love that evil man, not even his mama."

"But you had two children with Donald Scruggs, didn't you?" I knew that this was one sure way to test the accuracy of the rumors I had heard from Aunt Nona.

"Never! Those boys were not his'in. He had nothing to do with that. He only thinks he did. I let him think it so he won't kill me. Naw, those babies were from me and Squirrel making love near the river."

"So, you hate the butterflies because years after you and Squirrel had two children together, he decided that it was too dangerous to keep seeing you … and that's the reason for your dislike of the butterflies?"

"I don't wanna talk no more," she said. She started the swing again and the sound of the rhythmic squeaking returned.

I waited several minutes while I considered what I might say to begin again.

"I love butterflies. They're so innocent and beautiful. They fill the world with so much color and emotion," I said.

Ruby put both of her feet down flat on the wooden floor of the porch. The swing stopped immediately. She turned and looked me squarely in the face.

"Those damn butterflies were there when Squirrel said it was over. Flitterin' 'round like they wuz sum'thin' special and all. I wuz hurtin' like hell and they wuz payin' no mind to my misery. And that ain't all," she said and turned away from me.

"What else? Did something else happen?" I asked.

"Those damn butterflies," she spoke softly now and I could see tears coming down her face again.

"They wuz there when my babies were killed. My babies were killed in that same place where they wuz created. God Almighty!" she screamed out.

I jumped a little. Her sudden outburst startled me.

"But I found Buster and Micah in the barn," I said. I knew that few people were aware that her sons actually drowned in that black swamp behind the barn. My daddy decided that he would guard the information he had received from the M.E.

"Donald took me out to the spot. That's when he had that Greesome woman out there. He toll me that she wuz in on it with that nigger, that she had helped him kill my babies. Right there where those butterflies were, flitterin' and dancin' like nothin' had ever happened to my boys. I lost it all right there, child. Ever' thing. Right there in that spot with those butterflies dancin' all around with joy. She deserved to die, and so did those butterflies."

# Chapter Forty-four

Mama was standing near the back door when I came into the yard. I was moving towards the back steps, hoping to slip into the house, unannounced, as it were.

"You escape from jail?" she asked.

I knew she had to be kidding me.

"Something like that. I didn't break out, if that's what you mean."

"Your father called and told me some of what transpired. He told me that Ruby Scruggs shot her husband in the foot, and then locked him in the closet at their house. It all sounded funny, in a way, but I know that it probably wasn't."

"Yes, ma'am, it does sound a little comical, but not funny, as you say. Mama," I said as I sat down on the back steps, "she's pathetic. I feel so sorry for her. I think she's crazy, too. Not the way I talk about Aunt Nona. I think the death of Ruby's sons has made her crazy."

Mama sat down on the top step. I was sitting a few steps below her. I turned sideways so that I could look at her while we talked.

"Losing your children like that is enough to make a body crazy. One day you'll know… well, I guess the truth is none of us will ever know what she feels like until we've suffered the same way. Goodness knows, I hope you never have to experience what she experienced."

"Where's Daddy now?"

"He's at the doctor's office with Donald Scruggs. He said he'd be there for a while, and then he wasn't sure what he was going to do."

She offered to fix me some lunch, but I told her I wasn't hungry. I told her that I was going to lie down for a little while, maybe take a nap. She felt my forehead and asked me if I was feeling okay. I told her I was fine, just a little tired from all of the morning's activities.

I couldn't sleep initially. I spent the first couple of hours re-examining all that happened. I went through the evidence again and tried to decide how it all fit together. Ruby almost confessed to killing Betty Ann Greesome. Almost. At the very least, she was there, or so it seemed to me. And maybe she had something to do with it. I didn't believe for a minute that she had anything to do with the death of her children. However, her husband was a different matter in that regard.

It just wouldn't all fit together. I had pieces of the story, but not a complete picture as yet. I wondered how Ralph Hines was involved. Why was Greesome disposed of? If she had been the leader of the therapy group, then who was in charge now? Was there someone else involved in this horrible mess? Too many questions—too few answers.

I had some answers, but I was still left with too much I could not explain.

I finally fell asleep and had a terrible dream about seeing butterflies dying in a forest fire. I saw Greesome in my dream, as well as Ralph Hines and Donald Scruggs, but there was another person off in the shadows of the trees. I couldn't see the face. It was one of those fitful dreams, where, when you finally awaken, you are relieved that it was only a dream.

It was close to supper time when I crawled from the bed. I was hungry at last. Mama fixed one of her all-vegetable suppers, plus biscuits. I ate two helpings of everything, including several biscuits.

After we had finished, Daddy told us that Donald Scruggs would be sleeping in one of the jail cells that night, maybe even longer. Daddy convinced him that it might be safer there than going home to Ruby. He also promised Scruggs that he would drive out to Ruby's and check on her. Daddy had been afraid that something else might happen between the two of them if Donald went home. He felt it safer if the two of them remained separated for the time being.

Then he told us that late in the afternoon some of Donald's brothers showed up at the jail demanding his release. Rumors were all over town that Daddy had arrested Donald, so they came downtown to make sure that justice was served. Daddy told us that it was funny when Donald got mad, and ran off all of his brothers. Even though he was lying in his cell with the door wide open, they couldn't understand why he was having to spend the night in the jail. It was too much for them to comprehend.

"And his foot?" I asked.

"Shot his little toe. Not much left of it. Hurts like—well, you can imagine. He'll survive."

"How long's he gonna stay at the jail?" Scottie said.

"Don't know. I can't put him up indefinitely. He'll have to go home sometime."

"And in the meantime?" I said.

"Well, I thought we'd all drive over to Ruby's and visit. Since I promised to check on her. You up for a trip?" Daddy was looking at Mama when he asked that question.

"All of us?" Mama said.

"Yes, ma'am. Let's make it a family affair. I think it might be good for Ruby to have contact with another woman, you, my dear … as well as an entire family. Might be good for her to see a family that's not dysfunctional."

"This family?" my mother asked, smiling at my father. It was a rare smile from her.

My mother attempted some humor. It was a unique moment in my young life. Perhaps there was still another side to her that I had not as yet uncovered or been exposed to. That being said, somewhere in her smile, I detected a hint of displeasure, none the less. My mama's reputation was firm, I thought on some fronts. One of those was that she wasn't much into visiting strangers in person, especially those who were poor.

She reluctantly agreed with Daddy, or somehow he won out in the circumstances surrounding the events of that momentous summer.

We all helped at clearing the table and washing the dishes. It took a good half-hour before we all climbed into the car. Scottie was the only one who finally protested his participation in this family trip. There was no way our parents would ever consider allowing him to remain home by himself. He put up a little fuss, but it was no use. They finally agreed that he could remain in the car once we arrived at Ruby's. He stopped complaining. He grabbed a handful of toy soldiers and climbed into the back seat with me.

On the ride over to Ruby Scruggs' house, Scottie wanted to know what the word *dysfunctional* meant. I smiled. Daddy laughed. Mama was stoic. Apparently, she did not consider his question humorous.

The dogs greeted our car as usual, but by now we were so used to being surrounded by barking dogs that we didn't give them a second thought. We exited the car and walked to the porch as if they were not there. Scottie remained steadfast in the backseat with his soldiers.

Mama was hesitant, but grabbed my daddy's arm and held on while we proceeded toward the front steps. The screen door slammed hard, announcing Ruby Scruggs' presence on her front porch. She stomped her foot a few times; the dogs quit barking, and then scurried off to their respective corners. I was impressed with Ruby's effective powers.

"Hope you don't mind some company, Mrs. Scruggs?" Daddy said.

"No, sir, Sheriff. Things is quiet around here with Donald off some-where, except for them dogs of his." She sat in the porch swing. She made no offer for us to sit, but we all sat anyway. Mama and Daddy sat in the plastic chairs available. I perched myself next to Ruby. I liked porch swings.

"That's one reason I came by," Daddy said after we were all sitting. "I didn't want you to worry about Donald."

"Hell, I ain't worried about him. God only knows what he's up to right now."

"I doubt if he's up to much. He's nursing an injured foot," Daddy said.

I sensed that my father, the Sheriff, was easing into the conversation, and he didn't want to say anything which might startle her. I heard him say once that when you deal with a person who is slightly out of tune, it is always helpful to gradually remind them of what has happened. For my thinking, Ruby Scruggs was slightly out of tune. Considering everything that had happened in the last few weeks, anyone would be out of tune, so to speak.

"He's always gettin' hisself into bad stuff," she said, turning to look directly at me for the first time since our arrival. "Yore hair looks mighty purdy this evening, little girl. Yore name is Clancy, ain't it?"

I could count on Ruby appreciating my red hair even if she had to have some confirmation regarding my identity. Ruby had a habit of needing to verify the folks around her before she could proceed in a conversation. This normally occurred after a period of time had elapsed between meeting the same people. Sometimes it happened after a day or more. Sometimes it might occur after only a few minutes had passed. I suppose it indicated a short attention span. It might also indicate something other than that.

"Yes, ma'am."

"Who's that woman sittin' over there?" she spoke in a subdued voice, but it was still loud enough for Mama to hear her.

"That's my mama," I said.

"Awh, git on. Why, she's purdy like you! But her hair ain't red," she sounded disappointed.

"No, ma'am, but her eyes are green like mine. Her hair used to be slightly red, back when she was a little girl. Her color changed over time."

"Whataya mean changed?"

"Mrs. Scruggs," Mama jumped into my conversation with Ruby, "when I was a girl my hair was what you would call auburn, a reddish-tint color. It wasn't at all like Clancy's, you know, really red."

"Oh. Shame ain't it? Red's such a purdy color. Yur child here has such lovely hair. I wish my hair wuz red."

"Why, Mrs. Scruggs, you have pretty hair," Mama lied, and we all knew it. Ruby Scruggs' locks looked as if she was wearing a bonafide mop head, and I'm being kind. At the very least, it was badly in need of washing. Combing or brushing would not have hurt it in the least.

"Thank ya for sayin' so, but I ain't washed it in days. I guess I jest been too busy to do it. Naw, that's not truthful. I ain't felt like doin' that. Too much goin' on. Yeah, too much stuff. My mama used to wash my hair, back when I wuz smallish."

"I'll help you wash your hair, Ruby. Why don't we go inside and do that now?" Mama said, surprising us all.

I cut my eyes to my daddy, he shrugged slightly, surprised at this offer from his wife. I don't think he was as stunned as I was.

"You'd do that fur me?" Ruby sounded shocked herself.

"I'd be happy to," Mama said, standing up and holding out her hand to Ruby while opening the screen door so that they could both go inside for the ritual.

"You come too, Miss Clancy. You come too," Ruby said.

She stepped out of the swing and extended her hand to me. I took it and we walked together into the house. Mama followed us. Daddy stayed on the porch with the dogs. Scottie was still mulling life over in the darkness of the backseat, but only doing that intermittently; my informed suspicion was that he was busy playing with his toy soldiers without considering much of anything else.

We followed her into the kitchen area.

"Mama always washed my hair at the kitchen sink cause our bathroom wuz so tiny," she informed us. "My bathroom is kinda tiny as well."

"This'll do nicely then, Ruby. It's okay if I call you Ruby?" Mama said.

"It's my name. I like it a damn sight better'n that gawd-awful Mrs. Scruggs."

"Ruby, we need some shampoo," Mama said.

"It's in the bathroom somewhere." She made no offer to go get it. She stood her ground by the kitchen sink in an awkward manner. It was an odd moment in what I thought was an odd scene, especially with my mother playing the central character.

"Clancy," Mama said to me directly, "go look for the shampoo, please."

I left, and a few minutes later returned with the bottle. Mama took it and began the process of wetting Ruby's hair and pouring the shampoo onto her head. She lathered it and began scrubbing her scalp. I could tell that she wasn't scrubbing as hard as she does mine. She was being gentle with Ruby.

I sat down in a kitchen chair and watched this surprising scene unfold. If someone had told me that my mother would be doing this domestic chore on behalf of Ruby Scruggs, I would immediately have known that such a person did not know my mother in any way. My mother washed her own hair. Once upon a time, when Scottie and I were quite small, probably toddlers, she washed our hair. That was years ago. In the last few years, I can only recall a few occasions when my brother came home completely filthy, head to toe, and she intentionally scrubbed his scalp. She did not trust him to clean his hair as required by the amount of dirt he had accumulated. No way he was going to sleep in his bed on her clean sheets, save a complete scrubdown prior to bedtime.

I was witnessing the exception to the rule.

I could tell that Ruby was enjoying this experience. I doubted if anyone since her mother had washed Ruby's hair.

Mama did it twice. She told Ruby that she thought her hair deserved extra special treatment, and that it would be good for her scalp to do it again. Ruby didn't say a word of argument, and allowed Mama to repeat what appeared to be considerable enjoyment for Ruby.

"Do you have a hair dryer?" Mama asked at the appropriate time.

"Naw, we ain't got none of that stuff, Mrs. Sheriff."

"Oh, Ruby, I'm sorry. I didn't even tell you my name. I'm Rachel."

"Rachel," Ruby repeated, as if trying to get a handle on that name.

"Rachel Evans, Ruby."

"Rachel Evans," she said. "That's a purdy name. So you must be Clancy Evans?"

"Yes, ma'am," I said.

"Little red-headed Clancy Evans. Purdy, real purdy."

Mama sent me after another towel, and it took me a while to find one clean enough. They all seemed to be used, but I finally found one that looked cleaner than most.

Ruby was sitting at the kitchen table when I returned with the almost clean towel. Mama stood behind her and rubbed her hair until it was nearly dry. That took several minutes.

"Rachel Evans, tell me why neither one of my boys had red hair?"

Mama looked at me as if to say, "What on earth do I say now?" Mama, of course, knew the correct answer to a question like that, but she wasn't quite sure how to explain it to Ruby.

"Well, it has to do with the way in which you are made and the way your —," she hesitated, no doubt considering what to say next. I knew that she was thinking about the rumors we had heard regarding the father of Ruby's children. I hadn't had a chance to tell Mama that those rumors were fact.

"Made how?" Ruby asked after Mama's pause lasted too long to suit Ruby.

I decided that an eleven year old girl's answer to the question might get closer to helping Ruby understand. Not that my mother didn't know the answer; she had plenty of education.

"Created," I said. "We're all created differently. Some of us have brown hair, some black, some blonde, and some red. And then when you get married, your husband brings how he was created and then there's this mix."

"A mix," she repeated as if she had never heard that before.

The truth was, I had never heard it explained quite like that before either.

"Clancy's right, Ruby. It's a mixture. Let's say that you have blonde hair and your husband has black hair, then some of your children could have blonde hair and some black."

"Or some brown," I added. Mama frowned at me. She was trying to keep it simple I think.

"So, anything's possible?" Ruby asked.

"No, not anything. Ruby, the color of our hair is in the genes we have. Genes determine everything about us. They carry the traits, like eye color, hair color, you know, stuff like that," Mama was working hard on her explanation.

"How's that?"

"Well, I have a gene that caused my eyes to be green. I was given that gene by my mother and my father when I was created. I had no control over it. But my parents determined the color of my eyes because of their genes," my mama said.

Mama was rubbing a little harder now as she tried to explain this subject to Ruby. Every now and then Ruby would say, "Oh," and Mama would just keep talking. I thought that Mama did a great job of unraveling a very complicated subject so that just about anyone could understand it. Well, almost anyone.

"So it's my fault that my boys didn't have red hair?"

# CHAPTER FORTY-FIVE

Mama and I took turns brushing Ruby's hair that night. I think she enjoyed it. Perhaps most women might enjoy such an experience. It can do the whole body good. I wasn't used to it, since my mother never offered to brush mine. Besides that, I was mostly too busy fishing. I did my own hair, washing and then letting it drip-dry of its own accord. My methodology permitted me to continue on my busy schedule while the hair dried itself. I simply permitted myself to suffer with the developing curls that naturally erupted from my routine. I didn't like the natural curls, but I managed to hide them most days. I tied my red locks back each day after a wash, keeping them hidden and out of the way while I did what I enjoyed, fishing for the most part.

It took a little over an hour before we had finally finished, and were ready to return to the front porch. Mama told me to go call Daddy to come inside so that he could see Ruby's hairdo. She hadn't done anything to it but wash, dry and brush it a few hundred times. However, Mama did take a few minutes to comb it into a rather nice shape or style, or what have you. It looked good, I must confess. I was surprised and pleased at what my mother had accomplished.

Mama had a reason for calling Daddy inside. She knew exactly how he was going to react. Some men would have simply said "Oh, you washed your hair. Very nice," and let it go at that. Not my daddy. He knew better than that. If he had said that, Mama would have killed him on the spot. But then, she knew he would never say that.

The three of us girls were standing in the small living room when Daddy entered.

"Wow!" he said, "Ruby, your hair looks beautiful."

Mama smiled broadly at him.

A large smile spread gradually over Ruby's face. She lowered her eyes, apparently embarrassed a little. I would bet that it had been a long time since a man had complimented her about anything.

"Thanks, Sheriff. It's just a wash," Ruby said softly.

"Maybe so, but it looks great. Do you feel better?"

"I reckon. Say, why don't I make us all some coffee or sumthin'?"

"Oh, you don't need—" Mama tried to say.

"It's the least I cud do fer you folks. I know … tea. I'll make us sum iced tea. That sounds better than coffee, don't it? Ya know, being the summer time and all. Sweet tea is wut I'll do fer ya."

She grabbed me and led me back into the kitchen.

"You can help me, Miss Clancy. Y'all jest sit yore selves down on the sofie, if ya can find a spot. Move those damn cats if need be."

Ruby seemed a little more alert now that her hair was clean. I followed her orders in the tea making, and after a few minutes we were all seated in the messy living room, sipping iced tea that was entirely too sweet even by Southern standards. I didn't dare ask for lemon. Mama would have been mortified. If it wasn't offered, we were told not to ask for anything. We endured the sweetness.

"Sheriff, do ya know where my husband is?" Ruby said, returning to a prior subject from earlier in the evening.

"That's another reason I came over tonight, Ruby. I wanted to tell you about Mr. Scruggs. He's sleeping in the jail tonight."

"Good," she said and laughed. "It's about time you arrested him."

"Oh, he's not arrested. He's just sleeping there."

"Whataya mean?"

"He's simply sleeping in one of the bunks at the jail tonight. I was afraid that you might shoot him again if he came home."

Mama and I winced when he said that. I thought he was being a little too honest. It was a funny line, but I dared not laugh, or smile.

"Probably right, Sheriff, even though it wuz an accident. He tried to take my gun, like I told ya. Even though he's got his own gun. Jest like mine, his is. Jest like mine. Said he needed to clean it or sumthin' stupid like that. He ain't ever cleaned a gun in his life. I told 'im that he ain't gonna git my gun twice. Told 'im to use his own gun from now on."

"He borrowed your rifle one other time?" Daddy said, fishing for something.

"Borrowed, hell! He stole it. Jest took it from the corner of the bedroom where I keeps it, without so much as a word of askin'. I didn't know it, though, not until we got home."

"Why did he need to use your rifle?" Daddy asked.

"I don't know why he took mine and not his. Oh, I know what he did with it, but he could've used his own and not mine."

"So what did he do with your rifle?" Daddy asked.

"He scared that woman."

"What woman?"

"That fat Greesome woman," she said.

"How did he scare her?"

Her eyes seem to glaze over at this point, and she stared off at something in the distance. This seemed to be a pattern she had whenever she was trying to recall something that happened in the past.

"He told me," she said, "that Greesome woman had helped that nigger kill my babies. I told 'im that we had to call ya, Sheriff, and have her arrested. But no, he wuz so smart he says that we need to scare her first, and then we call the sheriff."

I noticed that Ruby's eyes watered while she told us the situation.

She paused, rubbed her eyes with both of her fists, and then looked over at my mother. Mama took that as a clue to find a tissue for her to use on her eyes. Mama left and returned quickly with a handful of toilet paper. She gave it to Ruby. Ruby placed it in her lap and didn't use it on her eyes.

Ruby continued her remembrance.

"We drove over to that Greesome woman's apartment next to the church and she came out and got into the car, all silly like, like we wuz goin' out on the town or sumthin'. I never did know how Donald got her to git in that car. We talked about kidnappin' her and all. But hell, we didn't need to kidnap her, she just climbed in the stupid car. Why'd she do that, Sheriff? What ya reckon Donald said to her to git her in that car?"

"I don't know, Ruby."

"Me either, Sheriff. All so strange, I swear. If I live to a hunderd, I'll never understand folk. He never did 'splain that to me. I asked him at least a million times. Nothin'. He says it's none of my beeswax. God, I hate that expression."

"So what happened after she got into the car?"

"Well, we drove out to that place where all those damn butterflies wuz. That's where Donald said it happened. Where ..." she wiped her eyes hard again, this time using the toilet paper. "...where my boys were killed."

She stopped and this time Daddy just let her sit without asking her anything. I thought she was going to cry. Her eyes watered again, but there was no real crying. But she was feeling something strong, and I could tell that she was hurting more than a little.

"I'm sorry, Sheriff. I can't help feeling bad 'bout this whole mess, ya know. I miss my boys so damn much. Ya have no idea wut it's like to lose both yore childrun."

"You're right about that, Ruby," Daddy said to her, and I knew he meant it.

She slowly gathered some strength and continued her tale.

"I held the gun on Greesome and Donald tied her up. I think it wuz then she got really scared. I wuz enjoyin' it sumthin' fierce, Sheriff. I held my rifle on her while Donald tied her up and made her walk through the bushes to that mud hole behind the barn. Donald then made her git on her knees in that mud. She got mud all over her pretty dress and I laughed. I wuz enjoyin' it. She helped kill my babies. She deserved to have sum fear. Then Donald took some kind of box outta a sack and showed it to her and he laughed at her. I didn't understand none of that, Sheriff."

"Did he say anything to her?"

"Yeah, he talked and she cried. Lord, she cried. Screamed sum, too. But ain't no one gonna hear nothin' out there. I don't recall exactly what he said, Sheriff. He held up that box and made fun of her. But I got no memory of wut he said."

"Did she say anything about the box?"

"Naw, she never mentioned it. She jest begged fur her life, like we wuz gonna kill her. We never made no plans to kill her, Sheriff. I wouldn't have none of that. I never did believe Donald when he told me she and that nigger kilt my babies. No, sir. No part of that. I didn't like her none, but I never got the notion she wud kill anybody. Ya know how sum folks give the sense that they wud kill ya in second? Well, she never did that fur me. She maybe wuz there, but didn't kill nobody. And I told Donald that. He jest laughed and said not to worry 'bout that. Then he tells me to go put the barrel of my rifle in her mouth. I didn't want to do that. I figured she wuz scared enough by now and I wuz ready to take her back home. I figured she'd had enough. She wuz black with mud all over her legs and part of her dress. She'd had enough, Sheriff, fer sure. She wuz really scared. So, I says no to him."

I thought it was more than just interesting that Ruby's story tonight was a little different from the version she told me last night. This version was more amplified. I thought it better to let her say whatever she wanted to say rather than interrupt her flow. Daddy and I could talk later about the differences in her stories.

She looked toward the floor as if she was finished telling the story. We waited at least a minute or two to allow her time to say more. She was silent.

"What happened next, Ruby?" my dad said.

"Lord help me, Sheriff. He took the gun outta my hand and stuck that rifle barrel nearly down her throat. She gagged and acted like she cudn't breathe none. Then her eyes rolled back some and she fell over dead. Leastwise, I tho't she wuz dead. She looked dead. I think she had herself a heart attack right there in that mud. Ya know. Her face fell right in that black junk. He didn't show it much, but I could tell that Donald wuz scared sum. She weren't breathin' none and Donald said she didn't have no pulse. Anyhow, he told me to go lift up her head outta the mud, and when I did he stuck that rifle in her mouth again and he shot her."

"Why'd he do that, Ruby?"

"Meanness, Sheriff. He's damn mean. Heart attack weren't good enough fer him. No, he had to shoot her and git blood and junk all over my dress. I had mud and blood and … all over my dress and my shoes. That dress was practically new, don't ya know. Had it, I don't know, maybe a couple of years. It wuz my new favorite dress, but it wuz covered with mud and blood. My shoes as well. I went back to the car, took off my shoes and dress and tossed 'em into the trunk. Ya know, clean 'em up later. But I didn't wanna keep wearin' 'em any longer 'cause a wut had jest happened."

"Do you know what your husband was doing when you went to the car?" Daddy asked.

"He wuz buryin' that box of hers, leastwise that's wut he sed he wuz gonna do."

"And you didn't bury your dress and shoes, Ruby?" Daddy's question surprised me a little. He was actually suggesting that one of her details might have been wrong.

"No, sir, Sheriff. Not this time. I kep 'em, ya know, fer cleanin'. Clothes bein' so all-fired costly nowadays. Cum to think of it, they're still out there in the trunk now. I forgot all about them."

"You recall anything else about that night that Betty Ann Greesome died?" he asked.

"Jest ridin' home with a mean sonofabitch husband of mine. It wuz summertime, but ya know, I wuz cold ridin' back without a dress on, nothin' but bra and panties. It wuz a might cold, ya know. He never offered to do anything fer me. Never sed a word, the whole way home. Nary a word. When he gets that streak of meanness, he never notices nothin'. He wuz mean to shoot that woman like that, her bein' dead and all, I figured, ya know, already dead, most likely, why do that? No cause to do it, except meanness, Sheriff. And he used my gun, not his. I wudn't 'bout to let him have my gun again. Don't ya understand now?"

Daddy nodded his head slowly as if he understood. I wondered exactly what he understood, if there was anything completely clear in all of this. Mama sat down next to Ruby and put her arm around her. I felt sorry for Ruby. I had a strong feeling that she was telling us more of the truth tonight than what we had heard the might before. Her husband had used her grief and anger to make her do something she never would have done without his urging. But I was confused about the box. That was the one part of her story that didn't make any sense. I knew that the box had been hers. I couldn't understand why she didn't recognize the box. Maybe it had been too dark.

Still, one part of her story provided some clarification of what I had found on one of my excavations. That old sack containing a dress and some shoes were definitely from an earlier time, much earlier than this summer. That short line about her not burying her clothes *this time* clarified for me our earlier suspicions. Apparently that spot in the woods had been significant for Ruby for many years. Maybe just a little too significant.

I could tell that Daddy was in a bind about what to do with Ruby. He knew that he had to arrest her, but he also knew that she had suffered a lot already. She had probably suffered more than anyone, including Mr. Joe, at least up to this point. But then, my friend Mr. Joe had suffered in ways that Ruby would never suffer. Could I say the same thing about Ruby compared to him? Maybe suffering is simply no respecter of persons, no matter their station, their color, or their creed.

Mama must have read Daddy's mind. It was unusual for my mama to volunteer without being asked first. Washing Ruby's hair was not the only surprise we had that evening.

"I'll stay here with Ruby, if it's okay with Ruby," Mama said.

"Oh, that'd be nice, Rachel. Thank ya. It'd be nice to have sum company stay over fur a change. But ya don't really need bother yerself with it."

"Not a bother at all, Ruby," Mama said. "Maybe we can talk some more. You don't know much about me, do you?"

Daddy winked at me, gestured with his head toward the door, and offered a wry smile. Maybe I wasn't the only one learning something about Rachel Evans that summer.

Daddy and I walked through the front door and left the two women there. I caught the screen door as I followed my daddy onto the porch. I kept it from slamming.

Daddy didn't need a key to open the trunk of the Scruggs' old car. The whole locking mechanism was missing so that I could easily imagine the trunk lid made lots of noise when the car was moving, bouncing up and down on the Clancyville streets.

The dress and shoes were where Ruby said they were.

I watched Daddy place the evidence in a sack and then gently close the lid. He put the sack in the trunk of his official Sheriff's car, and then nodded at me as if to say that it was time to get in the car and head home.

We found Scottie asleep when Daddy and I climbed into the black-and-white.

"I'm confused about that box," I said.

"Me, too."

"And each time she tells that story about Miss Greesome, it's a little different," I said.

"What do you make of that? You believe she's lying intentionally to us?" Daddy asked.

"No, sir. I don't think so. I think the difference is that last night she didn't realize that Donald Scruggs was involved in the death of her sons."

"And where did she learn that tidbit?"

"Well, I had to point out to her that he must have been there since he knew that the two boys begged for their lives," I cut my eyes at him.

"Donald told her that?"

"That's what she said he said. So, I simply pointed that out to her, and her whole attitude changed."

"But what if Donald was just guessing about the boys begging? He could've just said it out of meanness."

"I didn't think of that. I thought it was a slip of his tongue."

"It might have been, but since we can't get inside his head, we don't know for sure, do we, Clancy Holmes, Ace Detective?"

"You think Mama will be okay tonight?"

"Your mama will be fine. She would never have volunteered if she didn't feel that she could handle the situation."

I stayed awake a long time that night thinking. I thought about Mr. Joe and wondered what he was focused on in that Dan River jail. I could easily imagine his overall concern about being found guilty of something he did not do. I thought about Donald Scruggs and how mean he was, especially to his wife as well as to other folks. My deep suspicion was that I was correct about Scruggs, and that he was involved somehow in the murder of Ruby's two boys. I had a strong impression that he had been present when they were killed.

Ralph Hines was also in my thoughts, but his role was not immediately clear to me. For my way of thinking, Hines was not intelligent enough to have much of role, at least not one of real leadership. So, I wondered how he fit into this whole mess.

But mostly I thought about Ruby, and how sad her life had been. I wondered what might happen to her eventually. I knew that Daddy would have to arrest her for her part in the death of Betty Ann Greesome. It was still unclear exactly what that part was. However, what we now knew, at least according to her latest story-version, placed her at the scene of the crime when Greesome was killed. I knew that my daddy would not want to arrest her and charge her. She was not the usual kind of criminal, if such a person existed. But despite my daddy's reticence with arresting and charging that poor woman, he would do it because he had to do it.

I finally fell asleep with all of those thoughts dancing inside my head.

Next morning I got dressed and stumbled down to breakfast about thirty minutes later than usual. Sarah was in the kitchen taking Mama's place at the stove. It had been a long time since Sarah had cooked breakfast in our home. The last time was when Mama was sick for a week in one of those bad winters where flu had landed nearly every-where in our county.

"Daddy already gone?"

"Yessum, he lit outta here like it wuz a fire or sumthin'. Yore mama done call'd and told me to tell him that Ruby Scruggs was gone, child."

"Gone where?"

"I don't know! Yore mama didn't say. All she said was that Ruby was gone. Yore daddy scrambled outta here like his pants wuz afire!" Sarah chuckled a little at her remark.

The phone rang and I beat Sarah to it.

"Hello," I said.

"Git the Sheriff to the phone!"

It was Ralph Hines. I knew that voice too well.

"He's not here now."

"Oh, Lord. Where'd he go?" Hines asked.

"I'm not sure. What's wrong?"

"We've got a crisis down here at the jail. You gotta find him. Ruby's got a rifle and—No! No! Don't shoot, Ruby. I'm putting the phone down—"

The line suddenly went dead. That was all I heard, but it was enough for me to know that something bad was happening downtown. I told Sarah that I was going to the jail, in case my daddy might call or come back to the house. I was guessing that he had gone over to retrieve Mama from the Scruggs' house.

I would have had Sarah call the dispatcher and have her contact Daddy that way, but I remembered that our dispatcher, Susan Chaney, had been out with a sick child.

I ran all the way to the jail. It took me less than ten minutes, and I was out of breath when I hurried through the door. No one was in the front office area. I heard voices coming from the cells. I entered where the door used to be. Daddy hadn't had time to replace it since the men of the town had broken it into small pieces.

Ruby was in the cell area with both Hines and her husband Donald. The two men were in a cell together and Ruby was holding a rifle on them. She was sitting across from the closed cell door that housed the two men. She was leaning against the wall. Her knees were bent with her feet flat against the floor. The rifle was resting on her right knee, held there by her right hand with her index finger touching the trigger. The barrel of her rifle was pointing toward the two men.

Her cheeks and eyes were wet. Apparently, she had been crying, but now she seemed to be fairly calm under the circumstances. Hines and Scruggs were anything but calm.

"You don't need to see this, Miss Clancy. You jest run along now. I've got business to take care of," Ruby spoke in a calm voice.

I noticed that her hair still looked nice. In fact, she was wearing a pair of seemingly clean blue jeans, a light yellow tank top underneath a large outer shirt, and some sandals on her feet. That oversized outer shirt was unbuttoned with its shirttail sagging onto the floor all around her.

"Git the sheriff, kid," Donald Scruggs yelled to me. Hines nodded furiously. He was apparently too frightened to speak.

I ignored Donald's directive.

"What kind of business, Ruby?"

"I'm gonna shoot me two dawgs," she said.

# CHAPTER FORTY-SIX

By the time Daddy and Mama arrived, our little jail was beginning to get crowded. Except for that lynch mob a few days ago, we usually didn't have this many in the jail at one time.

"Sheriff, you and your wife jest stay right where you are, okay? I got business here. Serious business. It's 'tween me and those two dirty old men in that cell."

Ruby had not altered her position in front of the cell since I had arrived. The rifle still rested across her knee with her hand holding it mostly by the trigger guard. Her finger had not moved from the trigger. She was ready to use it at a moment's notice.

She appeared to be calm, but looks can oftentimes be deceiving. Still, her demeanor was that of a person in control of herself, to say nothing of the situation at hand.

My parents were standing in the threshold. I was in front of them. It was easy enough for Ruby Scruggs to see us with her peripheral vision. However, her focus remained on the two men in the cell directly across from her.

I knew that my father wasn't about to go charging this woman for fear that the gun might go off and hit someone. He squatted down, and Mama and I backed up a little when he gestured with his hand for us to do so. He wanted us out of the line of fire as much as possible in such small quarters.

"Ruby, what kind of serious business do you have here with a rifle in hand?"

"Sheriff, I got to thinkin' last night about all that Miss Clancy and I has talked about. I's cum to the conclusion that my dear old sweet husband here, Mr. Donald Scruggs hisself, knows sum-thing 'bout the death of my boys. And this no-count skunk Ralph Hines does too! So, before I shoot them both, they gonna talk and answer sum questions."

"You've been here awhile, correct?" Daddy asked.

"Yessir, I has. Several minutes now, maybe half an hour or more."

"Have they said anything about the death of your sons?"

"Not yet. They been too busy yellin' and hollerin' and callin' me names. When they calms down, we gonna have this talk and they gonna tell me ever'thang they know 'bout my boys, and wut happened to 'em."

The two men were sitting on the bunk. Hines had his knees up against his chest while Scruggs had only one knee against his. His injured foot was extended out to the edge of the bunk. They both had their backs to the solid wall of the building. Neither of them appeared relaxed. At the threat from Ruby, they tried to move closer to the cement wall behind them, which was quite impossible at the moment. They were already pushing hard against it, and that particular wall was going nowhere. I could see the fear in their eyes.

"Okay, Ruby. Ask your questions," Daddy said.

"Sheriff!" Donald screamed out. "You can't let her do this! She's crazy. Craziest woman I ever knew! She's already shot me once. I ain't talkin.'"

Ruby lifted the rifle to her right eye with one swift motion. She obviously knew something about rifles and what to do with them if called upon.

"Oh, Lord. Ask yore questions, Ruby. I'll tell ya what I know," Hines pleaded.

"Shut up, Hines, ya idiot. Don't say a word! She's crazy," Donald said.

"Who kilt Buster?" she asked.

No one moved at first. Hines finally turned his head slowly and looked at Scruggs. He lifted his hand slightly and pointed to the man sitting next to him on the bunk. Nothing was said.

Seconds passed.

"He did," Hines said meekly after a few moments had gone by.

Scruggs slapped Hines viciously on the side of his head, and Hines went sprawling off the bunk and across the cell in our direction. Donald Scruggs had some strength, I'll say that for him.

"Ya stupid … I told ya to keep yore mouth shut!"

"Ya kilt my Buster, Donald? My first born?"

"Ruby, I told ya who kilt Buster, it wuz that nigger and that Greesome woman. I told ya all of that afore."

"You wuz there, jest like Clancy said."

"What duz that nosey kid know 'bout anything? No, I weren't there. I figured it all out, I tell ya. Ya see, I jest put two and two together and figured out who did it."

"You wuz there, ya lyin' snake! You wuz there. How else wud ya know that my babies begged and pleaded fur their lives? You told me they begged. How did you know that, if you wuz not there? Ya saw it all, didn't ya, Donald?"

"No, no. Ruby, honey, ya got it all wrong." He was smiling at her now and attempting some sweet talk, probably to convince her. It was rather disgusting, from my vantage point. I figured he was lying, and even a slightly deranged Ruby knew that as well.

She fired the rifle and the bullet caught him just below the knee cap in his good leg. The shot surprised us all. It was the sound that a rifle makes in a small area. Amplified, to say the least.

Mama gasped and jumped back toward the opened doorway. I stepped back as a reflex, and my Daddy flinched, and then, as if on impulse, moved ever so slightly in Ruby's direction. It was almost undetectable the way he moved so easily toward her.

"Awwwh!" Scruggs yelled and grabbed his leg as he rolled away from us, off of the bunk onto the cell floor. Hines didn't move a muscle. He appeared to be petrified.

"Ya stupid bitch! Ya shot me again!" Scruggs yelled.

"Ya lied," she said calmly.

"Oh, god it hurts!" he screamed in agony.

"It'll hurt again if ya keeps a lyin," she said and cocked the rifle.

"Okay, okay, ya bitch. I wuz there! I saw it all. That nigger and that woman kilt yore sons."

She fired again. If possible, I believed that the sound was even louder this time. Mama gasped again, this time a little louder. The bullet hit him in the right thigh. I had to admit that she was a good shot. No one could be that lucky two times in a row, even at the close distance she was from the two men. For my money, Ruby hit what she wanted to hit.

Daddy inched closer to her.

Scruggs grimaced again. He was writhing in pain on the cell floor, completely prone now. His left hand was holding his left knee and his right hand was pushing against his right thigh. He had probably forgotten his injured toe by this time.

"Tell me the truth, ya lyin' bastard!" she screamed at him.

"Hines killed Micah!"

"What?" she said.

"Hines, yore lover, he killed Micah!"

Hines stood up and looked around. There was no where for him to run. Ruby cocked the gun swiftly, then turned the rifle toward Hines. My daddy leaped from his crouched position and landed full-force on top of her. The gun went off and the bullet hit the concrete wall just above Hines' head. Daddy wrestled the rifle away from Ruby and rolled over onto his feet in one smooth motion. Ruby was lying on the floor crying.

I felt sorry for her.

Hines was standing in the corner of the cell whimpering. His pants were wet down the front, just below his belt and all the way to his knee. Scruggs was in serious pain on the cell floor.

"Let me outta here," Hines yelled.

"I don't think so," Daddy responded.

"You can't hold us here because of some crazy woman," he said.

"Watch me."

"I need a doctor," Scruggs grunted. I figured his pain was real.

"When you tell me the rest of the story, you'll get a doctor."

"You can't do that. That's ... that's ... illegal," he groaned.

"Maybe, but I want the truth. One of you is gonna talk, if not both."

"I ain't talkin," Hines said as if he were now in full control. "I want a lawyer."

Daddy cocked the rifle and pointed it in the general direction of Hines. It seemed to me that it was aimed somewhere in front of Hines' position.

"Whataya doin'? You're the sheriff. You can't shoot me."

"Ruby shot you. You think those two witnesses over there will testify against me?"

Daddy used his head to gesture in our direction. I waved a little at Hines. Mama nodded, as if in agreement with my daddy.

"Scruggs will tell them, he'll tell that you shot me."

"I don't think Mr. Scruggs is going to tell anybody anything, are you Donald?"

"Shoot the bastard," Donald yelped. "Go ahead and kill him for all I care."

"Looks like there are to be no witnesses to your story, Deputy Hines. Just you and me. It might turn out to be your word against mine. Who do you think the court will believe?"

Daddy lifted the rife and aimed at some lower part of Hines' body. There was a smile on my father's face. He was smiling at no one in particular.

"Okay, I killed Micah. I killed him. But Scruggs here, ... he killed Buster."

Ruby lifted her head from the floor. She then sat up, wiped her eyes and leaned against the wall behind her. This time her legs were straight out in front of her. She stared at Scruggs while the words of Hines tried to register with her. She was having trouble sorting out details, or so it seemed.

"Betty Ann Greesome and Joe Jenkins didn't kill anybody, did they?" Daddy asked.

"Naw. That nigger wasn't even there. We just used him. Seemed like a good thing to do, him being black and all. Greesome was there, but she was a wimp. She begged us not to do it."

"Why did you kill them?"

"They wuz scared of wut we was doin' and all. They wuz runnin' 'round screamin' and yellin'. At first we couldn't quiet 'em down. Scruggs smacked 'em a little, and they finally settled sum. Scruggs wuz worried that they might talk, them being youngins and all. We couldn't have none of that. But to tell ya the truth, I couldn't understand how Scruggs here could kill his own children, but he convinced me to kill the little one. I just choked him until he stopped breathing. That wuz easy. Scruggs did the same to Buster, then he hung 'im up in that nigger's barn to make it look like old Joe did it, ya know, some kind of sex crime or revenge against white folks," Hines said.

I could tell that Daddy was disgusted with the whole story. He was slowly shaking his head, as if wondering how they could do what they were confessing.

"They weren't his'in," Ruby said with tears in her eyes. "They belonged to you and me."

"What?" Hines said.

"They were yore's. Both of 'em wuz yore's."

"You never told me any different. Why didn't ya tell me?"

"I figur'd ya knew it. The whole town talked 'bout it."

"That wuz jest gossip, woman. You never said a word to me, not directly. Why didn't ya tell me?"

"Ya never asked. 'Cause you didn't love me. Ya jest wanted sex. Ya never loved me, even back when we got married. It wuz always sex. Always. Same thing. So, I never told ya the truth."

Hines seemed to be genuinely dumbfounded. It was the first time I had ever seen the man speechless.

"I wish you weren't hearing all of this," Mama whispered to me.

Hines looked at Scruggs, who lay groaning on the floor from the pain of his two new wounds.

"You knew, ya bastard! Didn't you? Ya knew that they wuz mine!" he screamed and jumped on top of Scruggs and began to hit him.

Daddy retrieved his keys from his desk in the front room, unlocked the cell, pulled Hines from Scruggs, and then put Deputy Hines in the other cell. While he was busy with Hines, Scruggs saw his opportunity to get away despite his leg wounds. He struggled to his feet, held onto the bars while he tried to move both of his injured legs, and headed slowly towards the open doorway. He was heading our direction, but not making good time.

When I heard the deafening sound of the revolver in that small jail room, I pulled Mama down and we both hit the floor hard. I looked up in time to see Scruggs fall face down right next to us. There was blood everywhere, even some on us. Donald Scruggs wasn't moving. Ruby had shot him in the head, and I could see tiny pieces of what I guessed to be his bloody skull all around me. There were a few fragments on my mother and me as well.

Mama gasped again and pulled my head close to her. She was doing her best to keep me from seeing what was inches away from us. I looked up from her protection every chance I got to see what might happen next.

I saw my daddy jerk the small revolver from Ruby's hand before she could shoot anyone else. My poor Daddy. He didn't want anyone to be killed, even Ralph Hines and Donald Scruggs, maybe the worst of the worst. Ruby had surprised him by bringing a rifle and a handgun to the party. She had apparently had the small weapon in the pocket of her blue jeans, and her long shirttail had helped to hide whatever bulge was there. She had definitely come prepared to take care of these two men. She finally got her chance. It was a small miracle that she failed to kill both of them.

I watched my father help her up, and then turn her so she faced the wall. He told her to place both of her hands above her head on the wall, and then he proceeded to check her for more weapons. He then gently guided her into the now vacant cell. Our small facility only had two cells for incarcerating criminals. We weren't really prepared for all of this, to say the least.

Daddy walked into the outer office and called the local funeral home. He told them what had happened, a short version. He suggested that they get in touch with the coroner as well. We waited in silence for the proper people to arrive. It took longer than I had thought it should. My limited experience informed me that when there was a dead body on hand, those proper, official people made good time in coming. Today was different, or so it seemed. It felt as if they took their own sweet time to arrive. But then again, I might have been wrong in my estimation of time. I simply wanted it all to be over with and done.

After Daddy had taken statements from both Mama and me, he told Mama to take me home. He said I had experienced enough today to fill a lifetime. As we were finally leaving, the ambulance personnel were taking what was left of Donald Scruggs' body away.

# CHAPTER FORTY-SEVEN

That night at supper Daddy told me that Ruby had begged him to let
her have a few minutes alone in a cell with Hines. Daddy told her that
he would love to do that, but that he couldn't. He knew that she wanted
to kill him. He told her the best he could do would be to grant them
some privacy while they occupied their separate cells. They would have
the entire night to talk.

I doubt if talking to Ralph Hines was what Ruby Scruggs had in
mind.

"I blame myself for the shooting," Daddy said.

"Nonsense, dear. You had no way of knowing what she was going
to do."

"I knew that she was a desperate woman. I just didn't do my job, and
search her thoroughly. If I handled her like a normal arrest, I would
have found that handgun. I could have prevented … the whole, damn
mess."

"Maybe some of it," I said, in his defense.

"Yeah, maybe some of it," he agreed.

"Well, you got the confessions. You solved the murders," Mama said.

"But can you use those confessions?" I asked.

"I think so. At least they were good enough for the judge to release
Mr. Joe."

"And you told him everything," Mama said to him.

"Well, I might have omitted that part about that other person holding the rifle and making some idle threats in an effort to get Hines and Scruggs to talk."

"Uh-uh," Mama said and nodded.

"Mr. Joe's home?" I said.

"Should be. Maybe we can go check on him after supper."

Scottie and I both grinned. That was the best news we had heard in quite some time.

"Scruggs dead?" Scottie asked.

"Scott!" Mama said in mock surprise. She was slowly getting used to our inappropriate, blunt discussions at the dinner table. I could tell that she still didn't like them.

"Yes," Daddy said, in answer to Scottie's question.

"So, what do you think will happen to Ruby?" I said.

"Mrs. Scruggs," Mama corrected me.

"I don't think she likes being called Mrs. Scruggs, Mama."

"Perhaps not, but you can't go around calling her by her first name. You're a child."

"But it's her name," Scottie said, trying to defend me.

"Listen, you two. I've already bent enough rules around here. Respect for adults will not change in this house! Do you understand me?"

We did, and said nothing more. We simply nodded our heads and wished that we were older.

Daddy waited for the smoke to clear before he answered my question.

"I plan to move her to the Dan River jail tomorrow. I don't think it's healthy for both Ralph Hines and Ruby Scruggs to be in the same general area of confinement in our small facility."

"You mean you don't think it's healthy for Ralph Hines," I said.

He smiled without answering.

"With the men prisoners?" Scottie asked.

"What?" Daddy asked.

"You said you were moving her to the Dan River jail. She gonna be placed in with the men?"

"There's a women's division. She'll be separate from the men," Daddy said.

"So Hines is safe?" I said.

"He's safe in jail here. Safe from Ruby."

"So Hines must be Squirrel," I offered my insight mainly to Daddy.

"I beg your pardon," he said.

"Ralph Hines is Squirrel," I repeated.

"What on earth are you talking about?" Mama said.

"Ruby—uh, Mrs. Scruggs said that she had an affair with a guy whose nickname was Squirrel. He was the father of both her sons."

"She told you all of that?" Mama was aghast.

"Yes, ma'am. So, is that true, Daddy?"

"Hines used to go by that nickname back in high school. He dropped it some time ago. At least that's what Aunt Nona told me."

We all smiled at his revelation. My daddy used Aunt Nona as a source for something he knew. My, oh my.

Daddy and I were sitting in the black-and-white waiting for Scottie and Mama to join us for our excursion to Mr. Joe's. I still had some questions regarding our now finished investigation. The murders of those two boys had been solved.

"I'm confused about the box, Daddy."

"Me, too."

"From the contents it obviously belonged to Ruby. And she said she buried it. Then she told us that when she and Scruggs took Greesome out to the swamp to frighten her, Scruggs buried a box. Were there two boxes?"

"Hmm. Good question. Maybe we need to do some more digging in the mud."

"Oh, Mama will love that," I said just as Mama was getting into the car.

"Mama will love what?" she said.

"Dirty clothes," I said.

"You're not going back to that mud hole, are you?"

"Afraid so, dear," Daddy said as we drove to Mr. Joe's farm.

We found Mr. Joe walking around the burned-out spot where his barn used to be. He waved when he saw us coming. He was smiling, quite a lot.

"Settling back in?" Daddy said.

"Yes, sir. Good to be home."

"You're using your good voice," I said.

"Yes, ma'am. I did a lot of thinking while I was in jail. I had plenty of time to think. Came to some conclusions about myself. Time to start being me, and time to stop pretending to be what others want me to be."

"Sounds like a lesson all of us should learn," Daddy said.

"Well, Sheriff Evans, it was a lesson that was a long time coming for me. But, I'm just glad that I learned it. Your daughter helped me."

I smiled and hugged Mr. Joe. It was good to have him back from Dan River. It was good to have him out of jail. I was happy that he was finally proven innocent of all the charges against him. I knew it, I knew it as surely as I knew my own innocence. I was also sorry that I had doubted him that one time. I regretted that. My first impression had been the correct one. All things considered, I was one happy girl.

"Most of the butterflies are dead, Mr. Joe," Scottie said.

"Maybe they'll come back."

"From the dead?" Scottie said.

"No, sir," Mr. Joe laughed, "not from the dead. Can't undo what's been done. I meant some new butterflies will return ultimately. Maybe they'll return to that same spot. Meanwhile, let's go down to the house and I'll make us all some sweet tea. I need some sweet tea. They sure don't know how to make sweet tea in that Dan River jailhouse."

We sat around on the front porch talking and sipping our sweet, iced tea. Mr. Joe knew how to make delicious Southern iced tea. I whispered to Daddy that this would be a good time to go check the mud hole for another box. He told me that it would be better to wait until tomorrow because of the evening shadows.

"What are you two plotting over there?" Mama said.

"Just the overthrow of the world, dear. No need to worry," Daddy said.

Some time around mid-morning the next day, Daddy and I drove out to Mr. Joe's place. We stopped at his house and asked him if he would like to join our search at the swamp. He agreed to help us, and we all headed to the burned-out foliage. The area had changed drastically. It was now just a sunken spot of black earth with ashes covering it. The mud was completely dried.

"Doesn't quite look the same," Mr. Joe said.

"I bet Bessie Mae misses it," I said.

"She came over and stared at it yesterday afternoon. Then she just turned around and headed back out to the pasture. I think she misses the cool liquid around her legs," Mr. Joe. said.

After a few minutes I found the spot where we had located the cigar box full of pictures. I put a stick in the ground to mark it. Then I walked over to the tree where I had found the sack with the dress and shoes inside. I marked that spot as well.

"Let's assume that Ruby buried the box over there where the stick is. Let's assume that she buried it prior to that evening when Betty Ann Greesome was brought here and died. But on that night, again, let's assume, Donald Scruggs had a box in his hand which Ruby didn't recognize. But, we assume, that Betty Ann Greesome did recognize it. So, after Greesome died of a heart attack, and then Scruggs shot her, Scruggs then buried the box that he had brought," I said, finishing off my assumptions.

"Okay, I'll go along with those assumptions. I'll add that the box most likely belonged to Betty Ann Greesome, which is why he was able to taunt her with it, that is, if Ruby's story holds water at that point and our assumptions prove to be on target," Daddy said.

"So where out here would … let's see," I said, moving around to the spot I wanted. "Ruby was over here by the tree burying something … she said … oh, no! That was the first time she talked to me and I think she got confused. She was mixing up her memories, at least I think that's what happened. I believe the correct version of the events is that years ago something happened out here between Ralph Hines and Ruby so that she buried the dress she wore to the prom along with her shoes in a hole inside a tree. But this summer, she removed a dress and shoes because they were splattered with the blood of Betty Ann Greesome when Donald shot Greesome. After she removed the dress from this summer, she put it into the trunk of their car along with the shoes."

"You surely did get yourself messed up in a lot of trouble, Miss Clancy," Mr. Joe said. "How old did you say you were?"

"Let's not talk about that," Daddy said. "I should've known better than to allow her to help me on this case."

"You're not suggesting that I didn't help you, are you?" I said.

"Hardly that, my dear," Daddy answered. "You helped quite a bit. I just don't know how my rating as a parent is going to be when all is said and done, when all the facts come out about this horrible stuff you were surrounded with this summer."

I had nothing to say about his near-confession.

"As I was saying, explaining … Ruby was likely over here somewhere, and Greesome was on the other side of the mud hole. So, Donald Scruggs must have been … where?"

The area was getting smaller as we discussed the story from the bits and pieces we had heard from Ruby, coupled with our assumptions.

"I think I found something over here," Mr. Joe said to us. We quickly joined him as he was digging up some of the hardened mud with his cane. He took the rubber tip off of the end so that he could dig better. Because of the dried mud from the fire and the absence of any recent rain, we could see something protruding from the ground.

"May I help you?" I said.

"Absolutely," Mr. Joe answered.

I dropped to my knees and began digging around the object he had spotted. It took several minutes, but we finally were able to free what turned out to be a second box. It was also wooden, but smaller than Ruby's. It had a latch on it, but no lock.

The three of us sat down near a tree and opened our new-found item. Much like the other box, this one had small artifacts which obviously meant something to its owner, pictures of naked children, and a small crucifix attached to a tiny, gold chain. Among the small artifacts was a Masonic ring, a pin which represented some sorority Daddy said, a music-clef pin, and a silver Bible inscribed on the back with *Love, Robbie.*

"I'll bet that's a music sorority, and it would seem to me that this box did, in fact, belong to one Betty Ann Greesome," Daddy said.

"That's why Ruby said that Donald was showing the box to Greesome before she died. And, for some reason, he was able to taunt her with it. But why? Or how? What's in this box that Scruggs could use … wait a minute, maybe that's how he got Greesome to get into the car that night. Remember, Ruby said that she didn't know how he was able to get the woman to come along so easily," I said.

"Could explain a lot, but doesn't answer the question of how Scruggs got his hands on that box," Daddy said. "That just might remain an unanswerable mystery."

"You two folks have gathered in a whole lot of information," Mr. Joe said.

"Much of that credit goes to this young lady, here," Daddy said, pointing in my direction. "She has a curious disposition about things. And speaking of curious things, which of these objects in this box were precious enough to Greesome to upset her? And why did he want to get rid of her? I assume that his whole plan was to kill her from the beginning. I don't believe Ruby was part of that plan."

"Maybe they were all precious to her," Mr. Joe said. "People hold onto things which become almost sacred to them. They usually keep them in a special place, like a jewelry box, or—"

"A nice little wooden box like this," I said, agreeing with my friend.

"Yes, ma'am, like that," Mr. Joe said.

"Too many unanswered questions for me, Daddy," I confessed. "I would like to know much that we may likely never know. I agree with you, I don't get the idea of killing Greesome. Scruggs' taunt may just have been some silly nothing that he learned through Hines, say. I doubt if Hines is going to answer any questions we might have."

"Well, at least it is over," Daddy said.

Mr. Joe nodded and you could tell that he was certainly relieved to be a free man again.

"I don't think so." I said, rather emphatically.

"What?" Daddy said. "You can give your curiosity a rest now, you know."

"What Scruggs, and Ruby, to some extent, did to Greesome was torture. Why did they do that to her? Just bring her out here and kill her. Why torture?" I asked.

"See what I have to put up with, Mr. Joe," he said. "She never lets a thing rest, like a dog with an old bone, she continually gnaws on it."

Daddy thought for a minute or so, and then shook his head.

"You tell me, Sherlock," he finally answered.

"I can only speculate, but that's about all. My guess is that she did something they didn't like. Greesome was part of that small church group, along with Hines. My best guess is that she did something that the group did not want her to do, or something that the group as a whole thought was wrong. Or she was going to do something they didn't want her to do. I think that they tortured her, that is, the group may have asked Scruggs to scare her into silence. Or, maybe scare her in order to stop her from doing something or to force her to go along with the rest of the group. Only Scruggs took it too far."

"But it was only Donald Scruggs and his wife that did this," Daddy said. "At least according to what Ruby told us."

"That's right. Ralph Hines wasn't involved in Greesome's death, as far as we know now. He may not have known anything about it. Scruggs lied to Ruby to get her to help him, for whatever reason," I said.

"So where are you going with this?" Daddy asked.

"I don't know, Daddy. But I can't help but feel that we're missing something here. Scruggs is dead. Greesome is dead. Oh yeah, did you ever check on those names I got from the pastor when he saw the people leaving that meeting?"

"Yes, ma'am. Both were dead ends. No one ever heard of them."

"Maybe they're from out of town," I said.

"Have to be far out of town. I called Richmond and they have nothing on either name. They must be from out of state."

"Can we check somewhere else?"

"Sure. I have a contact in Washington. She can help us search for them."

"Could be helpful." I said. "And, one other thing … I can't be certain that Donald and Ruby were at that meeting. If they were, they didn't say much, if anything. I would definitely recognize their voices, but … well, no such luck. I didn't see them and I can't put them in the church that night."

"Well, like I said, Clancy, we found out who killed Buster and Micah. We have an eye witness who saw Betty Ann Greesome die. The murders are solved, but the motives are still lingering a bit. And the criminal activity behind the murders is still basically unknown. We simply do not know who all the participants were, and are. And we don't know exactly how their little pornography network was connected. My guess is that it was associated with a much larger network. I'd say that most of that group you overheard at the church house has left Clancyville by now. Don't you think so, daughter?"

"Perhaps, but only if they're smart. Still, it would be nice to know where they were from. You know me, ever curious."

"Yeah, I know you, and one day that cat's gonna die."

"The one who has nine lives?" I asked.

"I think you've used up two or three of those lives already," Daddy said.

Mr. Joe smiled, and then winked at me.

# Chapter Forty-eight

The next night Mr. Joe Jenkins joined us for supper. Mama fixed an extra special meal to celebrate his release and to welcome him back to the community. I was pleased that it had all been her idea. She even baked a chocolate cake and had Sarah make a peach pie. We had some kind of celebration that night.

Mama fried chicken, fixed corn on the cob and green beans, made biscuits, and even prepared mashed potatoes for Scottie and me. It would be an understatement to say that it was all good. I thought it tasted especially good in light of Mr. Joe's presence, and his widely acclaimed innocence. Some of the good town folk would have to eat a lot of humble pie, as Sarah once said.

"What's the difference between a priest and a preacher?" Scottie asked.

"Why on earth would you ask a question like that?" Mama said.

"I was just wondering. I got into an argument with Turby the other day, and he said that there wasn't any difference. I thought there was."

"Well, some groups have a priest and some have what we call pastors or preachers. It all depends on what you believe, I suppose," Mama said.

"We have a pastor, right?" Scottie said.

"That's correct."

"Well, is there a difference between priests and pastors?"

"Priests usually wear a white collar around the neck," Mr. Joe said, "but then some pastors wear those too, but are not usually referred to as priests. Depends upon the tradition of the group, I reckon."

"I told Turby that the biggest difference was over women."

"I beg your pardon, young man," Mama said.

"I told Turby that the biggest difference—"

"I heard you the first time. What on earth do you mean by such a statement?" Mama said.

"Well, priests can't have women and preachers can."

Everyone laughed except Mama and Scottie.

"Scott, a priest usually cannot marry, while most pastors can get married," Daddy said for clarification. "However, there are priests in some traditions, some churches, who can be married. So, it's not always the case that a priest is denied the ability to marry. And, some people choose not to marry."

"Yeah, that's what I said. And that's what I told Turby."

"Well, then you told him correctly. There is a difference," Mama said.

"But he argued and said that wasn't so because Pastor Flowers didn't have a wife, and therefore he was just like a priest."

"But the difference is choice," Daddy said. "Like I said, some choose not to marry. Homer Flowers chooses to be single. A priest, say, in the Roman Catholic tradition, is single because of a promise he makes to remain single all of his life. I think they call it a vow. Isn't that true, Mr. Joe?"

"I believe so, Sheriff."

"Well, now that we have discussed the finer points of religious commitment, let's all go to the den, and I'll serve dessert," Mama said.

It was difficult choosing between the peach pie and the chocolate cake, so Scottie and I decided to have a piece of both. That was probably the smartest thing I had done in weeks. However, it wasn't too smart to eat that much dessert after having consumed fried chicken, corn, mashed potatoes and biscuits. I fell asleep during the after-dinner conversation with our special guest. I don't remember walking upstairs to my bedroom, so I guess my daddy must have carried me. It had been a long while since that had happened. I do remember my dreams that night. Scottie had become a priest, but was giving his religious group fits because he wanted to marry Melissa Jones. I decided against telling him about my dream. He hated Melissa Jones, he once said, and the inside word I got from the school last year was that Melissa Jones hated Scott Evans. Tit for tat, so to speak. But, it was an interesting dream.

I realize, of course, that the relating of these events from the early life of an eleven-year-old girl-child helping her father, the County Sheriff, to investigate and solve a crime as gruesome as this one was is unusual. Most eleven-year-old girls play with dolls or spend their time ignoring the boys, for the most part. But then, I was not a typical eleven-year-old girl. Now that I am grown and look back on all that happened that summer, I am not a little awed with the severity of each occurrence, with the development of our tenacious investigation, with the wonderful gift that was given to Joe Jenkins, as well as with the growth that took place in me because my father trusted in me. He allowed me to help him, and that was the best gift of all for me. I learned from my mistakes as well as from successes. Even now as I recall the specifics of that summer of my twelfth birthday celebration, I am convinced that my errors in judgment were not balanced by my relentless path to the hard-won discoveries. But, I did learn.

I need to tell the rest of the story.

Two weeks after we had that grand celebration for Mr. Joe's return to life among us, and the morning after we had celebrated Scottie's tenth birthday, Daddy and I were eating breakfast together. We had gathered at Mr. Joe's place to celebrate Scottie's big day. Scottie received a new fishing rig from our parents, and I gave him some additional tackle items to make sure his fishing equipment stayed ample. Uncle Walters sent him some money, which Mama immediately placed in the bank in Scottie's savings account. Uncle Walters sent his usual over-the-top monetary gift, and our mother knew that it was much too large for

Scottie to have at his young age. She did dole out a manageable amount from that generous gift so that my brother wouldn't feel cheated.

We dined sumptuously on an abundant picnic lunch Mama and Sarah packed, along with Scottie's favorite dessert—pound cake. Mr. Joe had made homemade ice cream, and we all had a delightful time together that day. I was still celebrating Mr. Joe's innocence and his release from jail.

The summer of 1973 was coming to an end with some wholesome goodness after all of the pain.

"Heard from Washington the other day. Forgot to tell you. Those two names you got from Pastor Flowers turned up very little. They were both elderly women from North Carolina," Daddy told me the next day as we were reflecting after breakfast.

Mama had already cleaned up and was somewhere else in the house with Sarah. Daddy and I were alone, sitting at the kitchen table. He was taking his time this morning before heading off to his office.

"Are you going to check with North Carolina?" I asked.

"Yes, ma'am, but I don't expect much. Elderly women are not the usual profile, I'm told, in cases like this. I think it's a dead-end, but I'll keep digging. Maybe you ought to check with Reverend Flowers again about those names. Maybe you heard him wrong."

Scottie walked through the room with his new fishing tackle, and continued on his way out the back door before I could respond to Daddy's suggestion.

"Hey! Where are you headed?" Daddy laughed at his son.

"Got to check this new equipment out. You comin' Clancy?"

"Wouldn't miss this for the world," I said. "We're off to the river. Tell Mama we'll be gone maybe a couple of hours, no more. Should be plenty of time for Scottie to catch a mess of fish with that new rig. Home about noon, I suppose," I said.

Mama came into the kitchen as we were leaving, told us to wait up before heading out. She had fixed us some leftovers from yesterday's celebratory feast. She then reminded us with her usual recitation of regulations involving walking, water, and a host of other notions which

I have conveniently forgotten. She then sent us off with one final surprising comment.

"If the fishing is good, then you can stay the day. We can dine on your catch for supper," she said, jolting us a little as we hurried down the back steps.

I was trying hard to remember a time when our mother had been so nice to us. I was coming up empty on that reflection. Maybe she was just glad it was over, the investigation, that is, or maybe, she was happy it had ended the way it ended. At any rate, Scottie and I were the recipients of her good will and we had the day to fish and sufficient food to satisfy.

Since that cataclysmic event at the jail involving Ruby Scruggs, Ralph Hines, and Donald Scruggs, along with Mr. Joe's later release, we hadn't been fishing at all. It was the longest stretch we had gone all summer, even in the midst of our investigation. We were long overdue for some good catfish.

We stopped at Mr. Joe's and talked awhile with him before we headed to our fishing hole. It was a little after ten by the time we were casting for some of those big cats. It felt like it was going to be another scorcher. I wanted Scottie to catch the first fish, so I cheated by not baiting my hook. He was too busy admiring his new equipment to notice the obvious discrepancy between our rigs. Besides, he would never have considered that I would do such a thing in order to ensure his success at catching the first fish.

It must have been at least fifteen minutes before Scottie landed the initial catfish of the morning. It was a beauty, one for the record book. It looked like it could have weighed at least a pound and a half, maybe two. He was smiling from ear to ear by the time he landed it. I was happy for him.

"Well, I guess that means it's broken in," he said with great pride.

"I'd say so. You gonna let me use it some?" I said.

"Sure, but not today. Today's she's all mine. Sorry, sis."

"I understand, Little Brother. Now. I'm gonna whip your tail and catch some fish. More than you, and bigger than anything you'll catch," I said.

I knew this type of challenge would get his juices flowing and he would likely out-fish me for the day, for sure.

I retrieved my line, baited it with a glob of chicken livers, and began catching catfish like I knew what I was doing. By the time the lunch hour had rolled around on us my stringer was heavy with seven catfish. Scottie had six. He had caught the first two, but after that I hit a streak of three in a row before he caught his next group. Then we alternated catching them before I finished out the morning with two straight big ones. He failed to land a small one just before we decided to break for lunch.

Since our fishing hole was partially shaded, we weren't as concerned as some fishermen might have been to be fishing in the heat of the day. The shade landed right over the largest part of the hole which had been so good to us for several years now.

We dined in fine style under a large oak a short distance from the river bank. We left our catfish stringers cooling in the Staunton River while we filled ourselves with delicious vittles. The day-old items from Scottie's birthday party tasted even better to me. I dozed off while Scottie ate two pieces of pound cake.

I had no problem giving the fish a break from our joint fishing exploits. I think I was a little tired as well.

I woke up when I heard a twig snap close to me.

"Hey, Pastor Flowers. Wait till you see the big cat I caught this morning!" Scottie called out, causing me to awaken from my nap. I waited on my eyes to adjust to the light. "Hello, Scottie, Clancy. I thought I heard someone talking as I was heading toward my spot on the river. I was going to ask if you children were having any luck, but I can tell from Scott's greeting that he has caught at least one whale of a fish," he said as he approached.

"Where's your tackle?" I said.

"Oh, that. It's over yonder. I wanted to see who it was that was out here."

He was dressed in his usual preacher-type clothing. I thought it odd that he would fish in a sport coat and tie. But what did I know about preachers and fishing.

"You usually dress like that when you fish?" I said.

"Oh, I have to sneak in some fishing time whenever I can. I was out visiting this morning, and thought I'd spend a few hours fishing this afternoon. Didn't have time to change clothes. Besides, I have a Nominating Committee meeting tonight. Say, you sure are inquisitive about me today, Clancy."

"I'm sorry, Pastor Flowers. I guess I have a suspicious nature. Forgive me. I just don't usually see people out fishing in their good, Sunday-type clothes."

Homer Flowers sat down under the tree next to us.

"Ah, that's okay. If I saw me coming along and saying that I was headed towards fishing, I'd ask a lot of questions too."

He chuckled to himself. For some reason, he thought that was funny. I didn't see the humor myself.

"So where is your spot on the river?" I asked.

"Down that direction," he said pointing back towards Mr. Joe's place, the direction in which we had come. I couldn't recall too many good spots along the river between this place and Mr. Joe's land. I knew this section of the river better than most folks. I had tried out many possible spots along the way, with limited success.

"Is it a good place?" I asked.

"Oh, yeah. The best. In fact, last week I caught over twenty in two days."

"Not bad," I said, "not bad at all. Maybe you could show us …," I caught myself before I said more. I remembered what I had told him about our secret spot, and I was almost about to break my own rules by asking to see someone else's secret fishing hole.

"Well, now that I know where your spot is, it would only be fair for me to show you mine. Come on," he said getting to his feet.

"Let me go get the fish first," Scottie said.

"It's not that far, Scottie. Just leave the fish and your gear here. You can come right back after I show you my place."

"No, sir," Scottie said. "The fish can stay, but not my new tackle. This is brand new. Birthday gift, yesterday. I ain't goin' nowhere without it.

And, tell you what, lettme show you the stringer of fish I caught this mornin."

Scottie headed back quickly toward the river away from our dining and snoozing spot under the large tree.

"Very well, then. Bring it along. So how old are you, Scott?" he called after my brother.

"Ten!" he turned, still walking, now backwards, and answered Pastor Flowers, as he beamed with great pride as if it were a major accomplishment. Pastor Flowers and I watched Scottie turn and run to the water's edge and retrieve his stringer. He walked back slowly toward us, holding the line of fish as high over his head as he could. I could easily tell that it was quite heavy for him to hold that high.

"We can leave our picnic stuff," I said.

"Yeah, I reckon it'll be safe. Not many people know of this spot. Still, the preacher found it," he whispered.

"Yeah, he did," I said, softly.

"You two coming?" Pastor Flowers called out to us. He had walked on ahead, leading the way to his fishing hole.

"Be right there," I shouted to Pastor Flowers. "Scottie's returning his stringer to the water."

I watched Scottie run back to the water's edge and drop his stringer into the river. There was no need to keep those fish out of the water for any length of time. We still had a few hours of quality fishing time before we would need to head home.

The two of us ran and caught up with Pastor Flowers.

We walked along with him until we came to a place in front of us where the river did an abrupt right-hand turn, then an abrupt left-hand turn, thus creating a small peninsula on the left-hand side of the river just below us. I had never noticed this spot. It had no appeal to me for some reason. And, I usually did not walk along the river in this direction. My trek was always southward, keeping the river on my right. Just a habit, I suppose. At any rate it seemed more natural to me.

"Well, there it is. That little place down there that juts out as the river turns twice. Good fishing down there. You wanna join me?"

Before either of us could answer him, the preacher shoved Scottie and all of his fishing gear into the water below us. Then he grabbed me from behind. He dragged me away from the river toward a grove of trees off to the right. I could hear Scottie splashing around in the water. I could only imagine that he was feverishly trying to save his new tackle and remain afloat in the deep water.

By the time Pastor Flowers had dragged me kicking some ten to fifteen feet from the riverbank, he was already wrapping a small cord around my chest and arms. I was struggling in vain against his powerful grip. He held me with one hand and continued to wrap the cord around my body with the other.

"What on earth are you doing, Pastor Flowers?" I finally said.

"Shut up, Clancy. I'm sick and tired of you interfering with my business. You've messed things up really well this summer. But, you've done it for the last time."

I tried to kick him, but he sidestepped, avoiding the hard thrust of my right foot. He then wrapped a heavy fishing line around my legs several times. This obviously thwarted my ability to use my feet as a weapon. After I was rendered completely helpless, he took a large ball of cotton from his pocket and stuffed it in my mouth. Then he tied a red bandanna around my mouth to keep the cotton inside. It gagged me at first.

"Don't swallow that cotton, little girl, or you'll choke to death," he said laughing a little.

I had that thought myself, already.

Off in the distance I could hear Scottie calling out. The preacher walked over to the edge of the river and then disappeared down the embankment to the water. In a few minutes he was climbing up the side of the hill dragging a wet Scottie. I was relieved when I saw my little brother roll over. He looked tired from struggling in the water. He then stood up and was about to thank the preacher for saving him from the river when he spotted me tied up, lying on the ground, close to a tree.

"What's goin'—" Scottie didn't get a chance to finish his question before the preacher threw him abruptly to the ground, and then tied his legs with what looked like the same heavy fishing line he had used on my legs. I could see from the short distance between us that my brother tried vigorously to resist, but the preacher slapped him hard two or three times in the face. Scottie then stopped fighting.

"What are you doin', Pastor Flowers? Have you lost your mind?" Scottie said, trying to be calm, but not quite understanding what was happening to us. Without answering, Flowers flipped Scottie over onto his stomach and then tied Scottie's hands behind his back.

"Doing?" he said, when he had finally tightened the last section of the line. "I'm getting rid of two brats who have just about ruined my life. Losing my mind? Not quite. I'm smart enough to outsmart the likes of you two."

"What on earth are you talkin' about, preacher?" Scottie was pleading with him now. I could tell that my brother sounded desperate, that he had no idea what Flowers was doing with us. It was easy to feel the fear mounting inside myself. I knew Scottie was feeling something of the same thing.

Unfortunately, I had some idea, but I was helpless to do anything by way of assisting my little brother.

"I'm talking about my business interests. Who do you think was behind that *therapy* group, Clancy Evans?" Flowers asked, directing his question to me.

Homer Flowers looked over at me when he asked that. He smiled. It was not a friendly smile, nor could I call it an evil one. The best description I could give it is to call it wicked. I had a sick feeling deep within.

"Never quite figured that one out, did you, little Miss Detective? See, you're not so smart. Always remember that you have to outsmart the bad guys. You have to out-think them. But that tidbit of wisdom won't do you any good now, will it?"

I watched him gag Scottie the same way he had silenced me. He then went behind a tree and retrieved a camera and a blanket. He laid out the blanket not far from Scottie's bound position, and then walked back over to my brother. He took a knife from his pocket and began cutting off Scottie's clothes. Once or twice he nicked Scottie. My brother grimaced a little but that was all.

Once he had removed all of his clothes, I could easily sense that my brother was not going to be as feisty as his usual demeanor was. Bound and quite naked, my brother was quiet and easily controlled by this man.

The preacher then dragged my naked brother over to the blanket and laid him on it. He began taking pictures. I was disgusted, but I also knew that I was next up for the photographic session.

Scottie rolled over and the preacher slapped him and told him to stay put and to keep his little eyes on the camera lens. I knew that my brother was completely embarrassed.

"Okay, Miss Clancy. Now it's time for you to join your brother," he said as he came at me with the knife. "Nothing sells like adolescent bondage. But, you wouldn't know about that, now would you? You may be keen in some aspects, but not about what sells, what real business is out there in the child pornography market. I'll make a small fortune with these pictures of you two."

Pastor Flowers laughed and began cutting my clothes.

# CHAPTER FORTY-NINE

I will never know what Pastor Homer Flowers had in mind for me and my brother that day. It was obvious that he was going to take several photographs of two naked children. My concern was what would likely take place after he had finished his photography; however, I could use my imagination well enough to have a general idea. I had only managed a brief glimpse of the sordid side of life by the age of eleven. He had just finished cutting my shirt off, nicking me three times with his penknife, when a friendly voice came out of nowhere and startled my attacker.

"Don't think you better keep doing that, Mr. Flowers," Mr. Joe said in that beautiful deep tone of his which I had grown to love.

The preacher turned around and stared at the approaching black man. The demeanor of our assailant was such that he obviously believed he was still in complete control of the situation. I am certain that Homer Flowers believed that. Body language speaks volumes.

"Oh, you poor old nigger. Well, are you here to rescue these children?" he said with a severe, condescending tone. He even swaggered a few steps towards Mr. Joe.

"Do they need rescuing?" Mr. Joe asked rather calmly, shifting his old wooden cane from his left hand to his right.

The preacher chuckled, "Well, they do seem to be in a bind."

He laughed at his own sordid humor.

"Then it looks like I'm here to rescue them," Mr. Joe said.

"Over my dead body, you black sonofabitch."

Homer Flowers charged Joe Jenkins with the small knife in his right hand, fully intending to kill him. At least that's what it looked like to me from the prone position and angle I had.

Mr. Joe stuck his cane in the preacher's gut, stopping him cold from his advancement. He then swiftly slapped Flowers' right hand with the same wooden weapon utilizing a horizontal chopping motion, much like a baseball player laying down a perfect bunt with a bat but with much more force behind it. The small knife dropped from the minister's hand and landed some five feet away from me.

The preacher regrouped faster than I had thought possible after Mr. Joe's initial blow to his belly. He charged Mr. Joe once more, like a bull running towards a matador. Mr. Joe sidestepped him and shoved him down to the ground. Homer grunted when he hit the hard surface. Mr. Joe was embarrassing him, and that wasn't setting too well with the minister. Slowly the preacher sat up on his knees as Mr. Joe walked over to him.

"You better finish me off, nigger-man. If you don't, I just might get up from here and beat you to death. Wouldn't that be something?"

Flowers sounded a little too assured with himself to suit me. Something was up.

Mr. Joe started to hit him again with his cane when the preacher pulled a small .38 from his pocket and fired twice into Mr. Joe's midsection. My heart sank as Mr. Joe fell face down to the ground. He didn't move. Scottie and I watched in horror as the preacher stood up and walked over to the unmoving Mr. Joe. I had the horrible feeling that he was going to shoot him again. I managed to sit up on my knees and to offer some guttural protest. It was loud enough for the preacher to hear me. He looked in my direction.

"And what do you think you're doing little girl? Going somewhere? I don't think so," he said as he walked slowly towards me, forgetting about the motionless man on the ground now behind him, forgetting Mr. Joe for the moment. Flowers believed he had all the time in the world. "Now maybe we won't be interrupted anymore by your so-called friends. Let's see, where was I? Oh yes, the knife."

He turned around a few times searching for his penknife. While Flowers was preoccupied with his search, I tried to get Scottie's attention, but I think my brother was too frightened, too embarrassed to move. At any rate, Scottie failed to look in my direction.

Homer now had found his blade, and was back cutting my jeans from the bottom up. Suddenly, two large, black hands embraced his neck like someone lifting a round object from a pedestal. Mr. Joe picked the preacher straight up from the ground and held him high. His feet were dangling, some five inches or more from the ground. While kicking and screaming, Flowers slashed wildly with the small knife in his right hand, but failed to land a blow on Mr. Joe. His movements gradually slowed to stillness. In just a few minutes he appeared to be dead, or unconscious. It seemed to me that Mr. Joe's mighty hands had choked the life out of my would-be attacker. After several minutes more, still holding the body of Flowers above the ground, Mr. Joe released him, allowing his lifeless form to fall to the grassy area like a pile of dirty clothes.

I could feel no sympathy for Reverend Homer Flowers.

Mr. Joe was breathing hard by now. He took the knife and cut the cords which were pressing my arms to my side. While I was working on the bandanna with my newly freed hands, Mr. Joe collapsed in front of me before he could unbind my legs.

"Mr. Joe!" I said, crawling in his direction while reaching for him. He was unconscious, but breathing.

I cut the fishing line from my legs. Then I used the knife to free Scottie. I took off the preacher's trousers and brought them to my brother. He was too glad to be alive at that point to worry so much about the fact that the pants were ten sizes too big. I took the preacher's shirt and put it on. My breasts had not developed too much as yet, but I still didn't want to walk around without some covering. I didn't even want to walk from Mossie's Point to our house without a shirt covering myself, even if it was still a hot August day. There are some things eleven-year-old ladies simply will not tolerate.

I called Daddy from Mr. Joe's house and told him that I believed it was really over now, that I had discovered some important details, and that he'd better send the Rescue Squad out to the Staunton River just past Mr. Joe's farm.

"There's been another death," I said, "maybe two."

We spent the better part of the afternoon in the Clancyville Family Practice. Dr. Abigail Smith-Johnson had only been in our town for a few months that year. She was fresh from her residency at Duke Medical, and this was the way in which she was paying off some of her school loans. Besides being attractive, she was a good doctor, or so I thought. Mama didn't care too much for her because she said that she was far too young. Daddy didn't say anything because he never went to the doctor anyway.

Dr. Smith-Johnson checked my brother and me as if we might be somebody special. It felt good to be treated that way. Scottie had to have six stitches total in two different places, while I needed only a thorough cleaning of a couple of places. She wanted to apply some sterile bandages over a place or two, but I refused. She ended up giving me some bandages to stick in the pockets of my jeans in case I changed my mind.

Scottie and I both were lucky, or so everybody said as the story was told and retold. For some reason, the gashes in Scottie's small body became larger and larger with each retelling of his adventure, as he recalled it. I chose not to talk a great deal about my encounter with the so-called man of the cloth.

Mama was so upset she couldn't speak for a considerable time. I found out later that it was this experience which caused her to question a little of her faith. She and God never were on the same terms after all of this, but I couldn't see where you could really blame God for what Homer Flowers did. I blamed Homer Flowers. I blamed him for most of what had happened in our little town that summer, once I knew that he was the driving force behind the whole sordid affair.

Daddy was about as calm as he ever was, but I could tell that he was relieved to know that we were okay, and that the investigation was finally over and done. All he had to do now was to finish the massive paperwork.

"Where's Mr. Joe?" I said, as we were finally able to leave the doctor's office. It was past suppertime.

"He's on his way," he paused and looked at his watch, "no, check that. He's at the hospital in Dan River by now. I'll go call and check on his status."

"If he makes it, do you think anyone will question the way Homer Flowers died?"

"Not while I'm sheriff. Self-defense, no questions asked. And he saved the life of my two children. I'll say I did it before I allow anything to happen to him."

Even though I would have been surprised if my daddy had said any-thing else, it was still good to hear him actually speak the words aloud.

When we called, Mr. Joe was already in surgery and they couldn't tell us anything. We sat around the house that evening just glad to be home together and all in one piece. Daddy called again around eight that evening. The surgery was over, but the doctor told him that the next thirty-six hours would be critical for the patient. He told him that if he believed in prayer, then he would recommend saying a few.

Daddy relayed the message to all of us, but no one said anything except Mama.

"I usually call the pastor when something like this occurs."

Everyone understood her thinking, but we had no words of wis-dom. There was a bad taste in our collective mouths, at least there was in mine. I don't think I had ever been so wrong in my young life about another person. My intuition had failed me, and that was a sobering thought. It's a great thing to have, this intuitive-thing, but I learned the hard way that there is no guarantee that a person is as they appear to be. Apparently, the world is full of people capable of convincing deceit. This most significant lesson nearly cost me my life, to say nothing of Scottie's. The jury was still out on what it might cost Mr. Joe.

Scottie retired to his room to play with his soldiers, and I wandered out to the front porch to look for stars. It was cloudy, naturally. There was a slight breeze coming in from the southwest. I sat down and leaned against the post next to the right-hand side of the steps. I considered sitting in the porch swing, but changed my mind. A few minutes later Daddy joined me on the steps.

"I think Mr. Joe is going to be fine, Clancy. He's strong for his age."

"Yes, sir. He's pretty strong."

"You have doubts, huh?"

"After this summer, I have doubts about … well, if I say everything, does that sound too pessimistic?"

He put his arm around my shoulders and pulled me close to his side. It was a gentle hug.

"I think you grew up too fast, little girl."

"I didn't know that there was a speed control on it."

He smiled.

"Any loose ends, or do you think you have the package together finally?" Daddy said, removing his arm from around me.

"Nothing really bothering me. Like you, I think Homer Flowers was the boss behind this whole scheme or whatever you call what they did, at least here in Clancyville. Say, what about those two women you were checking on?"

"Turns out that they were members of a church in Mooresville, North Carolina where Homer Flowers had served as pastor years ago. One has been dead for ten years, the other is in a nursing home close to Charlotte."

"So we don't know who those women I saw are. He gave me false names. We should have checked out those names earlier. That would have drawn suspicion to him. That was my fault," I confessed.

"Hey, I'm the Sheriff around here. That sort of thing is my job, not yours. We let those names slip through, didn't we?"

"Well, it doesn't matter now. And, I really don't know what I would have done if we had checked and discovered that those names were really bogus. I never would have suspected him. Of all the people … I mean he had me fooled, Daddy."

"Me, too. But I feel sorry for your mother. She really liked the man. The two of us are harder cases to win over. This sort of thing is truly hard on her."

"It's hard on all of us, but we'll recover. We usually do."

"It's been an interesting summer, huh?" he said.

"I might use other phrases to capture the essence of this summer. All things considered, yes, it's been, as you say, *interesting*. I don't want any more surprises for a while. I need some dull time before school begins, less excitement. Maybe you ought to go talk with Scottie about what happened to him. I think he was embarrassed about having his sister see him naked."

"We've already talked. He's okay. He just said he was sorry that he couldn't help you. He was worried about you."

"I was worried about me, too."

I could feel a tear coming on so I didn't say anything more. I didn't know what to say anyway. It's nice to have someone worry about you now and then, even if it is an aggravating-at-times little brother.

A few days later we all took a trip to Dan River Memorial Hospital to see our friend Joe Jenkins. He had just been transferred from ICU to a regular room that morning.

He looked tired from his trip down two floors, but his spirits were raised considerably when all four of us walked in.

His smile was the best part of the greeting. It was, in fact, the most encouragement I had received, other than my daddy's embrace on the front steps a few nights prior.

We stayed only a few minutes, and we didn't talk his head off during our brief encounter. Scottie hugged him gently, I thanked him for saving my life, and Daddy shook his hand for a long time without saying anything except that he hoped he got well soon. Mama was speechless but smiled a lot. She kissed him on the forehead. One more surprise from my mother. I think Mr. Joe understood our body language well enough. Some times you do not have to say a lot to express what is really heart-felt.

Daddy told us later that the doctor said Mr. Joe should be home before September. That was really some good news to hear. In the meantime, Scottie and I had just a few more days of fishing before the work would begin all over. Once school started, we could only fish on Friday afternoons and Saturdays. According to Mama's law book, it was illegal to fish the other days when school was in session. Scottie and I had found some devious ways to break that law on many occasions.

# CHAPTER FIFTY

There was a point during the summer of 1973 about which I have often wondered. It was the intervening time between the solution of the one mystery which had consumed most of my summer, and the birth of another mystery which was to consume most of the next several years of my life. In actual time it was almost exactly two weeks from one mystery solved to the beginning of the next. But now and then when I allow myself to wander back to that period, it seems much longer than a mere two weeks. I suppose that's because it was such a wonderful time for our family. It was also a time of anticipation for Mr. Joe Jenkins' return from the hospital.

Scottie and I were busy counting the days for Mr. Joe. We were depending heavily on that indirect word from Daddy that Mr. Joe would be coming home before September. As the time drew nearer, we began to guess at dates. Scottie selected August 22nd and I had chosen the 27th. He was much more of an optimist than I. At least that's partly the truth. My chief reason for selecting August 27th was that date was my birth date. I figured it would be a grand present to have Mr. Joe well and back home.

We both felt so strongly about our calendar selections, that we wagered a whopping seventy-five cents on our opinions, and decided that the winner would be the one who either hit the day exactly or was the closest one to it.

As it turned out, my pessimism won out by a mere day. Joe Jenkins came home on the twenty-fifth of August. I was seventy-five cents richer, but I never collected that wager. It wasn't because I didn't need the money, or that I forgave my little brother for being so foolish as to bet against the solid wisdom of his older and wiser sister. It was because my whole world changed on August 25, 1973, and collecting on a bet seemed trivial at best.

Daddy telephoned us from his office saying that he had just received word that Mr. Joe was home. He told Mama to get the cake and all the presents ready, that he would be home for an early lunch, and then we would all drive out to Mr. Joe's farm for a real homecoming celebration. Sarah was also invited to the gala event we had carefully planned.

I was upstairs changing my clothes for our welcome-home party at Mr. Joe's place, and Scottie was somewhere in the house playing with his soldiers or watching television. Mama was in the kitchen getting the cake ready for travel. She and I had just finished wrapping the last present. Sarah was ironing and humming that spiritual *Go Down, Moses*. I could hear her all the way up to my room with my door shut. It was a good old song, I thought. Good also to hear someone like Sarah singing it.

I heard three blasts before it dawned on me what they were. I ran to my window and could only see the front end of Daddy's car in our driveway. It appeared that the driver's side door was open. I heard another two shots ring out. I ran to my parent's bedroom because they had a window that looked directly down onto the driveway.

Daddy was lying face down about three feet or so from the car and the open door. He wasn't moving.

I heard someone yell, "Drive!" I could see some type of old yellow car speed away from our house. That would be the last time I saw that yellow car.

By the time I hit the back door and headed towards my daddy, Mama, Sarah, and Scottie were already outside next to him. Mama was on the ground holding his head in her lap. She was crying. Sarah was holding onto Scottie saying, "Oh, no, Lord Jesus. Oh, no." I don't remember what Scottie was doing, if anything.

I sat down next to my daddy's body and just watched the blood pour out of the wounds all over his chest. I was too numb to cry then, but I made up for it later.

I have a vague recollection that the funeral for my father was scheduled to be the day after my birthday. I remember my mother coming into my room to inform me of that horrible event forthcoming the next day.

"I'm guessing," she began, as she sat down on the edge of my bed, "that celebrating your birthday is not on your to-do list today."

My head was buried under two pillows. Despite the diminished acoustics, I could hear her clearly.

I came out from under my soft surroundings, turned over, and then straightened up as I shifted my body so I could lean against the bed's headboard. "You guessed right."

"Maybe later," she suggested.

"Doubtful," I said.

"You need anything?" she asked.

"Yeah, my daddy."

My mother nodded a few times, as if to say she understood and agreed. She then stood quickly, and left the room without another word.

I stayed in the house until the last day of August that year; that is, I remained there after I had attended a most horrible service for Bill Evans. I guess I survived the funeral, but I really don't recall it. I suppose there are some things a person has to block from memory because of the sheer pain.

People came to the house to comfort my mother, but I ignored them. Some tried to talk with me. I either refused to see them, making some lame excuse, or if I was forced to grant them an audience due to unavoidable circumstances, I paid no attention to whatever it was that they were saying. Scottie and I didn't talk that entire last week of the month. In fact, I had little to say to anyone except when Sarah broke me out of my doldrums toward the end of the week.

"Miss Clancy, has you been to see Mr. Joe?"

I hadn't thought about Mr. Joe since that most horrible day of my life.

"You know I haven't," I confessed.

"Well, child, you knows that he can't walk over here."

Sarah had a way of telling folks what they ought to do without saying it outright. She said no more to me that day, she just continued her cleaning while she hummed *Some Times I Feel Like a Motherless Child*. She had been humming that same tune all week, and I believe in some strange way it was helping me. She hummed mostly. Once during the week I actually heard her singing the words when she didn't think anyone was around. I sat down on the floor in the hall and listened intently. They were sad enough to touch me, especially the line, *a long way from home*.

I startled her a little when I spoke.

"What does that mean, Sarah?"

"Didn't know anyone wuz listenin', child."

She sang the line again for me, "*a long way from home*." It sounded mournful when she sang it.

"Does it mean that you feel homeless?"

"Sumthin' like that. 'Spose it means that you feels like you don't got no love, Miss Clancy. You know, away from home, away from love. Sumthin' like that."

"I feel a little like that, Sarah."

"Yessim, I reckon so."

"I mean, I know that I have love, but a big part of that love is gone."

"Yessim."

"If I sing that song, I change the words some, but it means the same. Doesn't it, Sarah?"

"Means exactly the same as I can tell, Miss Clancy."

On the last day of August I announced to my mother that I was going to visit Mr. Joe. Mama looked a little surprised, but I saw Sarah smile out of the corner of my eye. I was heading down the back steps when Mama called out to me as my feet touched the ground.

"I forgot to tell you something," she said. She was standing on the top step, holding the screen door.

I turned to face her, figuring that she was going to give me some of her wisdom about life. My mood was still on the dark side of despondency.

"It's called kaleidoscope," she said.

I was confused. "What are you talking about?"

"Butterflies," she said.

"Butterflies," I repeated, more of a question than a statement.

"I thought you might want to know that a cluster of butterflies is referred to as a kaleidoscope of butterflies. Sometimes they are called a swarm, but I much prefer kaleidoscope to swarm. Don't you agree, Clancy?"

She smiled. It felt as if this was the first time I could remember my mother actually talking with me, not at me. It suddenly dawned on me what she was saying.

"How did you know I was …?" I didn't finish my question.

My mother turned and was going back inside the house.

"I get around, Clancy. I'm not just another pretty face, you know."

It was a hot morning when I walked out to Mr. Joe's farm. I first noticed the butterflies when I was in sight of his house.

"Anybody home?" I called out.

"Yes, ma'am. Everybody's home here. Come in, come in."

Mr. Joe was sitting on the sofa reading a book. He took off his reading glasses and smiled. It was a warm and inviting smile. Then he stood up, moved a little closer to me as I entered his living room, and then he gave me a bear hug. It was a long hug, like he hadn't seen me in a long time, which was true enough. Maybe it was more than just that. It felt good to have someone hug me. I remembered another hug of recent vintage. No one at my house had hugged me since the day of the funeral. That was four days back. Mr. Joe's hug felt solid. Real.

"Come over here and sit down. I've missed you."

"Missed you, too. Are you feeling better?"

"I get stronger every day. Pretty good for an old man, huh?"

"Yes, sir, that's pretty good, even for a young man."

I noticed a slight smile from him as we sat.

"Family okay?" he asked.

"We're getting by. Nothing to brag about."

"Sorry I missed the funeral."

"I don't like funerals," I said.

"Me either. Had my share of 'em. Too much pain."

"Yeah," I said, and I could feel some tears from down deep. I rubbed my eye so that he couldn't see me cry. Something told me that he probably saw me do it and suspected what I was covering up, wily old man that he was.

I quickly decided to change the direction of our conversation.

"I have a question that's been bothering me … a little," I said.

"Ask," he said.

"I'm curious as to why you came over to the river the day you and Flowers got into that fight. What made you come?" I asked. "You didn't usually come over when Scottie and I were fishing. You could've, you had plenty of opportunities, but you seldom did. Why did you come that day?"

"Good question, Clancy. That's a really good question. I think it shows some serious thinking on your part. You think like a shrewd detective. In other words, what caused me to come check on my two favorite fishermen?"

"Yes sir, that would be the question," I confirmed.

"Or, in other words, why are you and Scottie alive now? All things being equal, and in light of who it was that came to kill you both, how is it that I would show up and take action?" Mr. Joe rephrased it once more.

"You keep answering my question with a question, or a series of questions all related. Tell me the answer now," I said.

He chuckled a little.

"Reverend Flowers came to see me a few times, but not too many, considering how many years he was the pastor here, I suppose. But, he came to visit me on enough occasions for me to ascertain his habits. He would drive his car a little past my house and park it over on the left side of the dirt road between my house and the barn. He would then walk back and …well, you get the picture. We'd visit some. But, on that day, that most important day, I happened to hear a car, so I looked out and watched him park in his usual spot, but instead of walking back to my house to visit me, he walked towards the river."

"That unusual? He told us that he did fish some."

"I never saw him fish. I never saw him carrying any fishing tackle. I had never seen him walk in that direction, past my barn, heading toward the river. I thought it strange, so I decided I might just investigate. Besides, I knew you two were at the river, fishing."

"That's it? You didn't suspect him of anything?"

"That's it, Clancy. He parked his car in that same spot, but failed to come visit me, like he had done on all previous occasions to my knowledge. Parked his car, and then walked in the wrong direction."

"And that's the difference between living and dying for me and Scottie?"

"Well, I should say that there is likely more to the story, but walking in the wrong direction is never a good thing when you do it around a curious body like me."

He smiled broadly and I returned the same to him. I wanted to say something, but I couldn't think of the right words to use. All of my good words failed me at that moment.

"They're back, you know," Mr. Joe said out of the blue, changing our subject once again.

"Who's back?"

"The butterflies. I told you they'd return."

"Yeah, I saw a few of them fluttering around me while I was comin' down the road."

"No, I mean a whole group of them are back."

"Oh," I said, with some excitement, "that reminds me of what I just learned. You remember me asking you if you knew what a group or cluster of butterflies was called?"

"I seem to recollect you questioning me about that," he said.

"Well, that group of butterflies is called a kaleidoscope. Isn't that something?"

"Indeed. A kaleidoscope. How 'bout that? That's a good word for what they create in those large numbers."

"Okay, so, you said that they, our kaleidoscope of butterflies, were back. Where?"

"Come on. Help an old man up and I'll show you."

He removed his cane from behind the front door and I put my arm around his waist to help him. We walked that way toward the spot where his barn used to be. When we got to the trail that used to take us to the flowers and ultimately to the swamp, Mr. Joe turned left instead of right.

"This is a different spot," I said.

"Things change. Sometimes life has to start over. Come on."

He was leading the way now. He seemed to be walking very well for a man who almost died a few weeks ago.

We came to a thicket of bushes and high grass. It was like a wall around us, taller than Mr. Joe's six foot frame. He and my daddy were both tall men.

"You go first, Miss Clancy. Come on. You go first."

We changed places and he pointed to the spot that he wanted me to walk through. It was a heavy thicket. It seemed to develop as if out of nowhere all the while we had spent our time trying to unravel our summer mystery. We both had to duck as we made our way through the underbrush.

We finally emerged on the other side. We were greeted by thousands of butterflies encircling the small grove of wildflowers which hadn't been burned. The fire hadn't reached this far back into the woods. The thicket we had plodded through was some type of still green vine mingled with fescue. The other three sides of the small wildflower orchard were protected by thick growths of late-summer honeysuckle. The sweet smell was intoxicating, both for Mr. Joe and me, as well as for the butterflies, most likely.

"Told you, Miss Clancy," Mr. Joe said.

"Beg your pardon?"

"I told you they'd come back. You just can't keep Mother Nature down for long. Some bad things happen. Horrible things. But you cannot kill all of the butterflies. Life keeps on going, Miss Clancy. We just have to decide if we're gonna go with it or not."

I hugged him as we stood there in the middle of the wildflowers surrounded by thousands of butterflies, our own kaleidoscope of loveliness. We stood there in that radiant colorful bath, all the while taking in that sweet honeysuckle odor. My heart was broken with the loss of my father, but the sight of the butterflies brought back just enough hope to keep me moving ahead. My eyes began to water again.

"We gonna make it, Miss Clancy."

"How do you know that?"

"Well, first off, we both been loved by good people. That makes you strong, you know. Real strong."

"But the butterflies make it without love," I offered. "How do they do it?"

"Well, it only appears that they make it without love. I suspect that the Creator has placed a special kind of love inside of them. Call it a zest-for-life love, or what a poet once said about butterflies. He referred to them as being intemperate."

"Is that a good thing, Mr. Joe?" I asked.

"Depends on how you define that word *intemperate*."

"How do you define it?"

"I like to think it means free, not controlled by someone, unrestrained. That's the way life should be for all things, all people, like the butterflies."

"I like that, Mr. Joe. I like that a lot. But, I'm wondering if it could also mean that they don't know when to quit … you know … coming back here after all of this tragedy, this destruction, this pain."

"Yes, ma'am. I think you've got something there. They just don't know when to quit. Like you, Clancy Evans, just like you."

God knows I hoped that Mr. Joe was right about that strong love and the intemperate butterflies. I held out my arms and watched several butterflies land on me. Maybe they thought I was a flower or something. It made me laugh, but only a little. It was the first time I had actually expressed any joy in many days. I might yet make it after all, if I could pattern my life after them, and be like the butterflies.

# About M. Glenn Graves

I began writing in earnest in 1992. It took several years to finish that first book, and then it took a few more years beyond that not-very-good-first-attempt to finally write a story that I was proud of. In that second story, I found my voice as a writer. I also found the main character of all of my novels thus far—Clancy Evans, the private investigator trying to discover the truth about whatever situation she finds herself involved in… usually a murder.

One of the aspects of writing a story I have learned along my journey as an author is that while I dearly love my main heroine, sometimes the story is driven largely by the other characters who show up unexpectedly. It is for me deliciously fun to have an unanticipated character arrive on the scene who then has a heavy or major influence on the story. I have found some wonderfully devilish characters in this manner. To be sure, Clancy Evans still has the largest impact on a story I write, but her friends, such as Rosey and Starnes and Rogers (and even her Uncle Walters), are vital parts of the narrative.

# A Request from Glenn...

Help me spread the word. If you found this book of value, please write a favorable review on Amazon.com and Goodreads.com. Also, consider recommending or passing this book onto a friend. Thank you!